Bessy Rane by Mrs Henry Wood

Ellen Price was born on 17th January 1814 in Worcester.

In 1836 she married Henry Wood, whose career in banking and shipping meant living in Dauphiné, in the South of France, for two decades. During their time there they had four children.

Henry's business collapsed and he and Ellen together with their four children returned to England and settled in Upper Norwood near London.

Ellen now turned to writing and with her second book 'East Lynne' enjoyed remarkable popularity. This enabled her to support her family and to maintain a literary career.

It was a career in which she would write over 30 novels including 'Danesbury House', 'Oswald Cray', 'Mrs. Halliburton's Troubles', 'The Channings' and 'The Shadow of Ashlydyat'.

Sadly, her husband, Henry died in 1866.

Ellen though continued to strive on. In 1867, she purchased the magazine 'Argosy', founded two years previously by Alexander Strahan. She was a prolific writer and wrote much of the magazine herself although she had some very respected contributors, amongst them Hesba Stretton and Christina Rossetti. Although she would gradually pare down writing for the magazine she continued to write novel after novel. Such was her talent that for a time she was, in Australia, more popular than Charles Dickens.

Apart from novels she was an excellent translator and a writer of short stories. 'Reality or Delusion?' is a staple of supernatural anthologies to this day.

Ellen Wood died of bronchitis on 10th February 1887. He estate was valued at a very considerable £36,000.

She is buried in Highgate Cemetery, London.

A monument to her in Worcester Cathedral was unveiled in 1916.

Index of Contents

CHAPTER I

THE ANONYMOUS LETTER

It was an intensely dark night. What with the mist that hung around from below, and the unusual gloom above, Dr. Rane began to think he might have done well to bring a lantern with him, to guide his steps up Ham Lane, when he should turn into it. He would not be able to spare time to pick his way there. A gentleman—so news had been brought to him—was lying in sudden extremity, and his services as a medical man were being waited for.

Straight down, on the road before him, at only half-a-mile distance, lay the village of Dallory; so called after the Dallory family, who had been of importance in the neighbourhood in the years gone by. This little off-shoot was styled Dallory Ham. The latter name had given rise to disputes amidst antiquarians. Some maintained that the word Ham was only a contraction of hamlet, and that the correct name would be Dallory Hamlet: others asserted that the appellation arose from the circumstance that the public green, or common, was in the shape of a ham. As both sides brought logic and irresistible proof to bear on their respective opinions, contention never flagged. At no very remote period the Ham had been a grassy waste, given over to stray donkeys, geese, and gipsies. They were done away with now that houses encircled it; pretty villas of moderate dimensions, some cottages and a few shops: the high-road ran, as it always had done, straight through the middle of it. Dallory Ham had grown to think itself of importance, especially since the time when two doctors had established themselves in it: Dr. Rane and Mr. Alexander. Both lived in what might be called the neck of the Ham, which was nearest to Dallory proper.

Standing with your face towards Dallory (in the direction the doctor was hastening), his house was on the right-hand side. He had only now turned out of it. Dallory Hall, to which place Dr. Rane had been summoned, stood a little beyond the entrance to the Ham, lying back on the right in its grounds, and completely hidden by trees. It was inhabited by Mr. North.

Oliver Rane had come forth in haste and commotion. He could not understand the message, excepting the one broad fact that Edmund North, Mr. North's eldest son, was supposed to be dying. The servant, who brought it, did not seem to understand it either. He spoke of an anonymous letter that had been received by Mr. North, of disturbance thereupon, of a subsequent encounter—a sharp, brief quarrel—between Edmund North and Mr. Alexander, the surgeon; and of some sort of fit in which Edmund North was now lying senseless.

Dr. Rane was a gentlemanly man of middle height and slender frame, his age about thirty. The face in its small regular features might have been held to possess a dash of effeminacy, but for the resolute character of the firm mouth and the pointed chin. His eyes—rather too close together—whiskers and hair, were of a reddish brown, the latter worn brushed aside from the forehead; his teeth were white and even: altogether a good-looking man; but one of rather too silent manners, of too inscrutable a countenance to be very pleasing.

"An anonymous letter!" Dr. Rane had repeated to himself, with a sort of groan, hastening from his house as one greatly startled, and pursued his course down the Ham. Glancing across at Mr. Alexander's house, he felt a momentary temptation to go over and learn particulars—if, haply, the surgeon should be at home. The messenger had said that Mr. Alexander flung out of Dallory Hall in a passion, right in the middle of the quarrel; hence the summons for Dr. Rane. For Mr. Alexander, not Dr. Rane, was the Hall's medical attendant: this was the first time the latter had been so called upon.

They had come to Dallory within a day of each other, these two doctors, in consequence of the sudden death of its old practitioner; each hoping to secure the practice for himself. It was Mr. Alexander who chiefly gained it. Both were clever men; and it might have been at least an even race between them, but for the fact that Mrs. North, of Dallory Hall, set her face resolutely against Dr. Rane. The reason was inexplicable, since he had been led to believe that he should have the countenance of Mr. and Mrs. North. She did her best in a covert way to prevent his obtaining practice, pushing his rival—whom she really despised, and did not care a tittle for—into favour. Her object might not be to drive Oliver Rane from the spot, but it certainly seemed to look like it. So Mr. Alexander had obtained the lion's share of the practice in the best families, Dr. Rane but little; as to the poor, they were divided between them pretty equally. Both acted as general practitioners, and Mr. Alexander dispensed his own medicines. The rivals were outwardly cordial with each other; but Dr. Rane, no doubt, felt an inward smart at his want of success.

The temptation to dash over to Mr. Alexander's passed with the thought; there was no time for it. Dr. Rane pursued his course until he came to Ham Lane, an opening on the right, into which he turned, for it was a nearer way to the Hall. A narrow lane, green and lovely in early summer, with wild flowers nestling on its banks, dog-roses and honeysuckles clustering in its hedges. Here was the need of the lantern. But Dr. Rane sped on without regard to inadvertent steps that might land him in the ditch. Some excitement appeared to be upon him, far beyond any that might arise from the simple fact of being called out to a gentleman in a fit; yet he was by temperament very self-possessed, one of the calmest-mannered men living. A stile in the hedge on the left, which he found as if by instinct, took him at once into the grounds of Dallory Hall; whence there came wafting to him the scent of hyacinths, daffodils, and other spring flowers in delicious sweetness, spite of the density of the night-air. Not that Dr. Rane derived much advantage from the sweetness; nothing could seem delicious to him just then.

It was more open here, as compared with the lane, and not so intensely dark. Three minutes of the same heedless pace in and out of the winding walks, when he turned a point, and the old stone mansion was before him. A long, grey, sensible-looking house, of only two stories high, suggesting spacious rooms within. Lights shone from some of the windows and through the fan-light over the entrance-door. One of the gardeners crossed Dr. Rane's path.

"Is that you, Williams? Do you know how young Mr. North is?"

"I've not been told, sir. There's something wrong with him, we hear."

"Is this blight?" called back the doctor, alluding to the curiously dark mist.

"Not it, sir. It's nothing but the vapour rising from the day's heat. It have been hot for the first day o' May."

The door yielded to Dr. Rane's hand, and he went into the hall it was of fair size, and paved with stone. On the left were the drawing-rooms, on the right the dining-room, and also a room that was called Mr. North's parlour; a handsome staircase of stone wound up at the back. All the doors were closed; and as Dr. Rane stood for a moment in hesitation, a young lady in grey silk came swiftly and silently down the stairs. Her figure was small and slight, her face fair, pale, gentle, with the meekest look in her dove-like grey eyes. Her smooth, fine hair, of an exceedingly light brown, was worn in curls all round the head, after the manner of girls in a bygone time. It made her look very young, but she was in reality thirty years of age; three months younger than Dr. Rane. Miss North was very simple in tastes and habits, and adhered to many customs of her girlhood. Moreover, since an illness seven years ago, her hair had never grown very long or thick. She saw Dr. Rane, and came swiftly to him. Their hands met in silence.

"What is this trouble, Bessy?"

"Oh, I am so glad you are here!" she exclaimed, in the soft, subdued tones characteristic of dangerous sickness in a house. "He is lying as though he were dead. Papa is with him. Will you come?"

"One moment," he whispered. "Tell me, in a word, what it all is. The cause, I mean, not the illness."

"It was caused by an anonymous letter to papa. Edmund—"

"But how could any anonymous letter to your papa have caused illness to Edmund?" he interrupted. And the tone of his voice was so sharp, and the dropping of her hand, clasped until then, so sudden, that Miss North thought he was angry with her, and glanced upwards through her tears.

"I beg your pardon, Bessy. My dear, I feel so grieved and confounded at this, that I am scarcely myself. It is to me utterly incomprehensible. What were the contents of the letter?" he continued, as they hastened upstairs to the sick-chamber. And Bessy North told him in a whisper as much as she knew.

The facts of the case were these. By the six o'clock post that same evening, Mr. North received an anonymous letter, reflecting on his son Edmund. His first wife, dead now just eight-and-twenty years, had left him three children, Edmund, Richard, and Bessy. When the letter arrived, the family had sat down to dinner, and Mr. North did not open it until afterwards. He showed it to his son Edmund, as soon as they were left alone. The charges it contained were true, and Edmund North jumped to the conclusion that only one man in the whole world could have written it, and that was Alexander, the surgeon. He went into a frightful passion; he was given to doing so on occasions; and he had, besides, taken rather more wine at dinner than was good for him—which also he was somewhat addicted to. As ill fate had it, Mr. Alexander called just at the moment, and Mr. North, a timid man in nervous health, grew frightened at the torrent of angry words, and left them together in the dining-room. There was a short, sharp storm. Mr. Alexander came out almost immediately, saying, "You are mad; you are mad. I will talk to you when you are calmer." "I would rather be mad than bad," shouted Edmund North, coming after him. But the surgeon had already let himself out at the hall-door; and Edmund North went back to the dining-room, and shut himself in. Two of the servants, attracted by the sounds of dispute, had been lingering in the hall, and they saw and heard this. In a few minutes Mr. North went in, and found his son lying on the ground, senseless, He was carried to his chamber, and medical men were sent for: Dr. Rane (as being the nearest), and two physicians from the more distant market town, Whitborough.

Edmund North was not dead. Dr. Rane, bending over him, saw that. He had not been well of late, and was under the care of Mr. Alexander. Only a week ago (as was to transpire later) he had gone to consult a physician in Whitborough, one of those now summoned to him. This gentleman suspected he had heart-disease, and warned him against excitement. But the family knew nothing as yet of this; neither did Oliver Rane. Another circumstance Edmund North had not disclosed. When sojourning in London the previous winter, he had been attacked by a sort of fit. It had looked like apoplexy more than heart; and the doctors gave him sundry injunctions to be careful. This one also, Dr. Rane thought, knowing nothing of the former, looked like apoplexy. Edmund North was a very handsome man, but a great deal too stout.

"Is he dead, Oliver?" asked the grieving father; who, when alone with the doctor, and unrestrained by the presence of his wife, often called him by his Christian name.

"No; he is not dead."

And, indeed, a spasm at that moment passed over the prostrate face. All the means that Oliver Rane could think of, and use, he tried with the best heart and efforts—hoping to recall the fast-fleeting life.

But when the two doctors arrived from Whitborough, Oliver Rane found he was not wanted. They were professionals of long standing, men of note in their local arena; and showed themselves condescendingly patronizing to the young practitioner. Dr. Rane had rather a strong objection to be patronized: he withdrew, and went to Mr. North's parlour. It was a dingy room; the shaded lamp on the table not sufficing to light it up. Red moreen curtains were drawn before the large French window that opened to the flower-garden at the side.

Mr. North was standing before the fire. He was a little shrivelled man with stooping shoulders, his scanty hair smoothed across a low, broad forehead, his lips thin and querulous; his eyes, worn and weary now, had once been mild and loving as his daughter Bessy's. Time and care and (as some people said) his second wife, had changed him. Oliver Rane thought he had never seen him look so shrunken, nervous, and timid as to-night.

"What a pity it was that you should have mentioned the letter to him, Mr. North!" began the doctor, speaking at once of what lay uppermost in his thoughts.

"Mentioned the letter to him!—why, it concerned him," was the surprised answer. "But I never gave a thought to its having this effect upon him."

"What was in the letter, sir?" was the doctor's next question, put with considerable gloom, and after a long silence.

"You can read it, Oliver."

Opening the document, he handed it to Dr. Rane. It looked like any ordinary letter. The doctor took it to the lamp.

"Mr. North,

"Pardon a friend who ventures to give you a caution. Your eldest son is in some sort of embarrassment, and is drawing bills in conjunction with Alexander, the surgeon. Perhaps a word from you would arrest this: it is too frequently the first step of a man's downward career—and the writer would not like to see Edmund North enter on such."

Thus, abruptly and without signature, ended the fatal letter. Dr. Rane slowly folded it, and left it on the table.

"Who could have written it?" he murmured.

"Ah, there it is!" rejoined Mr. North. "Edmund said no one could have done it but Alexander."

Standing over the fire, to which he had turned, Dr. Rane warmed his hands. The intensely hot day had given place to a cold night. His red-brown eyes took a dreamy gaze, as he mentally revolved facts and suppositions. In his private opinion, judging only from the contents of the letter, Mr. Alexander was the last man who would have been likely to write it.

"It is not like Alexander's writing," observed Mr. North.

"Not in the least."

"But of course this is in a thoroughly disguised hand."

"Most anonymous letters are so, I expect. Is it true that he and your son have been drawing bills together?"

"I gather that they have drawn one; perhaps two, Edmund's passion was so fierce that I could not question him. What I don't like is, Alexander's going off in the manner he did, without seeing me: it makes me think that perhaps he did write the letter. An innocent man would have remained to defend himself. It might have been written from a good motive, after all, Oliver! My poor son!—if he had only taken it quietly!"

Mr. North wrung his hands. His tones were feeble, meekly complaining; his manner and bearing were altogether those of a man who has been constantly put down and no longer attempts to struggle against the cares and crosses of the world, or the will of those about him.

"I must be going," said Oliver Rane, arousing himself from a reverie. "I have to see a poor man at Dallory."

"Is it Ketler?"

"Yes, sir. Goodnight. I trust you will have reason to be in better spirits in the morning."

"Goodnight, Oliver."

But the doctor could not get off at once. He was waylaid by a servant, who said madam wished to see him. Crossing the hall, the man threw open the doors of the drawing-room, a magnificent apartment. Gilded and gleaming mirrors; light blue satin curtains and furniture; a carpet softer and thicker than moss: and all kinds of bright and resplendent things were there.

"Dr. Rane, madam."

Mrs. North sat on a couch by the fire. In the house she was called Madam—out of the house, too, for that matter. A severely handsome woman, with a cold, pale, imperious face, the glittering jewels in her black hair looking as hard as she did. A cruel face, as some might have deemed it. When Mr. North married her, she was the widow of Major Bohun, and had one son. Underneath the chandelier, reading by its light, sat her daughter, a young lady whose face bore a strong resemblance to hers. This daughter and a son had been born since her second marriage.

"You wished to see me, Mrs. North?"

Dr. Rane so spoke because they took no manner of notice of him. Mrs. North turned then, with her dark, inscrutable eyes; eyes that Oliver Rane hated, as he hated the cruelty glittering in their depths, He believed her to be a woman unscrupulously selfish. She did not rise; merely motioned him to a seat with a haughty wave of her white arm: and the bracelets shone on it, and her ruby velvet dress gleamed with amazing richness. He sat down with perfect self-possession, every whit as independent as herself.

"You have seen this infamous letter, I presume, Dr. Rane?"

"I have."

"Who sent it?"

"I cannot tell you, Mrs. North."

"Have you no idea at all?"

"Certainly not. How should I have?"

"Could you detect no resemblance in the writing to any one's you know?"

He shook his head.

"Not to—for instance—Alexander's?" she resumed, looking at him steadfastly. But Dr. Rane saw with a sure instinct that Alexander's was not the name she had meant to speak.

"I feel sure that Mr. Alexander no more wrote the letter than—than you did, Mrs. North."

"Does it bear any resemblance to Richard North's?" she continued, after a faint pause.

"To Richard North's!" echoed the doctor, the words taking him by surprise. "No."

"Are you familiar with Richard North's handwriting?"

Oliver Rane paused to think, and then replied with a passing laugh. "I really believe I do not know his handwriting, madam."

"Then why did you speak so confidently?"

"I spoke in the impulse of the moment. Richard North, of all men, is the lest likely to do such a thing as this."

The young lady, Matilda North, turned round from her book. An opera cloak of scarlet gauze was on her shoulders, as if she were cold; she drew it closer with an impatient hand.

"Mamma, why do you harp upon Richard? He couldn't do it; papa told you so. If Dick saw need to find fault with any one, or tell tales, he would do it openly."

One angry gleam from madam's eyes as her daughter settled to her book again, and then she proceeded to close the interview.

"As you profess yourself unable to give me information or to detect any clue, I will not detain you longer, Dr. Rane."

He stood for a second, expecting, perhaps, that she might offer her hand. She did nothing of the sort, only bowed coldly. Matilda North took no notice of him whatever: she was content to follow her mother's teachings when they did not clash with her own inclination. Dr. Rane had ceased to marvel why he was held in disfavour by Mrs. North: to try to guess at it seemed a hopeless task. Neither could he imagine why she opposed his marriage with Bessy; for to Bessy and her interests she was utterly indifferent.

As he left the drawing-room, Bessy North joined him, and they went together to the hall-door. No servant had been rung for—it was one of Mrs. North's ways of showing contempt—and they stood together outside, speaking softly. Again the tears shone in Bessy's eyes: her heart was a very tender one, and she had loved her brother dearly.

"Oliver, is there any hope?"

"Do not distress yourself, Bessy. I cannot tell you one way or the other."

"How can I help distressing myself?" she rejoined, her hand resting quietly in both his. "It is all very well for you to be calm; a medical man meets these sad things every day. You cannot be expected to care."

"Can I not?" he answered; and there was a touch of passionate emotion in the usually calm tones. "If any effort or sacrifice of mine would bring back his health and life, I would freely make it. Goodnight, Bessy."

As he stooped to kiss her, quick, firm footsteps were heard approaching, and Bessy went indoors. He who came up was a rather tall and very active man, with a plain, but nevertheless an attractive face. Plain in its irregular features; attractive from its open candour and strong good sense, from the earnest, truthful look in the deep-set hazel eyes. People were given to saying that Richard North was the best man of business for miles round. It was so: and he was certainly, in mind, manners, and person, a gentleman.

"Is it you, Rane? What is all this trouble? I have been away for a few hours, unfortunately. Mark Dawson met me just now with the news that my brother was dying."

The voice would have been pleasing to a degree if only from its tone of ready decision: but it was also musical as voices seldom are, clear and full of sincerity. From the voice alone, Richard North might have been trusted to his life's end. Dr. Rane gave a short summary of the illness and the state he was lying in.

"Dawson spoke of a letter that had excited him," said Richard.

"True; a letter to Mr. North."

"A dastardly anonymous letter. Just so."

"An anonymous letter," repeated the doctor. "But the effect on your brother seems altogether disproportioned to the cause."

"Where is the letter? I cannot look upon Edmund until I have seen the letter."

Dr. Rane told him where the letter was, and went out. Richard North passed on to the parlour. Mr. North, sitting by the fire, had his face bent in his hands.

"Father, what is all this?"

"Oh, Dick, I am glad you have come!" and in the tone there sounded an intense relief, as if he who came brought with him strength and hope. "I can't make top or tail of this; and I think he is dying."

"Who is with him?—Arthur?"

"No; Arthur has been out all day. The doctors are with him still."

"Let me see the letter."

Mr. North gave it him, reciting at the same time the chief incidents of the calamity in a rambling sort of manner. Richard North read the letter twice: once hastily, to gather in the sense; then attentively, giving to every word full consideration. His father watched him.

"It was not so much the letter itself that excited him, Richard, as the notion that Alexander wrote it."

"Alexander did not write this," decisively spoke Richard.

"You think not?"

"Why, of course he did not. It tells against himself as much as against Edmund."

"Edmund said no one knew of the matter except Alexander, and therefore no one else could have written it. Besides, Dick, where is Alexander? Why is he staying away?"

"We shall hear soon, I daresay. I have faith in Alexander. Keep this letter jealously, father. It may have been right to give you the information it contains; I say nothing at present about that; but an anonymous writer is generally a scoundrel, deserving no quarter."

"And none shall he get from me," spoke Mr. North, emphatically. "It was posted at Whitborough, you see, Dick."

"I see," shortly answered Richard. He threw his coat back as if he were too hot; and moved to the door on his way to his brother's chamber.

Meanwhile Oliver Rane went down the avenue to the entrance-gates, and took the road to Dallory. He had to see a patient there: a poor man who was lying in danger. He threw his coat back, in spite of the chilling fog, and wiped his brow, as if the weather or his reflections were too hot for him.

"What a fool! what a fool!" murmured he, half aloud, apostrophizing, doubtless, the writer of the anonymous letter. Or, it might be, the unfortunate young man who had allowed it to excite within him so fatal an amount of passion.

The road was smooth and broad: a fine highway, well kept. For a short distance there were no houses, but they soon began. Dallory was a bustling village, both poor and rich inhabiting it. The North Works, as they were familiarly called, from the fact of Mr. North's being their chief proprietor, lay a little further on, and Dallory Church still beyond. It was a straggling parish at best.

Amidst the first good houses that Dr. Rane came to was one superior to the rest. A large, square, handsome dwelling, with a pillared portico close to the village pathway, and a garden behind it.

"I wonder how Mother Gass is to-night?" thought the doctor, arresting his steps. "I may as well ask."

His knock was answered by the lady herself, whom he had so unceremoniously styled "Mother Gass." A stout, comfortable-looking dame, richly dressed, with a face as red as it was good-natured, and a curiously-fine lace cap, standing on end with yellow ribbon. Mrs. Gass possessed neither birth nor breeding; she had made an advantageous match, as you will hear further on: she owned many good qualities, and was popularly supposed to be rich enough to buy up the whole of Dallory Ham. Her late husband had been uncle to Oliver Rane, but neither she nor Oliver presumed upon the relationship in their intercourse with each other. In fact they had never met until two years ago.

"I knew your knock, Dr. Rane, and came to the door myself. Step into the parlour. I want to speak to you."

The doctor did not want to go in by any means, and felt caught. He said he had no time to stay; had merely called, in passing, to ask how she was.

"Well, I'm better this evening: the swimming in the head is less. You just come in, now. I won't keep you two minutes. Shut the door, girl, after Dr. Rane."

This was to a smart housemaid, who had followed her mistress down the wide, handsome passage. Dr. Rane perforce stepped in, very unwillingly. He felt instinctively convinced that Mrs. Gass had heard of the calamity at the Hall and wished to question him. To avoid this he would have gone a mile any other way.

"I want to get at the truth about Edmund North, doctor. One of the maids from the Hall called in just now and said he had been frightened into a fit through some letter; and that you were fetched to him."

"Well, that is true," said the doctor, accepting the situation.

"My patience!" ejaculated Mrs. Gass. "What was writ in the letter? She said it was one of them enonymous things."

"So it was."

"Was it writ to himself?"

"No. To Mr. North."

"Well, now,"—dropping her voice—"was it about that young woman he got acquainted with? You know."

"No, no; nothing of that sort." And Dr. Rane, as the shortest way of ending the matter, gave her the details.

"There was not much in the letter," he said, in confidential tones. "No harm would have come of it but for Edmund North's frightful access of passion. If he dies, mind,"—the doctor added this in a dreamy tone, gazing out as if looking into the future—"if he dies, it will not be the letter that has killed him, but his own want of self-control."

"Don't talk of dying, doctor. It is to be hoped it won't come to that."

"It is, indeed."

"And Mr. Richard was not at home, the girl said!"

"Neither he nor Captain Bohun. Richard has just come in now."

Mrs. Gass would fain have kept him longer, but he told her the sick man Ketler was waiting for him. This man was one of the North workmen, who had been terribly injured in the arm; Dr. Rane hoped to save both arm and life.

"That receipt for the rhubarb jam Mrs. Cumberland promised: is it ever coming?" asked Mrs. Gass as Dr. Rane was quitting the room.

Turning back, he put his hat on the table and took out his pocketbook. Mrs. Cumberland had sent it at last. He selected the paper from amongst several others and handed it to her.

"I forgot to leave it when I was here this morning, Mrs. Gass. My mother gave it me yesterday."

Between them they dropped the receipt. Both stooped for it, and their heads came together. There was a slight laugh; in the midst of which the pocketbook fell on the carpet. Some papers fluttered out of it, which the doctor picked up and replaced.

"Have you got them all, doctor? How is the young lady's cold?"

"What young lady's?" he questioned.

"Miss Adair's."

"I did not know she had one."

"Ah, them lovely girls with their bright faces never show their ailments; and she is lovely, if ever one was lovely in this terrestial world. Goodnight to you, doctor; you're in a mortal hurry."

He strode to the street-door and it closed sharply after him. Mrs. Gass looked out of her parlour and saw the same smart maid hastening along the passage: a little too late.

"Drat it, wench! is that the way you let gentlefolk show themselves out?—scuttering to the door when they've got clean away from it. D'you call that manners?"

CHAPTER II

ELLEN ADAIR

The day promised to be as warm as the preceding one. The night and morning mists were gone; the sun shone hot and bright. Summer seemed to have come in before its time.

Two white gothic villas stood side by side just within the neck of Dallory Ham, a few yards of garden and some clustering shrubs between them. They were built alike. The side windows, facing each other over this strip of ground, were large projecting bay-windows, and belonged to the dining-rooms. These houses were originally erected for two maiden sisters. A large and beautiful garden lay at the back, surrounding the two villas, only a slender wire fence, that a child might have stepped over, dividing it. Entering the Ham from the direction of Dallory, these houses stood on the left; in the first of them lived Mrs. Cumberland, the mother of Oliver Rane. She had been married twice: hence the difference in name. The second house was occupied by Dr. Rane himself. They lay back with a strip of grass before them, the entrance-doors being level with the ground.

Let us go into the doctor's: turning the handle of the door without ceremony, as Dr. Rane's more familiar patients are wont to do. The hall is small, narrowing off at the upper end to a passage, and lighted with stained glass. On the left of the entrance is the consulting-room, not much larger than a closet; beyond it is the dining-room, a spacious apartment, with its bay-window, already spoken of, looking to the other house. Opposite the dining-room across the passage is the white-flagged kitchen; and the drawing-room lies in front, on the right of the entrance. Not being furnished it is chiefly kept shut up. A back-door opens to the garden.

Oliver Rane sat in his consulting-room; the Whitborough Journal, damp from the press, in his hand. It was just twelve o'clock and he had to go out, but the newspaper was attracting him. By seven o'clock that morning he had been at the Hall, and learnt that there was no material change in the patient lying there: he had then gone on, early though it was, to see the man, Ketler. The journal gave the details of Mr. North's seizure with tolerable accuracy, and concluded its account in these words: "We have reason to know that a clue has been obtained to the anonymous writer."

"A clue to the writer!" repeated Dr. Rane, his eyes appearing glued to the words. "I wonder if it's true?—No, no; it is not likely," came the quiet, contemptuous decision. "How should any clue—"

He stopped suddenly; rose from the chair, and stood erect and motionless, as if some thought had struck him. A fine man; almost as good-looking at a casual glance as another who was stepping in upon him. The front-door had opened, and this one was lightly tapped at. Dr. Rane paused before he answered it, and a fierce look of inquiry, as if he did not care to be interrupted, shot from his eyes.

"Come in."

A tall, slender, and very handsome man, younger than Dr. Rane, opened the door slowly. There was a peculiar refinement in his proud fair features; a dreamy look in his dark blue eyes. An attractive face at all times and seasons, whose owner it was impossible to mistake for anything but an upright, well-bred gentleman. It was Arthur Bohun; Captain Bohun, as he was very generally called. He was the only son of Mrs. North by her former marriage with Major Bohun, and of course stepson to Mr. North.

"Any admittance, doctor?"

"Always admittance to you," answered the doctor, who could be affable or not, as suited his mood. "Why don't you come in?"

He came in with his pleasant smile; a smile that hid the natural pride of the face. Oliver Rane put down the newspaper.

"Well, is there any change in Edmund North?"

"The very slightest in the world, the doctors think; and for the better," replied Captain Bohun. "Dick told me. I have not been in myself since early morning. I cannot bear to look on extreme suffering."

A ghost of a smile flitted across Dr. Rane's features at the avowal. He could understand a woman disliking to look on suffering, but not a man. And the one before him had been a soldier!

Captain Bohun sat down on an uncomfortable wooden stool as he spoke, gently throwing back his light summer overcoat. He imparted the idea of never being put out over any earthly thing. The movement displayed his cool white waistcoat, across which fell a dainty gold chain with its transparent sapphire seal of rare and costly beauty.

"You have begun summer early!" remarked the doctor, glancing at Captain Bohun's attire.

The clothes were of a delicate shade of grey; looking remarkably cool and nice in conjunction with the white waistcoat. Captain Bohun was always well dressed; it seemed a part of himself. To wear the rude and rough attire that some men affect nowadays, would have been against his instincts.

"Don't sit on that stool of penitence; take the patient's chair," said the doctor, pointing to an elbow-chair opposite the window.

"But I am not a patient."

"No. Or you'd be at the opposition shop over the way."

Arthur Bohun laughed. "It was of the opposition shop I came to speak to you—if I came for anything in particular, Where's Alexander? Is he keeping out of the way; or has he really gone to London as people say?"

"I know nothing about him," returned Dr. Rane. "Look here—I was reading the account they give in the newspaper. Is this last hint true?"—holding out the journal—"that a clue has been obtained to the writer of the letter?"

Arthur Bohun ran his eyes over the sentence to which the doctor's finger pointed.

"No, this has no foundation," he promptly answered. "At least so far as the Hall is concerned. As yet we have not found any clue whatever."

"I thought so. These newsmongers put forth lies by the bushel. Just as we might do, if we had to cater for an insatiably curious public. But I fear I must be going out."

Arthur Bohun brought down the fore-legs of the stool, which he had kept on the tilt, rose, and said a word of apology for having detained him from his patients. His was essentially a courteous nature, sensitively regardful of other people's feelings, as men of great innate refinement are sure to be.

They went into the dining-room, Dr. Rane having left his hat there, and passed out together by the large bay-window. The doctor crossed at once to a door in the wall that bound the premises at the back, and made his exit to the lane beyond, leaving Arthur Bohun in the garden.

A garden that on a summer's day seemed as a very paradise. With its clustering shrubs, its overhanging trees, its leafy glades, its shrubberies, its miniature rocks, its sweet repose, its sweeter flowers. Seated in a remote part of that which belonged to Mrs. Cumberland, was one of the loveliest girls that eye had ever looked upon. She wore a morning dress of light-coloured muslin, with an edging of lace at the neck and wrists. Slight, gentle, charming, with a peculiar look of grace and refinement, a stranger would have been almost startled at her beauty. It was a delightful face; the features clearly cut; the complexion soft, pure, and delicate, paling and flushing with every emotion. In the dark brown eyes there was a singularly sweet expression; the dark brown hair took a lustrously bright tinge in the sunlight.

A natural arbour of trees and branches had been formed overhead: she sat on a garden bench, behind a rustic table. Before her, at a short distance, a falling cascade trickled down the artificial rocks, and thence wound away, a tiny stream, amidst ferns, violets, primroses, and other wild plants. A plot of green grass, smooth and soft as the moss of the rocks, lay immediately at her feet, and glimpses of statelier flowers were caught through the trees. Their rich perfume came wafted in a sudden breeze to the girl's senses, and she looked up gratefully from her work; some small matter of silken embroidery.

And now you could see the singular refinement and delicacy of the face, the pleasant expression of the soft bright eyes. A bird lodged itself on a branch close by, and began a song. Her lips parted with a smile of greeting. By way of rewarding it, off he flew, dipped his beak into the running stream, and soared away out of her sight. As is the case sometimes in life.

On the table lay a handful of violets, picked short off at the blossoms. Almost unconsciously, as it seemed, her thoughts far away, she began toying with them, and fell insensibly into the French schoolgirls' play, telling off the flowers. "M'aime-t-il?" was the first momentous question; and then the pastime, a blossom being told off with every answer. "Oui. Non. Un peu. Beaucoup. Pas du tout. Passionnément." And so the round went on, until the last violet was reached. It came, as chance had it, with the last word, and she, in an access of rapture, her soft cheeks glowing, her sweet lips parting, caught up the flower and pressed it to her lips.

"Il m'aime passionnément!"

Ah, foolish girl! The oracle seemed as true as if it had come direct from heaven. But can we not remember the ecstasy such necromancy once brought to ourselves!

With her blushes deepening as she woke, startling, into reality; with a smile at her own folly; with a sense of maidenly shame for indulging in the pastime, she pushed the violets together, threaded a needleful of green floss silk, and went on soberly with her work. A few minutes, and then either eye or ear was attracted by something ever so far off, and she sat quite still. Quite still outwardly; but oh! the sudden emotion that rose like a lightning flash within! and she knew the footsteps. Every vein was tingling; every pulse throbbing; the pink on her cheeks deepened; the life blood of her heart rushed wildly on, and she pressed her hand upon her bosom to still it.

He was passing on from Dr. Rane's to the other house, when he caught a glimpse of her dress through the trees, and turned aside. Nothing could have been quieter or more undemonstrative than the meeting; and yet a shrewd observer, skilled in secrets, had not failed to read the truth—that both alike loved. Captain Bohun went up, calm as befitted a well-bred man: shaking hands after the fashion of society, and apparently with as little interest: but on his face the flush also shone with all its tell-tale vividness; the hand that touched hers thrilled almost to pain. She had risen to receive him: as calm outwardly as he, but her senses were in wild confusion.

She began to go on with her work again in a hurried, trembling sort of fashion when he sat down. The day, for her, had turned to Eden; all things seemed to discourse sweet music.

True love—passionate, pure love—is not fluent of speech, whatever the world may say, or poets teach. Dr. Rane and Miss North thought they loved each other: and so they did, after a sensible, sober manner: they could have conversed with mutual fluency for ever and a day; but their love was not this love. It is the custom of modern writers to ignore it: the prevailing fashion is to be matter-of-fact; realistic; people don't talk of love now, and of course don't feel it: the capacity for it has died out; habits have changed. It is false sophistry. We cannot put off human nature as we do a garment.

Captain Bohun was the first to break the silence. She had been content to live in it by his side for ever: it was more eloquent, too, than his words were.

"What a lovely day it is, Ellen!"

"Yes. I think summer has come: we shall scarcely have it warmer than this in July. And oh, how charming everything is!"

"Yes. Yesterday I had a ride of ten miles between green hedges in which the May is beginning to blossom. Envious darkness had shut out the world before I reached home again."

"And I sat out here all the afternoon," she answered—and perhaps she unconsciously spoke in pursuance of the thought, that she had sat out waiting and hoping for him. "Where did you go, Arthur?"

"To Bretchley. Some of my old brother officers are quartered there: and I spent the day with them. What's that for?"

He alluded to the piece of work. She smiled as she held it out in her right hand, on the third finger of which was a plain gold ring. A small piece of white canvas with a pink rose and part of a green leaf already worked upon it in bright floss silk.

"Guess."

"Nay, how can I? For a doll's cushion?"

"Oh, Arthur!" came the laughing exclamation. "If I tell you, you must keep counsel, mind that, for it is a secret, and I am working it under difficulties, out of Mrs. Cumberland's sight. Don't you think I have done a great deal? I only began it yesterday."

"Well, what's it for?" he asked, putting his hand underneath it as an excuse, perhaps, for touching the fingers that held it. "A fire-screen for pretty faces?"

The young lady shook her head. "It's for a kettle-holder."

"A kettle-holder! What a prosy ending!"

"It is for Mrs. Cumberland's invalid kettle that she keeps in her bedroom. The handle got hot a day or two ago, and she burnt her hand. I shall put it on some morning to surprise her."

A silence ensued. Half their intercourse was made up of pauses: the eloquent language of true love. Captain Bohun, thinking how sweet-natured was the girl by his side, played abstractedly with the blossoms lying on the table.

"What have you been doing with all these violets, Ellen?"

"Nothing," she replied; and down went the scissors. But that she stooped at once, Captain Bohun might have seen the sudden flush on the delicate face, and wondered at it: a flush of remembrance. Il m'aime passionnément. Well, so he did.

"Please don't entangle my silk, Captain Bohun."

He laughed as he put down the bright gold skein. "Shall I help you to wind it, Ellen?"

"Thank you, but we don't wind floss silk. It would deaden its beauty. Arthur! do you know that the swallows have come?"

"The swallows! Then this summer weather will stay with us, for those birds have a sure instinct. It is early for them to be here."

"I saw one this morning. It may be only an avant-courier, come to report on the weather to the rest."

She laughed lightly at her own words, and there ensued another pause. Captain Bohun broke it.

"What a shocking thing this is about Edmund North!"

"What is a shocking thing?" she asked, with indifference, going on with her work as she spoke. Arthur Bohun, who was busy again with the pale blue violets, scarcely as blue as his own eyes, lifted his face and looked at her.

"I mean altogether. The illness; the letter; the grief at home. It is all shocking."

"Is Edmund North ill? I did not know it."

"Ellen!"

Living in the very atmosphere of the illness, amidst its bustle, distress, and attendant facts, to Arthur Bohun it seemed almost impossible that she should be ignorant of it.

"Why, what has Rane been about, not to tell you?"

"I don't know. What is the matter with Edmund North?"

Captain Bohun explained the illness and its cause. Her work dropped on her knee as she listened; her face grew pale with interest. She never once interrupted him; every sympathetic feeling within her was aroused to warm indignation.

"An anonymous letter!" she at length exclaimed. "That's worse than a stab."

"A fellow, writing one of malice, puts himself beyond the pale of decent society: shooting would be too good for him," quietly remarked Captain Bohun. "Here comes a summons for you, I expect, Ellen."

Even so. One of the maids approached, saying Mrs. Cumberland was downstairs; and so the interview was broken up. Captain Bohun would perforce have taken his departure, but Miss Adair invited him in—to tell the sad story to Mrs. Cumberland. Only too glad was he of any plea that kept him by Ellen's side.

Putting her work away in her pocket, she took the arm that was held out, and they went wandering through the garden; lingering by the cascade, dreaming in the dark cypress walk, standing over the beds of beautiful flowers. A seductive time; life's summer; but a time that never stays, for the frosts of winter and reality succeed it surely and swiftly.

Nothing had been said between them, but each was conscious of what the other felt. Neither had whispered in so many words, "I love you." Ellen did not hint that she had watched for him the whole of the past livelong day with love's sick longing; he did not confess how lost the day had been to him, how worse than weary, because it did not bring him to her presence. These avowals might come in time, but they would not be needed.

Stepping in through the centre doors of the bay window, as Arthur Bohun had made his exit from the opposite one, they looked round for Mrs. Cumberland, and did not see her. She was in the drawing-room on the other side the small hall, sitting near the Gothic windows that faced the road. A pale, reticent, lady-like woman, always suffering, but making more of her sufferings than she need have done—as her son, Dr. Rane, not over-dutifully thought. Her eyes were light and cold; her flaxen hair, banded smoothly under a cap, was turning grey. But that Mrs. Cumberland was quite occupied with self, and very little with her ward, Ellen Adair, she might have noticed before now the suggestive intimacy between that young lady and Arthur Bohun.

"Captain Bohun is here, Mrs. Cumberland," said Ellen, when they entered. "He has some sad news to tell you."

"And the extraordinary part of the business is that you should not have heard it before," added Arthur, as he shook hands with Mrs. Cumberland.

Mrs. Cumberland's rich black silk gown rustled a very little as she responded to the greeting; but there was no smile on her grey face, her cold eyes wore no brighter light. In her way she was glad to see him: that is, she had no objection to seeing him; but gladness and Mrs. Cumberland seemed to have parted company. The suffering that arises from constant pain makes a self-absorbed nature doubly selfish.

"What is the news that Ellen speaks of, Captain Bohun?"

He stood leaning against the mantelpiece as he told the tale: told it systematically; the first advent of the anonymous letter to Mr. North; the angry, passionate spirit in which Edmund North had taken it up; his stormy interview with the surgeon, Alexander; the subsequent attack, and the hopelessness in which he was lying. For once Mrs. Cumberland was aroused to feeling sympathy in another's sufferings: she listened with painful interest.

"And it was Oliver who was called in first to Edmund North!" she presently exclaimed, with emphasis, as if unable to credit the fact.

"Yes."

"But how was it he did not step in here afterwards to tell me the news?" she added, resentfully.

Captain Bohun could not answer that so readily. Ellen Adair, ever ready to find a charitable excuse for the world, turned to Mrs. Cumberland.

"Dr. Rane may have had patients to see. Perhaps he did not return home until too late to come here."

"Yes, he did; I saw his lamp burning before ten o'clock," was Mrs. Cumberland's answer. "Ah! this is another proof that I am being forgotten," she went on, bitterly. "When a woman has seen fifty years of life, she is old in the sight of her children, and they go then their own way in the world, leaving her to coldness and neglect."

"But, dear Mrs. Cumberland, Dr. Rane does not neglect you," said Ellen, struck with the injustice of the complaint. "He is ever the first to come in and amuse you with what news he has."

"And in this instance he may have kept silence from a good motive—the wish to spare you pain," added Captain Bohun.

"True, true," murmured Mrs. Cumberland, her mind taking a more reasonable view of the matter. "Oliver has always been dutiful to me."

Departing, Captain Bohun crossed the road to Mr. Alexander's; a slight limp visible in his gait. The mystery that appeared to surround the surgeon's movements at present, puzzled him not a little; his prolonged absence seemed unaccountable. The surgery, through which he entered, was empty, and he opened the door leading from it to the house. A maid-servant met him.

"Is Mr. Alexander at home?"

"No, sir."

"Papa's gone to London," called out a young gentleman of ten, who came running along the passage, cracking a whip. "He went last night. They sent for him."

"Who sent for him?" asked Captain Bohun.

"The people. Mamma's gone too. They are coming home to-day; and mamma's going to bring me a Chinese puzzle and a box of chocolate if she had time to buy them."

Not much information, this. As Captain Bohun turned out again, he stood at the door, wishing he had a decent plea to take him over to Mrs. Cumberland's again. He was an idle man; living only in the sweet pastime of making that silent love.

But Mrs. North never suspected that he was making it, or knew that he was intimate at Mrs. Cumberland's. Still less did she suspect that Mrs. Cumberland had a young lady inmate named Ellen Adair. It would have startled her to terror.

CHAPTER III

IN MRS GASS'S PARLOUR

Early on the following morning the death-bell ringing out from the church at Dallory proclaimed to those who heard it that Edmund North had passed to his rest. He had never recovered consciousness, and died some thirty-six hours after the attack.

Amongst those who did not hear it was Oliver Rane. The doctor had been called out at daybreak to a country patient in an opposite direction, returning between eight and nine o'clock.

He sat at breakfast in the dining-room, unconscious of the morning's calamity. The table stood in front of the large bay-window.

"She has done it too much—stupid thing!" exclaimed Dr. Rane, cutting a slice of ham in two and apostrophizing his unconscious servant. "Yesterday it was hardly warmed through. Just like them!—make a complaint, and they rush to the other extreme. I wonder how things are going on there this morning?"

He glanced up towards the distant quarter where the Hall was situated, for his query had reference to Edmund North; and this gave him the opportunity of seeing something else: a woman stepping out of Mrs. Cumberland's dining-room. She was getting on for forty, tall as a may-pole, with inquisitive green eyes, sallow cheeks, remarkably thin, as if she had lost her teeth, and a bunch of black ringlets on either side of her face. She wore the white apron and cap of a servant, but looked one of a superior class. Emerging from the opposite window, she stepped across the wire fence and approached Dr. Rane.

"What does Jelly want now?" he mentally asked.

A curious name, no doubt, but it was hers. Fanny Jelly. When Mrs. Cumberland had engaged her as upper maid, she decided to call her by the latter name, Fanny being her own.

Jelly entered without ceremony—she was not given to observing much at the best of times. She had come to say that he need not provide anything for dinner; her mistress meant to send him in a fowl—if he would accept it.

"With pleasure, tell her," said Dr. Rane. "How is my mother this morning, Jelly?"

"She has had a good night, and is pretty tolerable," replied Jelly, giving a backward fling to her flying cap-strings. "The foreign letters have come in; two for her, one for Miss Adair."

Dr. Rane, not particularly interested in the said foreign letters, went on with his breakfast. Jelly, with characteristic composure, stood at ease just inside the window watching the process.

"That ham is dried up to fiddle-strings," she suddenly said.

"Yes. Phillis has done it too much."

"And I should like to have the doing of her!" spoke Jelly in wrathful tones. "It is a sin to spoil good food."

"So it is," said Dr. Rane.

"So that poor young man's gone!" she resumed, as he cracked an egg.

The doctor lifted his head quickly. "What young man?"

"Edmund North. He died at half-past seven this morning."

"Who says so?" cried Dr. Rane, a startled look crossing his face.

"The milkman told me: he heard the passing-bell toll out. You needn't be surprised, sir: there has been no hope from the first."

"But there has been hope," disputed the doctor. "There was hope yesterday at midday, there was hope last night. I don't believe he is dead."

"Well, sir, then you must disbelieve it," equably answered Jelly; but she glanced keenly at him from her green eyes. "Edmund North is as certainly dead as that I stand here."

He seemed strangely moved at the tidings: a quiver stirred his lips, the colour in his face faded to whiteness. Jelly, having looked as much as she chose, turned to depart.

"Then we may send in the fowl, sir?"

"Yes, yes."

He watched her dreamily as she crossed the low fence and disappeared within her proper domains; he pushed the neglected ham from him, he turned sick at the lightly done egg, of which the shell had just been broken. What, though he preferred eggs lightly done in calm times? calm times were not these. The news did indeed trouble him in no measured degree: it was so sad for a man in the prime of early life to be cut off thus. Edmund North was only a year or two older than himself: two days ago he had been as full of health and life, deep in the plans and projects of this world, thinking little of the next. Sad? it was horrible. And Dr. Rane's breakfast was spoiled for that day.

He got up to walk the room restlessly: he looked at himself in the glass; possibly to see how the news might have affected his features; in all he did there was a hurried, confused sort of motion, betraying that the mind must be in a state of perturbation. By-and-by he snatched up his hat, and went forth, taking the direction of the Hall.

"I ought to call. It will look well for me to call. It is a civility I owe them," he kept repeating at intervals, as he strode along. Just as though he thought in his inmost heart he ought not to call, and were seeking arguments to excuse himself from doing so.

How eager he was to be there and see and hear all that was transpiring, he alone knew. No power could have stopped him, whether to go were suitable or unsuitable; for he had a strong will. He did not take the lane this time, but went straight along the high-road, turning in at the iron gates, and up the chestnut avenue. The tender green of the trees was beautiful: birds sang; the blue sky flickered through the waving leaves. Winding on, Dr. Rane met Thomas Hepburn, the undertaker and carpenter: a sickly looking but intelligent and respectable man.

"Is it you, Hepburn?"

"Yes, sir; I've been in to take the orders. What an awful thing it is!" he continued in a low tone, glancing round at the closed windows, as if fearful they might detect what he was saying. "The scoundrel who wrote that letter ought to be tried for murder when they discover him. And they are safe to do that, sooner or later."

"The writer could have done no great harm but for Edmund North's allowing himself to go into that fatal passion."

"An anonymous writer is a coward," rejoined Hepburn with scorn. "They say there'll not be an inquest."

"An inquest!" repeated the doctor, to whom the idea had never occurred. "There's no necessity for an inquest."

"Well, doctor, I suppose the law would in strictness exact it. But Mr. North is against it, and it's thought his wishes will be respected."

"Any of the medical men can furnish a certificate of the cause of death. I could do it myself."

"Yes, of course. But I've no time to stay talking," added the undertaker. "Good-day to you, sir."

The next to come forth from the house was Alexander, the surgeon. Dr. Rane rubbed his eyes, almost thinking they deceived him. The brother practitioners shook hands; and Mr. Alexander—a little man with dark hair—explained what had seemed inexplicable.

It seemed that the very same evening delivery which brought Mr. North the anonymous letter, had brought one to Mr. Alexander. His was from London, informing him that he had been appointed to a post connected with one of the hospitals, and requesting him to go up at once for a few hours. Mr. Alexander made ready, sent for a fly, and started with his wife for the station, bidding the driver halt at Mr. North's iron gates. As he was in attendance at that time on Edmund North, he wished to give notice of his temporary absence. To be furiously attacked by Edmund North the moment he entered the doors, and as it seemed to him, without rhyme or reason, put Mr. Alexander into somewhat of a passion also. There was no time for elucidation, neither was a single word he said listened to, and the surgeon hastened out to his fly. He had returned by the first train this morning—London was not much more than an hour's journey by rail—and found that Edmund North had died of that self-same passion. Half paralyzed with grief and horror, Mr. Alexander hastened to the Hall; and was now coming from it, having fully exculpated himself in all ways in the sight of its master. Almost as fully he spoke now to Dr. Rane; in his grief, in his straightforward candour, nothing selfish or sinister could hide itself.

The transaction in regard to drawing the bill had been wholly Edmund North's, Some months ago he had sought Mr. Alexander, saying he was in want of a sum of money—a hundred pounds; he did not know how to put his hands just then upon it, not wishing to apply to his own family; would he, the surgeon, like a good fellow, lend it? At first, Mr. Alexander had excused himself; for one thing he had not the money—fancy a poor country surgeon with a hundred pounds loose cash, he said; but eventually he fell in with Edmund North's pleadings. A bill was drawn, both of them being liable, and was discounted by Dale, the lawyer, of Whitborough. When the bill had become due (about a week ago) neither of them could meet it; and the matter was arranged with Dale by a second bill.

"What I cannot understand is, how Edmund North, poor fellow, could have pitched upon me as the writer of that letter," observed the surgeon to Dr. Rane, when he had finished his recital. "He must have gone clean daft to think it. I had no reason for disclosing it; I did not fear but he would eventually meet the bill."

"I told them you could not have written it," quietly rejoined the doctor.

Mr. Alexander lifted his hand with angry emphasis. "Rane, I'd give a thousand pounds out of my pocket—if I were a rich man and had it—to know who wrote the letter and worked the mischief. I never disclosed the transaction to a living soul; I don't believe Edmund North did; besides ourselves, it was known only to the discounter. Dale is a safe man; so it seems a perfect mystery. And mark you, Rane—that letter was written to damage me at the Hall, not Edmund North."

Dr. Rane gazed at the other in great surprise. "To damage you?"

"It is the view I take of it. And so, on reflection, does Richard North."

"Nonsense, Alexander!"

"If ever the hidden particulars come to light, you will find that it is not nonsense, but truth," was the surgeon's answer. "I must have some enemies in the neighbourhood, I suppose; most professional men have; and they no doubt hoped to do for me with Mr. North. The Norths in a degree sway other people here, and so I should have lost my practice, and been driven away."

Oliver had raised his cane, and was lightly flicking the shrub by which he stood, his air that of one in deep thought.

"I confess I do not follow you, Alexander. Your ill-doing or well-doing is nothing to Mr. North; his son's of course was. If you lived by drawing bills, it could be no concern of his."

"Drawing bills on my own score would certainly be of no moment to Mr. North; but drawing them in conjunction with his son would be. Upon which of us would he naturally lay the blame? Upon a young, heedless man, as Edmund North was; or upon me, a middle-aged, established member of society, with a home and a family? The case speaks for itself."

Oliver Rane did not appear quite to admit this. He thought the probability lay against Mr. Alexander's theory, rather than with it. "Of course," he slowly said, "looking at it in that light, the letter would tell either way. But I think you must be wrong."

"No, I am not. Whoever wrote that missive did it to injure me. I seemed to see it, as by instinct, the minute Mr. North gave me the letter to read. If the motive was to drive me from Dallory, it might have been spared, and Edmund North saved, for I am going to quit it of my own accord."

"To quit Dallory?"

"In a month's time from this I and mine will have left it for London. The situation now given to me I have been trying for, under the rose, these six months past."

"But why do you wish to leave Dallory?"

"To better myself, as the servants say," replied Mr. Alexander, "and the move will do that considerably. Another reason is that my wife dislikes Dallory. Madam turned up her nose at us socially when we first settled here; and that, in a degree, kept the best society closed to Mrs. Alexander. She is well-born, has been reared a lady; and of course it was: enough to set her against the place. Besides, all our friends are in London; and so, you see, if my exit into the wilderness was what that anonymous individual was driving at, he might have gained his ends without crime, had he waited only a short time."

"I hate Mrs. North," dreamily spoke Dr. Rane; "and I am sure she hates me, though the wherefore to me is incomprehensible."

"Look there," spoke the surgeon, dropping his voice.

Both had simultaneously caught sight of Mrs. North. She was passing the shrubbery close by, and looked out at them. They raised their hats. Mr. Alexander made a movement to approach her; she saw it, and turned from him back to the dark wall with her usual sweeping step. So he remained where he was.

"She asked to see me on Tuesday night when I was leaving; wanting to know if I could tell her who wrote the letter," said Dr. Rane.

"She suspected me, I suppose."

"She appeared to suspect—not you, but some one else; and that was Richard North."

"Richard North!" ironically repeated Mr. Alexander. "She knows quite well that he is above suspicion; perhaps she was only trying to divert attention from some other person: she is made up of craft. Who knows but she wrote the letter herself?"

"Mrs. North!"

"Upon my word and honour, the thought is in my mind, Rane. If the motive of the letter were as you think—to do Edmund North damage with his father—I know of only one person who would attempt it, and that is Mrs. North."

Their eyes met: a strange light shone momentarily in Oliver Rane's. In saying that he hated Mrs. North, he spoke truth; but there was every excuse for the feeling, for it was quite certain that Mrs. North had long been working him what ill she could. His marriage with Bessy was being delayed, and delayed entirely through her covert opposition.

"That she is an entirely unscrupulous woman, and would stand at nothing, I feel sure," spoke Dr. Rane, drawing a deep breath. "But, as to the letter—"

"Well, as to the letter?" cried the surgeon, in the pause. "I don't say she foresaw that it would kill him."

"This would disprove your theory of its being written to damage you, Alexander."

"Not altogether. The damaging another, more or less, would be of no moment at all to Mrs. North; she would crush any one without scruple."

"I'm sure she would crush me," spoke Dr. Rane. "Heaven knows why; I don't."

"Well, if she did write the letter, I think her conscience must smite her as she looks at the poor dead man lying there. Good-day, Rane: I have not been home to see my little ones yet. Mrs. Alexander is remaining in town for a day or two."

In talking, they had walked slowly to the end of the avenue; Mr. Alexander passed through the gates, and took the road towards the Ham.

"I may as well go on at once, and see Ketler," thought Dr. Rane. "Time enough to call at the Hall as I return."

So he went on towards Dallory. Two gentlemen passed him on horseback, county magistrates, who were probably going to the Hall. The sight of them turned his thoughts to the subject of an inquest: he began speculating why Mr. North wished to evade it, and whether he would succeed in doing so. For his own part, he did not see that the case, speaking in point of law, called for one. Hepburn said it did; and he was supposed, as chief undertaker in Dallory, to understand these things.

Deep in reflection, the doctor strode on; when, in passing Mrs. Gass's house, a sharp tapping at the window saluted his ear. It came from that lady herself, and she threw up the sash.

"Just come in, will you, Dr. Rane? I want you for something very particular."

He felt sure she only wanted to question him about the death, and would a great deal rather have gone on: but with her red and smiling face inviting him in peremptorily, he did not see his way to refusing her.

"And so he is gone—that poor young man!" she began, meeting him in her smart dress and pink cap. "When I heard the death-bell ring out this morning, it sounded to me a'most like my own knell."

"Yes, he is gone—unhappily," murmured Dr. Rane.

"Well, now, doctor, the next thing is—what became of you yesterday?"

The change of subject appeared peculiar.

"Became of me?" repeated Dr. Rane. "How do you mean?"

"All the mortal day I was stuck at this parlour window, waiting to see you go by," proceeded Mrs. Gass. "You never passed once."

"Yes, I did. I passed in the morning."

"My eyes must have gone a-maying then, for they never saw you," was Mrs. Gass's answer.

"It was before my usual hour. I was called out early to a sick man in Dallory, and I took the opportunity to see Ketler at the same time."

"Then that accounts for the milk in the cocoa-nuts; and I wasted my time for nothing," was her good-tempered rejoinder.

"Why did you want to see me pass?"

Mrs. Gass paused for a moment before replying. She glanced round to see that the door was closed, and dropped her voice almost to a whisper.

"Dr. Rane, who wrote that fatal letter?"

"I cannot tell."

"Did you?"

Oliver Rane stared at her, a sudden flush of anger dyeing his brow. No wonder: the question, put with emphatic earnestness, seemed an assertion, almost like that startling reproach of Nathan to David.

"Mrs. Gass, I do not know what you mean."

"I see you don't relish it, doctor. But I am a plain body, as you know; and when in doubt about a thing, pleasant or unpleasant, I like to ask an explanation straight out."

"But why should you be in doubt about this?" he inquired wonderingly. "What can induce you to connect me with the letter?"

Mrs. Gass took her portly person across the room to a desk; unlocked it, and brought forth a folded piece of paper. She handed it to Dr. Rane.

It was not a letter; it could not be the copy of one: but it did appear to be the rough sketch of the anonymous missive that had reached Mr. North. Some of the sentences were written two or three times over; in a close hand, in a scrawling hand, in a reversed hand, as if the writer were practising different styles; in others the construction was altered, words were erased, others substituted. Oliver Rane gazed upon it as one in complete bewilderment.

"What is this, Mrs. Gass?"

"Is it not the skeleton of the letter?"

"No, certainly not. And yet—" Dr. Rane broke off and ran his eye over the lines again and again. "There is a similarity in some of the phrases," he suddenly said.

"Some of the phrases is identical," returned Mrs. Gass. "When Mr. Richard North was here yesterday, I got him to repeat over to me the words of the letter; word for word, so far as he remembered 'em, and I know 'em for these words. Whoever writ that letter to Mr. North, doctor, first of all tried his sentences and his hand, on this paper, practising how he could best do it."

"How did you come by this?"

"You left it here the night before last."

"I left it here!" repeated Dr. Rane, looking as if he mentally questioned whether Mrs. Gass was in her right senses.

"Yes. You."

"But you must be dreaming, Mrs. Gass."

"I never do dream—that sort of dreaming," replied Mrs. Gass. "Look here"—putting her stout hand, covered with costly rings, on his coat-sleeve—"didn't you upset your pocketbook here that night? Well, this piece of paper fell out of it."

"It could not have done anything of the sort," he repeated, getting flushed and angry again. "All the papers that fell out of my pocketbook I picked up and returned to it."

"You didn't pick this up; it must have fluttered away unseen. Just after you were gone I dropped my spectacle-case, and in stooping for it, I saw this piece of paper lying under the claw of the table."

"But it could not have come out of my pocketbook. Just tell me, if you please, Mrs. Gass, what should bring such a document in my possession?"

"That's just what I can't tell. The paper was not there before candle-light; I'll answer for that much; so where else could it have come from?"

The last words were not spoken as an assertion of her view, but as a question. Dr. Rane looked at her, she at him; both seeming equally puzzled.

"Had you any visitor last evening besides myself?" he asked.

"Not a soul. The only person that came into the parlour, barring my own servants, was Molly Green, under-housemaid at the Hall. She lived with me once, and calls in sometimes in passing to ask how I am. They sent her into Dallory for something wanted at the chemist's, and she looked in to tell me. The thing had just happened."

Dr. Rane's brow lost its perplexity: an easy smile, as if the mystery were solved, crossed his face. The hint recently given him by Mr. Alexander was in his mind.

"I'm glad you've told me this, Mrs. Gass. The paper was more likely to have been left by Molly Green than by me. It may have dropped from her petticoats."

"Goodness bless the man! From her petticoats! Why, she had run all the way from the Hall. And how was she likely to pick it up in that house—even though her gown had been finished off with fish-hooks?"

"What cause have I given you to suspect me of this?" retorted Dr. Rane in harsh tones.

"Only this—that I don't see where the paper could have come from but out of your own pocketbook," replied Mrs. Gass frankly. "I have no other reason to suspect you; I'd as soon suspect myself. It is just a mystery, and nothing else."

"Whatever the mystery may be, it is not connected with my pocketbook, Mrs. Gass," he emphatically said. "Did you mention this to Richard North?"

"No. Nor to anybody else. It was not a pleasant thing to speak of, you see."

"Not a pleasant thing for me, certainly, to be suspected of having dropped that paper. The culprit, an innocent one, no doubt, must have been Molly Green."

"I never was so brought up in all my life," cried the puzzled woman. "As to Molly Green—it must be just a fancy of yours, doctor, for it never can be fact."

Oliver Rane drew his chair a little nearer to Mrs. Gass, and whispered a word of the doubt touching Mrs. North. He only spoke of it as a doubt; a hint at most; but Mrs. Gass was not slow to take it.

"Heaven help the woman!—if it's her work."

"But this must not be breathed aloud," he said, taking alarm. "It may be a false suspicion."

"Don't fear me: it's a thing too grave for me to mix myself up in," was the reply: and to give Mrs. Gass her due, she did look scared in no slight degree. "Dr. Rane, I am sorry for saying what I did to you. It was the impossibility, as I took it, of anything's having left it here but that flutter of papers from your pocketbook. Whoever would have given a thought to Molly Green?"

Dr. Rane made no answer.

"She put her basket down by the door there, and came up the room to look at my geraniums; I held the candle for her. I remember she caught her crinoline on the corner of the iron fender, and it gave her a twist round. The idiots that girls make of themselves with them big crinolines! Perhaps it dropped from her then."

"Well, let us bury it in silence, Mrs. Gass; it is only a doubt at best," said the prudent but less eloquent physician. "You will allow me to take this," he added alluding to the paper. "I should like to examine it at leisure."

"Take it, and welcome," she answered; "I'm glad to be rid of it. As to burying it in silence, we had better, I expect, both do that."

"Even to Richard North," he enjoined rather anxiously.

"Even to Richard North. I have kept secrets in my day, doctor, and can keep 'em again."

Dr. Rane put the paper in his pocketbook, deposited that in the breast-pocket of his coat, and took his departure. But now, being a shrewd man, a suspicion that he would not have given utterance to for the whole world, lay on Dr. Rane—that it was more in accordance with probability that the paper had dropped out of his pocketbook than from Molly Green's petticoats, seeing they were not finished off with fish-hooks.

A heavy weight lying there on his breast! And he went along with a loitering step, asking himself how the paper could have originally come there.

CHAPTER IV

ALONE WITH THE TRUTH

Oliver Rane was in his bedchamber; a front apartment facing the road. It will be as well to give a word of description to this first floor, for it may prove needed as the tale goes on. It consisted of a large landing-place, its boards white and bare, with a spacious window looking to the side of the other house, as the dining-room beneath it did. Wide, low and curtainless was this window; giving, in conjunction with the bare floors and walls, a staring appearance to the place. Mrs. Cumberland's opposite landing (could you have seen it) presented a very different aspect, with its rich carpet, its statues, vases, bookcases, and its pretty window-drapery. Dr. Rane could not afford luxuries yet; or, indeed, superfluous furniture of any sort. The stairs led almost close to this window, so that in coming down from any of the bedrooms, or the upper floor, you had to face it.

To get into Dr. Rane's chamber—the best in the house—an ante-room had to be passed through, and its door was opposite the large window. Two chambers opened from the back of the landing: they faced the back lane that ran along beyond the garden wall. Above, in the roof, were two other rooms, both three-cornered. Phillis, the old serving-woman, slept on that floor in one of them, Dr. Rane on this: the house had no other inmates.

The ante-room had no furniture: unless some curious-looking articles lying on the floor could be called so. They seemed to consist chiefly of glass: jars covered in dust, a cylindrical glass-pump, and other things belonging to chemistry, of which science the doctor was fond. Certainly the architect had not made the most of this floor, or he would never have given so much space to the landing. But if this ante-room was not furnished, Dr. Rane's chamber was; and well furnished too. The walls were white and gold, the dressing-table and glass stood before the window and opposite the door. On the left was the fireplace; the handsome white Arabian bedstead was picked out with gold, and its hangings of green damask, matched the window drapery and the soft colours of the carpet.

Seated at the round table in the middle of the room, his hand raised to support his head, was Dr. Rane. He had only just come in, and it was now one o'clock—his usual dinner hour. It was that same morning mentioned in the last chapter, when he had quitted Mrs. Gass's house with that dangerous piece of paper weighing upon his pocket and his heart. He had been detained out. As he was entering the house of the sick man, Ketler, whom he had proceeded at once to see, a bustle in the street, and much wild running of women, warned him that something must have happened. Two men had fallen into the river at the back of the North Works; and excited people were shouting that they were drowned. Not quite: as Dr. Rane saw when he reached the spot: not beyond hope of restoration. Patiently the doctor persevered in his endeavours. He brought life into them at length; and stayed afterwards caring for them. After that, he had Ketler and other patients to see, and it was nearly one when he bent his steps towards home. In the morning he had said to himself that he would call at the Hall on his return; but he passed its gates; perhaps because it was his dinner hour, for one o'clock was striking.

Hanging up his hat in the small hall, leaving his cane in the corner—a pretty trifle with a gold stag for its handle—he was making straight for the stairs, when the servant, Phillis, came out of the kitchen. A little woman of some five-and-fifty years, with high shoulders, and her head carried forward. Her chin and nose were sharp now, but the once good-looking face was meek and mild, the sweet dark eyes were subdued, and the hair, peeping from beneath the close white cap, was grey. She wore a dark cotton gown and check apron. A tidy-looking, respectable woman, in spite of her unfashionable appearance.

"Is that you, sir? Them folks have been over from the brick-kilns, saying the woman's not so well to-day, if you'd please to go to her."

Dr. Rane nodded. He went on up the stairs and into his own room, the door of which he locked. Why? Phillis was not in the habit of intruding upon him, and there was no one else in the house. The first thing he did was to take the paper received from Mrs. Gass out of his pocketbook, and read it attentively twice over. Then he struck a match, set fire to it, and watched it consume away in the empty grate. A dangerous memento, whosesoever hand had penned it; and the physician did well, in the interests of humanity, to put it out of sight for ever. The task over, he leaned against the window-frame, and lapsed into thought. He was dwelling upon the death at Dallory Hall, and what it might bring forth.

Hepburn, the undertaker, was right. There was to be no inquest. So much Dr. Rane had learned from Richard North: who had hastened to the works on hearing of the accident to his men. The two Whitborough doctors had given the certificate of death: apoplexy, to which there had been a previous tendency, though immediately brought on by excitement: and nothing more was required by law. From a word spoken by Richard, Dr. Rane gathered that it was madam who had set her veto against an inquest. And quite right too; there was no necessity whatever for one, had been the comment made by Oliver Rane to Richard. But now—now when he was alone with himself and the naked truth: when there was no man at hand whose opinion it might be well to humour or deceive: no eye upon him save God's, he could not help acknowledging that had he been Mr. North, had it been his son who was thus cut off from life, he should have caused an inquest to be held. Ay, ten inquests, an' the law would have allowed them; if by that means he might have traced the letter home to its writer.

Quitting the window, he sat down at the table and bent his forehead upon his hand. Never in his whole life had anything so affected him as this death: and it was perhaps natural that he should set himself to see whether, or not, any sort of excuse might be found for the anonymous writer.

He began by putting himself in idea in the writer's place, and argued the point for him: for and against. Chiefly for; it was on that side his bias leaned. It is very easy, as the world knows, to find a plea for those in whom we are interested or on whom misfortune falls; it is so natural to indulge for their sakes in a little sophistry. Such sophistry came now to the help of the physician.

"What need had Edmund North to fly into a furious passion?" ran the self-argument. "Only a madman might have been expected to do so. There was nothing in the letter that need have excited him, absolutely nothing. It was probably written with a very harmless intention; certainly the writer never could have dreamt that it might have the effect of destroying a life."

Destroying a man's life! A flush passed into Oliver Rane's face at the thought, dyeing neck and brow. And, with it, recurred the words of Hepburn—that the writer was a murderer and might come to be tried for it. A murderer! There is no other self-reproach under heaven that can bring home so much anguish to the conscience. But—could a man be justly called a murderer if he had never had thought or intention of doing anything of the kind?

"Halt here," said Dr. Rane, suddenly speaking aloud, as if he were a special pleader arguing in a law court. "Can a man be called a murderer who has never had the smallest intention of murdering—who would have flown in horror from the bare idea? Let us suppose it was—Mrs. North—who wrote the letter? Alexander suspects her, at any rate. Put it that she had some motive for writing it. It might have been a good motive—that of stopping Edward North in his downward career, as the letter intimated—and she fancied this might be best accomplished by letting his father hear of what he, in conjunction with Alexander, was doing. According to Alexander, she does not interfere openly between the young men and their father; it isn't her policy to do so: and she may have considered that the means she took were legitimate under the circumstances. Well, could she for a moment imagine that any terrible consequences would ensue? A rating from Mr. North to his son, and the matter would be over. Just so: she was innocent of any other thought. Then how could she be thought guilty?"

Dr. Rane paused. A book lay on the table: he turned its leaves backwards and forwards in abstraction, his mind revolving the subject. Presently he resumed.

"Or—take Alexander's view of the letter—that it was written to damage him with Mr. North and the neighbourhood generally. Madam—say again—had conceived a dislike to Alexander, wished him dismissed from the house, but had no plea for doing it, and so took that means of accomplishing her end. Could she suspect that the result would be fatal to Edmund North? Would she not have shrunk with abhorrence from writing the letter, had she foreseen it? Certainly. Then, under these circumstances, how can a man—I mean a woman—be responsible, legally or morally, for the death? It would be utterly unjust to charge her with it. Edmund North is alone to blame. Clearly so. The case is little better than one of unintentional suicide."

Having arrived at this view of the subject—so comforting for the unknown writer—Dr. Rane rose briskly, and began to wash his hands and brush his hair. He took a note-case from his pocket, in which he was in the habit of entering his daily engagements, to see at what hour he could most conveniently visit the brick-fields, in compliance with the message received. The sick woman was in no danger, as he knew, and he might choose his own time. In passing through the ante-room—a room, by the way, generally distinguished as the Drab Room, from the unusual colour of the hideous walls—he took up one of the glass jars, requiring it for some purpose downstairs. And then he noticed something that displeased him.

"Phillis!" he called, going out to the landing: "Phillis!" And the woman, a very active little body, came running up.

"You have been sweeping the Drab Room?"

"It was so dirty, sir."

"Now look here," he cried, angrily. "If you sweep out a room again, when I tell you it is not to be swept, I'll keep every place in the house locked up. Some of the glass here is valuable, and I won't run the risk of having it broken with your brooms and brushes."

Down went Phillis, taking the reproof in silence. As Dr. Rane crossed the landing to follow her, his eyes fell on his mother's house through the large window. The window opposite was being cleaned by one of the servants: at the window of the dining-room underneath, his mother was sitting. It reminded Dr. Rane that he had not been in to see her for nearly two days; not since Edmund North—

Suddenly a sense of the delusive nature of the sophistry he had been indulging, flashed into his brain, and the truth shone out distinct and bare. Edmund North was dead; had been killed by the anonymous letter. But for that fatal letter he had been alive and well now. A sickening sensation, as of some great oppression, came over Oliver Rane, and his nerveless fingers dropped the jar.

Out ran Phillis, lifting her hands at the crash of glittering particles lying in the passage. "He has broken one himself now," thought she, referring to the recent reproof.

"Sweep the pieces carefully into a dust-pan, and throw them away," said her master as he passed on. "The jar slipped out of my fingers."

Phillis stared a minute, exhausting her surprise, and then turned away for the dust-pan. The doctor went on to the front-door, instead of into the dining-room, as Phillis expected.

"Sir," she called out, hastening after him, "your dinner's waiting. Will you not take it now?"

But Dr. Rane passed on as though he had not heard her, and shut the door loudly.

He turned into his mother's house. Not by the open window; not by stepping over the slight fence; but he knocked at the front-door, and was admitted as an ordinary visitor. Whether it was from having lived apart for so many years of their lives, or that a certain cordiality was wanting in the disposition of each, certain it was that Dr. Rane and his mother observed more ceremony with each other than usually obtains between mother and son.

Mrs. Cumberland sat at the open dining-room window just as he had seen her from his staircase landing; a newspaper lay behind her on a small table, as if just put down. Ellen Adair, as might be heard, was at the piano in the drawing-room, playing, perhaps from unconscious association, and low and softly as it was her delight to play, the "Dead March in Saul." The dirge grated on the ears of Dr. Rane.

"What a melancholy performance!" he involuntarily exclaimed; and Mrs. Cumberland looked up, there was so much irritation in his tone.

He shook hands with his mother, but did not kiss her, which he was not accustomed to do, and stood back against the broad window, his face turned to it.

"You are a stranger, Oliver," she said. "What has kept you away?"

"I have been busy. To-day especially. They had an accident at the works—two men were nearly drowned—and I have been with them all the morning."

"I heard of it. Jelly brought me in the news; she seems to hear everything. How fortunate that you were at hand!"

He proceeded, rather volubly for him, to give particulars of the accident and of the process he adopted to recover the men. Mrs. Cumberland looked and listened with silent, warm affection; but that she was a particularly undemonstrative woman, she would have betrayed it in her manner. In her eyes, there was not so fine and handsome and estimable a man in all Dallory as this her only son.

"Oliver, what a dreadful thing this is about Edmund North! I have not seen you since. Why did you not come in and tell me the same night?"

He turned his eyes on her for a moment in surprise, and paused.

"I am not in the habit of coming in to tell you when called out to patients, mother. How was I to know you wished it?"

"Nonsense, Oliver! This is not an ordinary thing: the Norths were something to me once. I have had Edmund on my knee when he was a baby; and I should have liked you to pay me the attention of bringing in the news. It appears to be altogether a more romantic event than one meets with every day, and such things, you know, are of interest to lonely women."

Dr. Rane made no rejoinder, possibly not having sufficient excuse for his carelessness. He stood looking dreamily from a corner of the window. Phillis, as might be seen from there, was carrying away the fowl prepared for his dinner, and a tureen of sauce. Mrs. Cumberland probably thought he was watching with critical curiosity the movements of his handmaid. She resumed:

"They say, Oliver, there has been no hope of him from the first."

"There was very little. Of course, as it turns out, there could have been none."

"And who wrote the letter? With what motive was it written?" proceeded Mrs. Cumberland, her grey face bent slightly forward, as she waited for an answer.

"It is of no use to ask me, mother. Some people hold one opinion, some another; mine would go for little."

"They are beginning now to think that it was not written at all to injure Edmund, but Mr. Alexander."

"Who told you that?" he asked, a sharper accent discernible in his tone.

"Captain Bohun. He came in this morning to tell me of the death. Considering that I have no claim upon him, that a year ago I had never spoken to him, I must say that Arthur Bohun is very kind and attentive to me. He is one in a thousand."

Perhaps the temptation to say, "It's not for your sake he is so attentive," momentarily assailed Oliver Rane. But he was good-natured in the main, and he knew when to be silent, and when to speak: no man better. Besides, it was no business of his.

"I entertain a different opinion," he observed, referring to the point in discussion. "Of course it is all guess work as to the writer's motive: there can be no profit in discussing it, mother: and I must be going, for my dinner's waiting. Thank you for sending me the chicken."

"A moment yet, Oliver," she interposed, as he was moving away. "Have you heard that Alexander is going to leave?"

"Yes: he was talking to me about it this morning."

If ever a glow of light had been seen lately on Mrs. Cumberland's marble face, it was seen then. The tightly-drawn features had lost their grey tinge.

"Oliver, I could go down on my knees and thank Heaven for it. You don't know how grieved I have felt all through these past two years, to see you put into the shade by that man, and to know that it was I who had brought you here! It will be all right now. New houses are to be built, they say, at the other end of the Ham, and the practice will be worth a great deal. I shall sleep well to-night."

He smiled as he shook hands with her; partly in affection, partly at her unusual vehemence. In passing the drawing-room, Ellen Adair happened to be coming out of it, but he went on. She supposed he had not observed her, and spoke.

"Ah! how do you do, Miss Adair?" he said, turning back, and offering his hand. "Forgive my haste; I am busy to-day."

And before she had time to make any reply, he was gone; leaving an impression on her mind, she could not well have told why or wherefore, that he was ill at ease; that he had hastened away, not from pressure of work, but because he did not care to talk to her.

If that feeling was possessing Dr. Rane, and had reference to the world in general, and not to the young lady in particular, it might not have been agreeable to him to encounter an acquaintance as he turned out of his mother's house. Mr. Alexander was swiftly passing on his way towards home from the lower part of the Ham, and stopped.

"I wish I had never said a syllable about going away until I was off," cried he in his off-hand manner—a pleasanter and more sociable manner than Dr. Rane's. "The news has been noised abroad, and the whole place is upon me; asking this, that, and the other. One man comes and wants to know if I'll sell my furniture; another thinks he'd like the house as it stands. My patients are up in arms;—say I'm doing it to kill them. I shall have some of them in a fever before the day's over."

"Perhaps you won't go, after all," observed Dr. Rane.

"Not go! How can I help going? I'm elected to the post. Why, it's what I've been looking out for ever so long—almost ever since I came here. No, no, Rane: a short time, and Dallory Ham will have seen the last of me."

He hastened across the road to his house, like a man who has the world's work on his busy shoulders. Dr. Rane's thoughts, as he glanced after him, reverted to the mental argument he had held in his chamber, and he unconsciously resumed it, putting himself in the place of the unknown, unhappy writer, as before.

"It's almost keener than the death itself—if the motive was to injure Alexander in his profession, or drive him from the place—to know that he, or she—Mrs. North—might have spared her pains! Heavens! what remorse it must be!—to commit a crime, and then find there was no necessity for doing it!"

Dr. Rane passed his white handkerchief over his brow—the day was very warm—and turned into his house. Phillis once more placed the dinner on the table, and he sat down to it.

But not a mouthful could he swallow; his throat felt like so much dried-chip, and the food would not go down. Phillis, who was coming in for something or other, saw him leave his plate and rise from table.

"Is the fowl not tender, sir?"

"Tender?" he responded, as though the sense of the question had not reached him, and paused. "Oh, it's tender enough: but I must go off to a patient. Get your own dinner, Phillis."

"Surely you'll come back to yours, sir?"

"I've had as much as I want. Take the things away."

"I wonder what's come to him?" mused the woman as his quick steps receded from the house, and she was left with the rejected dishes. A consciousness came dimly penetrating to her hazy brain that there was some change upon him. What it was, or where it lay, she did not define. It was unusual for his strong firm fingers to drop a glass; it was still more unusual for him to explain cause and effect. "The jar slipped from my fingers." "I've had as much as I want. I must go off to a patient." It was quite out of the order of routine for Dr. Rane to be explanatory to his servant on any subject whatever: and perhaps it was his having been so in these two instances that impressed Phillis.

"How quick he must have eaten his dinner!"

Phillis nearly dropped the dish. The words were spoken close behind her, and she had believed herself alone in the house. Turning, she saw Jelly, standing half in, half out of the window.

"Well, I'm sure!" cried Phillis, in wrath. "You needn't come startling a body in that way, Mrs. Jelly. How did you know but the doctor might be at table?"

"I've just seen him go down the lane," returned Jelly, who had plenty of time for gossiping with her neighbours, and had come strolling over the fence now with no other object. "Has he had his dinner? It's but the other minute he was in at our house."

"He has had as much as he means to have," answered Phillis, her anger evaporating, for she liked a gossip also. "I'm sure it's not worth the trouble of serving meals, if they are to be left in this fashion. It was the same thing at breakfast."

Jelly recollected the scene at breakfast; the startled pallor on Dr. Rane's face, when told that Edmund North was dead: she supposed that had spoiled his appetite. Her inquisitive eyes turned unceremoniously to the fowl, and she saw that the merest slice off the wing was alone eaten.

"Perhaps he is not well to-day," said Jelly.

"I don't know about his being well; he's odder than I ever saw him," answered Phillis. "I shouldn't wonder but he has had his stomach turned over them two half-drowned men."

She carried the dinner-things across to the kitchen. Jelly, who assisted at the ceremony, as far as watching and talking went, was standing in the passage, when her quick eyes caught sight of two small pieces of glass. She stooped to pick them up.

"Look, Phillis! You have been breaking something. It's uncommonly careless to leave the bits about."

"Is it!" retorted Phillis. "Your eyes are in everything. I thought I took 'em all up," she added, looking on the ground.

"What did you break?"

"Nothing. It was the doctor. He dropped one of them dusty glass jars down the stairs. It did give me a start. You should have heard the smash."

"What made him drop it?" asked Jelly.

"Goodness knows," returned the older woman. "He's not a bit like himself to-day; it's just as if something had come to him."

She began her dinner as she spoke, standing, her usual mode of taking it. Jelly, following her free-and-easy habits, stood against the door-post, apparently interested in the progress of the meal. They presented a contrast, these two women, the one a thin, upright giantess, the other a dwarf stooping forward. Jelly, a lady's-maid, held herself of course altogether above Phillis, an ignorant (as Jelly would have described her) servant-of-all-work, though condescending to drop in for the sake of gossip.

"Did you happen to hear how the doctor found Ketler?"

"As if I should be likely to hear!" was Phillis's retort. "He'd not tell me, and I couldn't ask. My master's not one you can put questions to, Jelly."

A silence ensued. The gossip apparently flagged to-day. Phillis had it chiefly to herself, for Jelly vouchsafed only a brief remark now and again. She was engaged in the mental process of wondering what had come to Dr. Rane.

CHAPTER V

RETROSPECT

There must be a little retrospect to make things intelligible to the reader; and it may as well be given at once.

Mr. North, now of Dallory Sail, had got on entirely by his own industry. Of obscure, though in a certain way respectable, parentage, he had been placed as apprentice to a firm in Whitborough. It was a firm in extensive work, not confining itself to one branch. They took contracts for public buildings, small and large: did mechanical engineering; had planned one of the early railways. John North—plain Jack North he was known as, then—remained with the firm when he was out of his time, and got on in it. Steady and plodding, he rose from one step to another; and at length, in conjunction with one who had been in the same firm, he set up for himself. This other was Thomas Gass. Gass had not risen from the ranks as North had: his connections were good, and he had received a superior education; but his friends were poor. North and Gass, as the new firm called itself, began business near to Dallory; quietly at first—as all people, who really expect to get on, generally do begin. They rose rapidly. The narrow premises expanded; the small contracts grew into large ones. People said luck was with them—and in truth it seemed so. The Dallory works became noted in the county, employing quite a colony of people: the masters were respected and sought after. Both lived at Whitborough; Mr. North with his wife and family; Mr. Gass a bachelor.

Thomas Gass had one brother; a clergyman. Their only sister, Fanny, a very pretty girl, had her home with him in his rectory, but she came often to Whitborough on a visit to Thomas. Suddenly it was announced to the world that she had become engaged to marry a Captain Rane, entirely against the wish of her two brothers. She was under twenty. Captain Rane, a poor naval man on half-pay, was almost old enough to be her grandfather. Their objection lay not so much in this, as in himself. For some reason or other, neither of them liked him. The Reverend William Gass forbid his sister to think of him; Mr. Thomas Gass, a fiery man, swore he would never afterwards look upon her as a sister, if she persisted in thus throwing herself away.

Miss Gass did persist. She possessed the obstinate spirit of her brother Thomas, though without his fire. She chose to take her own way, and married Captain Rane. They sailed at once for Madras; Captain Rane having obtained some post there, connected with the Government ships.

Whether Miss Gass repented her marriage, her brothers had no means of learning: for she, retaining her anger, never wrote to them during her husband's lifetime. It was a very short one. Barely a twelvemonth had elapsed after the knot was tied, when there came a pitiful letter from her. Captain Rane had died, just as her little son Oliver (named after a friend, she said) was born. Thomas Gass, to whom the letter had been specially written, gathered that she was left badly off; though she did not absolutely say so. He went into one of his angry moods, and tossed the epistle across the desk to his partner. "You must do something for her, Gass," said John North when he had read it. "I never will," hotly affirmed Mr. Gass. "Fanny knows what I promised if she married Rane—that I would never help her during my lifetime or after it. She knows another thing—that I am not one to go from my word. William may help her if he likes; he has not much to give away, but he can have her home to live with him." "Help the child, then," suggested Mr. North, knowing further remonstrance to be useless. "No," returned obstinate Thomas Gass; "I'll stick to the spirit of my promise as well as the letter." And Mr. North bent his head again—he was going over some estimates—feeling that the affair was none of his. "I don't mind putting the boy in the tontine, North," presently spoke the junior partner. "The tontine!" echoed John North in surprise, "what tontine?" "What tontine?" returned the hard man—though in truth he was not hard in general, "why, the one that you and others are getting up; the one you have just put your baby, Bessy, into; I know of no other tontine." "But that will not benefit the boy," urged Mr. North: "certainly not now; and the chances are ten to one against its ever benefiting him in the future." "Never mind; I'll put him into it," said Mr. Gass, whose obstinacy always came out well under opposition. "You want a tenth child to close the list, and I'll put him into it." So into the tontine Oliver Rane, unconscious infant, was put.

But Mrs. Rane did not further trouble either of her brothers; or, as things turned out, require assistance from them. She remained in India; and after a year married a Government chaplain there, the Reverend George Cumberland, who possessed some private property. Little, if any, communication took place afterwards between her and her brothers; she cherished resentment for old grievances, and would not write to them. And so the sister and the brothers seemed to fade away from each other from henceforth. We all know how relatives, parted by time and distance, become estranged, disappearing almost from memory.

Whilst the firm, North and Gass, was rising higher and higher in wealth and importance, the wife of its senior partner died. She left three children, Edmund, Richard, and Bessy. Subsequently, during a visit to London, chance drew Mr. North into a meeting with a handsome young woman, the widow of Major Bohun. She had not long returned from India, where she had buried her husband. A designing, attractive syren, who began forthwith to exercise her dangerous fascinations on plain, unsuspicious Mr. North. She had only a poor pittance; what money there was belonged to her only child, Arthur; a little lad: sent out of sight already to a preparatory school. Report had magnified Mr. North's wealth into something fabulous; and Mrs. Bohun did not cease her scheming until she had caught him in her toils and he had made her Mrs. North.

Men do things sometimes in a hurry, only to repent of them at leisure. That Mr. North had been in a hurry in this case was indisputable—it was just as though Mrs. Bohun had thrown a spell over him; whether he repented when he woke up and found himself with a wife, a stepmother for his children at home, was not so certain. He was a sufficiently wise man in those days to conceal what he did not want known.

Whom he had married, beyond the fact that she was the widow of Major Bohun, he did not know from Adam. For all she disclosed about her own family, in regard to whom she maintained an absolute reticence, she might have dropped from the moon, or "growed" like Topsy; but, from the airs and graces she assumed, Mr. North might have concluded they were dukes and duchesses at least. Her late husband's family were irreproachable, both in character and position. The head of it was Sir Nash Bohun, representative of an ancient baronetcy, and elder brother of the late major. Before the wedding tour was over, poor Mr. North found that his wife was a cold, imperious, extravagant woman, not to be questioned by any means if she so chose. When her fascinations were in full play (while she was only Mrs. Bohun) Mr. North had been ready to think her an angel. Where had all the amiability flown to? People do change after marriage somehow. At least, there have been instances known of it.

A little circumstance occurred one day that—to put it mildly—had surprised Mr. North. He had been given to understand by his wife that Major Bohun died suddenly of sunstroke; she had certainly told him so. In talking at a dinner-party at Sir Nash Bohun's with some gentlemen not long from India, he and Mr. North being side by side at the table after the ladies had retired, the subject of sunstrokes came up. "My wife's former husband, Major Bohun, died of one," innocently observed Mr. North. "Died of what?" cried the other, putting down his claret-glass, which he was conveying to his mouth. "Of sunstroke," repeated Mr. North. "Bohun did not die of sunstroke," came the impulsive answer; "who told you he died of that?" "She did—my wife," was Mr. North's answer. "Oh!" said his friend; and took up his claret again. "Why, what did he die of, if it was not sunstroke?" asked Mr. North, with curiosity. "Well,—I—I don't know; I'd rather say no more about it," was the conclusive reply: "of course Mrs. North must know better than I." And nothing more would he say on the subject.

They were staying at this time at Sir Nash Bohun's. In passing through London after the Continental wedding trip on their way to Whitborough, Sir Nash had invited them to make his house their resting-place. Not until the day following his conversation at the dinner-table had Mr. North an opportunity of questioning his wife; but, that some false representation, intentionally or otherwise, had been made to him on the subject of her late husband's death, he felt certain. They were alone in her dressing-room. Mrs. North, who had a great deal of beautiful black hair, was standing before the glass, doing something to a portion of it, when her husband suddenly accosted her. He called her by her Christian name in those first married days. It was a very fine one.

"Amanda, you told me, I think, that Major Bohun died of sunstroke."

"Well?" she returned carelessly, occupied with her hair.

"But he did not die of sunstroke. He died of—of something else."

Mr. North had watched women's faces turn to pallor, but never in his whole life had he seen so livid a look of terror as now overspread his wife's. Her hair dropped from her nerveless hands.

"Why, what is the matter?" he exclaimed.

She murmured something about a spasm of the heart, to which she was subject: an excuse, as he saw. Another moment, and she had recovered her composure, and was busy with her hair again.

"You were asking me something, were you not, Mr. North?"

"About Major Bohun: what was it he died of—-if it was not sunstroke?"

"But it was of sunstroke," she said, in a sharp, ringing accent, that would have required only a little more to be a scream. "What else should he die of suddenly in India's burning climate? He went out in the blazing midday sun, and was brought home dead!"

And nothing more, then or afterwards, did Mr. North learn. Her manner rendered it impossible to press the subject. He might have applied to Sir Nash for information, but an instinct prevented his doing so. After all, it did not matter to him what Major Bohun had died of, Mr. North said to himself and determined to forget the incident. But that some mystery must have attended Major Bohun's death, some painful circumstances which could blanch his wife's face with sickly terror, remained on Mr. North's mind as a fact not to be disputed.

Mrs. North effected changes. Almost the very day she was taken home to Whitborough, she let it be known that she should rule with an imperious will. Her husband became a very reed in her hands; yielding passively to her sway, as if all the spirit he had ever owned had gone out of him. Mrs. North professed to hate the very name of trade; that any one with whom she was so nearly connected should be in business, brought her a sense of degradation and a great deal of talk about it. The quiet, modest, comfortable home at Whitborough was at once given up for the more pretentious Manor Hall at Dallory Ham, which happened to be in the market. And they set up there in a style that might have more properly belonged to the lord-lieutenant of the county. Perhaps it was her assumption of grandeur indoors and out, combined with the imperious manner, the like of which had never before been seen in the simple neighbourhood, that caused people to call her "Madam." Or, it might have been to distinguish her from the first Mrs. North.

In proportion as Mrs. North made herself hated and feared by her husband, his children, and the household, so did she become popular with society. It sometimes happens that the more fascination a woman displays to the world, the more unbearable is she in her own house. It was the case here. Madam put on all her attractions when out-of-doors; she visited and dressed and dined; and gave fêtes again at Dallory Hall utterly regardless of expense. Little wonder that she swayed the neighbourhood.

Not the immediate neighbourhood. With the exception of the Dallory family (and they did not live there always), there was not a single person she would have visited. A few gentle-people resided at Dallory Ham; Mrs. North did not condescend to know any of them. People living at a greater distance she made friends with, but not those around her; and with as many of the county families as would make friends with her. The pleasantest times were those when she would betake herself off on long visits, to London or elsewhere: they grew to be looked forward to.

But the most decided raid made by Mrs. North was on her husband's business connections. Had Thomas Gass been a chimney-sweeper, she could not have treated him with more intense contempt. Thomas Gass had his share of sense, and pitied his partner far more than he would have done had that gentleman gone in for hanging instead of second marriage. Mr. Gass was a very wealthy man now; and had built himself a handsome and comfortable residence in Dallory.

But, as the years went on, he was doomed to furnish food himself to all the gossips within miles. Dallory rose from its couch one fine morning, to hear that Thomas Gass, the confirmed old bachelor, had married his housekeeper. Not one of your "lady-housekeepers," but a useful, good, hard-working damsel, who had passed the first bloom of youth, and had not much beauty to recommend her. It was a nine days' wonder. Of course, however much the neighbours might solace their feelings by ridiculing him and abusing her, they could not undo the marriage. All that remained to them was, to make the best of it; and by degrees they wisely did so. The new Mrs. Gass glided easily into her honours. She made an excellent wife to her ailing husband—for Thomas Gass's health had begun to fail before his marriage—she put on no airs of being superior to what she was; she turned out to be a thoroughly capable woman of business, giving much judicious advice to those about her: she was very good to the sick and suffering, caring for the poor, ready to give a helping hand wherever and whenever it might be needed. In spite of her fine dresses, which sat ludicrously upon her, and of her manner of talking, which she did not attempt to improve; above all, in spite of their own prejudices, Dallory grew to like and respect Mrs. Gass, and its small gentle-people admitted her to their houses on an equality.

And so time and years went on, Mr. North withdrawing himself more and more from personal attendance on the business, which seemed to have grown utterly distasteful to him. His sons had become young men. Edmund was a civil engineer: by profession at least, not much by practice. Never in strong health, given to expensive and idle habits, Edmund North was generally either in trouble abroad, or leading a lazy life at home, his time being much divided between going into needless passions and writing poetry. Richard was at the works, the mainspring of the business. Mr. Gass had become a confirmed invalid, and could not personally attend to it; Mr. North did not do so. There was only Richard—Dick, as they all called him; but he was a host in himself. Of far higher powers than Mr. North had ever possessed, cultivated in mind, he was a thorough man of business, and at the same time a finished gentleman. Energetic, persevering, firm in controlling, yet courteous and considerate to the very lowest, Richard North was loved and respected. He walked through life doing his duty by his fellow-men: striving to do it to God. He had been tried at home in many ways since his father's second marriage, and borne all with patient endurance: how much he was tried out of home, he alone knew.

For a long time past there had been trouble in the firm, ill-feeling between the two old partners; chiefly because Mr. North put no limit to the sums he drew out for his private account. Poor Mr. North at length confessed that he could not help it: the money was wanted by his wife: though how on earth she contrived to get rid of so much, even with all her extravagance, he could not conceive. Mr. Gass insisted on a separation: John North must withdraw from the firm; Richard might take his place. Poor Mr. North yielded meekly. "Don't let it get abroad," he only stipulated, speaking as if he were half heartbroken, which was nothing new; "I should not like the world to know that I was superseded." They respected his wishes, and the change was made privately: very few being aware that the senior partnership in the firm had passed into the hands of a young man. Thenceforth Mr. North ceased to have any control in the business; in fact, to have any actual connection with it. Dallory suspected it not: Mrs. North had not the faintest idea of it. Richard North signed the cheques as he had done before, "North and Gass:" and perhaps the bank at Whitborough alone knew that he signed them now as principal.

Richard was the scape-goat now. Mr. North's need of money, or rather his wife's, did not cease: the sum arranged to be paid to him as a retiring pension—a very liberal sum, and Mr. Gass grumbled at it—seemed to be as nothing; it melted in madam's hands like so much water. Richard was constantly appealed to by his father; and responded generously, though it crippled him.

The next change came in the shape of Mr. Gass's death. The bulk of his property was left to his wife; a small portion, comparatively speaking, to charities and servants; two thousand pounds to Richard North. He also bequeathed to his wife his interest in the business, which by the terms of the deed of partnership he had power to do. So that his share of the capital was not drawn out, and the firm remained, actually as well as virtually, North and Gass. People generally supposed that the "North" was Mr. North; and madam went into a world of indignation at her husband's name being placed in conjunction with "that woman's." In the years gone by, Mr. North had had a nice time of it, finding it a difficult matter to steer his course between his partner and madam, and give offence to neither. Madam had never condescended to notice Thomas Gass's wife in the least degree: she took to abusing her now, asking her husband how he could suffer himself to be associated with her. Mr. North, when goaded almost beyond endurance, had hard work to keep his tongue from retorting that it was not himself that was associated with her, but Richard.

Mrs. Gass showed her good sense in regard to the partnership, as she did in most things. She declined to interfere actively in the business. Richard North went to her house two or three times a-week to keep her cognizant of what was going on; he consulted her opinion on great matters, just as he had consulted her husband's. She knew she could trust to him. Ever and anon she would volunteer some advice to himself personally: and it was invariably good advice. It could not be concealed from her that large sums (exclusively Richard's) were ever finding their way to the Hall, and for this she took him to task. "Stop it, Mr. Richard," she said—always as respectful to him as she had been in her housekeeping days: "Stop it, sir. Their wants are like a cullender, the more water you pour into it the more you may. It's doing them no good. An end must come to it some time, or you'll be in the workhouse. The longer it goes on, the more difficult it will be to put an end to, and the harder it will be for them." But Richard, sorely tried between prudence and filial duty, could not bring himself to stop it so easily; and the thing went on.

We must now go back to Mrs. Cumberland. It was somewhat singular that, the very week Thomas Gass died, she should make her unexpected appearance at Dallory. But so it was. Again a widow, she had come home to settle near her brother Thomas. She arrived just in time to see him put into his coffin. The other brother, William, had been dead for years. Mrs. Gass, who knew all about the estrangement, received her with marked kindness, and heartily offered her a home for the future.

Yet that was declined. Mrs. Cumberland preferred to have a home of her own, possessing ample means to establish one in a moderate way. She gave a sketch of her past life to Mrs. Gass. After her marriage with the Reverend George Cumberland, they had remained for some time at his chaplaincy in the Madras presidency; but his health began to fail, and he exchanged to Australia. Subsequently to that, years later, he obtained a duty in Madeira. Upon his death, which occurred recently, she came to England. Her only son, Oliver Rane, had been sent home at the age of seven, and was placed with a tutor in London. When the time came for him to choose a profession he decided on the medical, and qualified himself for it, studying in London, Paris, and Vienna. He passed all the examinations with great credit, including that of the College of Physicians. He next paid a visit to Madeira, remaining three months with his mother and stepfather, and then came home and established himself in London, with money furnished by his mother. But practice does not always come quickly to young beginners, and Oliver Rane found his means lessening. He had a horror of debt, and wisely decided to keep out of it: taking a situation as assistant, and giving up the expensive house he had entered on. This had just been effected when Mrs. Cumberland returned. For the present she let her son remain as he was: Oliver had all a young man's pride and ambition, and she thought the discipline might do him good.

Mrs. Cumberland took on lease one of the two handsome gothic villas on the Ham, and established herself in it; with Jelly for a waiting-maid, and two other servants. This necessitated spending the whole of her income, which was a very fair one. A portion of it would die with her, the rest was willed to her son Oliver.

In the old days when she was Fanny Gass, and Mr. North, plain John North—Jack with his friends—they were intimate as elder brother and young sister. If Mrs. Cumberland expected this agreeable state of affairs to be resumed, she was destined to find herself mistaken. Madam set her scornful face utterly against Mrs. Cumberland: just as she had against others. It did not matter. Mrs. Cumberland simply pitied the underbred woman: her health was very delicate, and she did not intend to visit any one. The gentle-people of the neighbourhood called upon her; she returned the call, and there the acquaintance ended. When invitations first came in, she wrote a refusal, explaining clearly and courteously why she was obliged to do so—that her health did not allow her to visit. If she and Mr. North met each other, as by chance happened, they would linger in conversation, and be happy in the reminiscences of past days.

Mrs. Cumberland had thus lived on in retirement for some time, when the medical man who had the practice of Dallory Ham, and some of that of Dallory, died suddenly. She saw what an excellent opportunity it would be for her son to establish himself, if he would but take up general practice, and she sent a summons for him. When Oliver arrived in answer to it, he entered into the prospect warmly; left his mother to make arrangements, and returned to London, to superintend his removal. Mrs. Cumberland went to Mr. North, and obtained his promise to do what he could to further Oliver's interests. It was equivalent to an assurance of success—for Dallory Hall swayed its neighbours—and Mrs. Cumberland did not hesitate to secure the gothic villa adjoining her own, which happened to be vacant, believing that the future practice would justify it. In a week's time Oliver Rane came down and took possession.

But fate was against him. Dr. Rane said treachery. A young fellow whom he knew in London had told a medical friend—a Mr. Alexander—of this excellent practice that had fallen in at Dallory, and that Rane was hoping to secure it for himself. What was Dr. Rane's mortification when, upon arriving at the week's end at Dallory Ham to take possession, he found another there before him. Mr. Alexander had arrived the previous day, was already established in an opposite house, and had called on every one. Dr. Rane went over and reproached him with treachery—they had not previously been personally acquainted. Mr. Alexander received the charge with surprise; he declared that the field was as open to him as to Dr. Rane—that if he had not thought so, nothing would have induced him to enter it. He spoke his true sentiments, for he was a straightforward man. An agent in Whitborough had also written up to tell him of this opening; he came to look at it, and decided to try it. The right to monopolize it, was no more Dr. Rane's, he urged, than it was his. Dr. Rane took a different view, and said so: but contention would not help the matter now, and he could only yield to circumstances. So each held to his right in apparent amicability, and Dallory had two doctors instead of one; secret rivals from henceforth.

Not for a moment did Oliver Rane think Mr. Alexander could long hold out against him, as he had secured, through his mother, the favour of Dallory Hall. Alas, a very short time showed him that this was a mistake; Dallory Hall turned round upon him, and was doing what it could to forward his rival. Mrs. Cumberland went to Mr. North, seeking an explanation. He could only avow the truth—his wife, who was both master and mistress, had set her face against Oliver, and was recommending Alexander. "John, you promised me," urged Mrs. Cumberland, "I know I did, and I'd keep to it if I could," was Mr. North's mournful answer; "but no one can hold out against her." "Why should she have taken this dislike to Oliver?" rejoined Mrs. Cumberland. "Heaven knows; a caprice, I suppose. She sets herself against people without reason: she has never taken to either Richard or Bessy; and only a little to Edmund. If I can do anything for Oliver under the rose, I'll do it. I have every desire to help him, Fanny, in remembrance of our friendship of the old days."

Mrs. Cumberland carried home news of her non-success to Oliver. As to madam, she simply ignored him, bestowing her patronage upon his rival. How bitterly the slight touched his heart, none but himself could tell. Mrs. Cumberland resented it; but ah, not as he did. A sense of wrong was ever weighing upon his spirit, and he thought Fate was against him. One puzzle remained on his mind unsolved—what he could have done to offend Mrs. North.

Mr. Alexander obtained a fair practice: Dr. Rane barely sufficient to keep himself. His wants and those of the old servant Phillis were few. Perhaps the entire fault did not lie with madam. Alexander had a more open manner and address than Dr. Rane, and they go a long way with people; he was also an older man, and a married man, and was supposed to have had more experience. A sense of injury rankled ever in Oliver Rane's heart; of injury inflicted by Alexander. Meanwhile he became engaged to Bessy Rane. During an absence from home of madam's, the doctor grew intimate at the Hall, and an attachment sprang up between him and Bessy. When madam returned, his visits had to cease, but he saw Bessy at Mrs. Gass's and elsewhere.

I think that is all the retrospect that need be gone into. It brings us down to the present time, the period of the anonymous letter and Edmund North's death. Exactly two years ago this same month, May, the rival doctors had appeared in Dallory Ham; and now one of them was about to leave it.

One incident must be told, bearing on something that has been related, and then the chapter shall close.

The summer of the past year had been a very hot one. A labouring man, working on Mr. North's grounds, suddenly fell; and died on the spot. Mr. Alexander, summoned hastily, thought it must have been sunstroke. "That is what my father died of," remarked Captain Bohun, who stood with the rest. Mr. North turned to him: "Do you say your father died of sunstroke, Arthur?" "Yes, sir, that is what he died of. Did you not know it?" was the ready reply. "You are sure of that?" continued Mr. North. "Quite sure, sir," repeated Arthur, turning his dreamy blue eyes full upon his stepfather, in all their proud truthfulness.

Mr. North knew that he spoke in the sincerity of belief. Arthur Bohun possessed in an eminent degree the pride of his father's race. That innate, self-conscious sense of superiority that is a sort of safeguard to those who possess it: the noblesse oblige feeling that keeps them from wrong-doing. It is true, Arthur Bohun held an exalted view of his birth and family: in so far as that his pride in it equalled that of any man living or dead. He was truthful, generous, honourable; the very opposite in all respects to his mother. Her pride was an assumed pride; a despicable, false, contemptible pride, offensive to those with whom she came into contact. Arthur's was one that you admired in spite of yourself. Of a tarnish to his honour, he could almost have died; to bring disgrace on his own name or on his family, would have caused him to bury his head for ever. Sensitively regardful of other people's feelings, courteous in manner to all, he yet unmistakably held his own in the world. His father had been just the same; and in his day was called "Proud Bohun."

To have asserted that Major Bohun died of sunstroke, had any doubt of the fact lain on his mind, would have been simply impossible to Arthur Bohun. Therefore, Mr. North saw that, whatever the mystery might be, regarding the real cause of Major Bohun's death, Arthur was not cognizant of it.

CHAPTER VI

WATCHING THE FUNERAL

In Mrs. Gass's comfortable dining-room, securely ensconced behind the closed blinds, drawn to-day, sat that lady and a visitor. It was the day of the funeral of Edmund North; and Mrs. Gass had put on mourning out of respect to the family: a black silk gown and white net cap. It need not be said that the change improved her appearance greatly: she looked, as she herself would have phrased it, genteel to-day. This was her favourite sitting-room; she rarely used any other: for one thing it gave her the opportunity of seeing the movements of her neighbours. The drawing-room faced the garden at the back: a large and beautiful apartment, opening to the smooth green lawn.

The visitor was Mrs. Cumberland. For once in her life Mrs. Cumberland emerged from her shell of indifference and condescended to show a little of the curiosity of ordinary people. She had come to Mrs. Gass's to see the funeral pass: and that lady made much of her, for their meetings were rare. Mrs. Cumberland was also in black silk: but she rarely wore anything else. The two women sat together, talking in subdued voices of bygone times: not that they had known each other then; but each had interest in the past. Mrs. Gass was full of respect, never presuming on her elevation; though they were sisters-in-law, she did not forget that she had once been only a servant in Mrs. Cumberland's family. They had little in common, though, and the topics of conversation exhausted themselves. Mrs. Cumberland was of a silent nature, not at all given to gossip in general. She began to think the waiting long. For the convenience of two mourners, who were coming from a distance, the funeral had been put off until four o'clock.

"Holidays don't improve the working class—unless they've the sense to use 'em as they ought," observed Mrs. Gass. "Just look at them three, ma'am. They've been at the tap—and more shame to 'em! They'd better let Mr. Richard catch his eye upon 'em. Putting themselves into that state, when he is following his brother to the grave."

She alluded to some men belonging to the Dallory Works, closed to-day. They had taken more than was becoming, and were lounging against the opposite shutters, quarrelling together. Mrs. Gass could bear it no longer; in defiance of appearances she drew up the blind and dashed open the window.

"Are you three men not ashamed of yourselves? I thought it was you, Dawson! When there's any ill-doing going on, you're safe to be in it. As to you, Thomas, you'll not like to show your face tomorrow. Don't come to me again, Smith, to beg grace for you of Mr. Richard North."

The men slunk away and disappeared down an entry. Mrs. Gass, in one sense of the word, was their mistress; at any rate, their master's partner. She closed the window and drew down the blind.

"Are the men paid for to-day, or do they lose it?" asked Mrs. Cumberland.

"They're paid, ma'am, of course. It would be very unjust to dock them when the holiday's none of their making. Neither Mr. Richard nor me would like to be unjust."

"And he—Richard—seems to act entirely for his father."

Mrs. Gass coughed. "Mr. North is took up with his garden, and that; he don't care to bother his head about business. It's better in younger hands."

Another pause. Mrs. Cumberland felt weary.

"Is this funeral ever coming?" she exclaimed. "There seems to be some delay."

"It was a late hour to fix it for, ma'am. Old Sir what's-his-name wrote word he couldn't be here before the afternoon; so they put it off to four o'clock for his convenience."

Mrs. Cumberland looked up inquiringly. She did not understand.

"I mean young Bohun's relatives, ma'am. Madam's brother-in-law by her first husband."

"Sir Nash Bohun! Is he coming?"

"Sir Nash; that's the name," remarked Mrs. Gass. "I know when Mr. Richard said it, it put me in mind of grinding the teeth."

"What could have induced them to ask him?" wondered Mrs. Cumberland. "He is no relative."

"It sounds grand to have him, ma'am—and that's all she thinks of," returned Mrs. Gass, with slighting allusion to madam. "Or maybe, as it was an uncommon death, they want to make it an uncommon funeral. I look upon it as no better than a murder."

"It is very strange about that piece of paper," observed Mrs. Cumberland.

She lowered her voice as she spoke, as if the subject would not bear the broad light of day. Any surprise, greater than appeared in Mrs. Gass's face at hearing it could not well be imagined.

"Ma'am! Did he tell you of that?"

"Did who tell me?"

"Your son."

They looked questioningly at each other; both unconscious that they were alluding to two totally different circumstances. Cross-purposes are sometimes productive of more evil than straightforward ones.

It appeared that a night or two after Edmund North's death, Captain Bohun found in his own desk a sheet of folded notepaper in an envelope. It contained a few words in Edmund's handwriting, not apparently addressed to any one in particular, but to the world in general. No date was added, but the ink looked fresh, as if it had recently been written.

"When the end comes, make no fuss with me, but bury me quietly out of sight.—E. N."

Captain Bohun, not having the faintest idea as to who put it in his desk, or how it came there, carried it to Richard North. Richard showed it to his father. Thence it spread to the house, and to one or two others. Opinions were divided. Mr. North thought his ill-fated son had intended to allude to his own death: must have felt some foreshadowing of it on his spirit. On the contrary, Arthur Bohun and Richard both thought that it was nothing more than one of his scraps of poetry: and this last idea was at length adopted. Arthur Bohun had related the circumstance to Mrs. Cumberland, and it was this she meant to speak of to Mrs. Gass. Mrs. Gass, who knew nothing about it, thought, quite naturally, that she spoke of the paper found on her carpet.

"Of course it might have been nothing more than some ideas he had dotted down, poor fellow, connected with his nonsensical poetry," slightingly observed Mrs. Cumberland, who was the first to continue speaking: "Richard North and Captain Bohun both hold to that opinion. I don't. It may be that I am inclined to look always on the gloomy side of life; but I can only think he was alluding to his own death."

"'Twas odd sort of poetry," cried Mrs. Gass, after a pause and a stare.

"The only curious part about it to my mind is, that it should have been found in Arthur Bohun's desk," pursued Mrs. Cumberland, the two being still delightfully unconscious that they were at the cross-purposes. "He says he has not left his desk unlocked at all, that he is aware of—but of course he might have done so. Why Edmund North should have chosen to put it there, is a mystery."

"What has Captain Bohun's desk to do with it?" inquired Mrs. Gass, beginning to feel a little at sea.

"The paper was found in Captain Bohun's desk. Though why Edmund North should have placed it there, remains a mystery."

"Ma'am, whoever told you that, must have been just trying to deceive you. It was found on this carpet."

"Found on this carpet!"

"On this very blessed carpet, ma'am. Right back under the claw of that centre dining-table."

Again they gazed at each other. Mrs. Cumberland thought her friend must be dreaming.

"But you are quite mistaken, Mrs. Gass. The paper—note, or whatever it was—could not have been on this carpet at all: nor in your house, in fact. Captain Bohun discovered it in his desk three days ago, and he has not the slightest idea as to how it came there. Mr. North took possession of it, and it has never since been out of his hands."

"My dear lady, they have been mystifying of you," cried Mrs. Gass. "Seeing's believing. The paper was first found by me. By me, ma'am, on this carpet, and it was the same night that Edmund North was first took; not an hour after the fit."

Mrs. Cumberland made no reply. She was drifting into the conclusion that all the circumstances had not been related to her.

"I picked the paper up myself," continued Mrs. Gass, straightforwardly anxious for the truth. "I kept it safe here for a day and a night, ma'am, waiting to give it back to your son: what I thought was that he had dropped it out of his pocketbook. I never spoke of it to a single soul, and as soon as I had the opportunity I gave it up to him. If it was found in Captain Bohun's desk afterwards—why, Dr. Rane, or somebody else must have put it there. Ma'am, if, as I conclude, you've heard about the paper from your son, I wonder he did not tell you this."

"What paper was this?" inquired Mrs. Cumberland, a dim idea arising in her mind that they could not be talking of the same thing.

"It was the copy of that anonymous letter."

"The copy of the anonymous letter!"

"Leastways, its skeleton."

Rapidly enough came elucidation now. Without in the least intending to break faith with Dr. Rane, or with her own resolution to keep the matter secret, Mrs. Gass told all she knew, with one exception. Led on by the miserable, but very natural misapprehension that Mrs. Cumberland was a depositary of the secret as well as herself, she spoke, and had not the least idea that she was betraying trust. That exception was the hinted suspicion that madam might have been the writer. Mrs. Cumberland sat listening, still as a statue.

"And you thought that—this rough copy of the letter—was dropped by Oliver?" she exclaimed at length, moved out of her usual calmness.

"What else could I think?" debated Mrs. Gass. "Dr. Rane had let fall some papers from his pocketbook five minutes before, and I picked this up as soon as he had gone. I'm sure I never so much as gave a thought to Molly Green—though she had come straight from the Hall. Dr. Rane said it might have dropped from her petticoats: but it was a puzzle to me how; and it's a puzzle still."

A keen, inquiring glance shot from the speaker's eyes with the last words. It was momentary and not intentional; nevertheless, something in it caused Mrs. Cumberland's heart to quail. A greyer hue spread over her grey face; a cold shade of recollection deadened her heart. Captain Bohun had told her of Mr. Alexander's theory: that the letter was written to damage himself.

"I am sorry I spoke of this, ma'am," struck in Mrs. Gass. "More particular that it should have been you: you'll naturally tell Dr. Rane, and he will say I know how to keep secrets—just about as the jackdaws keep theirs. It was your telling of the other paper that misled me."

"I am quite safe," answered Mrs. Cumberland, with a sickly smile. "The matter's nothing to me, that I should speak of it again."

"Of course not, ma'am. After all Halloa! here it comes!"

This sudden break was caused by the roll of a muffled drum, first advent of the advancing funeral procession. Edmund North had belonged to a local military corps, and was to be attended to the grave with honours. Mrs. Gass drew up the white blind an inch above the Venetian, which enabled them to look out unseen. The road suddenly became lined with spectators; men, women and children collecting one hardly knew from whence.

The band came first—their instruments in rest; then the muffled drum, on which its bearer struck a note now and again. The hearse and three mourning coaches followed, some private carriages, and the soldiers on foot. And that was all: except some straggling spectators in the rear, with Hepburn the undertaker and his men on either side the black coaches. The hearse was exactly opposite Mrs. Cumberland when the band struck up the Dead March in Saul. Suddenly there flashed across her a recollection of the morning, only a very few days ago, when Ellen Adair had been playing that same dirge, and it had grated on Oliver's ear. Her eyes fixed themselves on the hearse as it passed, and she saw in mental vision the corpse lying within. In another moment, the music, her son, the dead, and the fatal letter, all seemed to blend confusedly in her brain: and Mrs. Cumberland sat, down white and faint, and almost insensible. The lady of the house, her eyes riveted on the window, made her comments and suspected nothing of the indisposition.

"Mr. North in the first coach with his white hankecher held to his nose. And well he may hold it, poor berefted gentleman! Mr. Richard is sitting by the side of him. Captain Bohun's on the opposite seat:— and—who's the other? Why! it's young Sidney North. Then they've sent for him from college, or wherever it is he stays at: madam's doings, I'll lay. What a little whipper-snapper of a fellow it is!—like nobody but himself. He'll never be half the man his stepbrothers are."

Mrs. Gass's remarks ceased with the passing of the coach. In her curiosity she did not observe that she received no response. The second coach came in sight, and she began again.

"An old gent, upright as a dart, with snow-white hair and them features called aquiline! A handsome face, if ever I saw one; his eyes as blue and as fine as Captain Bohun's. There's a likeness between 'em. It must be his uncle, Sir Nash. A young man sits next him with a white, unhealthy face; and the other two—why, if I don't believe it's the young Dallorys!"

There was no reply. Mrs. Gass turned to see the reason. Her visitor was sitting back in a chair, a frightfully grey shade upon her face and lips.

"My patience! Don't you feel well, ma'am?"

"I am a little tired," replied Mrs. Cumberland, smiling languidly as she roused herself. "Looking out at passing things always fatigues me."

"Now, don't you stir, ma'am; I'll tell it off to you," came the rejoinder, spoken with sympathy. "There's only one coach more. And that have but two inside it—the doctors from Whitborough," added Mrs. Gass. "I wonder they didn't invite Mr. Oliver—the first called in to the poor young man—and Alexander. Not thought good enough by madam, perhaps, to be mixed with all these dons."

She looked after the swiftly passing pageantry with lingering admiration. Mrs. Cumberland sat still in the chair and closed her eyes, as if all interest in the funeral—and in life too, for that matter—had passed away.

The procession wound along: through the long straggling village street, past the Dallory Works, an immense group of buildings that lay on the left, and so to the church. It was the only church in the parish, inconveniently distant for some of the inhabitants. Dallory Ham spoke about building one for itself; but that honour had not yet been attained to. In a corner of the large churchyard lay Mrs. North, Mr. North's first wife and Edmund's mother. The new grave was dug by her side.

Amidst the spectators, numbers of whom had collected in the burial ground, stood Jelly. Very much no doubt to the astonishment of her mistress, had she seen her. To peep surreptitiously from behind blinds, was one thing; but to stand openly staring in the churchyard, was another; and Mrs. Cumberland would assuredly have ordered her away. Jelly had come to it with a cousin of hers, Susan Ketler, the wife of the sick man who was being attended by Dr. Rane. Jelly had curiosity enough for ten ordinary women—which is saying a great deal—and would not have missed the sight for the world.

It was soon over: our burial service is not a long one: and the coaches and mourners moved away again, leaving the field in possession of the mob. A rush ensued to obtain a view of the coffin, as yet scarcely sprinkled with earth. Jelly and her friend approached, and the former read the inscription.

"Edmund, son of John North and of Mary, his first wife. Died May 3rd, 18—, aged 33."

"I should not have put 'died,' but 'murdered,' if it was me had the writing of it," spoke Mrs. Ketler.

"And so should I, Susan," significantly replied Jelly. "Here! let's get out of this throng."

Jelly, in her loftiness of stature and opinion, was above the throng literally and figuratively; but it was dense and troublesome. Neither death nor funeral had been of an ordinary description; and others besides the great unwashed were crowding there. The two women elbowed their way out, and passed back down the broad highway to Ketler's house in Dallory. He was one of the best of the North workmen, earning good wages; and the family lived in comfort.

Ketler was in the parlour, sitting up for the first time. Under Dr. Rane's skilful treatment he was getting rapidly better. A child sat on his knee, held by his able arm; the rest were around. The children had wanted, as a matter of course, to go out and see the funeral. "No," said their father; "they might get playing, and that would be unseemly." He was a short, dark, honest-looking man; a good husband and father. Jelly sat talking for a short time, and then rose to leave.

But she was not allowed to do so. To let her depart at that hour without first partaking of tea, would have been a breach of hospitality that the well-to-do workpeople of Dallory would never hear of. Jelly, too easily persuaded where gossip was concerned, took off her bonnet, and the tray was brought in.

Cups of beer induce men to a long sitting; cups of tea women. Jelly sat on, oblivious of the lapse of time. The chief topic of conversation was the anonymous letter. Jelly found to her surprise and anger, that here, the prevailing belief was that it had been written by a clerk named Wilks, who was in the office of Dale the lawyer, and might have, become cognizant of the transaction between his master, Mr. Alexander, and Edmund North.

"Who told you that, Ketler?" sharply demanded Jelly, fixing her indignant eyes on the man.

"I can't rightly say who told me," replied Ketler; "it's the talk of the place. Wilks denies it out and out; but when he's in his evening cups—and that's not seldom—he does things that next morning he has no recollection of. Doctor Rane laughed at me, though, for saying so: a lawyer knows better than to let private matters get out to his clerks, says the doctor. But he don't know that Tim Wilks as some of us do."

"Well, I would not say too much about it's being Tim Wilks, if I were you, Ketler," cried Jelly, in suppressed wrath, brushing the crumbs from her black gown. "You might find yourself in hot water."

And then Ketler suddenly remembered that Wilks was her particular friend, so he turned the subject.

Jelly tore herself away at last, very unwillingly: gossip and tea-drinking formed her idea of an earthly paradise. Night was setting in; a light, beautiful night, the moon sailing majestically in the sky.

Just past the gates of Dallory Hall, in a bend of the road where the overhanging trees on either side gave it a lonely appearance at night: and by day too, for that matter: no dwelling of any sort being within view, stood a bench at the side of the path. It was a welcome resting-place to tired wayfarers; it was no less welcome to wandering lovers in their evening rambles. As Jelly went hastening on, a faint sound of voices broke upon her ear from this spot, and she arrested her steps instinctively. The chance of pouncing unexpectedly upon a pair exchanging soft vows, was perfectly delightful to Jelly; especially if it should happen to be a pair who had no business to exchange them.

Stealing softly along, went she, until she came to the turning, and then she looked cautiously round. The projecting bushes favoured her. To do Jelly justice, it must be affirmed that she had neither malice nor ill-will in her nature; rather the contrary; but a little innocent prying into her neighbours' affairs presented an irresistible temptation. What, then, was her astonishment to see—not a dying swain and his mistress, side by side: but her own mistress, Mrs. Cumberland, seated on the bench in an agony of grief, and Dr. Rane standing with folded arms before her.

Jelly, great at divining probabilities, easily comprehended the situation. Her mistress must have stayed to take tea with Mrs. Gass, and encountered her son in walking home.

To come down upon lovers with a startling reprimand was one thing; to intrude upon her mistress and Dr. Rane would be quite another. Jelly wished she had not gone stealing up like a mouse, and felt inclined to steal back again.

But the attitude and appearance of Mrs. Cumberland riveted her to the spot. Her face, never so grey as now, as seen in the moonlight, was raised to her son's, its expression one of yearning agony; her hands were lifted as if imploring some boon, or warding off some fear. Jelly's eyes opened to their utmost width, and in her astonishment she failed to catch the purport of the first low-breathed words.

"I tell you, you are mistaken, mother," said Dr. Rane in answer, his own voice ringing out clearly enough in the still night; though it nevertheless bore a hushed tone. "Is it probable? Is it likely? I drop the copy of the letter out of my pocketbook! What next will you suppose me capable of?"

"But—Oliver,"—and the voice was raised a little—"how else could it have been found upon her carpet?"

"I have my theory about that," he rejoined with decision. "Mother, come home: I will tell you more then. Is this a fitting time or place to have thus attacked me?"

Air, voice, action, were sharp, with authority, as he bent and took her hand. Mrs. Cumberland, saying something about "having been surprised into speaking," rose from the bench. Jelly watched them along the road; and then sat down on the bench herself to recover her amazement.

"What on earth docs it mean?"

Ah! what did it mean? Jelly was pretty sharp, but she was afraid to give full range to her thoughts. Other steps fell on her ear. They proved to be those of Mr. Alexander.

"Is it you, Jelly! Waiting for your sweetheart?"

Jelly rose. "Standing about to look at funerals, and such things, tires one worse than a ten-mile run."

"Then why do you do it?"

"One fool makes many," returned Jelly with composure. "Sir, I'd like to know who wrote that letter."

"It strikes me the letter was written by a woman."

"A woman!" echoed Jelly, in genuine surprise. "Good gracious, Mr. Alexander!"

"They are go sharp upon us at times, are women," he continued, smiling. "Men don't attack one another."

"And what woman do you suspect, sir?" cried Jelly, in her insatiable curiosity.

"Ah! there's the rub. I have been speaking of women in general, you see. Perhaps it was you?"

"Me!" exclaimed Jelly.

Mr. Alexander laughed. "I was only joking, Jelly. Goodnight."

But Jelly, sharp Jelly, rather thought he had not been joking, and that the suspicion had slipped out inadvertently.

She went straight home. And when she arrived there, Mrs. Cumberland was seated by the drawing-room fire, her face calm and still as usual, listening to the low sweet singing of Ellen Adair.

And Oliver Rane had passed in to his own house with his weight of care. Half wishing that he could exchange places with Edmund North in Dallory churchyard.

The two guests, Sir Nash Bohun and his son, were departing from Dallory Hall. They had arrived the previous afternoon in time to attend the funeral, had dined and slept there, and were now going again. Their coming had originated with Sir Nash. In his sympathy with the calamity—the particulars of which had been written to him by his nephew, Arthur Bohun—Sir Nash had proposed to show his concern and respect for the North family by coming with his son to attend the funeral. The offer was accepted; albeit Mrs. North was not best pleased to receive them. From some cause or other, madam had never been anxious to court intimacy with her first husband's brother: when thrown into his society, there was something in her manner that almost seemed to say she did not feel at ease with him.

Neither at dinner last night nor at breakfast this morning had the master of the house been present; the entertainment of the guests had fallen on Richard North as his father's representative. Captain Bohun was of course with them; also the rest of the family, including madam. Madam played her part gracefully in black crape elaborately set off with jet. For once in her life she was honest and did not affect to feel the grief for Edmund that she would have felt for a son.

Sitting disconsolately before the open window of his parlour was Mr. North. His black clothes looked too large for him, his whole air was that of one who seems to have lost interest in the world. It is astonishing how aged, as compared with other moments, men will look in their seasons of abandonment. While we battle with our cares, they spare the features in a degree: but in the abandonment of despair, when all around seems dreary, and we are sick and faint because to fight longer seems impossible, then look at the poor sunken face!

The room was dingy; it has already been said; rather long but narrow; and it seemed uncared for. Opposite the fireplace stood an old secretaire filled with seeds and papers relating to gardening, and near it was a closet-door. This closet—but it was more a small, dark passage than a closet—had an opposite door opening to the dining-room. But, if the parlour was dingy, the capacious window and the prospect on which it looked, brightened it. Stretching out before it, broad and large, was the gay parterre of many-coloured flowers, Mr. North's only delight for years past. In the cultivation of these flowers, he had found a refuge from life's daily vexations and petty cares. Heaven is merciful, and some counterbalancing interest to long-continued sorrow is often supplied to us.

Mr. North sat looking at his flowers. He had been sitting there for the past hour, buried in reflections that were not pleasant, and the morning was getting on. He thought of his embarrassments: those applications for money from madam, that he strove to hide from his well-beloved son Richard, and that made the terror of his life. They were apt to come upon him at the most unexpected times, in season and out of season; it seemed to him that he was never free from them; could never be sure at any moment she would not come down upon him the next. For the past few days the house had been, so to say, sacred from these carping concerns; even she had respected the sorrow in it; but with this morning, the return to everyday life, business and the world resumed its sway. Mr. North was looked upon as a man perfectly at his ease in money matters; "rolling in wealth," people would say, as they talked of the handsome portion his two daughters might expect on their wedding-day. Local debts, the liabilities of ordinary life, were kept punctually paid; Richard saw to that; and perhaps no one in the whole outer world, excepting Mrs. Gass, suspected the truth and the embarrassment. Mr. North thought of his other son, he who had gone from his view for ever; but the edge of grief was wearing off, though he was as eager as ever to discover the anonymous writer.

But there is a limit to all things—I don't know what would become of some of us if there were not—and the mind cannot dwell for ever upon its own bitterness. Unhappy topics, as if in very weariness, gradually drifted away from Mr. North's mind, and were replaced by thoughts of his flowers. How could it be otherwise, when their scent came floating to him through the broad open window in delicious perfume. The colours charmed the eye, the aroma took captive the senses. Spring flowers, all; and simple ones. Further on, beyond the trees that bounded the grounds, a fine view was obtained of the open country over Dallory Ham. Hills and dales, woods and sunny plains, with here and there a gleam of glistening water, lay under the distant horizon. Mr. North looked not at the landscape, which was a familiar book to him, but at his flowers.

The spring had been continuously cold and wet, retarding the appearance of these early flowers to a very late period. For the past week or two the weather had been lovely, and the flowers seemed to have sprung up all at once. A little later the tulip beds would be in bloom. A rare collection; a show for the world to flock to. Later on still, the roses would be out, and many thought they were the best show of all. And so the year went on, the flowers replacing each other in their loveliness.

Sadness sat on them to-day: for we see things, you know, in accordance with our own mood, not as they actually are. Mr. North rose with a sigh and stood at the open window. Only that very day week, about this time in the morning, his eldest son had stood there with him side by side. For this was the eighth of May. "Poor fellow!" sighed the father, as he thought of this.

Some one went sauntering down the path that led round from the front of the house, and disappeared beyond the trees; a short, slight young man. Mr. North recognized his son Sidney; madam's son as well as his own; and he gave a sigh almost as profound as the one he had given to the lost Edmund. Sidney North was dreadfully dissipated, and had already caused a great deal of trouble. It was suspected—and with truth—that some of madam's superfluous money went to this son. She had brought him up badly, fostering his vanity, indulging him in everything. By the very way in which he walked now—his head moodily lowered, his gait slouching, his hands thrust into his pockets, Mr. North judged him to be in some dilemma. He had not wished him to be summoned home to the funeral; no, though the dead had stood to him as half-brother; but madam took her own way and wrote for him. "He'll be a thorn in her side if he lives," thought the father, his reflections unconsciously going out to that future time when he himself should be no more.

The door opened, and Richard came in. Mr. North stepped back from the window at which he had been standing.

"Sir Nash and his son are going, sir. You will see them first, will you not?"

"Going already! Why—I declare it is past eleven! Bless me! I hope I have not been rude, Dick? Where are my boots?"

The boots were at hand, ready for him. He put them on, and hid his slippers out of sight in the closet. What with his present grief, and his disinclination for society, or, as he called it, company, that for some time had been growing upon him, Mr. North had held aloof from his guests. But he was one of the last men to show incivility, and it suddenly struck him that perhaps he had been guilty of it.

"Dick, I suppose I ought to have been at the breakfast-table?"

"Not at all, my dear father; not at all. Your remaining in privacy is perfectly natural, and I am sure Sir Nash feels it to be so. Don't disturb yourself: they will come to you here."

Almost as he spoke they entered, Captain-Bohun with them. Sir Nash was a very fine man with a proud face, that put you in mind at once of Arthur Bohun's, and of the calmest, pleasantest, most courteous manners possible. His son was not in the least like him; a studious, sickly man, his health delicate, his dark hair scanty. James Bohun's time was divided between close classical reading and philanthropic pursuits. He strove to have what he called a mission in life: and to make it one that might do him some service in the next world.

"I am so very sorry! I had no idea you would be going so soon: I ought to have been with you before this," began Mr. North in a flutter.

But the baronet laid his hands upon him kindly, and calmed the storm. "My good friend, you have done everything that is right and hospitable. I would have stayed a few hours longer with you, but James has to be in London this afternoon to keep an engagement."

"It is an engagement that I cannot well put off," interposed James Bohun in his small voice that always sounded too weak for a man. "I would not have made it, had I known what was to intervene."

"He has to preside at a public missionary meeting," explained Sir Nash. "It seems to me that he has something or other of the kind on hand every day in the year. I tell him that he is wearing himself out."

"Not every day in the year," spoke the son, taking the words literally. "This is the month for such meetings, you know, Sir Nash."

"You do not look strong," observed Mr. North, studying James Bohun.

"Not in appearance perhaps, but I'm wiry, Mr. North: and we wiry fellows last the longest. What sweet flowers," added Mr. Bohun, stepping to the window. "I could not dress myself this morning for looking at them. I longed to open the window."

"And why did you not?" sensibly asked Mr. North.

"I can't do with the early morning air, sir. I don't accustom myself to it.

"A bit of a valetudinarian," remarked Sir Nash.

"Not at all, father," answered the son. "It is as well to be cautious."

"I sleep with my window open, James, summer and winter. But we all have our different tastes and fancies. And now, my good friend," added the baronet, taking the hands of Mr. North, "when will you come and see me? A change may do you good."

"Thank you; not just yet. Thank you all the same, Sir Nash; but later—perhaps," was Mr. North's answer. He knew that the kindness was meant, the invitation sincere; and of late he had grown to feel grateful for any shown to him. Nevertheless he thought he should never accept this.

"I will not receive you in that hot, bustling London: it is becoming a penance to myself to stay there. You shall come to my place in Kent, and be as quiet as you please. You've never seen Peveril: it cannot boast the charming flowers that you show here, but it is worth seeing. Promise to come."

"If I can. Later. Thank you, Sir Nash; and I beg you and Mr. Bohun to pardon me for all my seeming discourtesy. It has not been meant so."

"No, no."

They walked through the hall to the door, where Mr. North's carriage waited. The large shut-up carriage. Some dim idea was pervading those concerned that to drive to the station in an open dog-cart would be hardly the right thing for these mourners after the recent funeral.

Sir Nash and his son stepped in, followed by Captain Bohun and Richard North, who would accompany them to the station. As Mr. North turned indoors again after watching the carriage away, he ran against his daughter Matilda, resplendent in glittering black silk and jet.

"They have invited you to visit them, have they not, papa?"

"They have invited me—yes. But I shall be none the nearer going there, Matilda."

"Then I wish you would, for I want to go," she returned, speaking imperiously. "Uncle Nash asked me. He asked mamma, and said would I accompany her: and I should like to go. Do you hear, papa? I should like to go."

It was all very well for Miss Matilda North to say "Uncle Nash." Sir Nash was no relation to her whatever: but that he was a baronet, she might have remembered it.

"You and your mamma can go," said Mr. North with animation, as the seductive vision of the house, relieved of madam's presence for an indefinite period, rose mentally before him.

"But mamma says she shall not go."

"Oh, does she?" he cried, his spirits and the vision sinking together. "She'll change her mind perhaps, Matilda. I can't do anything in it, you know."

As if to avoid further colloquy, he passed on to his parlour and shut the door sharply. Matilda North turned into the dining-room, her handsome black silk train following her, her discontented look preceding her. Just then Mrs. North came downstairs, a coquettish, fascinating sort of black lace hood upon her head, one she was in the habit of wearing in the grounds. Matilda North heard the rustle of the robes, and looked out again.

"Are you going to walk, mamma?"

"I am. Have you anything to say against it?"

"It would be all the same if I had," was the pert answer. Not very often did Matilda North gratuitously retort upon her mother; but she was in an ill humour: the guests had gone away much sooner than she had wished or expected, and madam had vexed her.

"That lace hood is not mourning," resumed Miss Matilda North, defiantly viewing madam from top to toe.

Madam turned the hood and the haughty face it encircled on her presuming daughter. The look was enough in itself; and what she might have said was interrupted by the approach of Bessy.

"Have you any particular orders to give this morning, madam?" Bessy asked of her stepmother—whom she as often called madam as mamma, the latter word never meeting with fond response from Mrs. North to her.

"If I have I'll give them later," imperiously replied madam, sweeping out at the hall-door.

"What has angered her now?" thought Bessy. "I hope and trust it is nothing connected with papa. He has enough trouble without having to bear ill-temper."

Bessy North was housekeeper. And a troublesome time she had of it! Between madam's capricious orders, issued at all sorts of inconvenient hours, and the natural resentment of the servants, a less meek and patient spirit would have been worried beyond endurance. Bessy made herself the scape-goat; labouring, both by substantial help and by soothing words, to keep peace in the household. None knew how much Bessy did, or the care that was upon her. Miss Matilda North had never soiled her fingers in her life, never done more than ring the bell, and issue her imperious orders after the fashion of madam, her mother. The two half-sisters were a perfect contrast. Certainly they presented such outwardly, as witness this morning: the one not unlike a peacock, her ornamented head thrown up, her extended train trailing, and her odds and ends of jet gleaming; the other a meek little woman in a black gown of some soft material with some quiet crape upon it, and her smooth hair banded back—for she wore it plain to-day.

On her way to the kitchens, Bessy halted at her father's sitting-room, and opened the door quietly. Mr. North was standing against the window-frame, half inside the room half out of it.

"Can I do anything for you, papa?"

"There's nothing to be done for me, child. What time do we dine to-day, Bessy?" he asked, after a pause.

"I suppose at six. Mrs. North has not given orders to the contrary."

"Very well. I'll have my luncheon in here, child."

"To be sure. Dear papa, you are not looking well," she added, advancing to him.

"No? Looks don't matter much, Bessy, when folk get to be as old as I am. A thought comes over me at odd moments—that it is good to grow ugly, and yellow, and wrinkled. It makes us wish to become young and fair and pleasant to the sight again: and we can only do that through immortality. Through immortality, child."

Mr. North lifted his hand, the fingers of which had always now a trembling sort of movement in them, to his shrivelled face, as he repeated the concluding words, passing it twice over the weak, scanty brown hair that time and care had left him. Bessy kissed him fondly, and quitted the room with a sigh, one sad thought running through her mind.

"How sadly papa is breaking!"

Mrs. North swept down the broad gravel-walk leading from the entrance, until she came to a path on the left, which led to the covered portion of the grounds: where the trees in places grew so thick and close that shade might be had at midday. This part of the grounds was near the dark portion of the Dallory highway, already mentioned (where Jelly had surprised her mistress and Oliver Rane in the moonlight the past night), only the boundary hedges being between them. It was a sweet spot, affording retirement from the world and shelter from the fierce rays of the sun. Madam was fond of frequenting this spot: and all the more so because sundry loop-holes gave her the opportunity of peering out beyond. She could see all who passed to and from the Hall, without being herself seen. One high enclosed wall was especially liked by her; concealed within its shade, quietly resting on one of its rustic seats, she could hear as well as see. Before she had quite gained this walk, however, her son Sidney crossed her path. A young man of twenty now, undersized, insufferably vain, fast, and conceited. His face might be called a pretty face: his auburn curls were arranged after the models in a hairdresser's window; his very blue unmeaning eyes had no true look in them. Sidney North as like neither father nor mother: like no one but his own contemptible self; madam looked upon him as next door to an angel; he was her well-beloved. There can be no blindness equal to that of a doting mother.

"My dear, I thought you had gone with them to the station," she said.

"Didn't ask me to go; Dick and Arthur made room for themselves, not for me," responded Sidney, taking his pipe from his mouth to speak, and his voice was as consequential as his mother's.

A frown crossed madam's face. Dick and Arthur were rather in the habit of putting Sidney in the shade, and she hated them for it. Arthur was her own son, but she had never regarded him with any sort of affection.

"I'm going back this afternoon, mamma."

"This afternoon! No, my boy; I can't part with you to-day."

"Must," laconically responded Sidney, puffing away at his pipe. And madam had come to learn that it was of no use saying he was to stay if he wanted to go. "How much tin can you let me have?"

"How much do you want?"

"As much as you can give me."

His demands for money seemed to be as insatiable as madam knew her husband found hers. The fact was beginning to give her some concern. Only two weeks ago she had despatched him all she could afford: and now here he was, asking again. A slight frown crossed her brow.

"Sidney, you spend too much."

"Must do as others do," responded Sidney.

"But, my sweet boy, I can't let you have it. You don't know the trouble it causes."

"Trouble!—with those rich North Works to draw upon!" cried Sidney. "The governor must be putting by mines of wealth."

"I don't think he is, Sidney. He always pleads poverty; says we drain him. I suppose it's true."

"Flam! All old paters cry that. Look at Dick—the loads of gold he must be netting. He gets his equal share, they say; goes thirds with the other two."

"Who says it?"

"A fellow told me so yesterday. It's an awful shame that Dick should be a millionaire, and I obliged to beg for every paltry coin I want! There's not so many years between us."

"Dick has his footing at the works, you see," observed madam. "Let him! I wouldn't have you degrade yourself to it for the world. He's fit for nothing but work; has been brought up to it; and we can spend."

"Just so," complacently returned the young man. "And you must shell out liberally for me this afternoon, mamma."

Without further ceremony of adieu or apology, Mr. Sidney North sauntered away. Madam proceeded to her favourite shaded walk, where she kept her eyes looking out on all sides for intruders, friends or enemies. On this occasion she had the satisfaction of being gratified.

Her arms folded over the black lace shawl she wore, its hood gathered on her head, altogether very much after the fashion of a Spanish mantilla, and her train with its crape and jet falling in stately folds behind her, madam had been pacing this retreat for the best part of an hour, when she caught sight, through the interstices of the leaves, of two ladies slowly approaching. The one she recognized at once as Mrs. Cumberland; the other she did not recognize at all. "What a lovely face!" was her involuntary thought.

A young, fair, lovely face. The face of Ellen Adair.

CHAPTER VIII

MADAM'S LISTENING CLOSET

Many years before, when the Reverend George Cumberland held his chaplaincy in Madras, there were two friends also there with whom he was intimate—Major Bohun and Mr. Adair. The latter held a civil appointment under Government. At that time, Mr. Adair was not married. Later, this gentleman went to Australia: Mr. and Mrs. Cumberland also went there. Mr. Adair had married in the course of time. His wife died, leaving one little child, a daughter: who was, despatched to England for her education. Upon its completion, William Adair wrote and begged Mrs. Cumberland to receive her: he thought it probable that he should be returning home; and if so, it would not be worth while for Ellen to go out to him. Mrs. Cumberland consented, and the young lady became an inmate of her house at Dallory Ham. Very liberal terms were offered by Mr. Adair: but this was a matter entirely between himself and Mrs. Cumberland.

Holding herself, as she did, so aloof from her neighbours, there was little wonder in madam's having remained unconscious of the fact that some months ago, nearly twelve now, a young lady had come to reside with Mrs. Cumberland. Part of the time Mrs. Cumberland had been away. Madam had also been away: and when at home her communication with Dallory and Dallory Ham consisted solely in being whirled through its roads in a carriage: no one indoors spoke unnecessarily in her hearing of any gossip connected with those despised places; and to church she rarely went, for she did not get up in time. And so the sweet girl, who had for some time now been making Arthur Bohun's heart's existence, had never yet been seen or heard of by his mother.

For Mrs. Cumberland to be seen abroad so early was something marvellous; indeed, she was rarely seen abroad at all. On this morning she came out of her room between eleven and twelve o'clock, dressed for a walk; and bade Ellen Adair prepare to accompany her. Ellen obeyed, silently wondering. The truth was, Mrs. Cumberland had picked up a very unpleasant doubt the previous day, and would give the whole world to lay it to rest. It was connected with her son. His assurances had partly pacified her, but not quite: and she determined to have a private word with Mr. North. Ellen, walking by her side along the road, supposed they were going in to Dallory. Mrs. Cumberland kept close to the hedge for the sake of the shade: as she brushed the bench in passing, where she had sat the past night, a slight shudder seized her frame. Ellen did not observe it; she was revelling in the beauty of the sweet spring day. The gates of Dallory Hall gained, Mrs. Cumberland turned in. Ellen Adair wondered more and more; but Mrs. Cumberland was not one to be questioned at will on any subject.

On they came, madam watching with all her eyes. Mrs. Cumberland was in her usual black silk attire, and walked with the slow step of an invalid. Ellen wore a morning dress of lilac muslin. It needed not the lilac parasol she carried to reflect an additional lovely hue on that most lovely face. A stately, refined girl, as madam saw, with charming manners, the reverse of pretentious.

But as madam, fascinated for once in her life, gazed outwards, a certain familiarity in the face dawned upon her senses. That she had seen it before, or one very like it, became a conviction to her. "Who on earth is she?" murmured the lady to herself—for madam was by no means stilted in her phrases in leisure moments.

"Are you going to call at the Hall, Mrs. Cumberland?" inquired Ellen, venturing to ask the question at length in her increasing surprise. And every word could be distinctly heard by madam, for they were very close to her.

"I think so," was the answer, given in hesitating tones. "I—I should like to tell Mr. North that I feel for his loss."

"But is it not early to do so—both in the hour of the day, and after the death?" rejoined Ellen, with deprecation.

"For a stranger it would be; for me, no. I and John North were once as brother and sister. Besides, I have something else to say to him."

Had Miss Adair asked what the something else was—which she would not have presumed to do—Mrs. Cumberland might have replied that she wished again to enlist the Hall's influence on behalf of her son, now that Mr. Alexander was about to leave. A sure indication that it was not the real motive that was drawing her to the Hall, for she was one of those reticent women who rarely, if ever, observe candour even to friends. Suddenly she halted.

"I prefer to go on alone, Ellen. You can sit down and wait for me. There are benches about in the covered walks."

Mrs. Cumberland went forward. Ellen turned and began to walk towards the entrance-gates with the lingering step of one who waits. Mrs. Cumberland had gone well on, when she turned and called.

"Ellen."

But Ellen did not hear.

"Ellen! Ellen Adair!"

A louder call, this, falling on the warm summer air, echoing in the curious ears covered by the lace mantilla. Mrs. North gave a quick, sharp start. It looked very like a start of terror.

"Ellen Adair!" she repeated to herself, her eyes, in their fear, flashing out on the beautiful face, to see whether she could trace the resemblance now. "Ellen Adair? Good Heavens!"

Ellen had turned at once. "Yes, Mrs. Cumberland."

"Do not go within sight of the road, my dear. I don't care that all the world should know I am calling at Dallory Hall. Find a bench and sit down, as I bade you."

Obedient as it was in her nature to be, the young lady turned into one of the side paths, which brought her within nearer range of madam's view. She, madam, with a face from which every atom of colour had faded, leaving it white as ashes, stood still as a statue, as one confounded.

"I see the likeness: it is to him," she muttered. "Can he have come home?"

Ellen Adair passed out of sight and hearing. Madam, shaking herself from her fear, turned with stealthy steps to seek the house, keeping in the private paths as long as possible, which was a more circuitous way. Madam intended, unseen, to make a third at the interview between her husband and Mrs. Cumberland. The sight of that girl's face had frightened her. There might be treason in the air.

Mrs. Cumberland was already in Mr. North's parlour. Strolling out amongst his flowers, he had encountered her in the garden, and taken her in through the open window. Madam arriving a little later, passed through the hall to the dining-room. Rather inopportunely, there sat Bessy, busy with her housekeeping books.

"Take them elsewhere," said madam, with an imperious sweep of the hand.

She was not in the habit of giving a reason for any command whatever: let it be reasonable or the contrary, the rule was to hear and obey. Bessy gathered her books up and went away, madam fastening the bolt of the door after her.

Then she stole across the soft Turkey carpet and slipped into the closet already spoken of, that formed a communication—though never used—between the dining-room and Mr. North's parlour. The door opening to the parlour was unlatched, and had been ever since he put his slippers inside it an hour ago. When her eyes became accustomed to the darkness, madam saw them there; she also saw one or two of his old brown gardening coats hanging on the pegs. Against the wall was a narrow table with an unlocked desk upon it, belonging to herself. It was clever of madam to keep it there. Opening the lid silently, she pulled up a few of its valueless papers, and let them appear. Of course, if the closet were suddenly entered from the parlour—a most unlikely thing to happen, but madam was cautious—she was only getting something from her desk. In this manner she had occasionally made an unsuspected third at Richard North's interviews with his father. Letting the lace hood slip off, madam bent her ear to the crevice of the door, and stood there listening. She was under the influence of terror still: her lips were drawn, her face wore the hue of death.

Apparently the ostensible motive of the interview—Mrs. Cumberland's wish to express her sympathy for the blow that had fallen on the Hall—was over; she had probably also been asking for Mr. North's influence in favour of her son. The first connected words madam caught were these:—

"I will do what I can, Mrs. Cumberland. I wished to do it before, as you know. But Mrs. North took a dislike—I mean took a fancy to Alexander."

"You mean took a dislike to Oliver," corrected Mrs. Cumberland. "In the old days, when you were John North without thought of future grandeur, and I was Fanny Gass, we spoke out freely to each other."

"True," said poor Mr. North. "I've never had such good days since. Ah, what a long time it seems to look back to! I have grown into an old man, Fanny, older in feeling than in years; and you—you wasted the best days of your life in a hot and unhealthy climate."

"Unhealthy in places and at certain seasons," corrected Mrs. Cumberland. "My husband was stationed in the beautiful climate of the Blue Mountains, as we familiarly call the region of the Neilgherry Hills. It is pleasant there."

"Ay, I've heard so. Getting the cool breezes and all that."

"People used to come up there from the hot plains to regain their lost health," continued Mrs. Cumberland, whose thoughts were apt to wander back to the earlier years of her exile. "Ootacamund is resorted to there, just as the colder seaside places are here. But I and Mr. Cumberland were stationary."

"Ootacamund?" repeated Mr. North, struck with the name. "Ootacamund was where my wife's first husband died; Major Bohun."

"No, he did not die there," quietly rejoined Mrs. Cumberland.

"Was it not there? Ah! well, it does not matter. One is apt to confuse these foreign names and places in the memory."

Mrs. Cumberland made no rejoinder, and a momentary silence ensued. Madam, who with the mention of the place, Ootacamund, bit her lip almost to bleeding, bent forward, and looked through the opening of the door. She could just see the smallest portion of the cold, calm, grey face, and waited in sickening apprehension of what the next words might be. They came from Mrs. Cumberland and proved an intense relief, for the subject was changed for another.

"I am about to make a request to you, John: I hope you will grant it for our old friendship's sake. Let me see the anonymous letter that proved so fatal to Edmund. Every incident connected with this calamity is to me so full of painful interest!" she continued, as if seeking to apologize for her request. "As I lay awake last night, unable to sleep, it came into my mind that I would ask you to let me see the letter."

"You may see it, and welcome," was Mr. North's ready reply, as he unlocked a drawer in his old secretaire, and handed the paper to her. "I only wish I could show it to some purpose—to someone who would recognize the handwriting. You won't do that."

Mrs. Cumberland answered by a sickly smile. Her hands trembled as she took the letter, and Mr. North noticed how white her lips had become—as if with some inward suspense or emotion. She studied the letter well, reading it three times over; looking at it critically in all lights. Madam in the closet could have struck her for her inquisitive curiosity.

"You are right, John," she said, with an unmistakable sigh of relief as she gave the missive back to him; "I certainly do not recognize that handwriting. It is like no one's that I ever saw."

"It is a disguised hand, you see," he answered. "No doubt about that: and accomplished in the cleverest manner."

"Is it true that poor Edmund had been drawing bills in conjunction with Alexander?"

"Only one. He had drawn a good many I'm afraid during his short lifetime in conjunction with other people, but only one with Alexander—which they got renewed. No blame attaches to Alexander; not a scrap of it."

"Oliver told me that."

"Ay. I have a notion that poor Edmund did not get into this trouble for his own sake, but to help that young scamp, his brother."

"Which brother?"

"Which brother!" echoed Mr. North, rather in mockery. "As if you need ask that. There's only one of them who could deserve the epithet, and that's Sidney. An awful scamp. He is but twenty years of age, and he is as deep in the ways of a bad world as though he were forty."

"I am very sorry to hear you say it. Whispers go abroad about him, as I dare say you know, but I would rather not have heard them confirmed by you."

"People can't say much too bad of him. We have Mrs. North to thank for it: it is all owing to the way she has brought him up. When I would have corrected his faults, she stepped in between us. Oftentimes have I thought of the enemy that sowed the tares amidst the wheat in his neighbour's field."

"The old saying comes home to many of us," observed Mrs. Cumberland with a suppressed sigh, as she rose to leave. "When our children are young they tread upon our toes, but when they grow older they tread upon our hearts."

"Ay, ay! Don't go yet," added Mr. North. "It is pleasant in times of sorrow to see an old friend. I have no friends now."

"I must go, John. Ellen Adair is waiting for me, and will find the time long. And I expect it would not be very agreeable to your wife to see me here. Not that I know wherefore, or what I can have done to her."

"She encourages no one; no one of the good old days," was the confidential rejoinder. "There's no fear of her; I saw her going off towards the shrubberies—after Master Sidney, I suppose. She takes what she calls her constitutional walks there. They last a couple of hours sometimes."

As Mr. North turned to put the letter into the drawer again, he caught sight of a scrap of poetry that had been found in Arthur Bohun's desk. This he also showed his visitor. He would have kept nothing from her; she was the only link left to him of the days when he and the world (to him) were alike young. Had Mrs. Cumberland stayed there till night, he would then have thought it too soon for her to depart.

"I will do all I can for your son, Fanny," said Mr. North, as they stood for a moment at the glass-doors. "I like Oliver. He is a steady, persevering fellow, and I'll help him on if I can. If I do not, the fault will not lie with me. You understand?" he added, looking at her.

Mrs. Cumberland understood perfectly—the fault would lie with madam. She nodded in answer.

"Mr. Alexander is going, John—as you know. Should Oliver succeed in getting the whole of the practice—and there's nothing to prevent it—he will soon be making a large income. In that case, I suppose he will be asking you to give him something else."

"You mean Bessy. I wish to goodness he had her!" continued Mr. North impulsively; "I do heartily wish it sometimes. She has not a very happy life of it here. Well, well; I hope Oliver will get on with all my heart; tell him so from me, Fanny. He shall have her when he does."

"Shall he!" ejaculated madam from her closet, and in her most scornfully defiant tone—for the conversation had not pleased her.

They went strolling away amidst the flowers, madam peering after them with angry eyes. She heard her husband tell Mrs. Cumberland to come again; to come in often; whenever she would. Mr. North went on with her down the broad path, after they had lingered some minutes with the sweet flowers. In strolling back alone, who should pounce upon Mr. North from a side path but madam!

"Was not that woman I saw you with the Cumberland, Mr. North?"

"It was Mrs. Cumberland: my early friend. She came in to express her sympathy at my loss. I took it as very kind of her, madam."

"I take it as very insolent," retorted madam. "She had some girl with her when she came in. Who was it?"

"Some girl!" repeated Mr. North, whose memory was anything but retentive. "Ah yes, I remember: she said her ward was waiting for her."

"Who is her ward?"

"The daughter of a friend whom they knew in India, madam. In India or Australia; I forget which: George Cumberland was stationed in both places. A charming young lady with a romantic name: Ellen Adair."

Madam toyed with the black lace that shielded her face. "You seem to know her, Mr. North."

"I have seen her in the road; and in coming out of church. The first time I met them was in Dallory, one day last summer, and Mrs. Cumberland told me who she was. That is all I know of her, madam—as you seem to be curious."

"Is she living at Mrs. Cumberland's?"

"Just now she is. I—I think they said she was going out to join her father," added Mr. North, whose impressions were always hazy in matters that did not immediately concern him. "Yes, I'm nearly sure, madam: to Australia."

"Her father—whoever he may be—is not in Europe then?" slightingly spoke madam, stooping to root up mercilessly a handful of blue-bells.

"Her father lives over yonder. That's why the young lady has to go out to him."

Madam tossed away the rifled flowers and raised her head to its customary haughty height. The danger had passed. "Over yonder" meant, as she knew, some far-off antipodes. She flung aside the girl and the interlude from her recollections, just as ruthlessly as she had flung the blue-bells.

"I want some money, Mr. North."

Mr. North went into a flutter at once. "I—I have none by me, madam."

"Then give me a cheque."

"Nor cheque either. I don't happen to have a signed cheque in the house, and Richard is gone for the day."

"What have I repeatedly told you—that you must keep money by you; and cheques too," was her stern answer. "Why does Richard always sign the cheques? Why can't you sign them?"

She had asked the same thing fifty times, and he had never been goaded to give the true answer.

"I have not signed a cheque since Thomas Gass died, except on my own private account, madam; no, nor for long before it. My account is overdrawn. I shan't have a stiver in the bank until next quarter-day."

"You told me that last week," she said contemptuously. "Draw then upon the firm account."

He shook his head. "The bank would not cash it."

"Why?"

"Because only Richard can sign. Oh dear, this is going over and over the old ground again. You'll wear me out, madam. When Richard took the management at the works, it was judged advisable that he should alone sign the business cheques—for convenience' sake, madam; for convenience' sake. Gass's hands were crippled with gout; I was here with my flowers."

"I don't care who signs the cheques so that I get the money," she retorted in rude, rough tones. "You must give me some to-day."

"It is for Sidney; I know it is for Sidney," spoke Mr. North tremulously. "Madam, you are ruining that lad. For his own sake some check must be put upon him: and therefore I am thankful that to-day I have no money to give."

He took some short hurried steps over the corners of paths and flower-beds, with the last words, and got into his own room. Madam calmly followed. Very sure might he be that she would not allow him to escape her.

Ellen Adair, waiting for Mrs. Cumberland, had not felt the time long. Very shortly after she was left alone, the carriage came back from the station, bringing Arthur Bohun: Richard had been left at

Whitborough. Captain Bohun got out at the gates, intending to walk up to the house. Ellen saw him come limping along—the halt in his gait was always more visible when he had been sitting for any length of time—and he at the same time caught sight of the bright hues of the lilac dress gleaming through the trees.

Some years back, the detachment commanded by Arthur Bohun was quartered in Ireland. One ill-starred night it was called out to suppress some local disturbances, and he was desperately wounded: shot, as was supposed, unto death. That he would never be fit for service again; that his death, though it might be lingering, was inevitable; surgeons and friends alike thought. For nearly two years he was looked upon as a dying man: that is, as a man who could not possibly recover. But Time, the great healer, restored him; and he came out of his sickness and danger with only a slight limp, more or less perceptible. When walking slowly, or when he took any one's arm, it was not seen at all. Mrs. North (who was proud of her handsome and distinguished son, although she had no love for him) was wont to tell friends confidentially that he had a bullet in his hip yet—at which Arthur would laugh.

The sight of the lilac dress caused him to turn aside. Ellen rose and stood waiting; her whole being was thrilling with the rapture the meeting brought. He took her hand in his, his face lighting.

"Is it indeed you, Ellen! I should as soon have expected to see a fairy here."

"Mrs. Cumberland has gone to call on Mr. North. She told me to wait for her."

"I have been with Dick to take my uncle and James to the station," spoke Captain Bohun, pitching upon it as something to say, for his tongue was never too fluent when alone with her. "He has been asking me to go and stay with him."

"Sir Nash has?"

"Yes. Jimmy invites no one; he is taken up with his missionaries, and that."

"Shall you go?"

Their eyes met as she put the question. Go! away from her!

"I think not," he quietly answered. "Not at present. Miss Bohun's turn must come first: she has been writing for me this long time."

"That's your aunt."

"My aunt. And a good old soul she is. Won't you walk about a little, Ellen?"

She took the arm he held out, and they paced the covered walks, almost in silence. The May birds were singing, the budding leaves were green. Eloquence enough for them: and each might have detected the beating of the other's heart. Madam had her ear glued to that closet-door, and so missed the sight. A sight that would have made her hair stand on end.

Minutes, for lovers, fly on swift wings. When Mrs. Cumberland appeared, it seemed that she had been away no time. Ellen went forward to meet her: and Captain Bohun said he had just come home from the station. Mrs. Cumberland, absorbed in her own cares, complaining of fatigue, took little or no notice of him: he strolled by their side up the Ham. Standing at Mrs. Cumberland's gate for a moment in parting, Oliver Rane came so hastily out of his house that he ran against them.

"Don't knock me down, Rane," spoke Arthur Bohun in his lazy but very pleasing manner.

"I beg your pardon. When I am in a hurry I believe I am apt to drive on in a blindfold fashion."

"Is any one ill, Oliver?" questioned his mother.

"Yes. At Mrs. Gass's. I fear it is herself. The man who brought the message did not know."

"You ought to keep a horse," spoke Captain Bohun, as the doctor recommenced his course. "So much running about must wear out a man's legs."

"Oughts go for a great deal, don't they?" replied the doctor, looking back. "I ought to be rich enough to keep one, but I'm not."

Captain Bohun wished them good-day, and they went indoors. Ellen wondered at hearing that Mrs. Cumberland was going out again. Feeling uneasy—as she said—about the sudden illness, she took her way to the house of Mrs. Gass, in spite of the fatigue she had been complaining of. A long walk for her at any time. Arrived there she found that lady in perfect health; it was one of her servants to whom Oliver had been summoned. The young woman had scalded her hand and arm.

"I was at the Hall this morning, and Mr. North showed me the anonymous letter," Mrs. Cumberland took occasion to say. "It evidently comes from a stranger; a stranger to us. The handwriting is quite strange."

"So much the better, ma'am," heartily spoke Mrs. Gass. "It would be too bad to think it was wrote by a friend."

"Oliver thinks it was madam," pursued Mrs. Cumberland, lowering her voice. "At least—he has not gone so far as to say he thinks it, but that Mr. Alexander does."

"That's just what he said to me, ma'am. Alexander thought it, he said, but that he himself didn't know what to think, one way or the other. As well, perhaps, for us not to talk of it: least said is soonest mended."

"Of course. But I cannot help recalling a remark once innocently made by Arthur Bohun in my hearing: that he did not know any one who could imitate different handwritings so well as his mother. Did you"— Mrs. Cumberland looked cautiously round—"observe the girl, Molly Green, take her handkerchief from her pocket whilst she stood here?"

"I didn't see her with any handkercher," was the answer, given after a slight pause. "Shouldn't think the girl has one. She put her basket on the sideboard there, to come forward to my geraniums, and stood stock still while she looked at 'em. I don't say she didn't go to her pocket; but I never saw her do it."

"It might have been so. These little actions often pass unnoticed. And it is so easy for any other article to slip out unseen when a handkerchief is drawn from a pocket," concluded Mrs. Cumberland in a suppressed, almost eager tone. Which Mrs. Gass noticed, and did not quite like.

But there is still something to relate of Dallory Hall. When madam followed her husband through the glass-doors into his parlour, an unusually unpleasant scene ensued. For once Mr. North held out resolutely. He had no other resource, for he had not the money to give her, and did not know where to get it. That it was for Sidney, he well believed; and for that reason only would have denied it to the utmost of his feeble strength. Madam flounced out in one of her worst moods. Mrs. Cumberland's visit and the startling sight of Ellen Adair had brought to her unusual annoyance. As ill-luck had it, she encountered Bessy in the hall, and upon her vented her temper. The short scene was a violent one. When it was over, the poor girl went shivering and trembling into her father's parlour. He had been standing with the door ajar, shrinking almost as much as Bessy, and utterly powerless to interfere.

"Oh, child! if I could only save you from this!" he murmured, as they stood together before the window, and he fondly stroked the head that lay on his breast. "It's cue of the troubles that are wearing me out, Bessy: wearing me out before my time."

Bessy North was patient, meek, enduring; but meekness and patience can both be tried beyond their strength.

"Oliver Rane wants you: you know that, Bessie. If he could see his way to keeping you, you should go to him tomorrow. Ay! though your poor brother has just been put into his grave."

Bessy lifted her head. In these moments of emotion, the heart speaks out without reticence.

"Papa, I would go to Oliver as he is now, and risk it," she said through her blinding tears. "I should not be afraid of our getting on: we would make shift together, until better times came. He spoke a word of this to me not long ago, but his lips were sealed, he said, and he could not press it."

"He thought he had not enough for you?"

"He thought you would not consider it so. I should, papa. And I think those who bravely set out to struggle on together, have as much happiness in their makeshifts and economies as others who begin with a fortune."

"We'll see; we'll see, Bessy. I should like you to try it, if you are not afraid. I'll talk to Dick. But—mind!— not a word here," he added, glancing round to indicate the precincts of Mrs. North. "We shall have to keep it to ourselves if we would not have it frustrated. I wonder how much Oliver makes a year."

"Not much; but he is advancing slowly. He has talked to me about it. What keeps one will keep two, papa."

"He comes into about two hundred a-year when his mother dies. And I fear she won't live long, from what she tells me. Poor Fanny! Not that I'd counsel any one to reckon on dead men's shoes, child. Life's uncertain: he might die before her."

"He would not reckon on anything but his own exertions, papa. He told me a secret—that he is engaged on a medical work, writing it all his spare time. It is quite certain to become a standard work, he says, and bring him good returns. Oh! papa, there will be no doubt about our getting on. Let us risk it!"

She spoke in a bright, hopeful tone—her mild eyes shining. Mr. North caught a little of the glad spirit, and resolved—Dick being willing: sensible Dick—that they should risk it.

CHAPTER IX

IN LAWYER DALE'S OFFICE

Whitborough was a good-sized, bustling town, sending two members to parliament. In the heart of it lived Mr. Dale, the lawyer, who did a little in money-lending as well. He was a short stout man, with a red face and no whiskers, nearly bald on the top of his round head; and he usually attired himself in the attractive costume of a brown tail coat and white neckcloth.

On this same morning which had witnessed the departure of Sir Nash Bohun and his son from Dallory Hall, Mr. Dale, known commonly amongst his townsfolks as Lawyer Dale—was seated in his office at Whitborough. It was a small room, containing a sort of double desk, at which two people might face each other. The lawyer's seat was against the wall, his face to the room; a clerk sometimes sat, or stood on the other side when business was pressing. Adjoining this office was one for the clerks, three of whom were kept; and clients had to pass through their room to reach the lawyer's.

Mr. Dale was writing busily. The clock was on the stroke of twelve, and a great deal of the morning's work had still to be done, when one of the clerks came in: a tall, thin, cadaverous youth with black hair, parted into a flat curl on his forehead.

"Are you at home, sir?"

"Who is it?" asked Mr. Dale, growling at the interruption.

"Mr. Richard North."

"Send him in."

Richard came in; a fine looking man in his mourning clothes; the lawyer could not help thinking so. After shaking hands—a ceremony Mr. Dale liked to observe with all his clients, when agreeable to them—he came from behind his desk to seat himself in his elbow-chair of red leather, and gave Richard a seat opposite. The room was small, the desk and other furniture large, and they sat very close together. Richard held his hat on his knee.

"You guess, no doubt, what has brought me here, Mr. Dale. Now that my ill-fated brother is put out of our sight in his last resting-place, I have leisure and inclination to look into the miserable event that sent him there. I shall spare neither expense nor energy in discovering—if it may be—the traitor."

"You allude to the anonymous letter."

"Yes. And I have come to ask you to give me all the information you can about it."

"But, my good sir, I have no information to give. I don't possess any."

"I ought to have said details of the attendant circumstances. Let me hear your history of the transaction from beginning to end: and if you can give me any hint as to the writer—that is, if you have formed any private opinion about him—I trust you will do so."

Mr. Dale could be a little tricky on occasion; he was sometimes engaged in transactions that would not have borne the light of day, and that most certainly he would never have talked about. On the other hand, he could be honest and truthful where there existed no reason for being the contrary: and this anonymous letter business came under the latter category.

"The transaction was as open and straightforward as possible," spoke the lawyer—and Richard, a judge of character and countenances, saw he was speaking the truth. "Mr. Edmund North came to me one day some short time ago, wanting me to let him have a hundred pounds on his own security. I didn't care to do that—I knew about his bill transactions, you see—and I proposed that some one should join him. Eventually he came with Alexander the surgeon, and the matter was arranged."

"Do you know for what purpose he wanted the money?"

"For his young brother, Sidney North. A fast young man, that, Mr. Richard," added the lawyer in significant tones.

"Yes. Unfortunately."

"Well, he had got into some secret trouble, and came praying to Mr. Edmund to get him out of it. Whatever foolish ways Edmund North had wasted money in, there's this consolation remaining to his friends—that the transaction which eventually sent him to his grave was one of pure kindness," added the lawyer warmly. "'My father has enough trouble,' he remarked to me; 'with one thing and another, his life's almost worried out of him; and I don't care that he should hear what Master Sidney's been up to, if it can be kept from him.' Yes; the motive was a good one."

"How was it he did not apply to me?" asked Richard.

"Well—had you not, just about that time, assisted your brother Edmund in some scrape of his own?"

Richard North nodded.

"Just so. He said he had not the face to apply to you so soon again; should be ashamed of himself. Well, to go on, Mr. Richard North. I gave him the money on the bill; and when it became due, neither he nor Alexander could meet it: so I agreed to renew it. Only one day after that, the anonymous letter found its way to Dallory Hall."

"You are sure of that?"

"Certain. The bill was renewed on the 30th of April; here, in this very room. Mr. North received the letter on the 1st of May."

"It was so. By the evening post."

"So that, if the transaction got wind through that renewing, the writer did not lose much time about it."

"Well now, Mr. Dale, in what way could that transaction have got wind, and who heard of it?"

"I never spoke of it to a human being," impetuously cried the lawyer. And Richard North again felt sure that he spoke the truth.

"The transaction, from the beginning, was known only to us three men: Edmund North, the surgeon, and myself. I don't believe either of them mentioned it at all. I know I did not. It's just possible Edmund North might have told his stepbrother Sidney how he got the money—the young scamp. I beg your pardon, Mr. Richard; I forgot he was your brother also."

"It would be to Sidney's interest to keep it quiet," remarked Richard. "Our men at the works have a report amongst them—I know not where picked up, and I don't think they know either—that the writer was your clerk, Wilks."

"Nonsense!" contemptuously rejoined the lawyer. "I've heard the report also. Why should Wilks trouble his head about it? Don't believe anything so foolish."

"I don't believe it," returned Richard North. "Wilks could have no motive whatever for it, as far as I can see. But I think that he may have become cognizant of the affair, and talked of it abroad."

"Not one of my clerks knew anything about it," protested Mr. Dale. "I've three of 'em: Wilks and two others. You don't suppose, sir, I take them into my confidence in all things."

"But, is it quite impossible that any one of them—say Wilks—could have found it out surreptitiously?" urged Richard.

"Wilks has nothing surreptitious about him," said the lawyer. "He is too shallow for it. A thoroughly useful clerk, but a man without guile."

"I did not mean to apply the word to him personally. I'll change it if you like. Could Wilks, or either of the other two, have accidentally learnt this, without your knowledge? Was there a possibility of it? Come, Mr. Dale; be open with me. Even if it were so, no blame would attach to you."

"It is just this," answered Mr. Dale: "I don't see how it was possible for any one of them to have learnt it; and yet at the same time, I see no other way in which it could have transpired. That's the candid truth. I lay awake one night for half-an-hour, turning the puzzle over in my mind. Alexander says he never opened his lips about it; I know I did not; and poor Edmund North went into his fatal passion thinking Alexander wrote the letter, because he said Alexander alone knew of it; a pretty sure proof he had not talked about it himself."

"Which brings us back to your clerks," remarked Richard North. "They might have overheard a few chance words when the bill was renewed."

"I'm sure the door was shut," debated Mr. Dale, in a tone as if he were not sure, but rather sought to persuade himself that he was so. "Only Wilks was in, that morning; the other two had gone out."

"Rely upon it that's how it happened. The door could not have been quite closed."

"Well, I don't know. I generally shut it myself, and carefully too, when important clients are in here. I confess," honestly added Mr. Dale, "that it's the only explanation I can see in the matter. If the door was unlatched, Wilks might have heard. I had him in last night, and taxed him with it. He denies it out and out: says that, even if the affair had come to his knowledge, he knows his duty better than to have talked about it."

"I don't doubt that he does, when in his sober senses. But he is not always in them."

"Oh, come, Mr. Richard North, it is not as bad as that."

Richard was silent. If Mr. Dale was satisfied with his clerk and his clerk's discretion, he had no desire to render him otherwise.

"He takes too much now and then, you know, Mr. Dale; and he may have dropped a word in some enemy's hearing: who perhaps caught it up and then wrote the letter. Would you mind my questioning him?"

"He is not here to be questioned, or you might do it and welcome," replied Mr. Dale. "Wilks is lying up to-day. He has not been well for more than a week past; could hardly do his work yesterday."

"I'll take an opportunity of seeing him then," said Richard. "My father won't rest until the writer of this letter has been traced; neither, in truth, shall I."

The lawyer said good-morning to his visitor, and returned to his desk. But ere he recommenced work, he thought over the chief subject of their conversation. Had the traitor been Wilks, he asked himself. What Richard North had said was perfectly true—the young man sometimes took too much after work was over. But Mr. Dale had hitherto found no reason to complain of his discretion; and, difficult as it seemed to find any other loophole of suspicion, he finally concluded that he had no reason to do so now.

Meanwhile Richard North walked back to Dallory—it was nearly two miles from Whitborough. Passing his works, he continued his way a little further, to a turning called North Inlet, in which were some houses, large and small, chiefly tenanted by his workpeople. In one of these, a pretty cottage standing back, lodged Timothy Wilks. The landlady was a relative of Wilks's, and as he paid very little for his two rooms, he did not mind the walk once a-day to and from Whitborough.

"Good-morning, Mrs. Green. Is Timothy Wilks in?"

Mrs. Green, an ancient matron in a mob-cap, was on her knees, whitening the door-step. She rose at the salutation, saw it was Richard North, and curtsied.

"Tim have just crawled out to get a bit o' sunshine, sir. He's very bad to-day. Would you please to walk in, Mr. Richard?"

Amidst this colony of his workpeople he was chiefly known as "Mr. Richard." Mrs. Green's husband was timekeeper at the North Works.

"What's the matter with him?" asked Richard, as he stepped over the threshold and the bucket to the little parlour.

"Well, sir, I only hope it's not low fever; but it looks to me uncommon like it."

"Since when has he been ill?"

"He have been ailing this fortnight past. The fact is, sir, he won't keep steady," she added in deploring tones. "Once a-week he's safe to come home the worse for drink, and that's pay night; and sometimes it's oftener than that. Then for two days afterwards he can't eat; and so it goes on, and he gets as weak as a rat. It's not that he takes much drink; it is that a little upsets him. Some men could take half-a-dozen glasses a'most to his one."

"What a pity it is!" exclaimed Richard.

"He had a regular bout of it a week or so ago," resumed Mrs. Green; who once set off on the score of Timothy's misdoings, never knew when to stop. It was so well known to North Inlet, this failing of the young man's, that she might have talked of it in the market-place and not betrayed confidence. "He had been ailing before, as I said, Mr. Richard; off his food, and that; but one night he caught it smartly, and he's been getting worse ever since."

"Caught what smartly?" asked Richard, not posted up in North Inlet idioms.

"Why, the drink, sir. He came home reeling, and give his head such a bang again the door-post that it knocked him back'ards. I got him up somehow—Green was out—and on to his bed, and there he went off in a dead faint. I'd no vinegar in the house: if you want a thing in a hurry you're sure to be out of it: so I burnt a feather up his nose, and that brought him to. He began to talk all sorts of nonsense then, about doing 'bills,' whatever that might mean, and old Dale's money-boxes, running words into one another like mad, so that you couldn't make top or tail of it. I'd never seen him as bad as this, and got frightened."

She paused to take breath, always short with Mrs. Green. The words "doing bills" struck Richard North. He immediately perceived that hence might have arisen the report—for she had no doubt talked of this publicly—that Timothy Wilks was the traitor. Other listeners could put two and two together as well as he.

"I thought I'd get in the vinegar, in case he went off again," resumed Mrs. Green. "And when I was running round to the shop for it—leastways walking, for I can't run now—who should I meet, turning out of Ketler's but Dr. Rane. I stopped to tell him, and he said he'd look in and see Tim. He's a kind man in sickness, Mr. Richard."

"Did Dr. Rane come?" asked Richard.

"Right off, sir, there and then. When I got back he had put cloths of cold water on Tim's head. And wasn't Tim talking! You might have thought him a show-man at the fair. The doctor wrote something on paper with his pencil and sent me off again to Stevens the druggist's, and Stevens he gave me a little bottle of white stuff ta bring back. The doctor gave Tim some of it in a teacup of cold water, and it sent him into a good sleep. But he has never been well, sir, since then: and now I misdoubt me but it will end in low fever."

"Do you remember what night this was?" asked Richard.

"Ay, that I do, sir. For the foolish girls was standing out by twos and threes, making bargains with their sweethearts to go a-maying at morning dawn. I told 'em they'd a deal better stop indoors to mend their stockings. 'Twas the night afore the first of May, Mr. Richard."

"The evening of the day the bill was renewed," thought Richard. He possessed the right clue now. If he had entertained any doubt of Wilks before, this set it at rest.

"Did any of the neighbours hear Tim talking?" he asked.

"Not a soul but me and Dr. Rane here, sir. But I believe he had been holding forth to a room-full at the Wheatsheaf. They say he was in part gone when he got there. Oh, it does make me so vexed, the ranting way he goes on when the drink's in him. If his poor father and mother could look up from their graves, they'd be fit to shake him in very shame. Drink is the worst curse that's going, Mr. Richard—and poor Tim's weak head won't stand hardly a drop of it."

She had told all she knew. Richard North stepped over the bucket again, remarking that he might meet Tim. Sure enough he did so. In taking a cross-cut to the works, he came upon him, leaning against the wooden railings that bordered a piece of waste land. He looked very ill: Richard saw that: a small, slight young man with a mild, pleasant countenance and inoffensive manners. His mother had been a cousin of Mrs. Green's, but superior to the Greens in station. Timothy would have held his head considerably above North Inlet, but for being brought down both in consequence and pocket by his oft-recurring failing.

Kindly and courteously, but with a resolute tone not to be mistaken, Richard North entered on his questioning. He did not suspect Wilks of having written the anonymous letter; he told him this candidly; but he suspected, nay, knew, that it must have been written by some one who had gathered certain details from Wilks's gossip. Wilks, weak and ill, acknowledged that the circumstance of the drawing of the bill; or rather the renewing of one; had penetrated to his hearing in Mr. Dale's office; but he declared that he had not, as far as he knew, repeated it again.

"I'd no more talk of our office business, sir, than I'd write an anonymous letter," said he, much aggrieved. "Mr. Dale never had a more faithful clerk about him than I am."

"I dare say you would not, knowingly," was Richard's rejoinder. "Answer me one question, Wilks. Have you any recollection of haranguing the public at the Wheatsheaf?"

Mr. Wilks's reply to this was, that he had not harangued the public at the Wheatsheaf. He remembered being at the house quite well, and there had been a good deal of argument in the parlour; chiefly, he thought, touching the question as to whether masters in general ought not to give holiday on the first of May. There had been no particular haranguing on his part, he declared; and he could take his oath that he never opened his lips there about what had come to his knowledge. One thing he did confess, on being pressed by Richard—that he had no remembrance of quitting the Wheatsheaf, or of how he reached home. He retained a faint idea of having seen Dr. Rane's face bending over him later, but could not say whether it was dream or reality.

Nothing more could be got out of Timothy Wilks. That the man was guiltless of intentional treachery was as undoubted as that the treachery had occurred through his talking. Richard North bent his steps to the Wheatsheaf, to hold conference with Packerton, the landlord of that much-frequented hostelrie.

And any information that Packerton could give, he was willing to give; but it amounted to little. Richard wanted the names of all who went into the parlour on the night of the 30th of April, during the time that Wilks was there. The landlord mentioned as many as he could remember; but said that others might have gone in and out. One man—who looked like a gentleman and sat by Wilks—was a stranger, he said; he had never seen him before or since. This man grew quite friendly with Wilks, and went out with him, propping up his steps. Packerton's son, a smart youth of thirteen, going out on an errand, had overtaken them on their way across the waste ground. (In the very path where Richard had only now encountered Wilks.) Wilks was holding on by the railings, the boy said, talking with the other as fast as he could talk, and the other was laughing. Richard North wished he could find out who this man was, and where he might be seen; for, of all the rest mentioned by the landlord, not one was at all likely to have written the anonymous letter. Packerton's opinion was that Wilks had not spoken of the matter there; he was then hardly "far enough gone" to have committed the imprudence.

"But I suppose he was when he left you," said Richard.

"Yes, sir, I'm afraid he might have been. He could talk; but every bit of reason had gone out of him. I never saw anybody but Wilks just like this when they've taken too much."

Again Richard North sought Wilks, and questioned him who this stranger, man or gentleman, might be. He might as well have questioned the moon. Wilks had a hazy impression of having been with a tall, thin, strange man: but where, or when, or how, he knew not.

"I'll ask Rane what sort of a condition Wilks was in when he saw him," thought Richard.

But Richard could not carry out his intentions until night. Business claimed him for the rest of the day, and then he went home to dinner.

Dr. Rane was in his dining-room that night, the white blind drawn before the window, and writing by the light of a shaded candle. Bessy North had said to her father that Oliver was busy with a medical work from which he expected good returns when published. It was so. He spared himself no labour; over that, or anything else: often writing far into the small hours. He was a patient, persevering man: once give him a chance of success, a fair start on life's road, and he would be sure to go on to fortune. He said this to himself continually; and he was not mistaken. But the chance had not come yet.

The clock was striking eight, when the doctor heard a ring at his door-bell, and Phillis appeared, showing in Richard North. A thrill passed through Oliver Rane; perhaps he could not have told why or wherefore.

Richard sat down and began to talk about Wilks, asking what he had to ask, entering into the question generally. Dr. Rane listened in silence.

"I beg your pardon," he suddenly said, remembering his one shaded candle. "I ought to have asked for more light."

"It's quite light enough for me," replied Richard. "Don't trouble. To go back to Wilks: Did he say anything about the bill in your hearing, Rane?"

"Not a word; not a syllable. Or, if he did, I failed to catch it."

"Old Mother Green says he talked about 'bills,'" said Richard. "That was before you saw him."

"Does she?" carelessly remarked the doctor. "I heard nothing of the kind. There was no coherence whatever in his words, so far as I noticed: one never pays much attention to the babblings of a drunken man."

"Was he quite beside himself?—quite unconscious of what he said, Rane?"

"Well, I am told that it is the peculiar idiosyncrasy of Wilks to be able to talk and yet to be unconscious for all practical purposes, and for recollection afterwards. Otherwise I should not have considered him quite so far gone as that. He talked certainly; a little; seemed to answer me in a mechanical sort of way when I asked him a question, slipping one word into another. If I had tried to understand him, I don't suppose I could have done so. He did not say much; and I was away from him a good deal about the house, looking for water and rags to put on his head."

"Then you heard nothing about it, Rane?"

"Absolutely nothing."

The doctor sat so that the green shade of the candle happened to fall on his face, making it look very pale. Richard North, absorbed in thought about Wilks, could not have told whether the face was in shadow or in light. He spoke next about the stranger who had joined Wilks, saying he wished he could find out who it was.

"A tall thin man, bearing the appearance of a gentleman?" returned Dr. Rane. "Then I think I saw him, and spoke to him."

"Where?" asked Richard with animation.

"Close to your works. He was looking in through the iron gates. After quitting Green's cottage, I crossed the waste ground, and saw him standing at the gates, under the middle gas-lamp. I had to visit a patient down by the church, and took the nearer way."

"You did not recognize him?"

"Not at all. He was a stranger to me. As I was passing, he turned and asked me whether he was going right for Whitborough. I pointed to the high-road and told him to keep straight on. Depend upon it, this was the same man."

"What could he have been looking in at my gates for?" muttered Richard. "And what—for this is of more consequence—had he been getting out of Wilks?"

"It seems rather curious altogether," remarked Dr. Rane.

"I'll find this man," said Richard, as he got up to say goodnight; "I must find him. Thank you, Rane."

But after his departure Oliver Rane did not settle to his work as before. A man, once interrupted, cannot always do so. All he did was to pace the room restlessly with bowed head, as a man in some uneasy dream. The candle burnt lower, the flame grew above the shade, throwing its light on his face, showing up its lines and angles. But it was not any brighter than when the green shade had cast over it its cadaverous hue.

"Edmund North! Edmund North!"

Did the words in all their piteous, hopeless appeal come from him? Or was it some supernatural cry in the air?

CHAPTER X

PUT TO HIS CONSCIENCE

A fine morning in June. Lovely June; with its bright blue skies and its summer flowers. Walking about amidst his rose-trees, was Mr. North, a rake in his hand. He fancied he was gardening; he knew he was trifling. What did it matter?—his face looked almost happy. The glad sunshine was overhead, and he felt as free as a bird of the air.

The anonymous letter, that had caused so much mischief, was passing into a thing of the past. In spite of Richard North's efforts to trace him out, the writer remained undiscovered. Timothy Wilks was the chief sufferer, and bitterly resentful thereon. To have been openly accused of having sent it by at least six persons out of every dozen acquaintances he met, disturbed the mind and curdled the temper of ill-starred Timothy Wilks. As to the general public, they were beginning to forget all about the trouble—as it is in the nature of a faithless public to do. Only in the hearts of a few individuals did the sad facts remain in all their sternness; and of those, one was Jelly.

Poor Mr. North could afford to be happy to-day, and for many days to come. Bessy also. Madam had relieved them of her presence yesterday, and gone careering off to Paris with her daughter. They hoped she might be away for weeks. In the seductive freedom of the home, Richard North had stayed late that morning. Mr. North was just beginning to talk with him, when some one called on business, and Richard shut himself up with the stranger. The morning had gone on; the interview was prolonged; but Richard was coming out now. Mr. North put down the rake.

"Has Wilson gone, Richard?"

"Yes, sir."

"What did he want? He has stayed long enough."

"Only a little business with me, father," was Richard's answer in his filial care. It had not been agreeable business, and Richard wished to spare his father.

"And now for Bessy, sir?" he resumed, as they paced side by side amongst the sweet-scented roses. "You were beginning to speak about her."

"Yes, I want to talk to you. Bessy would be happier with Rane than she is here, Dick."

Richard looked serious. He had no objection whatever to his sister's marrying Oliver Rane: in fact, he regarded it as an event certain to take place, sooner or later; but he did not quite see that the way was clear for it yet.

"I have no doubt of that, father."

"And I think, Dick, she had better go to him now, whilst we are at liberty to do as we please at home."

"Now!" exclaimed Richard.

"Yes; now. That is before madam comes back again. Poor Edmund is only just put under the sod; but—considering the circumstances—I think the memory of the dead must give place to the welfare of the living."

"But how about ways and means, sir?"

"Ay: how about ways and means. Nothing can be spared from the works at present, I suppose, Dick."

"Nothing to speak of, sir."

Mr. North had felt ashamed even to ask the question. In fact, it was more a remark than a question, for he knew as well as Richard did that there was no superfluous money to draw upon.

"Of course not, Dick. Rane gets just enough to live upon now, and no more. Yesterday, after madam and Matilda had driven off, I was at the front-gates when Rane passed. So he and I got talking about Bessy. He said his income was small now, but that of course it would considerably augment as soon as Alexander had left. As he and Bessy are willing to try it, I don't see why they should not do so, Dick."

Richard gave no immediate reply. He had a rose in his hand and was looking at it absently, deep in thought. His father continued:

"It's not as if Rane had no expectations whatever. Two hundred a-year must come to him at his mother's death. And—Dick—have you any idea how Mrs. Gass's will is left?"

"Not the least, sir."

"Oliver Rane is the nearest living relative to her late husband, Mrs. Cumberland excepted. He is Thomas Gass's own nephew—and all the money was his. It seems to me, Dick, that Mrs. Gass is sure to remember him: perhaps largely."

"She may do so."

"Yes; and I think will do so. Bessy shall go to him; and be emancipated from her thraldom here."

"Oliver Rane has no furniture in his house."

"He has some. The dining-room and his bedroom are as handsomely furnished as need be. We can send in a little more. There are some things at the Hall that were Bessy's own mother's, and she shall have them. They have not been thought much of here, Dick, amidst the grand things that madam has filled the house with."

"She'll make a fuss, though, at their being removed," remarked Dick.

"Let her," retorted Mr. North, who could be brave as the best when two or three hundred miles lay between him and madam. "Those things were your own dear mother's, Dick; she bought them with her own money before she married me, and I have always regarded them as heir-looms for Bessy. It's just a few plain solid mahogany things, as good as ever they were. It was our drawing-room furniture in the early days, and it will do for their drawing-room now. When Rane is making his six or seven hundred a-year, they can buy finer if they choose. We thought great things of it; I know that."

Richard smiled. "I remember once when I was a very little fellow, my mother came in and caught me drawing a horse on the centre-table with pen-and-ink. The trouble she had to get the horse out!—and the whipping I had!"

"Poor Dick! She did not whip often."

"It did me good, sir. I have been scrupulously careful of furniture ever since."

"Ah, nothing like the lessons of early childhood for making an impression," spoke Mr. North. "'Spare the rod and spoil the child!' There was never a truer saying than that."

"Then you really intend them to marry at once," said Richard, returning to the question.

"I do," replied Mr. North in more decisive tones than he usually spoke. "They both wish it: and why should I hold out against them? Bessy's thirty this year, you know, Dick: if girls are not wives at that age, they begin to think it hard. It's better to marry tolerably young: a man and woman don't shake down into each other's ways if they come together late in life. You are silent, Dick."

"I was thinking, sir, whether I could not manage a couple of hundred pounds for them from myself."

"You are ever generous, Dick. I don't know what we should all do without you."

"The question is—shall I give it over to them in money, or spend it for them in furniture?"

"In money; in money, Dick," advised Mr. North. "The furniture can be managed; and cash is cash. Spend it in chairs and tables and it seems as if there were nothing tangible to show for it."

Richard smiled. "It strikes me that the argument lies the other way, sir. However, I think it will be better to do as you advise. Bessy shall have two hundred pounds handed to her after her marriage, and they can do what they consider best with it."

"To be sure; to be sure, Dick. Let them be married. Bessy has a miserable life of it here; and she'll be thirty on the twenty-ninth of this month. Oliver Rane was thirty the latter end of March."

"Only thirty!" cried Richard. "I think he must be more than that, sir."

"But he's not more," returned Mr. North. "I ought to know; and so ought you, Dick. Don't you remember they are both in the tontine? All the children put into that tontine were born in the same year."

"Oh, was it so? I had forgotten," returned Richard carelessly, for the tontine had never troubled him very much. He could just recollect that when they were children he and his brother were wont to teaze little Bessy, saying if she lived to be a hundred she would come into a fortune.

"That was an unlucky tontine, Dick," said Mr. North, shaking his head. "Of ten children who were entered for it, only three remain. The other seven are dead. Four of them died in the first or second year."

"How came Oliver Rane to be put into the tontine?" asked Richard. "I thought he came to life in India—and lived there for the first few years of his life. The tontine children were all Whitborough children."

"Thomas Gass did that, Richard. When he received news that his sister had this baby—Oliver—he insisted upon putting him into the tontine. It was a sort of salve to Tom Gass's conscience; at least I thought so: what his sister and the poor baby wanted then was money—not to be put into a useless tontine. Ah, well, Rane has got on without any one's assistance, and I dare say will flourish in the end."

Richard glanced at his watch; twelve o'clock; and increased his pace; a hundred and one things were wanting him at the works. Mr. North walked with him to the gate.

"Yes, it's all for the best, Dick. And we'll get the wedding comfortably over while madam's away."

"What has been her motive, sir, for opposing Bessy's engagement to Rane?"

"Motive!" returned Mr. North. "Do you see that white butterfly, Dick, fluttering about?—as good ask me what its motive is, as ask me madam's. I don't suppose she has any motive—except that she is given to opposing us all."

Richard concluded it was so. Something might lie also in Bessy's patient excellence as a housekeeper; madam, ever selfish, did not perhaps like to lose her.

As they reached the iron gates, Mrs. Cumberland passed, walking slowly. She looked very ill. Mr. North arrested her, and began to speak of the projected marriage of Oliver and Bessy. Mrs. Cumberland changed colour and looked almost frightened. Unobservant Mr. North saw nothing. Richard did.

"Has Oliver not told you what's afoot?" said the former. "Young men are often shyer in these matters than women."

"It's a very small income for them to begin upon," she observed presently, when Mr. North had said his say—and Richard thought he detected some private objection to the union. "So very small for Bessy— who has been used to Dallory Hall."

"It won't always remain small," said Mr. North. "His practice will increase when Alexander goes; and he'll have other money, may be, later. Oh, they'll get on, Fanny. Young couples like to be sufficiently poor to make struggling upwards a pleasure. I dare say you married upon less."

"Of course, if you are satisfied—it must be all right," murmured Mrs. Cumberland. "You and Bessy."

She drew her veil over her grey face, said good-morning, and moved away. Not in the direction of Dallory—as she was previously walking—but back to the Ham. Mr. North turned into his grounds again; Richard went after Mrs. Cumberland.

"I beg your pardon," he said—he was not as familiar with her as his father was—"will you allow me a word. You do not like this proposed marriage. Have you anything to urge against it?"

"Only for Bessy's sake. I was thinking of her."

"Why for Bessy's sake?"

There was some slight hesitation in Mrs. Cumberland's answer. She appeared to be drawing her veil straight.

"Their income will be so small. I know what a small income is, and therefore I feel for her."

"Is that all your hesitation, Mrs. Cumberland?—the narrowness of the income?"

"All."

"Then I think, as my father says, you may safely leave the decision with themselves. But—was this all?" added Richard: for an idea to the contrary had taken hold of him. "You have no personal objection to Bessy?"

"Certainly it was all," was Mrs. Cumberland's reply. "As to any personal objection to Bessy, that I could never have. When Oliver first told me they were engaged, I thought how lucky he was to win Bessy North; I wished them success with all my heart.

"Forgive me, Mrs. Cumberland. Thank you. Good-morning."

Reassured, Richard North turned, and strode hastily away in the direction of Dallory. He fancied she had heard Bessy would have no fortune, and was feeling disappointed on her son's account. It struck him that he might as well confirm this; and he wheeled round.

Mrs. Cumberland had gone on and was already seated on the bench before spoken of, in the shady part of the road. Richard, in a few concise words, entering into no details of any sort, said to her that his sister would have no marriage portion.

"That I have long taken as a matter of course; knowing what the expenses at the Hall must be," she answered with a friendly smile. "Bessy is a fortune in herself; she would make a good wife to any man. Provided they have sufficient for comfort—and I hope Oliver will soon be making that—they can be as happy without wealth as with it, if your sister can only think so. Have you—pardon me for recalling what must be an unpleasant topic, Richard—have you yet gained any clue to the writer of that anonymous letter?"

"Not any. It presents mystery on all sides."

"Mystery?"

"As it seems to me. Going over the various circumstances, as I do on occasion when I have a minute to myself, I try to fit the probability into another, and I cannot compass it. We must trust to time, Mrs. Cumberland. Good-morning."

Richard raised his hat, and left her. She sat on with her pain. Mrs. Cumberland was as strictly rigid a woman in tenets as in temperament; her code of morality was a severe one. Over and over again had she asked herself whether—it is of no use to mince the matter any longer—Oliver had or had not written that anonymous letter which had killed Edmund North: and she could not answer the question. But, if he had done it, why then surely he ought not to wed the sister. It would be little less than sin.

Since this secret trouble had been upon her, more than a month now, her face had seemed to assume a greyer tinge. How grey it looked now, as she sat on the bench, passers-by saw, and almost started. One of them was Mr. Alexander. Arresting his quick steps—he always walked quickly—he inquired after her health.

"Not any better and not much worse," she answered. "Complaints, such as mine, are always tediously prolonged."

"They are less severe to bear, however, than sharper ones," said the doctor, willing to administer a grain of comfort if he could. "What a lovely day! And madam's off for a couple of months, I hear."

"Have the two any connection with each other, Mr. Alexander?"

"I don't know," he said laughing. "Her presence makes winter at the Hall, and her absence its sunshine. If I had such a wife, I'm not sure that I should think it any sin to give her an overdose of laudanum some day, out of regard to the general peace. Did you hear of her putting Miss Bessy's wrist out?"

"No."

"She did it, then. Something sent her into a passion with Miss Bessy; she caught her hand and flung it away so violently that the wrist began to swell. I was sent for to bind it up. Why such women are allowed to live, I can't imagine."

"I suppose because they are not fit to die," said Mrs. Cumberland. "When are you leaving?"

"Sometime in July, I think, or during August. I enter on my new post the first of September, so there's no especial hurry in the matter."

Mrs. Cumberland rose and continued her slow way homewards. Passing her own house, she entered that of her son. Dr. Rane was engaged with a patient, so she went on to the dining-room and waited.

He came in shortly, perhaps thinking it might be another patient, his face bright. It fell a little when he saw his mother. Her visits to him were so exceedingly rare that some instinct whispered him nothing pleasant had brought her there. She rose and faced him.

"Oliver, is what I hear true—that you are shortly to be married?"

"I suppose it is, mother," was his answer.

"But—is there no impediment that should bar it?" she asked in a whisper.

"Well—as to waiting, I may wait to the end, and not find the skies raining gold. If Bessy's friends see no risk in it, it is not for me to see it. At any rate, this will be a more peaceful home for her than the Hall."

"I am not talking of waiting—or of gold—or of risk, Oliver," she continued solemnly, placing both her hands on his arm. "Is there nothing on your mind that ought to bar this marriage? Is your conscience at rest? If—wait and let me speak, my son; I understand what you would say; what you have already told me—that you were innocent—and I know, that I ought to believe you. But a doubt continually flashes up in my mind, Oliver; it is not my fault; truth knows my will is good to bury it for ever. Bear with me a moment; I must speak. If the death of Edmund North lies at your door, however indirectly it was caused, to make his sister your wife will be a thing altogether wrong; little less than a sin in the sight of Heaven. I do not accuse you, Oliver; I suggest this as a possible case; and now I leave it with you for your own reflection. Oh, my son, believe me—for it seems to me as though to-day I spoke with a prophet's inspiration! If your conscience tells you that you were not innocent, to bring Bessy North home to this roof will be wrong, and I think no blessing will rest upon it."

She was gone. Before Oliver Rane in his surprise could answer a word, Mrs. Cumberland was gone. Passing swiftly out at the open window, she stepped across the garden and the wire-fence, and so entered her own home.

CHAPTER XI

A QUIET WEDDING

Apparently Dr. Rane found nothing on his conscience that could present an impediment, and the preparation for the wedding went quietly on. Secretly might almost be the better word. In their dread lest the news should reach madam in her retreat over the water, and bring her back to thwart it, those concerned deemed it well to say nothing; and no suspicion of what was afloat transpired to the world in general.

Bessy—upon whom, from her isolated position, having no lady about her, the arrangements fell—was desired to fix a day. She named the twenty-ninth of June, her birthday. After July should come in, there was no certainty about madam's movements; she might come home, or she might not, and it was necessary that all should be over by that time, if it was to be gone through in peace. The details of the ceremony were to be of the simplest nature: Edmund North's recent death and the other attendant and peculiar circumstances forbidding the usual gaiety. The bridal party would go to church with as little ceremony as they went to service on Sundays, Bessy in a plain silk dress and a plain bonnet. Mr. North would give his daughter away, if he were well enough; if not, Richard. Ellen Adair was to be bridesmaid; Arthur Bohun had offered himself to Dr. Rane as best man. It might be very undutiful, but Arthur enjoyed stealing a march on madam as much as the best of them.

Mrs. Cumberland was no doubt satisfied with regard to the scruples she had raised, since she intended to countenance the wedding, and go to church. Dr. Rane and his bride would drive away from the church-door to the railway-station at Whitborough. The bridal tour was to last one week only. The doctor did not care to be longer away from his patients, and Bessy confessed that she would rather be at home, setting her house in order, than prolonging her stay at small inns in Wales. But for the disconcerting fact of madam's being in Paris, Dr. Rane would have liked to take Bessy across the Channel and give her her first glimpse of the French capital. Under madam's unjust rule, poor Bessy had never gone anywhere: Matilda North had been taken half over the world.

The new household arrangements at Dr. Rane's were to be accomplished during their week's absence: the articles of furniture—that Mr. North chose to consider belonged to Bessy—to be taken there from the Hall; the new carpet, Mrs. Cumberland's present, to be laid down in the drawing-room; Molly Green to enter as helpmate to Phillis. Surely madam would not grumble at that? Molly Green, going into a temper one day at some oppression of madam's, had given warning on the spot. Bessy liked the girl, and there could be no harm in engaging her as her own housemaid.

One of those taken into the secret had been Mrs. Gass. Richard, who greatly respected her in spite of her grammar, and liked her also, unfolded the news. She received it in silence: a very rare thing for Mrs. Gass to do. Just as it had struck Richard in regard to Mrs. Cumberland, so it struck him now—Mrs. Gass did not quite like the tidings.

"Well, I hope they'll be happy," she said at length, breaking the silence, "and I hope he deserves to be. I hope it with all my heart. Do you think he does, Mr. Richard?"

"Rane? Deserves to be happy? For all I see, he does. Why should he not?"

"I don't know," answered Mrs. Gass, looking into Richard's face. "Oliver Rane is my late husband's nephew, but he's three parts a stranger to me, except as a doctor; for he attends here, you know, sir,—as is natural—and not Alexander. Is he truthful, Mr. Richard? Is he trustworthy?"

"He is, for anything I know to the contrary," replied Richard North, a little wondering at the turn the conversation was taking. "If I thought he was not, I should be very sorry to give Bessy to him."

"Then let us hope that he is, Mr. Richard, and wish 'em joy with all our hearts."

That a doubt was lying on Mrs. Gass's mind, in regard to the scrap of paper found in her room, was certain. Being a sensible woman, it could only be that—when surrounding mists had cleared away—she should see that the only likely place for it to have dropped from, was Dr. Rane's pocketbook. Molly Green had been subjected to a cross-examination, very cleverly conducted, as Mrs. Gass thought, which left the matter exactly as it was before. But the girl's surprise was so genuine, at supposing any receipt for making plum-pudding (for thus had Mrs. Gass put it) could have been dropped by her, that Mrs. Gass's mind could only revert to the pocketbook. How far Oliver Rane was guilty, whether guilty at all, she was quite unable to decide. A doubt remained in her mind, though she was glad enough to put it from her. One thing struck her as curious, if not suspicious—that from the hour she had handed him over the paper to this, Dr. Rane had never once spoken of the subject to her. It almost seemed to Mrs. Gass that an innocent man would have done so, though it had only been to say, I have found no clue to the writer.

And if a little of the same doubt rose to Richard North during his interview with Mrs. Gass, it was due to her manner. But he was upright himself, unsuspicious as the day. The impression faded again; and he came away believing that Mrs. Gass, zealous for the Norths' honours, rather disapproved of the marriage for Bessy, on account of the doctor's poverty.

And so, there was no one to give a word of warning where it might have been effectual, and the day fixed for the wedding drew on. After all, the programme was not strictly carried out, for Mr. North had one of his nervous attacks, and could not go to church.

At five minutes past nine o'clock, in the warm bright June morning, the Dallory Hall carriage drove up to Dallory Church. Richard North, his sister, and Arthur Bohun were within it. The forms and etiquette usually observed at weddings were slighted here, else how came Arthur Bohun, the bridegroom's best man, to come to church with the bride? What did it matter? Closely in its wake came up the other carriage—which ought to have been the first. In after days, when a strange ending had come to the marriage life of Oliver Rane and his wife, and Oliver was regarded with dread, assailed with reproach, people said the marriage had been the Norths' doings more than his. At any rate, Bessy was first at church, and both were a little late.

But Mr. North was not the only one who failed them; the other was Mrs. Cumberland. She assigned no reason for absenting herself from the ceremony, excepting a plea that she did not feel equal to it— which her son believed or not, as he pleased. Her new bright dress and bonnet were spread out on the bed; but she never as much as looked at them: and Ellen Adair found that she and Dr. Rane had to drive to church alone, in the hired carriage, arriving there almost simultaneously with the other party.

Richard North conducted his sister up the aisle, the bridegroom following close on their steps. Ellen Adair and Captain Bohun, left behind, walked side by side. Bessy wore a pretty grey silk and plain white bonnet: she had a small bouquet in her hand that the gardener, Williams, had arranged for her, Ellen Adair was in a similar dress, and looked altogether lovely. Mr. Lea, the clergyman, stood ready, book in hand. The spectators in the church—for the event had got wind at the last moment, as these events almost always do, and many came—rose up with expectation.

Of all the party, the bridegroom alone seemed to suffer from nervousness. His answering voice was low, his words were abrupt. It was the more remarkable, because he was in general so self-contained and calm a man. Bessy, always timid and yielding, spoke with gentle firmness; not a shade of doubt or agitation seemed to cross her. But there occurred a frightful contretemps.

"The ring, if you please," whispered the officiating clergyman to the bridegroom at that part of the service where the ring was needed.

The ring! Oliver Rane felt in his waistcoat-pocket, and went into an agony of consternation. The ring was not there. He must have left it on his dressing-table. The little golden symbol had been wrapped in white tissue paper, and he certainly remembered putting it into his waistcoat-pocket. It was as certainly not there now: and he supposed he must have put it out again.

"I have not got the ring!" he exclaimed hurriedly.

To keep a marriage ceremony waiting while a messenger ran a mile off for the ring and then ran a mile back again, was a thing that had never been heard of by the clergyman or any other of the startled individuals around him. What was to be done? It was suggested that perhaps some one present could furnish a ring that might suffice. Ellen Adair, standing in her beauty behind the bride, gently laid down the glove and bouquet she was holding, took off her own glove, and gave Oliver Rane a plain gold ring from her finger: one she always wore there. Arthur Bohun alone knew the history of the ring; the rest had never taken sufficient interest in her to inquire it; perhaps had never noticed that she wore one.

The service proceeded to its end. Had Oliver Rane gone a pilgrimage to all the jewellers' shops in Whitborough, he could not have chosen a more perfectly fitting wedding-ring than this. When they went into the vestry, Bessy, agitated by the mishap and the emotional position altogether, burst into tears, asking Ellen how she came by a wedding-ring.

The history was very simple. It arose—that is the possession of the ring—through the foolish romance of two young girls. Ellen and one of her schoolfellows named Maria Warne had formed a sincere and lasting, attachment to each other. At the time of parting, when Ellen was leaving school for Mrs. Cumberland's, each had bought a plain gold ring to give the other, over which eternal friendship had been vowed, together with an undertaking to wear the ring always. Alas, for time and change! In less than six months afterwards, Ellen Adair received notice of the death of Maria Warne. The ring had in consequence become really precious to Ellen; but in this emergency she had not scrupled to part with it.

As they came out of the vestry, Ellen found herself face to face with Jelly. The clerk, and the two women pew-openers, and the sexton, considering themselves privileged people, pressed up where they chose: Jelly, who of course—living with Mrs. Cumberland—could not be at all confounded with the common spectators, chose to press with them. Her face was long and serious, as she caught "hold of Miss Adair.

"How could you, Miss Ellen?" she whispered. "Don't you know that nothing is more unlucky than for a bride to be married with anybody else's wedding-ring?"

"But it was not a wedding-ring, Jelly. Only a plain gold one."

"Anyway it was unlucky for you. We have a superstition in these parts, Miss Ellen, that if a maid takes off a ring from her own finger to serve at a pinch for a bride, she will never be a wife herself. I wouldn't have risked it, miss."

Ellen laughed gaily, Jelly's dismay was so real and her face so grave. But there was no time for more. Richard held out his arm to her; and Oliver Rane was already taking out his bride. Close up against the door stood Mr. North's carriage, into which stepped the bride and bridegroom.

"My shawl! where's the shawl?" asked Bessy, looking round.

She had sat down upon it; and laughed gaily when Oliver drew it out. This shawl—a thin cashmere of quiet colours—was intended to be thrown on ere they reached the station. Her silk dress covered with that, and a black lace veil substituted for the white one on her bonnet, the most susceptible maid or matron who might happen to be travelling, would never take her for a bride.

Arthur Bohun deliberately flung an old white satin slipper after the carriage—it struck the old coachman's head, and the spectators shouted cheerily. Richard was going to the works. He placed Ellen in the carriage that had brought her.

"Will you pardon me, if I depute Captain Bohun to see you safely home instead of myself, Miss Adair? It is a very busy day at the works, and I must go there. Arthur, will you take charge of this young lady?"

What Ellen answered, she scarcely knew. Captain Bohun entered the carriage. The situation was wholly unexpected: and if their hearts beat a little faster in the tumult of the moment's happiness, Richard at least was unconscious of it.

"It is the first wedding I ever was at," began Ellen, feeling that she must talk to cover the embarrassment of the position. Both were feeling it: and moved as far apart from each other as if they had quarrelled: she in one corner, he in the further one opposite. "Of course it had been arranged that I should go home with Mrs. Cumberland."

"Is she ill?"

"Dr. Rane thinks it is only nervousness: he said so as we came along. I had to come with him alone. I am sure the people we passed on the road, who had not heard about Bessy thought it was I who was going to be married to him, they stared so into the carriage."

Ellen laughed as she said it. Arthur Bohun, drinking in draughts of her wondrous beauty, glanced at her meaningly, his blue eyes involuntarily betraying his earnest love.

"It may be your turn next, Ellen."

She blushed vividly, and looked from the window as though she saw something passing. He felt tempted there and then to speak of his love. But he had a keen sense of the fitness of time and place; and she had been placed for these few minutes under his protection: it seemed like putting him on his honour, as schoolboys say. Besides, he had fully made up his mind not to speak until he saw his way clear to marry.

Ellen Adair brought her face round again. "Jelly is in a terrible way about the ring, foretelling all sorts of ill-luck to every one concerned, and is thankful it did not happen to her. Will Bessy keep my ring always, do you think? Perhaps she would not be legally married if she gave it me back and took to her own—when it is found?"

Arthur Bohun's eyes danced a little. "Perhaps not," he replied in the gravest tones. "I don't know what they, would have done without it, Ellen."

"I did not tell Bessy one thing, when she asked me about it in the vestry. I will never tell her if I can help it—that Maria Warne is dead. How was it Mr. North did not come?"

"Nervousness too, in my opinion. He said he was ill."

"Why should he be nervous?"

"Lest it should come to his wife's ears that he had so far countenanced the marriage as to be present at it."

"Can you tell why Mrs. North should set her face against it?"

"No. Unless it is because other people have wished it. I should only say as much to you, though, Ellen: she is my mother."

The implied confidence sounded very precious in her ears. She turned to the window again.

"I hope they will be happy. I think there is no doubt of it. Bessy is very sweet-tempered and gentle."

"He is good-tempered too."

"Yes, I think so. I have seen very little of him. There's Mrs. Gass!"

They were passing that lady's house. She sat at the open window; a grand amber gown on, white satin ribbons in her cap. Leaning out, she shook her handkerchief at them in violent greeting, just as though they had been the bride and bridegroom. As Ellen drew back in her corner after bowing, her foot touched something on the carpet at the bottom of the carriage.

"Why! what is this?"

They both stooped at once. It was the wedding-ring enclosed in its tissue paper. Captain Bohun unfolded the paper.

"Dr. Rane must have lost it out of his pocket as we went along," cried Ellen. "He said, you know, that he felt so sure he had put it in. What is to be done with it?"

"Wear it instead of your own until they come back again," said Arthur. "Bessy can then take her choice of the two."

Accepting the suggestion without thought of dissent, Ellen took off her right glove and held out the other hand for the ring. He did not give it. Bending forward, he took her right hand and put it on for her.

"It fits as well as my own did."

Their eyes met. He had her hand still, as if trying how far the ring fitted. Her sweet face was like a damask rose.

"I trust I may put one on to better purpose some day, Ellen," came the murmuring, whispered, tremulous words. "Meanwhile—if Bessy does not claim this, remember that I have placed it on your finger."

Not another syllable, not another look from either. Captain Bohun sat down in his corner; Ellen in hers, her hot face bent over the glove she was putting on, and fully believing that earth had changed to Paradise.

CHAPTER XII

JELLY'S INDISCRETION

The days went on, and Dr. Rane's house was being made ready for the reception of the bride. No time could be lost, as the wedding tour was intended to be so short a one. As Jelly said, They would be at home before folk could look round. Mrs. Cumberland presented the new carpet for the drawing-room; the furniture that had been the first Mrs. North's, arrived from Dallory Hall. Molly Green arrived with it, equally to take up her abode in the house of Dr. Rane. The arranging of these things, with the rest of the preparations, was carried on with a considerable amount of bustle and gossip, Jelly being at the doctor's house continually, and constituting herself chief mistress of the ceremonies. Phillis and Molly Green, with native humility, deferred to her in all things.

It was said in a previous chapter that Jelly was one of those who retained an interest in the anonymous letter. She had a special cause for it. Jelly in her propensity to look into her neighbours' affairs, was given to taking up any mysterious cause, and making it her own. Her love of the marvellous was great, her curiosity insatiable. But Jelly's interest in this matter was really a personal one and concerned herself. It was connected with Timothy Wilks.

Amongst Jelly's other qualities and endowments, might be ranked one that was pre-eminent—love of admiration. Jelly could not remember to have been without an "acquaintance" for above a month at a time since the days when she left off pinafores. No sooner did she quarrel with one young man and dismiss him, than she took up another. Dallory wondered that of all her numerous acquaintances she had never married: but, as Jelly coolly said, to have a suitor at your beck and call was one thing, and to be tied to a husband was quite another. So Jelly was Jelly still; and perhaps it might be conceded that the fault was her own. She liked her independence.

The reigning "acquaintance" at this period happened to be Timothy Wilks. Jelly patronized him; he was devoted to her. There was a trifling difference in their ages—some ten years probably, and all on Jelly's side—but such a disparity had often happened before. Jelly had distinguished Tim by the honour of taking him to be her young man; and when the damaging whisper fell upon him, that he had probably written the anonymous letter resulting in the death of Edmund North, Jelly resented the aspersion far more than Timothy did. "I'll find out who did do it, if it costs me a year's wages and six months' patience," avowed Jelly to herself in the first burst of indignation.

But Jelly found she could not arrive at that satisfactory result any sooner than other people. It is true, she possessed a slight clue that they did not, in the few memorable words she had overheard that moonlight night between her mistress and Dr. Rane, but they did not assist her. The copy of the letter was said to have dropped out of Dr. Rane's pocketbook on somebody's carpet, and he denied that it had so dropped. Neither more nor less could Jelly make of the matter than this: and she laboured under the disadvantage of not being able to speak of what she had overheard, unless she confessed that she had been a listener. Considering who had been the speakers, Jelly did not choose to do that. From that time until this, quite two months, had the matter rankled in Jelly's mind; she had kept her ears open and put cautious questions whenever she thought they might avail, and all to no purpose. But in this, the first week of July, Jelly had a little light thrown on the clue by Molly Green. The very day that damsel arrived at Dr. Rane's as helpmate to Phillis, and Jelly had gone in with her domineering orders, the conversation happened to turn on plum-pudding—Phillis having made a currant-dumpling for dinner, and let the water get into it—and Molly Green dropped a few words which Jelly's ears caught up. They were only to the effect that Mrs. Gass had asked her whether she did not let fall on her carpet a receipt for making plum-pudding, the night of Edmund North's attack; which receipt Mrs. Gass had said, might have belonged to madam, and been brought from the Hall by Molly Green's petticoats. Jelly put a wary question or two to the girl, and then let the topic pass without further comment. That same evening she betook herself to Mrs. Gass, acting craftily. "Where's that paper that was found on your carpet the night Edmund North was taken?" asked Jelly boldly. Upon which Mrs. Gass was seized with astonishment so entire that in the moment's confusion she made one or two inconvenient admissions, just stopping short of the half-suspicion she had entertained of Dr. Rane.

In the days gone by, when Mrs. Gass was a servant herself, Jelly's relatives—really respectable people—had patronized her. Mrs. Gass was promoted to what she was; but she assumed no fine airs in consequence, as the reader has heard, and she and Jelly had remained very good friends. Vexed with herself for having incautiously admitted that the paper found was the copy of the anonymous letter, Mrs. Gass turned on Jelly and gave her a sharp reprimand for taking her unawares, and for trying to pry into what did not concern her. Jelly came away, not very much wiser than she went, but with a spirit of unrest that altogether refused to be soothed. She dared not pursue the inquiry openly, out of respect to her mistress and Dr. Rane, but she resolved to pump Molly Green. This same Molly was niece to the people with whom Timothy Wilks lodged, and rather more friendly with the latter gentleman than Jelly liked.

On the following morning when Jelly had swallowed her breakfast, she went into the next house with her usual want of ceremony. Phillis and Molly Green were on their knees laying down the new carpet in the drawing-room, tugging and hammering to the best of their ability, their gowns pinned round their waists, their sleeves up to the elbows; Phillis little and old, and weak-looking; Molly a comely girl of twenty, with rosy cheeks.

"Well, you must be two fools!" was Jelly's greeting, after taking in appearances. "As if you could expect to put down a heavy Brussels yourselves! Why didn't you get Turtle's men here? They served the carpet, and they ought to put it down."

"They promised to be here at seven o'clock this morning, and now it's nine," mildly responded Phillis, her pleasant dark eyes raised to Jelly's. "We thought we'd try and do it ourselves, so as to be able to get the table and chairs in, and the room finished. Perhaps Turtles have forgot it."

"I'd forget them, I know, if it was me, when I wanted to buy another carpet," said Jelly, tartly.

But, even as she spoke, a vehicle was heard to stop at the gate. Inquisitive Jelly looked from the window, and recognized it as Turtle's. It seemed to contain one or two pieces of new furniture. Phillis did not know that any had been coming, and went out. Molly Green rose from her knees, and stood regarding the carpet. This was Jelly's opportunity.

"Now, then!" she cried sharply, confronting the girl with imperious gesture. "Did you drop that, or did you not, Molly Green?"

Molly Green seemed quite bewildered by the address—as well she might be. "Drop what?" she asked.

"That plum-pudding receipt on Mrs. Gass's parlour carpet."

"Well, I never!" returned Molly after a pause of surprise. "What is it to you, Jelly, if I did?"

Now the girl only spoke so by way of retort; in a spirit of banter. Jelly, hardly believing her ears, accepted it as an admission that she had dropped it. And so the two went floundering on, quite at cross-purposes.

"Don't stare at me like that, Molly Green. I want a straightforward answer. Did it drop from your skirts?"

"It didn't drop from my hands. As to staring, it's you that's doing that, Jelly, not me."

"Where had you picked up the receipt? Out of Mr. Edmund North's room?"

"Out of Mr. Edmund North's room!" echoed Molly in wonder. "Whatever should have brought me doing that?"

"It was the night he was taken ill."

"And if it was! I didn't go a-nigh him."

A frightful thought now came over Jelly, turning her quite faint. What if the girl had gone to her aunt Green's that night and picked the paper up there? In that case it could not fail to be traced home to Timothy Wilks.

"Did you call in at your aunt's that same evening, Molly Green?"

"Suppose I did?" retorted Molly.

"And how dare you call in there, and bring—bring—receipts away with you surreptitious?" shrieked Jelly in her anger.

Molly Green stooped to pick up the hammer lying at her feet, speaking quietly as she did so. Some noise was beginning to be heard outside, caused by Turtle's men getting a piano into the house, and Phillis talking to them.

"I can't think what you are a-driving at, Jelly. As to calling in at aunt's, I have a right to do it when I'm out, if time allows. Which it had not that night, at any rate, for I never went nowhere but to the druggist's and Mrs. Gass's. I ran all the way to Dallory, and ran back again; and I don't think I stopped to speak to a single soul, but Timothy Wilks."

Jelly's spirits, which had been rising, fell to wrath again at the name. "You'd better say you got it from him, Molly Green. Don't spare him, poor fellow; whiten yourself."

Molly was beginning to feel just a little wrathful in her turn. Though Jelly was a lady's-maid and superior to herself with her red arms and rough hands, that could be no reason for attacking her in this way.

"And what if I did get it from him, pray? A plum-pudding prescription's no crime."

"But a copy of an anonymous letter is," retorted Jelly, the moment's anger causing her to forget caution. "Don't you try to brazen it out to me, girl."

"WHAT?" cried Molly, staring with all her eyes.

But in a moment Jelly's senses had come back to her. She set herself coolly to remedy the mischief.

"To think that my mind should have run off from the pudding-receipt to that letter of poor Mr. Edmund's! It's your fault, Molly Green, bothering my wits out of me! Where did you pick up the paper? There. Answer that; and let's end it."

Molly thought it might be as well to end it; she was growing tired of the play: besides, here were Turtle's men coming into the room to finish the carpet.

"I never had the receipt at all, Jelly, and it's not possible it could have dropped from me: that's the blessed truth. After talking to me, just as you've done, and turning me inside out, as one may say, Mrs. Gass as good as confessed that it might have fell out of her own bundle of receipts that she keeps in the sideboard drawer."

Slowly, Jelly arrived at a conviction that Molly Green, in regard to knowing nothing about the paper, must be telling the truth. It did not tend to lessen her anger.

"Then why on earth have you been keeping up this farce with me? I'll teach you manners with your betters, girl."

"Well, why did you set upon me?" was the good-humoured answer. "There's no such great treason in dropping a plum-pudding-receipt, even if I had done it—which I didn't. I don't like to be brow-beat for nothing: and it's not your place to do it, Jelly."

Jelly said no more. Little did she suspect that Mr. Richard North, leaning against the door-post of the half-open drawing-room door, whilst he watched the movements of the men, had heard every syllable of the colloquy. Coming round to see what progress was being made in the house, before he went to the works for the day, it chanced that he arrived at the same time as Turtle's cart. The new piano was a present from himself to Bessy.

Turtle's men leaving the piano in the hall, went into the room to finish the carpet, and Jelly came out of it. She found her arm touched by Mr. Richard North. He motioned her into the dining-room: followed, and closed the door.

"Will you tell me the meaning of what you have just been saying to Molly Green?"

The sudden question—as Jelly acknowledged to herself afterwards—made her creep all over. For once in her life she was dumb.

"I heard all you said, Jelly, happening to be standing accidentally at the door. What was it that was dropped on Mrs. Gass's carpet the night of my brother's illness?"

"It—was—a receipt for making plum-pudding, sir," stammered Jelly, turning a little white.

"I think not, Jelly," replied Richard North, gazing into her eyes with quiet firmness. "You spoke of a copy of an anonymous letter; and I am sure, by your tone, you were then speaking the truth. As I have overheard so much, you must give me a further explanation."

"I'd have spent a pound out of my pocket, rather than this should have happened," cried Jelly, with much ardour.

"You need not fear to tell me. I am no tattler, as you know."

Had there been only the ghost of a chance to stand out against the command, Jelly would have caught at it. But there was none. She disclosed what she knew: more than she need have done. Warming with her subject, when the narrative had fairly set in—as it was in Jelly's gossiping nature to warm—she also told of the interview she had been a partial witness to between Mrs. Cumberland and the doctor, and the words she had overheard.

Richard North looked grave—startled. He said very little: only cautioned Jelly never to speak of the subject again to other people.

"I suppose you will be asking Mrs. Gass about it, sir," cried Jelly, as he was turning to leave.

"I shall. And should be thankful to hear from her that it really was nothing more than a receipt for plum-pudding, Jelly."

Jelly's head gave an incredulous toss. "I hope you'll not let her think that I up and told you spontaneous, Mr. Richard. After saying to her that I should never open my lips about it to living mortal, she'd think I can't keep my word, sir."

"Be at ease, Jelly; she shall not suppose I learnt it by any thing but accident."

"And I am glad he knows it, after all!" decided Jelly to herself, as she watched him away up the Ham. "Perhaps he'll now be able to get at the rights and the wrongs of the matter."

Richard North walked along, full of trouble. It could not be but that he should have taken up a suspicion that Oliver Rane—now his brother-in-law—might have been the author of the anonymous letter. How, else, could its copy have dropped from his pocketbook—if, indeed, it had so dropped? Jelly had not thrown so much as a shadow of hint upon the doctor; either she failed to see the obvious inference, or controlled herself to caution: but Richard North could put two-and-two together. He went straight to Mrs. Gass's, and found that lady at breakfast in her dining-room, with window thrown up to the warm summer air.

"What is it you, Mr. Richard?" she cried, rising to shake hands. "I'm a'most ashamed to be found breakfasting at this hour; but the truth is, I overslept myself: and that idiot of a girl never came to tell me the time. The first part of the night I had no sleep at all: 'twas three o'clock before I closed my eyes."

"Were you not well?" asked Richard.

"I'd a touch of my pain; nothing more. Which is indigestion, Dr. Rane says: and he's about right. Is it a compliment to ask you to take some breakfast, Mr. Richard? The eggs are fresh, and here's some downright good tea."

Richard answered that it would be only a compliment; he had breakfasted with his father and Arthur Bohun before leaving home. His eyes ran dreamily over the white damask cloth, as if he were admiring what stood on it; the pretty china, the well-kept silver, the vase of fresh roses. Mrs. Gass liked to have things nice about her, although people called her vulgar. In reality Richard saw nothing. His mind was absorbed with what he had to ask, and with how he should ask it.

In a pause, made by Mrs. Gass's draining her cup of tea, Richard North bent forward and opened the communication, speaking in low and confidential tones.

"I have come to you thus early for a little information, Mrs. Gass. Will you kindly tell me what were the contents of the paper that was found here on your carpet, the night of Edmund's seizure?"

From the look that Mrs. Gass's countenance assumed at the question, it might have been thought that she was about to have a seizure herself. Her eyes grew round, her cheek and nose red. For a full minute she made no answer.

"What cause can you have to ask me that, Mr. Richard? You can't know nothing about it."

"Yes, I can; and do. I know that such a paper was found; I fear it was a copy of the anonymous letter. But I have come to you for particulars."

"My patience!" ejaculated Mrs. Gass. "To think you should have got hold of it at last. Who in the world told you, sir?"

"Jelly. But—"

"Drat that girl!" warmly interposed Mrs. Gass. "Her tongue is as long as from here to yonder."

"But not intentionally, I was about to add. I overheard her say a chance word, and I insisted upon her disclosing to me what she knew. There is no blame due to Jelly, Mrs. Gass."

"I say Yes there is, Mr. Richard. What right has she to blab out chance words about other folk's business? Let her stick to her own. That tongue of hers is worse than a steam-engine; once set going, it won't be stopped."

"Well, we will leave Jelly. It may be for the better that I should know this. Tell me all about it, my dear old friend."

Thus adjured, Mrs. Gass spoke; telling the tale from the beginning. Richard listened in silence.

"He denied that it came out of his pocketbook?" was the first remark he made.

"Denied it out and out. And then my thoughts turned naturally to Molly Green; for no other stranger had been in the room but them two. He said perhaps she had brought it in her petticoats from the Hall; but I don't think it could have been. I'm afraid—I'm afraid, Mr. Richard—that it must have dropped from his pocketbook."

Their eyes met: each hesitating to speak out the conviction lying at heart, notwithstanding there had been confidential secrets between them before to-day. Richard was thinking that he ought not to have married Bessy—at least, until it was cleared up.

"Why did you not tell me, Mrs. Gass?"

"It was in my mind to do so—I said a word or two—but then, you see, I couldn't think it was him that wrote it," was her answer. "Mrs. Cumberland told me she saw the anonymous letter itself; Mr. North showed it her; and that it was not a bit like any handwriting she ever met with. Suppose he is innocent— would it have been right for me to come out with a tale, even to you, Mr. Richard, that he might have been guilty?"

On this point Richard said no more. All the talking in the world now could not undo the marriage, and he was never one to reproach uselessly. Mrs. Gass resumed.

"If I had spoke ever so, I don't suppose it would have altered things, Mr. Richard. There was no proof; and, failing that, you wouldn't have liked to say anything at all to Miss Bessy. Any way they are man and wife now."

"I hope—I hope he did not write it!" said Richard, fervently.

Mrs. Gass gave a sweep with her arm to all the china together, as she bent her earnest face nearer to Richard's.

"Let's remember this much to our comfort, Mr. Richard: if it was him, he never thought to harm a hair of your brother's head. He must have wrote it to damage Alexander. Oliver Rane has looked upon Alexander as his mortal enemy—as a man who did him a right down bad turn and spoilt his prospects— as a man upon whom it was a'most a duty to be revenged."

"Do you think this?" cried Richard, rather at sea.

"No; but I say he thinks it. He never meant worse nor better by the letter than to drive Alexander away from the place where, as Rane fancies, he only had a footing by treachery. That is, if he wrote it. Sometimes I think he did, and sometimes I think he didn't."

"What is to be done?"

"Nothing. You can do nothing. You and me must just bury it between us, sir, for Miss Bessy's sake. It would be a nasty thing for her if a whisper of this should go abroad, let him be as innocent as the babe unborn. They are fond of one another, and it would just be a cruelty to have stopped the marriage with this. He is a well-intentioned man, and I don't see but what they'll be happy together. Let us hope that he has made his peace with the Lord, and that it won't be visited upon him."

"Amen!" Was the mental response of Richard North.

CHAPTER XIII

COMING HOME

Dashing up to Dallory Hall, just a week and a day after the wedding, came Mrs. North. Madam had learnt the news. Whilst she was reposing in all security in Paris, amidst a knot of friends who had chosen to be there at that season, Matilda North happened to take up a Times newspaper of some two or three days old, and saw the account of the marriage: "Oliver Rane, M.D., of Dallory Ham to Bessy, daughter of John North, of Dallory Hall, and of Elizabeth, his first wife." Madam rose up, her face flaming, and clutched the journal: she verily believed Miss Matilda was playing a farce upon her. No: the announcement was there in plain black and white. Making her hasty arrangements to quit the French capital, she came thundering home: and arrived the very day that Dr. and Mrs. Rane returned.

A letter had preceded her. A letter of denouncing wrath, that had made her husband shake in his shoes. Poor Mr. North looked tremblingly out for the arrival, caught a glimpse of the carriage and of madam's face, and slipped out by the back-door into the fields. Where he remained wandering about for hours.

So madam found no one to receive her. Richard was at the works, Captain Bohun had been out all the afternoon.

Nothing increases wrath like having no object to expend it on; and madam foiled, might have sat for a picture of fury. The passion that had been bubbling higher and higher all the way from Paris, found no escape at boiling point.

One of the servants happened to come in her way; the first housemaid, who had been head over Molly Green. Madam stopped her; bit her lips for calmness, and then inquired particulars of the wedding with a smooth face.

"Was it a runaway match, Lake?"

"Goodness, no, madam!" was Lake's answer, who was apt to be outspoken, even to her imperious mistress. "Things were being got ready for a month beforehand; and my master would have gone to church to give Miss Bessy away himself, but for not being well. All us servants went to see it."

Little by little, madam heard every detail. Captain Bohun was best man; Mr. Richard took out Miss Adair, who was bridesmaid, and looked lovely. The bride and bridegroom drove right away from the church-door. Captain Bohun went back in the carriage with Miss Adair; Mr. Richard went off on foot to the works. Miss Bessy—leastways Mrs. Oliver Rane now—had had some furniture sent to her new home from the Hall, and Molly Green was there as housemaid. That Lake should glow with intense gratification at being enabled to tell all this, was only in accordance with frail humanity: she knew what a dose it was for madam; and madam was disliked in the household more than poison. But Lake was hardly prepared for the ashy, tint that spread over madam's features, when she came to the part that told of the homeward drive of her son with Ellen Adair.

The girl was in the midst of her descriptions when Arthur Bohun came in. Madam saw him sauntering lazily up the gravel-drive, and swept down in her fine Parisian costume of white-and-black brocaded silk, lappets of lace floating from her hair. They met in the Hall.

"Why! is it you, mother?" cried Arthur in surprise—for he had no idea the invasion might be expected so soon. "Have you come home?"

He advanced to kiss her. Striving to be as dutiful as she would allow him to be, he was willing to observe all ordinary relations between mother and son: but of affection there existed none. Mrs. North drew back from the offered embrace, and haughtily motioned him to the drawing-room. Matilda sat there, sullen and listless: she was angry at being brought away summarily from Paris.

"Why did I assist at Bessy's wedding?" replied Arthur, parrying the attack with light good humour, as he invariably strove to do on these occasions. "Because I liked it. It was great fun. Especially to see Rane hunting in every pocket for the ring, and turning as red as a salamander."

"What business had you to do such a thing?" retorted madam, her face dark with the passion she was suppressing. "How dared you do it?"

"Do what, madam?"

Madam stamped a little. "You know without asking, sir; personally countenance the wedding."

"Was there any reason why I should not do so? Bessy stands to me as a sister: and I like her. I am glad she is married, and I hope sincerely they'll have the best of luck."

"I had forbidden the union with Oliver Rane," stamped madam. "Do you hear?—forbidden it. You knew that as well as she did."

"But then, don't you see, mother mine, you had no particular right to forbid it. If Matilda, there, took it into her head to marry some knight or other, you would have a voice in the matter, for or against; but Bessy was responsible to her father only."

"Don't bring my name into your nonsense, Arthur," struck in Matilda, with a frown.

Madam, looking from one to the other, was biting her lips.

"They had the wedding whilst you were away that it might be got over quietly," resumed Arthur, in his laughing way, determined not to give in an inch, even though he had to tell a home truth or two. "For my part, mother, I have never understood what possible objection you could have to Rane."

"That is my business," spoke Mrs. North. "I wish he and those Cumberland people were all at the bottom of the sea. How dared you disgrace yourself, Arthur Bohun?"

"Disgrace myself?"

"You did. You, a Bohun, to descend to companionship with them! Fie upon you! And you have been said to inherit your father's pride."

"As I hope I do, in all proper things. I am unable to understand your distinctions, madam," he added, laughingly. "Rane is as good as Bessy, for all I see. As good as we are."

Madam caught up a hand-screen, as if she would have liked to throw it at him. Her hand trembled, with emotion or temper.

"There's some girl living with them. They tell me you went home with her in the carriage!"

Arthur Bohun suddenly turned his back upon them, as if to see who might be coming, for distant footsteps were heard advancing. But for that, madam might have seen a hot flush illumine his face.

"Well? What else, mother? Of course I took her home—Miss Adair."

"In the face and eyes of Dallory!"

"Certainly. And we had faces and eyes out that morning, I can tell you. It is not every day a Miss North gets married."

"How came you to take her home?"

"Dick asked me to do so. There was no one else to ask, you see. Mrs. Gass cheered us in going by, as if we had been an election. She had a shining yellow gown on and white bows in her cap."

His suavity was so great, his determination not to be ruffled so evident, that Mrs. North felt partly foiled. It was not often she attacked Arthur; he always met it in this way, and no satisfaction came of it. She could have struck him as he stood.

"What is the true tale about the ring, Arthur?" asked Matilda, in the silence come to by Mrs. North. "Lake says Oliver Rane really lost it."

"Really and truly, Matty."

"Were they married without a ring?"

"Some one present produced one," he replied carelessly, in his invincible dislike to mention Ellen Adair before his mother and sister: a dislike that had ever clung to him. Did it arise from the reticence that invariably attends love, this feeling?—or could it have been some foreshadowing, some dread instinct of what the future was to bring forth?

"How came Dr. Rane to lose the ring?"

"Carelessness, I suppose. We found it in the carriage, going home. He must have dropped it accidentally."

"Peace, Matilda! Keep your foolish questions for a fitting time," stormed madam. "How dare you turn your back upon me, Arthur? What money has gone out with the girl?"

Arthur turned to answer. In spite of his careless manner, he was biting his lips with shame and vexation. It was so often he had to blush for his mother.

"I'm sure I don't know, if you mean with Bessy; it is not my business that I should presume to ask. Here comes Dick: I thought it was his step. You can inquire of him, madam."

Richard North looked into the drawing-room, unconscious of the storm awaiting him. Matilda sat back in an easy-chair tapping her foot discontentedly; Arthur Bohun toyed with a rose at the window; madam, standing upright by the beautiful inlaid table, her train sweeping the rich carpet, confronted him.

But there was something about Richard North that instinctively subdued madam; she had never domineered over him as she did over her husband, and Bessy, and Arthur; and at him she did not rave and rant. Calm always, sufficiently courteous to her, and yet holding his own in self-respect, Richard and madam seldom came to an issue. But she attacked him now: demanding why this iniquity—the wedding—had been allowed to be enacted.

"Pardon me, Mrs. North, if I meet your question by another," calmly spoke Richard. "You complain of my sister's marriage as though it were a wrong against yourself. What is your reason?"

"I said it should not take place."

"Will you tell me why you oppose it?"

"No. It is sufficient that, to my mind, it did not present itself as suitable. I have resolutely set my face against Dr. Rane and his statue of a mother, who presumes to call the Master of Dallory Hall John! And I forbade Bessy to think of him."

"But—pardon me, Mrs. North—Bessy was not bound to obey you. Her father and I saw no objection to Dr. Rane."

"Was it right, was it honourable, that you should seize upon my absence to marry her in this indecent manner?—before Edmund was cold in his grave?"

"Circumstances control cases," said Richard. "As for marrying her whilst you were away, it was done in the interests of peace. Your opposition, had you been at home, would not have prevented the marriage; it was therefore as well to get it over in quietness."

A bold avowal. Richard stood before madam when he made it, upright as herself. She saw it was useless to contend: and all the abuse in the world would not undo it now.

"What money has gone out with her?"

It was a question that she had no right to put. Richard answered it, however.

"At present, not any. To-morrow I shall give Rane a cheque for two hundred pounds. Time was, madam, when I thought my sister would have gone from us with twenty thousand."

"We are not speaking of what was, but of what is," said madam, an unpleasant sneer on her face. "Mr. North—to hear him speak—cannot spare the two hundred."

"Quite true; Mr. North has it not to spare," said Richard. "It is I who give it to my sister. Drained though we constantly are for money, I could not, for very shame, suffer Bessy to go to her husband quite penniless."

"She has not gone penniless," retorted madam, brazening the thing out. "I hear the Hall has been dismantled for her."

"Oh, mother!" interposed Arthur in a rush of pain.

"Hold your tongue; it is no affair of yours," spoke Mrs. North. "A cartload of furniture has gone out of the Hall."

"Bessy's own," said Richard. "It was her mother's; and we have always considered it Bessy's. A few trifling mahogany things, madam, that you have never condescended to take notice of, and that never, in point of fact, have belonged to you. They have gone with Bessy, poor girl; and I trust Rane will make her a happier home than she has had here."

"I trust they will both be miserable," flashed madam.

Equable in temper though Richard North was, there are limits to endurance; he found his anger rising, and quitted the room abruptly. Arthur Bohun went limping after him: in any season of emotion, he was undeniably lame.

"I would beg your pardon for her, Dick, in all entreaty," he whispered, putting his arm within Richard's, "but that my tongue is held by shame and humiliation. It was an awful misfortune for you all when your father married her."

"We can only make the best of it, Arthur," was the kindly answer. "It was neither your fault nor mine."

"Where is the good old pater?"

"Hiding somewhere. Not a doubt of it."

"Let us go and find him, Dick. He may be the better for having us with him to-day. If she was not my mother—and upon my word and honour, Richard, I sometimes think she is not—I'd strap on my armour and do brave battle for him."

The bride and bridegroom were settling down in their house. Bessy, arranging her furniture in her new home, was busy and happy as the summer day was long. Some of the mahogany things were terribly old-fashioned, but the fact never occurred to Bessy. The carpet was bright; the piano, Richard's present, and a great surprise, was beautiful. It was so kind of him to give her one—she who was only a poor player at best, and had thought of asking madam to be allowed to have the unused old thing in the old schoolroom at Dallory Hall. She clung to Richard with tears in her eyes as she kissed and thanked him. He kissed her again, and gave his good wishes for her happiness, but Bessy thought him somewhat out of spirits. Richard North handed over two hundred pounds to them: a most acceptable offering to Dr. Rane.

"Thank you, Richard," he heartily said, grasping his brother-in-law's hand. "I shall be getting on so well shortly as to need no help for my wife's sake or for mine." And Richard knew that he was anticipating the period when the other doctor should have left, and the whole practice be in his own hands.

It was on the third or fourth morning after their return, that Dr. Rane, coming home from seeing his patients, met his fellow-surgeon, arm-in-arm with a stranger. Mr. Alexander stopped to introduce him.

"Mr. Seeley, Rane," he said. "My friend and successor."

Had a shot been fired at Dr. Rane, he could scarcely have felt more astounded. In the moment's confused blow, he almost stammered.

"Your successor? Here?"

"My successor in the practice. I have sold him the goodwill, and he has come down to be introduced."

Dr. Rane bowed. The new doctor put out his hand. That same day Dr. Rane went over to Mr. Alexander's and reproached him.

"You might at least have given me the refusal had you wanted to sell it."

"My good fellow, I promised it to Seeley ages ago," was the answer. "He knew I had a prospect of the London appointment: in fact, helped me to get it."

What was to be said? Nothing. But Oliver Rane felt as though a bitter blow had again fallen upon him, blighting the fair vista of the future.

"Don't be down-hearted, Oliver," whispered Bessy, hopefully, as she clung around him when he went in and spoke of the disappointment. "We shall be just as happy with a small practice as a large one. It will all come right—with God's blessing on us."

But Oliver Rane, looking back on a certain deed of the past, felt by no means sure in his heart of hearts that the blessing would be upon them.

CHAPTER I

OF WHAT WAS, AND OF WHAT MIGHT BE

Bessy Rane sat at the large window of her dining-room in the coming twilight. Some twelve months had elapsed since her marriage, and summer was round again. Her work had dropped on her lap: it was that of stitching some wristbands for her husband: and she sat inhaling the sweet scent of the flowers, and watching Jelly's movements in Mrs. Cumberland's dining-room, facing her. Jelly had a candle in her hand, apparently searching for something. Bessy leaned forward to pluck a sprig of sweet verbena, and sat on tranquilly.

At the table behind her sat Dr. Rane, writing as fast as the waning light would permit him. Some unusual and peculiar symptoms had manifested themselves in a patient he had been recently attending, and he was making them and the case into a paper for a medical publication, in the hope that it would bring him back a remunerative guinea or two.

"Oliver, I am sure you can't see," said Bessy presently, looking round.

"It is almost blindman's holiday, dear. Will you ring for the lamp?"

Mrs. Rane rose. But, instead of ringing for the lamp, she went up to him, and put her hand on his shoulder persuasively.

"Take a quarter-of-an-hour's rest, Oliver. You will find all the benefit of it; and it is not quite time to light the lamp. Let us take a stroll in the garden."

"You are obstructing what little light is left, Bessy; standing between me and the window."

"Of course I am. I'm doing it on purpose. Come, Oliver! You ought to know a great deal better than I do that it is bad to try the eyes, sir. Please, Oliver."

Yielding to her entreaties, he pushed the paper from him with a sigh of weariness, and they stepped from the window into the garden. Bessy passed her hand within his arm; and, turning towards the more secluded paths, they began to converse with one another in low tones.

Many a twilight half-hour had they thus paced together of late, talking together of what was and of what might be. The first year of their marriage had not been one of success in a pecuniary point of view; for Dr. Rane's practice did not improve. He earned barely sufficient for their moderate wants. Bessy, as cash-keeper, had a difficulty in making both ends meet. But the fact was not known; never a syllable of it transpired from either of them. Dr. Rane was seen out and about a great deal, going to and fro amongst his patients; and the world did not suspect that his returns were so small.

The new surgeon, Seeley, had stepped into all Mr. Alexander's practice, and was flourishing. Dr. Rane's, as before, was chiefly confined to the lower classes, especially those belonging to the North Works; and from certain circumstances, these men were not so supplied with funds as they had been, and consequently were not so well able to pay him. That Dr. Rane was bitterly mortified at not getting on better, for his wife's sake as well as his own, could not be mistaken. Bessy preached of hope cheerfully; of a bright future yet in store; but he had lost faith in it.

It seemed to Dr. Rane that everything was a failure. The medical book he had been engaged upon with persevering industry at the time of his marriage, from which he had anticipated great things both in fame and fortune, had not met with success. He had succeeded in getting it published; but as yet there were no returns. He had sacrificed a sum of money towards its publication; not a very large sum, it is true, but larger than they could afford, and no one but themselves knew how it had crippled them. Bessy said it would come back some day with interest; for the present they had only to keep up a good heart and live frugally.

Poor Bessy herself had one grief that she never spoke of even to him—the want of offspring. There had been no prospect of it whatever; and she so loved children! As week after week, month after month went by, her disappointment was very keen. She was beginning to grow a little reconciled to it now; and became only the more devoted to her husband.

Mrs. Rane was an excellent manager in the household, spending the smallest fraction that she could, consistently with comfort. It had not yet come to the want of that. At the turn of the previous winter old Phillis became ill and had to leave; and Bessy had since kept only Molly Green. By a fortunate chance Molly understood cooking; she had become a really excellent servant. At the small expense they lived at now, Dr. Rane might perhaps have managed to continue to meet it whilst he waited patiently for better luck; but he did not intend to do anything of the sort. His only anxiety was to remove to another place, as far away from Dallory Ham as possible.

Whether this thirst for migration would have arisen had his practice become successful, cannot be told. We can only record things as they were. With the disappointment—and other matters—lying upon him, the getting away from Dallory had grown into a wild, burning desire, that never left him by night or day. That one fatal mistake of his life seemed to hang over him like a curse. It is true that when he penned the letter so disastrous in its result, he had no more intention in his heart of slaying or killing than had the paper he wrote on; he had only thought of putting Alexander into disfavour at Dallory Hall; but it had turned out otherwise, and Dr. Rane felt that he had a life to answer for. He might have borne this; and at any rate his running away from Dallory would neither lessen the heart's burden nor add to it; but what he could not bear was the prospect of detection. Not a day passed but he saw some one or other whose face tacitly reminded him that such discovery might take place. He felt sure that Mrs. Gass still suspected him of having written the letter; he knew that his mother doubted it; he gathered a half suspicion of Jelly; he had more than half one of Richard North; and how many others there might be he knew not. Ever since the time when he had returned from his marriage trip, he thought there had been an involuntary constraint in Richard's manner to him; it could not be fancy. As to Jelly, the way he sometimes caught her green eyes observing him, was enough to give the shivers to a nervous man, which Dr. Rane was not. How he could have committed the fatal mistake of putting that copy of the miserable letter into his pocketbook, he never knew. He had tried his writing and his sentences on two or three pieces of paper, but he surely thought he had torn all up and burnt the pieces. Over and over again, looking back upon his carelessness, he said to himself that it was Fate. Not carelessness, in one sense of the word. Carelessness if you will, but a carelessness that he could not go from in the arbitrary dominions of Fate. Fate had been controlling him with her iron hand, to bring his crime home to him; and he could not escape it. Whatever it might have been, however—Fate, or want of caution—it had led to his being a suspected man by some few around him; and continue to live amongst them he would not. Dr. Rane was a proud man, liking in an especial degree to stand well in the estimation of his fellows; to have such a degradation as this brought publicly home to him would well-nigh kill him with shame. Rather than face it he would have run away to the remotest quarter of the habitable globe.

And he had quite imbued Bessy with the wish for change. She only thought as he thought. Never suspecting the true reason of his wish to get away and establish himself elsewhere, she only saw how real it was. Of this they talked, night after night, pacing the garden paths. "There seems to have been a spell of ill-luck attending me ever since I settled in this place," he would say to her; "and I know it won't be lifted whilst I stop here." He was saying it this very night.

"I hate the place, Bessy," he observed, looking up at the bright evening star that began to show itself in the clear blue sky. "But for my mother and you I should never have stayed in it. I wish I had the money to buy a practice elsewhere. As it is, I must establish one."

"Yes," acquiesced Bessy. "But where? The great thing is—what other place to decide upon."

Of course that was the chief thing. Dr. Rane looked down and kept silence, pondering various matters in his mind. He thought it had better be London. A friend of his, one Dr. Jones, who had been a fellow-student in their hospital days, was doing a large practice as a medical man in the neighbourhood of New York: he wanted assistance, and had proposed to Dr. Rane to go over and join him. Nothing in the world would Dr. Rane have liked better; and Bessy was willing to go where he went, even to quit her native land for good; but Dr. Jones did not offer this without an equivalent, and the terms he named, five hundred pounds, were quite beyond the reach of Oliver Rane. So he supposed it must be London. With the two hundred pounds that he hoped to get for the goodwill of his own practice in Dallory Ham—at this very moment he was trying to negociate with a gentleman for it in private—-he should set up in London, or else purchase a small share in an established practice. Anything, anywhere, to get away, and to leave the nightmare of daily-dreaded discovery behind him!

"Once we are away from this place, Bessy, we shall get on. I feel sure of it. You won't long have to live like a hermit, from dread of the cost of entertaining company, or to look at every sixpence before you lay it out."

"I don't mind it, Oliver. You know how sorry I should be if you thought of giving up our home here for my sake."

"But I don't; it's for my own as well," he hastily added. "You can't realize what it is, Bessy, for a clever medical man—and I am that—to be beaten back for ever into obscurity; to find no field for his talents; to watch others of this generation rising into note and usefulness. I have not got on here! Madam has schemed to prevent it. Why she should have patronized Alexander; why she should patronize Seeley; not for their sakes, but to oppose me; I have never been able to imagine. Unless it was that my mother, when Fanny Gass, and Mr. North were intimate as brother and sister in early life."

"And madam despises the Gass family and ours equally. It was a black-letter day for us all when papa married her."

"That is no reason why she should have set her face against me. It has been a fatal blight on me: worse than you and the world think for, Bessy."

"I am sure you must have felt it so," murmured Bessy. "And she would have stopped our marriage if she could."

"Whoever succeeds me here will speedily make a good practice of it. You'll see. She has kept me from doing it. There's one blessed thing—her evil influence cannot follow us elsewhere."

"I should like to become rich and have a large house, and get poor papa to live with us," said Bessy hopefully. "Madam is worrying him into his grave with her cruel temper. Oh, Oliver, I should like him to come to us!"

"I'm sure I wouldn't object," replied Dr. Rane good-naturedly. "How they will keep up the expenses at Dallory Hall if this strike is prolonged, I cannot think. Serve madam right!"

"Do you hear much of the trouble, Oliver?"

"Much of it! Why, I hear nothing else. The men are fools. They'll cut their own throats as sure as a gun. Your brother Richard sees it coming."

"Sees what?" asked Bessy, not exactly understanding.

"Ruin," emphatically replied Dr. Rane. "The men will play at bo-peep with reason until the trade has left them. Fools! Fools!"

"It's not the poor men, Oliver. I have lived amongst them—some of them at any rate—since I was a child, and I don't like to hear them blamed. It is that they are misled. Misled by the Trades' Unions."

"Nonsense!" replied Dr. Rane. "A man who has his living to earn ought not to allow himself to be misled. There's his work to hand; let him do it. A body of would-be autocrats might come down on me and say, 'Oliver Rane, we want you to join our society: which forbids doctors to visit patients except under its own rules and regulations.' Suppose I listened to them?—and stayed at home, and let Seeley, or any one else, snap up my practice, and awoke presently to find my means of living irrevocably gone?—nothing left for me but the workhouse? Should I deserve pity? Certainly not."

Bessy laughed a little. They were going in, and she—still keeping her hand within his arm—coaxed him yet for another moment's recreation into the drawing-room. Sitting down to the piano in the fading light—the piano that Richard had given her—she began a song that her husband was fond of, "O Bay of Dublin." That sweet song set to the air of "Groves of Blarney," by the late Lady Dufferin. Bessy's voice was weak and of no compass, but it was true and rather sweet; and she had that, by no means common, gift of rendering every word as distinctly heard as though it were spoken: so that her singing was pleasant to listen to. Her husband liked it. He leaned against the window-frame, now as she sang, in a deep reverie, gazing out on Dallory Ham, and at the man lighting the roadside lamps. Dr. Rane never heard this song but he wished he was the emigrant singing it, with some wide ocean flowing between him and home.

"What's this, I wonder?"

Some woman, whom he did not recognize, had turned in at his gate and was ringing the door-bell. Dr. Rane found he was called out to a patient: one of the profitless people as usual.

"Piersons want me, Bessy," he looked into the room to say. "The man's worse. I shall not be long."

And Bessy rose when she heard the street-door closed.

Taking a duster from the drawer, she carefully passed it over the keys before closing her piano for the night. Very much did Bessy cherish her drawing-room and its furniture. They did not use it very much: not from fear of spoiling it, but because the other room with its large bay window seemed the more cheerful; and people feel more at ease in the room they usually sit in. Bessy took as much pride in her house as though it had been one of the grandest in all Dallory: happy as a queen in it, felt she. Stepping lightly over the drawing-room carpet—fresh as the day when it came out of Turtle's warehouse—touching, with a gentle finger, some pretty thing or other on the tables as she passed, she opened the door and called to the servant.

"Molly, it is time these shutters were shut."

Molly Green, in an apology of a cap tilted on her hair, and a white muslin apron, came out of the kitchen. Molly liked to be as smart as the best of them, although she had all the work to do. Which all was not very much when aided by her mistress's good management.

"You had better light the hall-lamp," added Mrs. Rane, as she went upstairs.

It was tolerably light still. Bessy often did what she was about to do—namely, draw down the window-blinds; it saved Molly trouble. The wide landing was less bare than it used to be; at the time of Dr. Rane's marriage he had covered it with some green drugget, and put a chair and a book-shelf there. It still looked too large, still presented a contrast to the luxuriously furnished landing of Mrs. Cumberland's opposite, especially when the two wide windows happened to be open; but Bessy thought her own quite good enough. Of the two back-rooms, one had been furnished as a spare bedchamber; the other had not much in it besides Bessy's boxes that had come from the Hall. Richard had spoken kindly to her about this last chamber. "Should any contingency arise; sickness, or other; that you should require its use, Bessy," he said, "and Rane does not find it quite convenient to spare money for furniture, let me know, and I'll do it for you." She had thanked him gratefully: but the contingency had not come yet.

Into this back-room first went Bessy, passed by her boxes, closed the window, and drew the white blind down. From thence into the next chamber—a pretty room with chintz curtains to the window and the Arabian bed. Dr. Rane was very particular about having plenty of air in his house, and would have every window open all day long. Next, Bessy crossed the landing again to her own chamber. She had to pass through the drab room (as may be remembered) to get to it. The drab room was in just the same state that it used to be; Dr. Rane's glass jars and other articles used in chemistry lying on one side its bare floor. Formerly they were strewed about anywhere: under Bessy's neat rule they were gathered into a small space. Sometimes Bessy thought she should like to make this her own sitting and work-room: its window looked towards the fields beyond Dallory Ham. Often, when she first came to the house, she would softly say to her heart, "What a nice day-nursery it would make!" She had left off saying it now.

Taking some work from a drawer in her own room, which was what she went up for—for she knew that Oliver would tell her to leave off if she attempted to stitch the wristbands by candle-light—she stood for a minute at the window and saw some gentleman, whom she did not recognize, turn out of Mr. Seeley's, and go towards Dallory.

"A fresh patient," she thought to herself, with a sigh very like envy. "He gets them all. I wish a few would come to Oliver."

As she watched the stranger up the road, something in his height and make put her in mind of her dead brother, Edmund. All her thoughts went back to the unhappy time of his death, and to the letter that had led to it.

"It's very good of Oliver to comfort me, saying he could not in any case have lived long—and I suppose it was so," murmured Bessy; "but that does not make it any the less shocking. He was killed. Cut off without warning by that wicked, anonymous letter. And I don't believe the writer will be ever traced now: even Richard seems to have cooled in the pursuit, since he discovered it was not the man he had suspected."

Close upon the return of Dr. and Mrs. Rane after their marriage, the tall, thin stranger who had been seen with Timothy Wilks the night before the anonymous letter was sent, and whom Richard North and others fully believed to have been the writer, was discovered. It proved to be a poor artist, travelling the country to take sketches—who was sometimes rather too fond of being a boon companion with whatever company he might happen to fall into. Hovering here some days, hovering there, in pursuit of his calling, he at length made his headquarters at Whitborough. Hearing he was suspected, he came forward voluntarily, and convinced Richard North that he at least had had nothing to do with the letter. Richard's answer was that he quite believed him. And perhaps it was Richard North's manner at this time, coupled with a remark he made to the effect that "it might be better to allow all speculation on the point to rest," that first gave Dr. Rane the idea of Richard's suspicion of himself. Things had been left at rest since then: and oven Bessy, as we see, thought her brother was growing cold.

Turning from the window with a sigh, given to the memory of her dead brother, she passed through the ante-room to the landing on her way downstairs. Mrs. Cumberland's landing opposite gave forth a brilliant light as usual—for that lady liked to burn many lamps in her hall and staircases—and Ann, the housemaid, was drawing down the window blind. Mrs. Rane's window had never had a blind.

Molly Green was taking the supper-tray into the dining-room when she went down. Bessy hovered about it, seeing that things were as her husband liked them. She put his slippers ready, she drew his arm-chair forward; ever solicitous for his comfort. To wait on him and make things pleasant for him was the great happiness of her life. After that she sat down and worked by lamplight, awaiting his return.

Whilst Dr. Rane, walking forth to see his patient and walking home again, was buried in an unpleasant reverie, like a man in a dream. That one dreadful mistake lay always with heavier weight upon him at the solitary evening hour. Now and again he would almost fancy he should see Edmund North looking out at him from the roadside hedges or behind trees. At any sacrifice he must get away from the place, and then perhaps a chance of peace might come to him: at least from this ever-haunting dread of discovery. He would willingly give the half of his remaining life to undo that past dark night's work.

There was trouble amongst the Dallory workpeople. It had been looming in the distance for some time before it came. No works throughout the kingdom had been more successfully carried on than the North Works. The men were well paid; peace and satisfaction had always reigned between them and their employers. But when certain delegates, or emissaries, or whatever they may please to call themselves, arrived stealthily at Dallory from the Trades' Unions, and took up stealthy abode in the place, and whispered stealthy whispers into the ears of the men, peace was at an end.

It matters not to trace the working of these insidious whispers, or how the poison spread. Others have done it far more effectively and to the purpose than I could do it. Sufficient to say that the Dallory workpeople caught the infection prevailing amongst other bodies of men—which the public, to its cost, has of late years known too much of—and they joined the ranks of the disaffected. First there had been doubt, and misgiving, and wavering; then agitation; then dissatisfaction; then parleying with their master, Richard North; then demands to be paid more and do less work. In vain Richard, with his strong sense, argued and reasoned: showing them, in all kindness, how mistaken was the course they were entering on, and what must come of it. They listened with respect, for he was liked and esteemed; but they would not give in. It had been privately told Richard that much argument and holding-out had been carried on with the Trades' Union emissaries, some of whom were ever hovering over Dallory like birds of prey: the workmen wanting to insist on the sense of Richard North's views of things, the others speciously disproving it. But it came to nothing. The workmen yielded to their despotic rulers as submissively as others have done, and Richard's words were set at nought. They were like so many tame sheep blindly following their leader. The agitation, beginning about the time of Bessy North's marriage, continued for many months; it then came to an issue; and for several weeks now, the works had been shut up.

For the men had struck. North and Gass had large contracts on hand, and they could not be completed. Unless matters took a speedy turn, masters and men would alike be ruined. The ruin of the first involved that of the last.

Mrs. Gass took things more equably than Richard North. In one sense she had less need to take them otherwise. Her prosperity did not depend on the works. A large sum of hers was certainly invested in them; but a larger was in other and safe securities. If the works and their capital went to ruin, the only difference it would make to Mrs. Gass was, that she would have so much the less money to leave behind her when she died. In this sense therefore Mrs. Gass could take things calmly: but in regard to the men's conduct she was far more outspoken and severe than Richard.

Dallory presented a curious scene. In former days, during work time not an idle man was to be found: the village had looked almost deserted, excepting for the children playing about. Now the narrow thoroughfares were blocked with groups of men; talking seriously, or chaffing with each other, as might be; most of them smoking, and all looking utterly sick of the passing hours. Work does not tire a man— or woman either—half as much as idleness.

At first the holiday was an agreeable novelty; the six days were each a Sunday, as well as the seventh; and the men and women lived in clover. Not one family in twenty had been sufficiently provident to put by money for a rainy day, good though their wages had been; but the Trades' Unions took care of their new protégés, and supplied them with funds. But as the weeks went on, and Richard North gave no sign of relenting—that is, of taking the men on again at their own terms—the funds did not come in so liberally. Husbands, not accustomed to being stinted; wives, not knowing how to make sixpence suffice for a shilling, might be excused if they felt a little put out; and they began to take things to the pawnbroker's. Mr. Ducket, the respectable functionary who presided over the interests of the three gilt balls at Dallory, rubbed his hands complacently as he took the articles in. Being gifted with a long sharp nose, he scented the good time coming.

One day, in passing the shop, Mrs. Gass saw three women in it. She walked in herself; and, without ceremony, demanded what they were pledging. The women slunk away, hiding their property under their aprons, and leaving their errand to be completed another time. That Mrs. Gass or their master, Richard North, should see them at this work, brought humiliation to their minds and shame to their cheeks. Richard North and Mrs. Gass had both told them (to their utter disbelief) that it would come to this: and to be detected in the actual fact of pledging, seemed very like defeat.

"So you've began, have you, Ducket?" commenced Mrs. Gass.

"Began what, ma'am?" asked Ducket; a little, middle-aged man with watery eyes and weak hair; always deferent in manner to the wealthy Mrs. Gass.

"Began what! Why, the pledging. I told 'em all they'd come to the pawnshop."

"It's them that have begun it, ma'am; not me."

"Where do you suppose it will end, Ducket?"

Ducket shook his head meekly, intimating that he couldn't suppose anything about it. He was naturally meek in disposition, and the brow-beating he habitually underwent in the course of business from his customers of the fairer sex had subdued his spirit.

"It'll just end in their pawning every earthly thing inside their homes, leaving them to the four naked walls," said Mrs. Gass. "And the next move 'll be into the work'us."

In the presence of Mrs. Gass, Ducket did not choose to show any sense of latent profit this wholesale pledging might bring to him. On the contrary, he affected to see nothing but gloom in the matter.

"A nice prospect for us rate-payers, ma'am, that 'ould be! Taxes be heavy enough, as it is, in Dallory parish, without having all these workmen and their families throw'd on us."

"If the taxes was of my mind, Ducket, they'd let the men starve, rather than help 'em. When able-bodied artisans have plenty of work to do, and won't do it, it's time they was taught a lesson. As sure as you and I are standing here, them misguided men will come to want a crust."

"Well, I'd not wish 'em as bad as that," said Ducket, who, apart from the hardness induced by his trade, was rather softhearted. "Perhaps Mr. Richard North 'll give in."

"Mr. Richard North give in!" echoed Mrs. Gass. "Don't upset your brains with perhapsing that, Ducket. Who ought to give in—looking at the rights and wrongs of the question—North and Gass, or the men? Tell me that."

"Well, I think the men are wrong," acknowledged the pawnbroker, smoothing down his white linen apron. "And foolish too."

Mrs. Gass nodded several times, a significant look on her pleasant face. She wore a top-knot of white feathers, and they bowed majestically with the movement.

"Maybe they'll live to see it, too. They will, unless their senses come back to 'em pretty quickly. Look here, Ducket: what I was about to say is this—don't be too free to take their traps in."

Ducket's face assumed a mournful cast, but Mrs. Gass was looking at him, evidently waiting for an answer.

"I don't see my way clear to refusing things when they are brought to me, Mrs. Gass, ma'am. The women 'ould only go off to Whitborough and pledge 'em there."

"Then they should go—for me."

"Yes, ma'am," rejoined the man, not knowing what else to say.

"I'm not particular squeamish, Ducket; trade's trade; and a pawnbroker must live as well as other people. I don't say but what the money he lends does sometimes a world of good to them that has no other help to turn to—and, maybe, through no fault of their own, poor things. But when it comes to dismantling homes by the score, and leaving families as destitute as ever they were when they came into this blessed world, that's different. And I wouldn't like to have it on my conscience, Ducket, though I was ten pawnbrokers."

Mrs. Gass quitted the shop with the last words, leaving Ducket to digest them. In passing North Inlet, she saw a group of the disaffected collected together, and turned out of her way to speak to them. Mrs. Gass was quite at home, so to say, with every one of the men at the works; more so than a lady of better birth and breeding could ever have been. She found fault with them, and commented on their failings as familiarly as though she had been one of themselves. Of the whole body of workpeople, not more than three or four had consistently raised their voices against the strike. These few would willingly have gone to work again, and thought it a terrible hardship that they could not do so; but of course the refusal of the majority to return practically closed the gates to all. Richard North could not keep his business going with only half-a-dozen pairs of hands in it.

"Well," began Mrs. Gass, "what's the time o' day with you men?"

The men parted at the address, and touched their caps. The "time o' day" meant, as they knew, anything but the literal question.

"How much longer do you intend to lead the lives of gentlefolk?"

"It's what we was a-talking on, ma'am—how much longer Mr. Richard North 'll keep the gates closed again' us," returned one whose name was Webb, speaking boldly but respectfully.

"Don't you put the saddle on the wrong horse, Webb; I told you that the other day. Mr. Richard North didn't close the gates again' you: you closed 'em again' yourselves by walking out. He'd open them to you tomorrow, and be glad to do it."

"Yes, ma'am, but on the old terms," debated the man, looking obstinately at Mrs. Gass.

"What have you to say again' the old terms?" demanded that lady of the men collectively. "Haven't they kept you and your families in comfort for years and years? Where was your grumblings then? I heard of none."

"But things is changed," said Webb.

"Not a bit of it," retorted Mrs. Gass. "It's you men that have changed; not the things. I'll put a question to yon, Webb—to all of you—and it won't do you any harm to answer it. If these Trade Union men had never come amongst you with their persuasions and doctrines, should you, or should you not, have been at your work now in content and peace? Be honest, Webb, and reply."

"I suppose so," confessed Webb.

"You know so," corrected Mrs. Gass. "It is as Mr. Richard said the other day to me—the men are led away by a chimera, which means a false fancy, Webb; a sham. There's the place"—pointing in the direction of the works—"and there's your work, waiting for you to do it. Mr. Richard will give you the same wages that he has always given; you say you won't go to work unless he gives more: which he can't afford to do. And there it rests; you, and him, and the business, all at a standstill."

"And likely to be at a standstill, ma'am," returned Webb, but always respectfully.

"Very well; let's take it at that," said Mrs. Gass, with equanimity. "Let's take it that it lasts, this state of things. What's to come of it?"

Webb, an intelligent man and superior workman, looked out straight before him thoughtfully, as if searching a solution to the question. Mrs. Gass, finding he did not answer, resumed:

"If the Trades' Unions can find you permanently in food and drink, and clothes and firing, well and good. Let 'em do it: there'd be no more to say. But if they can't?"

"They undertake to keep us as long as the masters hold out."

"And the money—where's it had from?"

"Subscribed. All the working bodies throughout the United Kingdom subscribe to support the Trades' Unions, ma'am."

"I heard," said Mrs. Gass, "that you were not getting quite as liberal a keep from the Trades' Unions as they gave you to begin upon."

"That's true," interrupted one named Foster, who very much resented the shortening of supplies.

Mrs. Gass gave a toss to her lace parasol. "I heard, too—I've seen, for the matter of that—that your wives had begun to spout their spare crockery," said she. "What'll you do when the allowance grows less and less till it comes to nothing, and all your things is at the pawnshop?"

One or two of them laughed slightly. Not at her figures of speech—the homely language was their own—but at the improbability of the picture she called up. It was a state of affairs impossible to arise, they answered, whilst they had the Trades' Unions at their backs.

"Isn't it," said Mrs. Gass. "Those that live longest 'll see most. There's strikes agate all over the country. You know that, my men."

Of course the men knew it. But for the general example set by others, they might never have struck themselves.

"Very good," said Mrs. Gass. "Now look here. You can see out before you just as well as I can, you men; your senses are as sharp as mine. When nearly the whole country goes on the strike, where are the subscriptions to come from for the Trades' Unions? Don't it stand to common reason that there'll be nobody to pay 'em? Who'll keep you then?"

It was the very thing wanted—that all the country should go on strike; for then the masters must give in, was the reply. And then the men stood their ground and looked at her.

Mrs. Gass shook her head; the feathers waved. She supposed it must be as Richard North had said—the men in their prejudice really could not foresee what might be looming in the future.

"It seems no good my talking," she resumed; "I've said it before. If you don't come to repent, my name's not Mary Gass. I'm far from wishing it; goodness knows; and I shall be heartily sorry for your wives and children when the misery comes upon 'em. Not for you; because you are bringing it deliberate on yourselves."

"We don't doubt your good wishes for us and our families, ma'am," spoke Webb. "But, if you'll excuse my saying it, you stand in the shoes of a master, and naturally look on from the masters' point of view. Your interests lie that way, ours this, and they're dead opposed to each other."

"Well, now, I'll just say something," cried Mrs. Gass. "As far as my own interest is concerned, I don't care one jot whether the works go on again, or whether they stand still for ever. I've as much money as will last me my time. If every pound locked up in the works is lost, it'll make no sort of difference to me, or my home, or my comforts—and you ought to know this yourselves. I shall have as much to leave behind me, too, as I care to leave. But, if you come to talking of interests, I tell you whose I do think of, more than I do of my own—and that's yours and Mr. Richard North's. I am as easy on the matter, on my own score, as a body can be; but I'm not so on yours or his."

It was spoken with simple earnestness. In fact Mrs. Gass was incapable of deceit or sophistry—and the men knew it. But they thought that, in spite of her honesty, she could only be prejudiced against the workmen; and consequently her words had no more weight with them than the idle wind.

"Well, I'm off," said Mrs. Gass. "I hope with all my heart that your senses will come to you. And I say it for your own sakes."

"They've not left us—that we knows on," grumbled a man in a suppressed, half-insolent tone, as if he were dissatisfied with things in general.

"I hear you, Jack Allen. If you men think you know your own business best, you must follow it," concluded Mrs. Gass. "The old saying runs, A wilful man must have his way. One thing I'd like you to understand: that when your wives and children shall be left without a potater to their mouths or a rag to their backs, you needn't come whining to me to help 'em. Don't you forget to bear that in mind, my men."

Waiting for her at home, Mrs. Gass found Richard North. That this was a very anxious time for him, might be detected by the thoughtful look his face habitually wore. It was all very well for Mrs. Gass, so amply provided for, to take existing troubles easily; Richard was less philosophical. And with reason. His own ruin—and the final closing of the works would be nothing less—might be survived. He had his profession, his early manhood, his energies to fall back upon; his capacity and character both stood pre-eminent: he had no fear of making a living for himself, even though it might be done in the service of some more fortunate firm, and not in his own. But there was his father. If the works were permanently closed, the income Mr. North enjoyed from them could no longer be paid to him. All Mr. North's resources, whether derived from them or from Richard's generosity, would vanish like the mists of a summer's morning.

"What's it you, Mr. Richard?" cried Mrs. Gass when she entered, and saw him standing near the window of her dining-room. "I wouldn't have stopped out if I'd known you were here. Some of the men have been hearing a bit of my mind," she added, sitting down behind her plants and untying her bonnet-strings. "It's come to pawning the women's best gowns now."

"Has it?" replied Richard North, rather abstractedly, as if buried in thought. "Of course it must come to that, sooner or later."

"Sooner or later it would come to pawning themselves, if hey could do it," spoke Mrs. Gass. "If this state of things is to last, they'll have nothing else left to pawn."

Richard wheeled round and took a chair in front of Mrs. Gass. He had come to make a proposition to her; one he did not quite approve of himself; and for that reason his manner was perhaps a little less ready than usual. Richard North had received from Mrs. Gass, at the time of her late husband's death, full power to act on his own responsibility, just as he had held it from Mr. Gass; but in all weighty matters he had made a point of consulting them: Mr. Gass whilst he lived, Mrs. Gass since then.

"It is a question that I have been asking myself a little too often for my own peace—how long this state of things will last, and what will be the end," said Richard in answer to her last words, his low tone almost painfully earnest. "The longer it goes on, the worse it will be; for the men and for ourselves."

"That's precisely what I tell 'em," acquiesced Mrs. Gass, tilting her bonnet and fanning her face with her handkerchief. "But I might just as well speak to so many postesses."

"Yes; talking will not avail. I have talked to them; and find it only waste of words. If they listen to my arguments and feel inclined to be impressed with them, the influences of the Trades' Union undo it all again. I think we must try something else."

"And what's that, Mr. Richard?"

"Give way a little."

"Give way!" repeated Mrs. Gass, pushing her chair back some inches in her surprise. "What! give 'em what they want?"

"Certainly not. That is what we could not do. I said give way a little."

"Mr. Richard, I never would."

"What I thought of proposing is this: To divide the additional wages they are standing out for. That is, offer them half. If they would not return to work on those terms, I should have no hope of them."

"And my opinion is, they'd not. Mr. Richard, sir, it's them Trade Union people that upholds 'em in their obstinacy. They'll make 'em hold out for the whole demands or none. What do the leaders of the Union care? It don't touch their pockets, or their comforts. So long as their own nests are feathered, the working man's may get as bare as boards. Don't you fancy the rulers 'll let our men give way half. It's only by keeping up agitation that agitators live."

"I should like to put it to the test. I have come here to ask you to agree to my doing it."

"And what about shortening the time that they want?" questioned Mrs. Gass.

"I should not give way there. It is impracticable. They must return on the usual time: but of the additional wages demanded I would offer half. Will you assent to this?"

"It will be with an uncommon bad grace," was Mrs. Gass's answer.

"I see nothing else to be done," said Richard North. "If only as a matter of conscience I should like to propose it. When it ends in a general ruin—which seems only too certain, for we cannot close our eyes to what is being enacted all over the country in almost all trades—I shall have the consolation of knowing that it is the men's own fault, not mine. Perhaps they will accept this offer. I hope so, though it will leave us little profit. If we can only make both ends meet, just to keep us going during these unsettled times, we must be satisfied. I am sure I shall be doing right, Mrs. Gass, to make this proposal."

"Mr. Richard, sir, you know that I've always trusted to your judgment, and shall do so to the end: anything you thought well to do, I should never dissuade you from. You shall make this offer if you please: but I know you'll be opening out a loophole for the men. Give 'em an inch, and they'll want an ell."

"If they come back it will be a great thing," argued Richard. "The sight of the works standing still; the knowledge that all it involves is standing still also, almost paralyzes me."

"Don't go and take it to heart at the beginning now," affectionately advised Mrs. Gass. "There's not much damage done yet."

Richard bent forward, painfully earnest. "It is of my father that I think. What will become of him if all our resources are stopped?"

"I'll take care of him till better times come round," said Mrs. Gass, heartily. "And of you, too, Mr. Richard; if you won't be too proud to let me, sir."

Richard laughed; a slight, genial laugh; partly in amusement, partly in gratitude. "I hope the better times will come at once," he said, preparing to leave. "At least, sufficiently good times to allow business to go on as usual. If the men refuse this offer of mine, they are made of more ungrateful stuff than I should give them credit for."

"They will refuse it," said Mrs. Gass, emphatically. "As is my belief. Not them, Mr. Richard, but the Trades' Unions for 'em. Once get under the thumb of that despotic body, and a workman daredn't say his soul is his own."

And Mrs. Gass's opinion proved to be correct. Richard North called his men together, and laid the concession before them; pressing them to accept it in their mutual interests. The men requested a day for consideration, and then gave their answer: rejection. Unless the whole of their demands were complied with, they unequivocally refused to return to work.

"It will be worse for them than for me in the long run," said Richard North.

And many a thoughtful mind believed that he spoke in a spirit of prophecy.

CHAPTER III

MORNING VISITORS

In the dining-room at Mrs. Cumberland's, with its window open to the garden and the sweet flowers, stood Ellen Adair. It was the favourite morning-room. Mrs. Cumberland, down in good time to-day, for it was scarcely eleven o'clock, had stepped into the garden, and disappeared amidst its remoter parts.

Ellen Adair, dressed in a cool pink muslin, almost as thin as gauze, stood in a reverie. A pleasant one, to judge by the soft blush on her face and the sweet smile that parted her lips. She was twirling the plain gold ring round and round her finger, thinking no doubt of the hour when it had been put on, and the words spoken with it. Bessy Rane had altogether refused to give back the ring she was married with, and Ellen retained the other.

The intimacy with Arthur Bohun, the silent love-making, had continued. Even now, she was listening lest haply his footsteps might be heard; listening with hushed breath and beating heart. Never a day passed but he contrived to call, on some plea or other, at Mrs. Cumberland's, morning, afternoon, or evening: and this morning he might be coming, for aught she knew. At the close of the past summer, Mrs. Cumberland had gone to the Isle of Wight for change of air, taking Ellen and her maid Jelly with her. She hired a secluded cottage in the neighbourhood of Niton. Singular to relate, Captain Bohun remembered that he had friends at Niton—an old invalid brother-officer, who was living there in great economy. On and off, during the whole time of Mrs. Cumberland's stay—and it lasted five months, for she had gone the beginning of September, and did not return home until the end of February—was Arthur Bohun paying visits to this old friend. Now for a day or two; now for a week or two; once for three weeks together. And still Mrs. Cumberland suspected nothing! It was as if her eyes were withheld. Perhaps they were: there is a destiny in all things, and it must be worked out. It is true that she did not see or suspect half the intimacy. A gentle walk once a-day by the sea was all she took. At other times Ellen rambled at will; sometimes attended by Jelly, alone when Jelly could not be spared. Captain Bohun took every care of her, guarding her more jealously than he would have guarded a sister: and this did a little surprise Mrs. Cumberland.

"We ought to feel very much obliged to Captain Bohun, Ellen," she said on one occasion. "It is not many a young man would sacrifice his time to us. Your father and his, and my husband, the chaplain, were warm friends for a short time in India: it must be his knowledge of this that induces him to be so attentive. Very civil of him!"

Ellen coloured vividly. Eminently truthful, she yet did not dare to say that perhaps that was not Captain Bohun's reason for being attentive. How could she hint at Captain Bohun's love, clear though it was to her own heart, when he had never spoken a syllable to her about it? It was not possible. So things went on in the same routine: he and she wandering together on the sea-shore: both of them living in a dream of Elysium. In February, when they returned home, the scene was changed, but not the companionship. It was an early spring that year, warm and genial. Many and many an hour were they together in that seductive garden of Mrs. Cumberland's, with its miniature rocks, its velvety grass; the birds sang and their own hearts danced for joy.

But Mrs. Cumberland's eyes were not to be always closed.

It was not to be expected that so lovely a girl as Ellen Adair should remain long without a declared suitor. Especially when there was a rumour that she would inherit a fortune—though how the latter arose people would have been puzzled to say. A gentleman of position in the neighbourhood; no other than Mr. Graves, son of one of the county members; began to make rather pointed visits at Mrs. Cumberland's. That his object was Ellen Adair, and that he would most likely ask her to become his wife, Mrs. Cumberland clearly saw. She wrote to Mr. Adair in Australia, telling him she thought Ellen was about to receive an offer of marriage, in every way eligible. The young man was of high character, good family, and large means, she said: should she, if the proposal came, accept it for Ellen. By a singular omission, which perhaps Mrs. Cumberland was not conscious of, she did not mention Mr. Graves's name. But the proposal came sooner than Mrs. Cumberland had bargained for: barely was this letter despatched—about which, with her usual reticence, she said not a word to any one—when Mr. Graves proposed to Ellen and was refused.

It was this that opened Mrs. Cumberland's eyes to the nature of the friendship between Ellen and Captain Bohun. She then wrote a second letter to Mr. Adair, saying Ellen had refused Mr. Graves in consequence, as she strongly suspected, of an attachment to Arthur Bohun—son of Major Bohun, whom Mr. Adair once knew so well. That Arthur Bohun would wish to make Ellen his wife, there could be, Mrs. Cumberland thought from observation, no doubt whatever: might he be accepted? In a worldly point of view, Captain Bohun was not so desirable as Mr. Graves, she added—unless indeed he should succeed to his uncle's baronetcy, which was not very improbable, the present heir being sickly—but he would have enough to live upon as a gentleman, and he was liked by every one. This second letter was also despatched to Australia by the mail following the one that carried the first. Having thus done her duty, Mrs. Cumberland sat down to wait for Mr. Adair's answer, tacitly allowing the intimacy to continue, inasmuch as she did not stop the visits of Arthur Bohun. Neither he nor Ellen suspected what she had done.

And with the summer there had come another suitor to Ellen Adair. At least another was displaying signs that he would like to become one. It was Mr. Seeley, the doctor who had replaced Mr. Alexander. Soon after Mrs. Cumberland's return from Niton in February, she had been for a week or two alarmingly ill, and Mr. Seeley was called in as well as her son. He had remained on terms of friendship at her house; and it became evident that he very much admired Miss Adair.

Things were in this state on this summer's morning, and Ellen Adair stood near the window twirling the plain gold ting on her finger. Presently she came out of her reverie, unlocked a small letter-case, and began to write in her diary.

"Tuesday.—Mrs. Cumberland talks of going away again. She seems to me to grow thinner and weaker. Arthur says the same. He thinks—"

A knock at the front-door, and Mr. Seeley was shown in. He paid a professional visit to Mrs. Cumberland at least every other morning. Not as a professional man, he told her; but as a friend, that he might see how she went on.

Miss Adair shook hands with him, her manner cold. He saw it not; and his fingers parted lingeringly from hers.

"Mrs. Cumberland is in the garden, if you will go to her," said Ellen, affecting to be quite occupied with her writing-case. "I think she wants to see you; she is not at all well. You will find her in the grotto, or somewhere about."

To this Mr. Seeley answered nothing, except that he was in no hurry, and would look after Mrs. Cumberland by-and-by. He was a dark man of about two-and-thirty, with a plain, honest face; straightforward in disposition and manner, timid only when with Ellen Adair. He took a step or two nearer Ellen, and began to address her in low tones, pulling one of his gloves about nervously.

"I have been wishing for an opportunity to speak to you, Miss Adair. There is a question that I—that I— should like to put to you. One I have very much at heart."

It was coming. In spite of Ellen Adair's studied coldness, by which she had meant him to learn that he must not speak, she saw that it was coming. In the pause he made, as if he would wait for her permission to go on, she felt miserably uncomfortable. Her nature was essentially generous and sensitive; to have to refuse Mr. Seeley, or any one else, made her feel as humiliated as though she had committed a crime. And she could have esteemed the man apart from this.

They were thus standing: Mr. Seeley looking awkward and nervous, Ellen turning red and white: when Arthur Bohun walked in. Mr. Seeley, effectually interrupted for the time, muttered a good-morning to Captain Bohun and went into the garden.

"What was Seeley saying, Ellen?"

"Nothing," she rather faintly answered.

"Nothing!"

Ellen glanced up at him. His face wore the haughty Bohun look; his mouth betrayed scorn enough for ten proud Bohuns put together. She did not answer.

"If he was saying 'nothing,' why should you be looking as you did?—with a blush on your face, and your eyes cast down?"

"He had really said as good as nothing, Arthur. What he might have been going to say, I—I don't know. He had only that moment come in."

"As you please," coldly returned Arthur, walking into the garden in his turn. "If you do not think me worthy of your confidence, I have no more to say."

The Bohun blood was bubbling up fiercely. Not doubting Ellen; not in resentment against her—at least only so in the moment's anger: but in indignation that Seeley, a common village practitioner, should dare to lift his profane eyes to Ellen Adair. Captain Bohun had suspected the man's hopes for some short time past; there is an instinct in these things; and he felt outrageous over it. Tom Graves's venture had filled him with resentment; but he at least was a gentleman and a man of position.

Ellen, wonderfully disturbed, gently sat down to write again; all she did was gentle. And the diary had a few sentences added to it.

"That senseless William Seeley! And after showing him as plainly as I could, that it is useless—that I should consider it an impertinence in him to attempt to speak to me. I don't know whether it was for the worst or the best that Arthur should have come in just at that moment. For the best because it stopped Mr. Seeley's nonsense; for the worst because Arthur has now seen and is vexed. The vexation will not last, for he knows better. Here they are."

Once more Ellen closed her diary. "Here they are," applied to the doctor and Mrs. Cumberland. They were walking slowly towards the window, conversing calmly on her ailments, and came in. Mrs. Cumberland sat down with her newspaper. As Mr. Seeley took his departure to visit other patients, Arthur Bohun returned. Close upon that, Richard North was shown in. It seemed that Mrs. Cumberland was to have many visitors that morning.

That Richard North should find his time hang somewhat on hand, was only natural; he, the hitherto busy man, who had often wished the day's hours doubled, for the work he had to do in it. Richard could afford to make morning calls on his friends now, and he had come strolling to Mrs. Cumberland's.

They sat down: Arthur in the remotest chair he could find from Ellen Adair. She had taken up a bit of light work, and her fairy fingers were deftly plying its threads. Richard sat near Ellen, facing Mrs. Cumberland. He could not help thinking how lovely Ellen Adair was: the fact had never struck him more forcibly than to-day.

"How is the strike getting on, Richard?"

Mrs. Cumberland laid down her newspaper to ask the question. No other theme bore so much present interest in Dallory. From the time that North and Gass first established the works, things had gone on with uninterrupted smoothness, peace and plenty reigning on all sides. No wonder this startling change seemed as a revolution.

"It is still going on," replied Richard. "How the men are getting on, I don't like to think about. The wrong way, of course."

"Your proposition, to meet them half-way, was rejected, I hear."

"It was."

"What do they expect to come to?"

"To fortune, I suppose," returned Richard. "To refuse work and not expect a fortune, must be rather a mistake. A poor look-out at the best."

"But, according to the newspapers, Richard, one-half the working-classes in the country are out on strike. Do you believe it?"

"A great number are out. And more are going out daily."

"And what is to become of them all?"

"I cannot tell you. The question, serious though it is, never appears to occur to the men or their rulers."

"The journals say—living so much alone as I do, I have time to read many of them, and I make it my chief recreation—that the work is leaving the country," pursued Mrs. Cumberland.

"And so it is. It cannot be otherwise. Take a case of my own as an example. A contract was offered me some days ago, and I could not take it. Literally could not, Mrs. Cumberland. My men are out on strike, and likely to be out; I had no means of performing it, and therefore could only reject it. That contract, as I happen to know, has been taken by a firm in Belgium. They have undertaken it at a cheaper rate than I could possibly have done it at the best of times: for labour is cheap there. It is quite true. The work that circumstances compelled me to refuse, has gone over there to be executed, and I and my men are playing in idleness."

"But what will be the end of it?" asked Mrs. Cumberland.

"The end of it? If you speak of the country, neither you nor I can foresee the end."

"I spoke of the men. Not your men in particular, but all those that we include under the name of British workmen: the great bodies of artisans scattered in the various localities of the kingdom. What is to become of these men if the work fails?"

"I see only one of three courses for them," said Richard, lifting his hand in some agitation, for he spoke from the depth of his heart, believing the subject to be of more awful gravity than any that had stirred the community for some hundreds of years. "They must eventually emigrate—provided the means to do so can be found; or they must become burdens upon public charity; or they must lie down in the streets and starve. As I live, I can foresee no better fate for them."

"And what of the country, if it comes to this?—if the work and the workmen leave it?"

Richard North shrugged his shoulders. It was altogether a question too difficult for him. He would have liked it answered from some one else very much indeed; just as others would.

"Lively conversation!" interposed Captain Bohun, in a half-satirical, half-joking manner, as he rose. It was the first time he had spoken. "I think I must be going," he added, approaching Mrs. Cumberland.

Richard made it the signal for his own departure. As they stood, saying adieu, Bessy Rane was seen for a moment at her own window. Mrs. Cumberland nodded.

"There's Bessy," exclaimed Richard. "I think I'll go and speak to her. Will you pardon me, Mrs. Cumberland, if I make my exit from your house this way?"

Mrs. Cumberland stepped outside herself, and Richard crossed the low wire fence that divided the two gardens. Arthur Bohun went to the door, without having said a word of farewell to Ellen Adair. He stood with it in his hand looking at her, smiled, and was returning, when Mrs. Cumberland came in again.

"Won't you come and say goodbye to me here, Ellen?"

The invitation was given in so low a tone that she gathered it by the form of the lips rather than by the ear; perhaps by instinct also. She went out, and they walked side by side in silence to the open hall-door. Dallory Ham, in its primitive ways and manners, left its house-doors open with perfect safety by day to the summer air. Outside, between the house and the gate, was a small bed planted with flowers. Arrived at the door, Captain Bohun could find nothing better to talk of than these, as he stood with her on the crimson mat.

"I think those lilies are finer than Mr. North's."

"Mrs. Cumberland takes so much pains with her flowers," was Ellen's answer. "And she is very fond of lilies."

They stepped out, bending over these self-same lilies. Ellen picked one. He quietly took it from her.

"Forgive me, Ellen," he murmured. "I am not a bear in general. Goodbye."

As they stood, her hand in his, her flushed face downcast, Mrs. North's open carriage rolled past. Madam's head was suddenly propelled towards them as far as safety permitted: her eyes glared: a stony horror sat on her countenance.

"Shameful! Disgraceful!" hissed madam. And Miss Matilda North, by her side, started up to see what the shame might be.

Arthur Bohun had caught the words—not Ellen—and bit his lips in a complication of feeling.

But all he did was to raise his hat—first to his mother, then to Ellen—as he went out at the gate. Madam flung herself back in her seat, and the carriage pursued its course up the Ham.

CHAPTER IV

THREE LETTERS FOR DR RANE

"You are keeping quality hours, Bessy—as our nurse used to say when we were children," was Richard North's salutation to his sister as he went in and saw the table laid for breakfast.

Mrs. Rane laughed. She was busy at work, sewing some buttons on a white waistcoat of her husband's.

"Oliver was called out at seven this morning, and has not come back yet," she explained.

"And you are waiting breakfast for him! You must be starving."

"I took some coffee when Molly had hers. How is papa, Richard?"

"Anything but well. Very much worried, for one thing."

"Madam and Matilda are back again, I hear?" continued Bessy.

"Three days ago. They have brought Miss Field with them."

"And madam has brought her usual temper, I suppose," added Bessy. "No wonder papa is suffering."

"That of course; it will never be otherwise. But he is troubling himself also very much about the works being stopped. I tell him to leave all such trouble to me, but it is of no use."

"When will the strike end, Richard?"

Richard shook his head. It was an unprofitable theme, and he did not wish to pursue it with Bessy. She had sufficient cares of her own, as he suspected, without adding to them. Three letters lay on the table, close to where Richard was sitting; they were addressed to Dr. Rane. His fingers began turning them about mechanically, quite in abstraction.

"I know the handwriting of two of them," remarked Bessy, possibly fancying he was curious on the point; "not of the third."

"The one is from America," observed Richard, looking at the letters for the first time.

"Yes; it's from Dr. Jones. He would like Oliver to join him in America."

"To join him for what?" asked Richard.

Bessy looked at him. She saw no reason why her brother should not be told. Dr. Rane wished it kept secret from the world; but this, she thought, could not apply to her good and trustworthy Richard. She opened her heart and told him all; not what they were going certainly to do, for ways and means were still doubtful, but what they hoped to be able to do. Richard, excessively surprised, listened in silence.

They had made up their minds to leave Dallory. Dr. Rane had taken a dislike to the place; and no wonder, Bessy added in a parenthesis, when he was not getting on at all. He intended to leave it as soon as the practice was disposed of.

"I expect this letter will decide it," concluded Bessy, touching one that bore the London postmark. "It is from a Mr. Lynch, who is wishing to find a practice in the country on account of his health. London smoke does not do for him, he tells Oliver. They have had a good deal of correspondence together, and I know his handwriting quite well. Oliver said he expected his decision to-day or tomorrow. He is to pay two hundred pounds and take the furniture at a valuation."

"And then—do I understand you rightly, Bessy?—you and Rane are going to America?" questioned Richard.

"Oh no," said Bessy with emphasis. "I must have explained badly, Richard. What I said was, that Dr. Jones, who has more practice in America than he knows what to do with, had offered a share of it to Oliver if he would join him. Oliver declined it. He would have liked to go, for he thinks it must be a very good thing; but Dr. Jones wants a large premium: so it's out of the question."

"But surely you would not have liked to emigrate, Bessy?"

She glanced into Richard's face with her meek, loving eyes, blushing a very little.

"I would go anywhere where he goes," she answered simply. "It would cost me pain to leave you and papa, Richard; especially papa, because he is old, and because he would feel it; but Oliver is my husband."

Richard drummed for a minute or two on the table-cloth. Bessy sewed on her last button.

"Then where does Rane think of pitching his tent, Bessy?"

"Somewhere in London. He says there is no place like it for getting on. Should this letter be to say that Mr. Lynch, takes the practice, we shall be away in less than a month."

"And you have never told us!"

"We decided to say nothing until it was a settled thing, and then only to you, and Mrs. Cumberland, and papa. Oliver does not want the world to know it sooner than need be."

"But do you mean to say that Rane has not told his mother?" responded Richard to this in some surprise.

"Not yet," said Bessy, folding the completed waistcoat. "It will be sure to vex her, and perhaps needlessly; for, suppose, after all, we do not go? That entirely depends upon the disposal of the practice here."

Bessy was picking up the threads in her neat way, and putting the remaining buttons in the little closed box, when Dr. Rane was heard to enter his consulting-room. Away flew Bessy to the kitchen, bringing in the things with her own loving hands—and, for that matter, Molly Green was at her upstairs work—buttered toast, broiled ham, a dainty dish of stewed mushrooms. There was nothing she liked so much as to wait on her husband. Her step was light and soft, her eye bright. Richard, looking on, saw how much she cared for him.

Dr. Rane came in, wiping his brow: the day was hot, and he tired. He had walked from a farm-house a mile beyond the Ham. A strangely weary look sat on his face.

"Don't trouble, Bessy; I have had breakfast. Ah, Richard, how d'ye do?"

"You have had breakfast!" repeated Bessy. "At the farm?"

"Yes; they gave me some."

"Oh dear! won't you take a bit of the ham, or some of the mushrooms, Oliver? They are so good. And I waited."

"I am sorry you should wait. No, I can't eat two breakfasts. You must eat for me and yourself, Bessy."

Dr. Rane sat down in his own chair at the table, turning it towards Richard, and took up the letters. Selecting the one from Mr. Lynch, he was about to open it when Bessy, who was now beginning her breakfast, spoke.

"Oliver, I have told Richard about it—what we think of doing?"

Dr. Rane's glance went out for a moment to his brother-in-law's, and met it. He made the best of the situation, smiled gaily, and put down the letter unopened.

"Are you surprised, Richard?" he asked.

"Very much, indeed. Had a stranger told me I was going to leave Dallory myself—and, indeed, that may well come to pass, with this strike in the air—I should as soon have believed it. Shall you be doing well to go, do you think, Rane?"

"Am I doing well here?" was the doctor's rejoinder.

"Not very, I fear."

"And, with this strike on, it grows worse. The wives and children fall ill, as usual, and I am called in; but the men have no money to pay me with. I don't intend to bring Bessy to dry bread, and I think it would come to that if we stayed here—"

"No, no; not quite to that, Oliver," she interposed. But he took no notice of her.

"Therefore I shall try my fortune elsewhere," continued Dr. Rane. "And if you would return thanks to the quarter whence the blow has originated, you must pay them to your stepmother, Richard. It is she who has driven me away."

Richard was silent. Dr. Rane broke the seal of Mr. Lynch's letter, and read it to the end. Then, laying it down, he took up the one from America, and read that. Bessy, looking across, tried to gather some information from his countenance; but Dr. Rane's face was one which, in an ordinary way, was not more easily read than a stone.

"Is it favourable news, Oliver?" she asked, as he finished the long letter, and folded it.

"It's nothing particular. Jones runs on upon politics. He generally gives me a good dose of them."

"Oh, I meant from Mr. Lynch," replied Bessy. "Is he coming?"

"Mr. Lynch declines."

"Declines, Oliver!"

"Declines the negotiation. And he is not much better than a sneak for giving me all this trouble, and then crying off at the eleventh hour," added Dr. Rane.

"It is bad behaviour," said Bessy, warmly. "What excuse does he make?"

"You can see what he says," said Dr. Rane, pushing the letter towards her. Bessy opened it, and read it aloud for the benefit of Richard.

Mr. Lynch took up all one side with apologies. The substance of the letter was, that a practice had unexpectedly been offered to him at the seaside, which he had accepted, as the air and locality would suit his state of health so much better than Dallory. If he could be of service in negotiating with any one else, he added, Dr. Rane was to make use of him.

It was as courteous and explanatory a letter as could be written. But still it was a refusal: and the negotiation was at an end. Bessy Rane drew a deep breath: whether of relief or disappointment it might have puzzled herself to decide. Perhaps it was a mixture of both.

"Then, after all, Oliver, we shall not be leaving!"

"Not at present, it seems," was Dr. Rane's answer. And he put the two letters into his pocket.

"Perhaps you will be thinking again, Oliver, of America, now?" said his wife.

"Oh no, I shall not."

"Does Dr. Jones still urge you to come?"

"Not particularly. He took my refusal as final."

She went on, slowly eating some of the mushrooms. Richard said nothing: this projected removal seemed to have impressed him to silence. Dr. Rane took up the remaining letter and turned it about, looking at the outside.

"Do you know the writing, Oliver?" his wife asked.

"Not at all. The postmark's Whitborough."

Opening the letter, which appeared to contain only a few lines, Dr. Rane looked up with an exclamation.

"How strange! How very strange! Bessy, you and I are the only two left in the tontine."

"What!" she cried, scarcely understanding him. Richard North turned his head.

"That tontine that we were both put into when infants. There was only one life left in it besides ourselves—old Massey's son, of Whitborough. He is dead."

"What! George Massey? Dead!" cried Richard North.

Dr. Rane handed him the note. Yes: it was even so. The other life had dropped, and Oliver Rane's and his wife's alone remained.

"My father has called that an unlucky tontine," remarked Richard. "I have heard it said that if you want a child to live, you should put it into a tontine, for the tontine lives are sure to arrive at a green old age, to the mutual general mortification. This has been an exception to the rule. I am sorry about George Massey. I wonder what he has died of?"

"Last long, in general, do you say?" returned Dr. Rane musingly. "I don't know much about tontines myself."

"Neither do I," said Richard. "I remember hearing of one tontine when I was a boy: five or six individuals were left in it, all over eighty then, and in flourishing health. Perhaps that was why my father and Mr. Gass took up with one. At any rate, it seems that you and Bessy are the only two remaining in this."

"I wonder if a similar condition of things ever existed before as for a man and his wife to be the two last in a tontine?" cried Dr. Rane, slightly laughing. "Bessy, practically it can be of no use to us conjointly; for before the money can be paid, one of us must die. What senseless things tontines are!"

"Senseless indeed," answered Bessy. "I'd say something to it if we could have the money now. How much is it?"

"Ay, by the way, how much is it? What was it that each member put in at first, Richard? I forget. Fifty pounds, was it? And then there's the compound interest, which has been going on for thirty years. How much would it amount to now?"

"More than two thousand pounds," answered Richard North, making a mental calculation.

Dr. Rane's face flushed with a quick hot flush: a light shone in his eye: his lips parted, as with some deep emotions. "More than two thousand pounds!" he echoed under his breath. "Two thousand pounds! Bessy, it would be like a gold-mine."

She laughed slightly. "But we can't get it, you see, Oliver. And I am sure neither of us wishes the other dead."

"No—no; certainly not," said Dr. Rane.

Richard North said good-day and left. Just before turning in at the gates of Dallory Hall, he met a gig containing Lawyer Dale of Whitborough, who was driving somewhere with his clerk; no other than Timothy Wilks. Mr. Dale pulled up, to speak.

"Can it be true that George Massey is dead?" questioned Richard as they were parting.

"It's true enough, poor fellow. He died yesterday: was ill but two days."

"I've just heard it at Dr. Rane's. He received a letter this morning to tell him of it."

"Dr. Rane did? I was not aware they knew each other."

"Nor did they. But they were both in that tontine. Now that George Massey's gone, Dr. Rane and his wife are the only two remaining in it. Rather singular that it should be so."

For a minute Mr. Dale could not recollect whether he had ever heard of this particular tontine; although, being a lawyer, he made it his business to know everything; and he and Richard talked of it together. Excessively singular, Lawyer Dale agreed, that a tontine should be practically useless to a man and his wife—unless one of them died.

"Very mortifying, I must say, Mr. Richard North; especially where the money would be welcome. Two thousand pounds! Dr. Rane must wish the senseless thing at Hanover. I should, I know, if it were my case. Good-morning."

And quiet Timothy Wilks, across whom they talked, heard all that was said, and unconsciously treasured it up in his memory.

Richard carried home the news to his father. Mr. North was seated at the table in his parlour, some papers before him. He lifted his hands in dismay.

"Dead! George Massey dead! Dick, as sure as we are here, there must be something wrong about that tontine! Or they'd never drop off like this, one after another."

"It's not much more than a week ago, sir, that I met George Massey in Whitborough, and was talking to him. To all appearance he was as healthy and likely to live as I am."

"What took him off?"

"Dale says it was nothing more than a neglected cold."

"I don't like it; Dick, I don't like it," reiterated Mr. North, "Bessy may be the next to go; or Rane."

"I hope not, father."

"Well—I've had it in my head for ever so long that that tontine is an unlucky one; I think it is going to be so to the end. We shall see. Look here, Dick."

He pointed to some of the papers before him; used cheques apparently; pushing them towards his son.

"They sent me word at the bank that my account was overdrawn. I knew it could not be, and asked for my cheques. Dick, here are four or five that I never drew."

Richard took them in his fingers. The filling up was in madam's handwriting: the signature apparently in Mr. North's.

"Do you give Mrs. North blank cheques ready signed, sir?"

"No, never, Dick. I was cured of that, years ago. When she wants money, I sometimes let her fill in the cheque, but I never sign it beforehand."

"And you think you have not signed these?"

"Think! I know I have not. She has imitated my signature, and got the money."

Richard's face grew dark with shame; shame for his stepmother. But that Mr. North was her husband, it would have been downright forgery. Probably the law, if called upon, might have accounted it so now. He took time for consideration.

"Father, I think—pardon me for the suggestion—I think you had better let your private account be passed over to me. Allow it to lie in my name; and make my signature alone available—just as it is with our business account. I see no other safe way."

"With all my heart; and be glad to do it," acquiesced Mr. North, "but there's no account to pass. There's no account to pass, Dick; it's overdrawn."

CHAPTER V

MADAM'S ADVICE

A dinner-party at Dallory Hall. Arthur Bohun was in his chamber, lazily dressing for it. Not a large party, this: half-a-dozen people or so, besides themselves; and the hour six o'clock. Two gentlemen, bidden to it, would have to leave by train afterwards: on such occasions dinner of necessity must be early.

Mr. North and Richard did not approve of madam's dinners at the most favourable times: now, with all the care of the strike upon them and the trouble looming in the distance if that strike lasted: the breaking up of their business, the failure of their means: they looked on these oft-recurring banquets as especially reprehensible. They were without power to stop them; remonstrance availed not with madam. Sometimes the dinners were impromptu, or nearly so, madam inviting afternoon callers at the Hall to stay, or bringing home a carriage-full of guests with her. As was partly the case on this day.

Captain Arthur Bohun, who liked to take most things easily, dressing included, stood hair-brush in hand. He had moved away from the glass, and was looking from the open window. His thoughts were busy. They ran on that little episode of the morning, when madam, passing in her carriage, had seen him with Ellen Adair, and had chosen to display her sentiments on the subject in the manner described. That it would not end there, Arthur felt sure; madam would inevitably treat him to a little more of her mind. It was rather a singular thing—as if Fate had been intervening with its usual cross purposes—for circumstances so to have ordered it that madam should still be in ignorance of their intimacy. Almost always when Mrs. Cumberland was at home, it chanced that madam was away; and, when madam was at the Hall, Mrs. Cumberland was elsewhere. Thus, during Mrs. Cumberland's prolonged stay at Niton, madam's presence blessed her household; the very week that that lady returned to Dallory Ham, madam took her departure, and had only recently returned. She had spent the interval in Germany. Sidney North, her well-beloved son, giving trouble as usual to all who were connected with him, had found England rather warm for him in early spring, and had betaken himself to Germany. His chief point of sojourn was Homburg, and madam, with her daughter Matilda, had been making it hers since the spring. Mr. North, in the relief her absence brought him, had used every exertion to supply her with the money she so rapaciously sent home for. It would appear that the accommodation had not been sufficient, for—as was soon to be discovered by Richard—the cheques shown to him by his father had been drawn by her at Homburg. And so, as Fate or Fortune had willed it, Mrs. North had been out of the way of watching the progress of the intimacy between her son and Ellen Adair.

A quick knock at the chamber-door, and madam swept in, a large crimson rose, just brought from the greenhouse, adorning her jet-black hair, her white silk gown rustling and trailing after her. As well as though she had already spoken, Arthur knew what she had come for. He thought that she was losing no time and must have hurried over her toilette purposely. The carriage had not long returned home, for she and Matilda had been to a distance, and remained out to luncheon. Arthur, not moving from where he was, began brushing his hair haphazard.

"I suppose I am late, madam?"

"Was it you that I passed this afternoon in Dallory Ham, talking to some girl?" began madam, taking no notice of his remark.

"It was me, safe enough; I had been calling on Mrs. Cumberland," replied Arthur, carelessly. "Dick also. By the way you stared, madam, I fancied you scarcely knew me."

A little banter. Madam might take it seriously, or not, as she chose. She went round to the other side of the dressing-table, and stood opposite him at the window.

"What girl were you talking to?"

"Girl! I was with Miss Adair."

"Who is she, Arthur?"

"She is Mrs. Cumberland's ward."

"What do you know of her?"

"I know her as being at Mrs. Cumberland's. I see her when I go there."

Was he really indifferent? Standing there brushing away at his hair lazily, his apparently supreme indifference could not be exceeded. Madam scanned his face in momentary silence; he was closely intent upon two sparrows, fighting over a reddening cherry on the branch of a tree.

"Fight away, young gentlemen; battle it out; you'll have all the better appetite for supper."

"Will you attend to me for a short time, Captain Bohun?" spoke madam, irritably.

"Certainly; I am attending," was the captain's ready answer.

Just for an instant madam paused. This was not one of the daily petty grievances that she made people miserable over, but a trouble to her of awful meaning, almost as of life or death. In this, her own grave interests, she could control her temper, and she thought it might be the better policy to do so whilst she dealt with it.

"Arthur, you know that you are becoming more valuable to me," she said, with calmness; and Arthur Bohun opened his surprised ears at the words and tone. "Since Sidney took up his abode away from England, and cannot come back to it, poor fellow, for the present you are all I have here. If I speak, it is for your welfare."

"Very good of you, I am sure," returned Arthur, seeing she waited for him to say something, and feeling how two-faced the words were, mother of his though she was. "What is it you wish to say?"

"It's about that girl, Miss—what do you call her?—Adair. Young men will be young men; soldiers especially; I know that; but wrong is wrong, and it cannot by the most ingenious sophistry be converted into right. It is quite wrong to play with these village girls, as you seem to be doing with Miss Adair."

Arthur threw back his head as though his pride were hurt. Madam had seen just the same movement in his father.

"I have no intention of playing with Miss Adair."

A gleam shot from her eyes—half fear, half defiance. She bit her lip, and went on in a still softer tone.

"You cannot mean anything worse, Arthur."

"I do not understand you, madam. Worse? Worse than what?"

"Anything serious. To play with village girls is reprehensible; but—"

"I beg your pardon, mother; this is quite unnecessary. The playing with village girls—whatever that may mean—is not a habit of mine, and never has been. The caution might be more appropriate if applied to your men-servants than it is to me."

"Allow me to finish, Arthur. To play with village girls is reprehensible; but to intend anything serious with one would be far more so in your case. Will you profit by the caution?"

"If you wish me to comprehend the word 'serious,' you must speak out. What does it mean?"

"It means marriage," she answered, with an outburst of temper—as far as tone might convey it. "I allude to this absurd intimacy of yours with Miss Adair. You must be intimate with the girl; your look and attitude, as I passed to-day, proved it."

"And if I did mean marriage, what then?"

He asked the question jokingly, laughing a little; but he was not prepared for the effect it had on his mother. Her eyes flashed fire, her lips trembled, her face turned white as death.

"Marriage! With her? You must be dreaming, Arthur Bohun."

"Not dreaming; joking," he said, lightly. "You may be at ease, madam; I have no intention of marrying any one at present."

"You must never marry Miss Adair."

"No?"

"Arthur Bohun, you are treating all this with mockery," she exclaimed, beginning to believe that he really was so; and the relief was great, though the tacit disrespect angered her. "How dare you imply that you could think seriously of these village girls?—only to annoy and frighten me."

"You must be easily frightened to-day, madam. I don't think I did imply it. As to Miss Adair—"

"Yes, as to Miss Adair," fiercely interrupted madam. "Go on."

"I was about to say that, in speaking of Miss Adair, we might as well recognize her true position. It is not quite respectful to be alluding to her as a 'village girl.' She is a lady, born and bred."

"Perhaps you will next say that she is equal to the Bohuns?"

"I do not wish to say it. Don't you think this conversation may as well cease, madam?" added Arthur, after a short pause. "Why should it have been raised? One might suppose I had asked your consent to my marriage, whereas you know perfectly well that I am a poor man, with not the slightest chance of taking a wife."

"Poor men get engaged sometimes, Arthur, thinking they will wait—and wait. Seeing you with that girl—the world calls her good-looking, I believe—I grew into an awful fright for your sake. It would be most disastrous for you to marry beneath your rank—a Bohun never holds up his head afterwards, if he does that; and I thought I ought to speak a word of warning to you. You must take a suitable wife when you do marry—one fitted to mate with the future Sir Arthur Bohun."

"To mate with plain Arthur Bohun. To call me the future Sir Arthur is stretching possibility very wide indeed, madam," he added, laughing.

"Not at all. You will as surely succeed as that I am telling you so. Look at that puny James Bohun! A few years at most will see the last of him."

"I hope not, for his father's sake. Any way, he may live long enough to marry and leave children behind him. Is your lecture at an end, madam?" he jestingly concluded. "If so, perhaps you may as well leave me to get my coat on, or I shall have to keep dinner waiting."

"I have another word," said madam; "your coat can wait. Miss Dallory dines here."

"Miss Dallory! I thought she was in Switzerland. Did she come over in a balloon to dine with us?"

"She is staying with her brother Frank. I and Matilda called at Ham Court just now and brought her with us."

"Did you bring him also?"

"I did not see him; they said he was not in the way. But now why do I mention this?"

"As a bit of gossip for me, I suppose. It's very good of you. My coat and dinner can certainly wait."

"I have brought Miss Dallory here for your sake, Arthur Bohun," was the rejoinder, spoken with emphatic meaning. "She is the young lady you will do well to think of as your future wife."

Madam went out of the room with much stately rustle, and swept downstairs. Another minute, and the door opened again to admit Richard North. Captain Bohun had not progressed further in dressing, or stirred from his place, but was leaning against the window-frame, whistling softly.

"Madam's in a way, is she not?" began Richard, in low tones. "My window was open, Arthur, and I was obliged to catch a word here and there. I made all kinds of noises, but you did not take the hint."

"She didn't; and I would as soon you heard as not," was Captain Bohun's answer. "You are ready, I see, Dick."

"The course of true love never did run smooth, you know," said Richard, laughing.

"And never will. Whenever I read of the old patriarchal days, in which a man had only to fix on a wife and bring her home to his tent; and look on all that has to be considered in these—money, suitability of family, settlements—I wonder whether it can be the same world. Madam need not fear that I have any chance of marrying."

"Or you wouldn't long be a bachelor?"

"I don't know about that."

"You don't know! Why, you do know, and so do I. I've seen how it is for some weeks now, Arthur."

"Seen what?"

Richard smiled.

"Seen what?"

"How it is between you and Ellen Adair."

"You think you have?"

"Think! You love her, don't you?"

Arthur Bohun put down the hair-brush gently, and moved to take up his coat.

"Dick, old fellow, whether it will come to anything between us or not, I cannot tell," he said, his voice strangely deep, his brow flushing with emotion, "but I shall never care for any one else as I care for her."

"Then secure her," answered Dick.

"I might be tempted to do it, in spite of my mother, had I the wherewithal to set up a home; but I haven't."

"You have more than double what Rane and Bessy have."

"Rane and Bessy! But Bessy is one in a thousand. I couldn't ask a wife to come home to me on that."

"Just as you think well, of course. Take care, though, you don't get her snapped up. I should fear it, if it were my case. Ellen Adair is the loveliest girl I ever saw, and I think her the sweetest, I could only look at her as we sat in Mrs. Cumberland's room this morning. Other men will be finding it out, Arthur, if they have not already done so."

Arthur never answered. He had gone back to his former post, and was leaning against the window-frame, looking out dreamily.

"Madam objects, I presume?"

"I presume she would, if I put it to her," assented Arthur, as if the proposition admitted of no dispute.

"I don't see why she should do so, or you, either."

"I'm afraid, Dick, we Bohuns have our full share of family pride."

"But Mr. Adair is, no doubt, a gentleman?"

"Oh yes. That is, not in trade," added Arthur, carelessly.

"Well, a gentleman is a gentleman," said Richard.

"Of course. But I take it for granted that he holds no position in the world. And we Bohuns, you know—"

Arthur stopped. Richard North laughed. "You Bohuns would like to mate only with position. A daughter, for example, of the Lord-Lieutenant of the county."

"Exactly," assented Arthur, echoing the laugh, but very much in earnest for all that. "Madam has been recommending Miss Dallory to my notice."

"Who?" cried Richard, rather sharply.

"Miss Dallory."

"You might do worse," observed Richard, after a pause.

"No doubt of that. She is downstairs."

"Who is downstairs?"

"She. So madam has just informed me."

"There's the gong."

"And be hanged to it!" returned Arthur, getting into his coat. "I wish to goodness madam did not give us the trouble of putting on dinner dress every other day! Neither are entertainments seemly in your house during these troubled times."

"What's more, I don't see how they will be paid for, if the trouble continues," candidly spoke Richard. "Madam must be uncommonly sanguine to expect it."

"Or careless," returned Arthur Bohun. "Dick, my friend, it's a bad sign when a man has no good word to give his mother."

That every grain of filial affection had long gone out of his breast and been replaced by a feeling akin to shame and contempt, Arthur Bohun was only too conscious of. He strove to be dutiful; but it was at times a hard task. Living under the same roof as his mother, her sins against manners and good feeling were brought under his notice perpetually; he was more sensitively alive to them than even others could be.

Since Arthur Bohun had quitted the army and recovered from the long sickness that followed on his wound, Dallory Hall had been his ostensible home. Latterly he had made it really so; for Dallory Ham contained an attraction from which he could not tear himself. Ellen Adair had his heart's best love: and, far from her he could not wander. A pure, ardent love, honourable as every true passion must be in an honourable man, but swaying his every action with its power. Sir Nash Bohun invited him in vain. His aunt, Miss Bohun, with whom he was a great favourite, wondered why he went so rarely to see her; or, when he did go, made his visit a flying one. Arthur Bohun possessed a few hundreds a-year: about four: just enough to keep him as a gentleman: and he had none of the bad habits that run away with young men's money. Miss Bohun would leave him fairly well off when she died: so he was at ease as to the future. One day, after he had been at Dallory Hall for a few months, he put a hundred-pound banknote into Richard North's hands.

"What is this for?" questioned Richard.

Arthur told him. The embarrassments in the Hall's financial department, caused by madam, were lightly touched on: this was Arthur's contribution towards his own share of the housekeeping. In the surprise of the moment, Richard North's spirit rose, and fought against it. Arthur quietly persisted.

"As long as I pitch my tent amongst you here, I shall hand over this sum every six months. To you, Dick; there's no one else to be trusted with it. If I gave it to Bessy, she would be safe to speak about it, and it might be wiled out of her."

"I never heard such nonsense in my life," cried Richard. "You will not get me to take it. I wouldn't countenance anything of the sort."

"Yes you will, Dick, Yon wouldn't like me to take up my abode at the Dallory Arms. I declare on my honour I shall do so, if I am forced to be as a guest at the Hall."

"But, Arthur—"

"Dick, my friend, there's no need of argument. I mean what I say. Don't drive me away. The Dallory Arms would not be a very comfortable home; and I should drift away, goodness knows where."

"As if one inmate, more or less, made any difference in our home expenses."

"As if it did not. I have no right or claim whatever to be living on your father. Don't make me small in my own eyes, frère Richard. You know that you'd feel the same in my place, and do the same. No one need know of this but our two selves, Dick."

Richard gave in: he saw that Arthur was resolute: and after all, it was just. So he took the banknote into account, and told his father about it; and Arthur Bohun stayed on, his conscience at peace. Once, in one of madam's furious onslaughts, when she spared no one, she abused her son for staying at the Hall, and living upon her. Upon her! Arthur parried the attack with careless good-humour, merely saying he was Dick's guest. When Dick turned him out of the Hall, he should go.

CHAPTER VI

MARY DALLORY

The guests waited in the drawing-room. Madam, with gracious suavity, was bestowing her smiles on all, after her manner in society, her white silk dress gleaming with richness. A slight frown crossed her brow, however, at the tardy entrance of her son and Richard North.

"We have waited for you," she said rather sharply. "Dinner has been announced."

Richard found his father did not intend to be present, and that he must act as host, which was nothing new. Glancing round the room, he was advancing to Miss Dallory—there was no married lady present excepting madam—when madam's voice rang out cold and clear.

"Take in Miss Field, Richard. Arthur, you will conduct Miss Dallory."

Now that was wrong according to the rules of etiquette. Miss Dallory, the great heiress, whose family was of some note in the county, should have fallen to Richard: Miss Field, a middle-aged lady, had only been Matilda North's governess. But madam had a way of enforcing her own commands: or, rather, of letting people know they might not be disputed. There was a moment's awkwardness: Richard and Arthur both stood with arrested footsteps; and then each advanced to the appointed lady. But Miss Dallory nearly upset it all: she turned from Captain Bohun to Richard, her hand outstretched.

"How do you do, Mr. North?"

He clasped it for a moment. Madam, who had a shrewd way of making guesses, and of seeing things that no one else saw, had gathered an idea long ago, that had Richard North's fortunes been in the ascendant, he might have forgotten the wide gulf separating him from Mary Dallory—she patrician-born, he plebeian—and asked her to step over it.

"I did not know you had returned, Miss Dallory, until a few minutes age," said Richard.

"No! I have been home two days."

They parted. Madam was sweeping on to the dining-room on the arm of a Colonel Carter, whose acquaintance she had made at Homburg, and the rest had to follow. Richard brought up the rear with Miss Field.

Miss Dallory, a rather tall and graceful girl of two-and-twenty, sat between Arthur Bohun and Richard North. She was not particularly handsome, but very pleasing. A fair-complexioned face with plenty of good sense in it, grey eyes rather deeply set, and soft dark-brown hair. Her manners were remarkably open: her speech independent. It was this perhaps—the pleasantness of the speech and manner—that made her a favourite with every one.

The Dallorys were very wealthy. There were three of them: Miss Dallory and her two brothers, John and Frank, both older than herself. They had been left orphans at an early age: their father's will having bequeathed his property almost equally amongst the three; the portion of it entailed on his elder son lay in another county. To the surprise of many people, it was found that he had left Dallory Hall to his daughter; so that, in point of fact, this Miss Dallory, sitting at Mr. North's dinner-table, was owner of the house. It had been the residence of the Dallorys during Mr. Dallory's lifetime: after his death, the trustees let it on lease to Mr. North. The lease had been purchased, so that Mr. North had no rent to pay for it. The lease, however, had now all but terminated. Madam hoped to be able to get it renewed:

perhaps that might be one of the reasons why she was now paying court to Mary Dallory. That young lady came into her property when she was one-and-twenty; and all power lay in her own hands. Nearly two years ago Miss Dallory had gone on the Continent with her aunt, Mrs. Leasom. Illness had prolonged Mrs. Leasom's stay there, and they had only just returned. Mrs. Leasom remained at her home in London; Miss Dallory came down at once to her younger brother's house—an extremely pretty place just beyond the Ham.

Dinner progressed. Miss Dallory talked chiefly to Richard, next to whom she sat; Arthur Bohun, on the other side, was rather silent and glum. She was telling them of her travels: and jestingly complaining of finding what she called a grand dinner, when she had thought Mrs. North was only bringing her to dine en famille. For her dress was nothing but a coloured muslin.

"Don't laugh at me, Mr. Richard North. If you had been living in a remote village of Switzerland for months, dining off bonilli and a tough chicken in your aunt's chamber, you would think this grandeur itself."

"I did not laugh," answered Richard. "It is a great deal grander than I like."

"Where is Mr. North?" she asked, slightly lowering her voice.

Richard shook his head. "The grandeur, as you call it, has tired him, Miss Dallory. He dines almost always in his own room: I join him as often as I can."

"I hear he is breaking," she continued, her deep grey eyes looking straight at Richard, pity and concern in their depths. "Frank says so."

"He is breaking sadly. The prolonged strain is too much for him."

Madam glanced down the table, and spoke in sharp tones.

"Are you attending to Miss Field, Richard?"

Miss Field was on his left hand: Miss Dallory on his right.

"Yes, madam. She heard," added he to Miss Dallory, scarcely moving his lips.

"And it was high treason, I suppose," rejoined that young lady, confidentially. "There have been changes in your home, Mr. Richard, since I was last here. Mr. North's first children were all in it, then."

"And now two of them have gone out of it. Bessy to another home: Edmund to—his last one."

"Ah, I heard all. How sad it must have been for you and Mr. North! John and Frank wrote me word that they followed him to the grave."

"Very sad for him as well as for us," assented Richard. "But he is better off."

"Who sent that wicked letter?"

Richard North dropped his glance on his plate as he answered, apparently intent on what was there. Miss Dallory's keen eyes had been on his: and she used to read a great deal that lay within them.

"There has been no discovery at all."

"It was thought to be Mr. Timothy Wilks, I believe."

"It was certainly not he," said Richard, rather hastily.

"No! He had at least something to do with the mischief, if he did not write the letter."

"Yes. But without intending evil. The next to leave the home here may be myself," he added.

"You!"

"Of course you have heard that our works are at a standstill? The men have struck."

"That's old news: I heard it in Switzerland."

"If we are not able to reopen them—and I begin to think we shall not be—I must go out into the world and seek employment elsewhere."

"Nonsense!"

"If you reflect for a moment, you will see that it is all sober earnest, Miss Dallory. When a man does not possess the means of living, he must work for one."

She said no more then. And when she spoke again the subject was changed.

"Is Bessy's marriage a happy one?"

"Very—as it seems to me. The worst is, Rane gets on as badly as ever in his profession."

"But why does he?"

"I know not. Except that madam undoubtedly works—always works—to keep him down."

"How wrong it is! He shall come and attend me. I will get up some headaches on purpose."

Richard laughed.

"We have had changes also, since you and I met," resumed Miss Dallory. "But not sad ones. I have become my own mistress in the world; am independent of every one. And Frank has taken up his abode at Ham Court for a permanency."

"I hope you intend to make a good use of your independence," said Richard, gravely.

"Of course. And I shall be independent; you may rely on that."

"We heard it rumoured some time ago that you were likely to lose your independence, Miss Dallory."

"I! In what way?"

"By getting married."

Their eyes met for a moment, and then dropped. Miss Dallory laughed lightly.

"Did the news penetrate as far as this? Well, it never was 'likely,' Mr. Richard North. A—gentleman asked me; but I had reason to suppose that he wanted my money more than he did myself, and so—nothing came of it."

"Who was he?"

"It would not be fair to tell you."

"Thank you for correcting me," spoke Richard, in his earnest way. "I ought to feel shame for asking. I beg your pardon; and his."

Happening to glance at the young lady, he saw that her face had turned crimson. A rare thing for Miss Dallory. She was too self-possessed to display emotion on light occasions.

"Have you seen Ham Court lately?" she resumed, looking up; the blushes making her very pretty.

"Not since your brother came to it. He has not been here long, you know. I called one day, but they said Mr. Dallory was out."

"The place is very nice now. He has made alterations, and done it up beautifully. You must come again."

"With pleasure," answered Richard. "How long shall you remain with him?"

"As long as he will have me. I am not going away yet. I shall make it my home. Frank has quiet tastes, and so have I: and we intend to live a Darby and Joan life together, and grow into an old maid and an old bachelor."

Richard smiled. "How is it Francis did not come with you this evening?"

"May I dare to tell you why?" she whispered. "When we saw madam's carriage driving up, Frank disappeared. 'Say I am out,' was his order to me. He and madam never got on well: as a little boy he was terribly afraid of her, and I think the feeling has lasted. When I went to put my bonnet on, I found him shut up in his room. He wished me joy of my visit, and promised to come and walk home with me in the evening."

Madam rose from table early. Something in the arrangements did not seem to suit her. It was a warm and lovely evening, and they went out on the lawn. Miss Dallory slipped round the corner of the house to the window of Mr. North's parlour.

It stood open and he sat just within it. Sat with his hands on his knees, and his head drooping. Miss Dallory started: not so much because his face was thin and worn, but at its hopeless expression. In her two years' absence, he seemed to have aged ten.

She stepped over the threshold, and gently laid her hands on his. He looked up as a man bewildered.

"Why—it—it cannot be Mary Dallory."

"It is Mary Dallory; come home at last. Won't you kiss me, dear Mr. North?"

He kissed her fondly. In the old days, when John North was supposed to be the most rising man, in a commercial point of view, in the county, Mr. Dallory had thought it worth while to court his friendship, and Mr. North had been asked to stand godfather to his little girl. Mary—after she lost her own parents—was wont to say she belonged to the Hall, and often would be there. Her aunt, Mrs. Leasom, who had been a Miss Dallory once, was left guardian to the children, with Ham Court as her residence until the younger son should be of age, to whom it would then lapse. But Mrs. Leasom spent a large portion of her time in London, and sometimes the children had not seen their native place, Dallory, for years together.

"When did you come home, my dear?"

"To England a week ago. To Ham Court only yesterday. Do you know that you are much changed?"

"Ay. There's nothing but change in this life, my dear. The nearer we approach the end of our days, the faster our sorrows seem to come upon us. I have had more than my share of them, and they have changed me. I see only one source of comfort left to me in the wide world."

"And that?" she asked, half kneeling at his feet.

"My dear son Richard. No one knows the son he has been to me; the sacrifices he has made. No one save God."

Miss Dallory gave no answer to this. He was lost in deep abstraction, thinking no doubt of his many troubles—for he always was thinking of them—when the person in question entered; Richard North. Miss Dallory rose and sat down on a chair decorously.

She remained only a minute or two now, and spent the time talking and laughing. Richard gave her his arm to take her back to the others. Miss Dallory apparently was in no hurry to go, for she lingered over some of the flower-beds.

"Is the strike a serious matter?" she questioned in a confidential tone.

"As serious as it is possible for any matter of the kind to be," replied Richard.

"You and your men were always on the best of terms: why did they become dissatisfied with you?"

"They never became dissatisfied with me. The Trades' Unions' agents stepped in and persuaded them they would be better off if they could work less time and be paid more wages. The men listened: it was only natural they should do so: and presented themselves with these new demands. I did not grant them, and they struck. That's the case in a nutshell, Miss Dallory."

"I suppose you would not grant them?"

"I would not grant them upon principle; I could not, because my profits did not allow it. I am quite certain that if I had given way, in a short time the men would have demanded more. The Trades' Unions will never allow them to be satisfied, until—"

"Until what?" she asked, for Richard had stopped.

"Until the country is ruined, and its trade has left it."

"It is a serious thing," she said—and she was very grave now. "I suppose you would take the men on again upon the old terms?"

"And be glad to do it."

"And they will not come?"

"No. I have offered to meet them half-way. It is of no use."

"Then I think those men deserve to learn what want of employment means," she returned warmly. "I thought your men were intelligent; I used to know many of them. When I go amongst them—and that may be tomorrow—-I shall ask them if they have taken leave of their senses. What does Mrs. Gass say to it all?"

Richard smiled a little. Mrs. Gass said more than he did, he answered, but it was equally useless.

"And I suppose it is the strike that is troubling Mr. North? I think him so very much changed."

"It troubles him, of course—and there are other things."

"Does it trouble you?" asked Miss Dallory, pointedly, as she looked straight at him.

"Trouble me!" he rejoined, surprised at the unnecessary question. "Why, it involves simply ruin, unless we can go on again. Ruin to me, and to my father with me. There's your brother."

They had reached the lawn at length, and saw Francis Dallory, who had come for his sister. He was a short, fair young man, with an open countenance. Madam had already appropriated him.

"Where's Arthur?" demanded madam, imperiously, as Miss Dallory came up on Richard's arm. "I thought he was with you."

Miss Dallory answered that she had not seen Arthur Bohun since quitting the dinner-table. No one had seen him, as far as madam could discover. She suspected he must have gone off somewhere to smoke; and would have liked to put his pipe behind the fire.

But the pipe was not in fault. Arthur Bohun, possibly thinking there were enough without him, had quietly made his escape, and gone for a stroll towards the Ham. It took him so near to Mrs. Cumberland's that he said to himself he might as well call and ask after the headache she had been suffering from in the morning.

Sophistry! Nothing but sophistry. Captain Arthur Bohun did not really care whether her headache was worse or better; until a moment ago he had not even remembered that she had complained of headache. The simple truth was, that he could not bear to rest for even one evening without a glimpse of Ellen Adair. No mother ever hungered for a lost child as he hungered for her presence.

They were at tea. Mrs. Cumberland, Ellen, and Mr. Seeley. When Jelly showed Captain Bohun in, the doctor was just taking his second cup. Ellen, who presided at the tea-tray, asked Captain Bohun if he would take some, and he rather shortly answered, No. Warfare lay in his mind. What business had that man to be sitting there on a footing of companionship with Ellen Adair?

Mrs. Cumberland's head was a little worse, if anything, she replied, thanking Captain Bohun for his solicitude in regard to it. Mr. Seeley had given her two draughts of something—ether, she believed—in the afternoon, but they had not done her head any good.

It might have come to a question as to which would sit out the other—for Mr. Seeley detected somewhat of the state of Arthur Bohun's mind, and resented it—but for the entrance of Dr. Rane. Dr. Rane appeared to have no present intention of leaving again, for he plunged into a hot discussion with his brother-practitioner, touching some difficult question in surgery, which seemed quite likely to continue all night, and Arthur Bohun rose. He would have remained willingly, but he was ever sensitive as to intruding, and fancied Mrs. Cumberland might wonder why he stayed.

As he went out, Francis Dallory and his sister were passing on their walk homeward. Captain Bohun turned with them, and went to the end of the Ham.

The shades of evening—nay, of night—had stolen over the earth as he went back again; the light night of summer. The north-west was bright with its opal tints; a star or two shone in the heavens. Dr. Rane was pacing his garden walks, his wife on his arm.

"Goodnight, Bessy!" he called out to her, whom he had always regarded as his stepsister.

"Goodnight, Arthur!" came the hearty rejoinder as Bessy recognized his voice.

Onwards a few steps—only a few—and it brought Arthur Bohun level with the window of Mrs. Cumberland's drawing-room. It was not yet lighted. At the window, standing very closely together, stood the other doctor and Ellen Adair. In Captain Bohun's desperate jealousy, he stared Ellen full in the face, and made no movement of recognition. Turning away with a contemptuous movement, plainly discernible in the dusk, he went striding on.

Shakespeare never read more truly the human heart than when he said that jealousy makes the food it feeds on. Arthur Bohun went home almost maddened; not so much with jealousy in its absolute sense, as with indignation at the doctor's iniquitous presumption. Could he have analyzed his own heart fairly, he would have found there full trust in the good faith of Ellen Adair. But he was swayed by man's erring nature, and yielded to it.

How innocent it all was! how little suggestive, could Captain Bohun only have read events correctly. There had been no invitation to tea at all; Mr. Seeley had gone in just as they began to take it, and was offered a cup by Mrs. Cumberland. As to being together at the window, Ellen had been standing there to catch the fading light for her wool-work, perhaps as an excuse for leaving him and Mrs. Cumberland to converse alone; and he had just come up to her to say goodnight as Captain Bohun passed.

If we could only divine the truth of these fancies when jealousy puts them before us in its false and glaring light, some phases of our lives might be all the happier in consequence. Arthur Bohun lay tossing the whole night long on his sleepless pillow, tormenting himself by wondering what Ellen Adair's answer to Seeley would be. That the fellow in his audacity was proposing to her as they stood at the window, he could have sworn before the Lord Chief Baron of England. It was a wretched night; his tumultuous thoughts were sufficient to wear him out. Arthur had Collins' "Ode to the Passions" by heart; but it never occurred to him to recall any part of it to profit now.

"Thy numbers, Jealousy, to nought were fixed,   Sad proof of thy distressful state.   Of differing themes the veering song was mixed: And now it courted Love; now, raving, called on Hate."

CHAPTER VII

LOVE AMONG THE ROSES

When Arthur Bohun rose the next morning, his senses had returned to him. That Ellen Adair's love was his, and that no fear existed of her accepting any other man, let him be prince or peasant, reason assured him. He wanted to see her; for that his heart was always yearning; but on this morning when, as it seemed, he had been judging her harshly, the necessity seemed overwhelmingly great. His impatient feet would have carried him to Mrs. Cumberland's immediately after breakfast; but his spirit was a little rebellious still, and kept him back. He would not betray his impatience, he thought; would not go down until the afternoon; and he began to resort to all sorts of expedients for killing time. He walked with Richard North the best part of the way to Dallory: he came back and wrote to his aunt, Miss Bohun; he went sauntering about the flower-beds with Mr. North. As the day wore on towards noon, his restless feet betook him to Ham Lane—which the reader has not visited since he saw Dr. Rane hastening through it on the dark and troubled night that opened this history. The hedges were green now, beautiful with their dog-roses of delicate pink and white, giving out the perfume of sweet-briar. Captain Bohun went along, switching at these same pleasant hedges with his cane. Avoiding the turning that would take him to Dallory Ham, he continued his way to another and less luxurious lane; the lane that skirted the back of the houses of the Ham, familiarly called by their inhabitants "the back lane." Strolling onwards, he had the satisfaction of finding himself passing the dead wall of Mrs. Cumberland's garden, and of seeing the roof and chimneys of her house. Should he go round and call? A few steps lower down, just beyond Dr. Rane's, was an opening that would take him there, a public-house at its corner. He had told himself he would not go until the afternoon, and now it was barely twelve o'clock; should he call, or should he not call?

Moving on, in his indecision, at a slow pace, he had arrived just opposite Dr. Rane's back garden door, when it suddenly opened, and the doctor himself came forth.

"Ah, how d'ye do?" said the doctor, rather surprised at seeing Arthur Bohun there. "Were you coming in this way? The door was bolted."

"Only taking a stroll," carelessly replied Captain Bohun. "How's Bessy?"

"Quite well. She is in the dining-room, if you'll come in and see her."

Nothing loth, Arthur Bohun stepped in at once, the doctor continuing his way. Mrs. Rane was darning stockings. She and Arthur had always been the very best of friends, quite brother and sister. Meek and gentle as ever, she looked, sitting there with her smooth, curling hair, and the loving expression in her mild, soft eyes! Arthur sat down and talked with her, his glance roving ever to that other house, seeking the form of one whom he did not see.

"Do you know how Mrs. Cumberland is this morning?" he inquired of Bessy.

"I have not heard. Mr. Seeley has been there; for I saw him in the dining-room with Ellen Adair."

Arthur Bohun's pulses froze to ice.

"I think they are both in the garden now."

"Are they?" snapped Arthur. "His patients must get on nicely if he idles away his mornings in a garden."

Bessy looked up from her darning. "I don't mean that Seeley's there, Arthur—I mean Mrs. Cumberland and Ellen."

As Bessy spoke, Jelly was seen to come out of Mrs. Cumberland's house, penetrate the trees, and return with her mistress.

"Some one has called, I suppose," remarked Bessy.

Captain Bohun thought the gods had made the opportunity for himself expressly. He went out, stepped over the small fence, and disappeared in the direction that Mrs. Cumberland had come from, believing it would lead him to Ellen Adair.

In the secluded and beautiful spot where we first saw her—but where we shall not often, alas! see her again—she sat. The flowers of early spring were out then; the richer summer flowers were blooming now. A natural bower of roses seemed to encompass her; the cascade was trickling softly as ever down the artificial rocks, murmuring its monotonous cadence; the birds sang to each other from branch to branch; glimpses of the green lawn and of brilliant flowers were caught through the trees. Ellen Adair had sometimes thought the spot beautiful as a scene in fairy-land. It was little less so.

She was not working this morning. An open book lay before her on the rustic table; her cheek was leaning on her raised hand, from which the lace fell back; a hand so suspiciously delicate as to betoken a want of sound strength in its owner. She wore a white dress, with a bow of pink ribbon at the throat, and a pink waistband. There were times, and this was one of them, when she looked extremely fragile.

A sound of footsteps. Ellen only thought it was Mrs. Cumberland returning, and read on. But there was a different sound in these steps as they gained on her ear. Her heart stood still, and then bounded on again tumultuously, her pulses tingled, her sweet face turned red as the blushing rose. Sunshine had come.

"Good-morning, Miss Adair."

In cold, resentful, haughty tones was it spoken, and he did not attempt to shake hands. The sunshine seemed to go in again with a sweep. She closed her book and opened it, her fingers fluttering. Captain Bohun put down his hat on the seat.

"I thought Seeley might be here," said he, seeking out a lovely rose, and plucking it carefully.

"Seeley!" she exclaimed.

"Seeley. I beg your pardon. I did not know I spoke indistinctly. SEELEY."

He stood and faced her, watching the varying colour of her face, the soft blushes going and coming. Somehow they increased his anger.

"May I ask if you have accepted him?"

"Ac—cepted him!" she stammered, in wild confusion. "Accepted what?"

"The offer that Seeley made you last night."

"It was not last night," she replied in a confused impulse.

"Oh, then it was this morning! May I congratulate you, or not?"

Ellen Adair turned to her book in deep vexation. She had been caught, as it were, into making the tacit admission that Mr. Seeley had made her an offer. And she was hurt at Arthur Bohun's words and tone. Had he no more trust in her than this? As she turned the leaves of the book in her agitation, the plain gold ring on her finger attracted his sight. He was chafing inwardly, but he strove to appear at careless ease, and sat down as far from her as the bench allowed.

"I would be honourable if I died for it," he remarked with indifference, looking at the rose. "Is it quite the thing for you to listen to another man whilst you wear that ring upon your finger?"

Ellen took it off and pushed it towards him along the table.

This frightened him. He turned as white as ashes. Until now, he had only been speaking in jealousy, not in belief. Her own face was becoming white, her lips were compressed to hide their trembling. And thus they sat for a minute or two. He looked at the ring, then looked at her.

"Do you mean it, Ellen?" he asked, in a voice that struggled with agitation, proving how very earnest he deemed the thing was becoming—whatever it might have begun in.

She made no answer.

"Do you wish to give me back this ring?"

"What you said was, I thought, equivalent to asking for it."

"It was not. You know better."

"Why are you quarrelling with me?"

Moving an inch nearer, he changed his tone to gentleness, bending his head forward.

"Heaven knows that it is bitter enough to do so. Have I cause, Ellen?"

Her eyes were bent down: the colour stole into her face again; a half-smile parted her lips.

"You know, Ellen, it is perfectly monstrous that a common man like Seeley should dare to cast his aspiring thoughts to you."

"Was it my fault?" she returned. "He ought to have seen that—that—I should not like it."

"What did you tell him?"

"That it was quite impossible; that he was making a mistake altogether. When he was gone, I complained to Mrs. Cumberland."

"Insolent jackanapes! Was he rude, Ellen?"

"Rude! Mr. Seeley!" she returned in surprise. "Quite the contrary. He has always been as considerate and deferential as a man can be. You look down on his position, Arthur, but he is as great a gentleman in mind as you are."

"I only despise his position when he would seek to unite you to it."

"It has been very wrong of you to make me confess this. I can tell you I am feeling anything but 'honourable,' as you put it just now. There are things that should never be talked about; this is one of them. Nothing can be more unfair."

Very unfair. Captain Bohun's right feeling had come back to him, and he could only assent to it. He began to feel a little ashamed of himself on more points than one.

"It shall never escape my lips, Ellen, whilst I breathe. Seeley's secret is safe for me."

Taking up the ring, he held it for a moment, as if examining the gold. Ellen rose and went outside. The interview was becoming a very conscious one. He caught her up near the cascade, took her right hand in his, and slipped the ring upon her third finger.

"How many times has it been off?" he asked.

"Never until to-day."

"Well, there it is again, Ellen. Cherish it still. I hope—that ere long—"

He did not finish, but she understood quite well what he meant. Their eyes met, and each read the impassioned love seated within the other; strangely pure withal, and idealistic as ever poet dreamed of. He strained the hand in his.

"Forgive my petulance, my darling."

Excepting the one sweet word and the lingering pressure of the hand; excepting that the variegated rose was transferred from his possession to hers, the interview had been wholly wanting in the fond signs and tokens that are commonly supposed to attend the intercourse of lovers. Captain Bohun had hitherto abstained from using them, and perhaps Heaven alone knew what the self-denial cost him. In his unusually refined nature he may have deemed that they would be unjustifiable, until he could speak out openly and say, Will you be my wife?

"What is your book, Ellen?" he asked, as she returned to take it up from the table.

"Longfellow."

"Longfellow! Shall I read some of it to you? can you remain out?"

"I can do so until one o'clock; luncheon-time."

They sat down, and he began "The Courtship of Miles Standish." The blue sky shone down upon them through the flickering leaves, the cascade trickled, the bees hummed in the warm air, the white butterflies sported with the buds and flowers: and Ellen Adair, her hands clasping that treasure they held, the rose, her eyes falling on it to hide their happiness, listened in wrapt attention, for the voice was sweeter to her than any out of heaven.

The words of another poet most surely were applicable to this period of the existence of Captain Bohun and Ellen Adair. One of them at least would acknowledge it amidst the bitterness of afterlife.

"Love took up the glass of Time, and turned it in his glowing hands; Every moment, lightly shaken, ran itself in golden sands."

It could not last—speaking now only of the hour. One o'clock came all too soon; when he had seemingly read about ten minutes; and Miles Standish had to be left in the most unsatisfactory condition. Ellen rose: she must hasten in.

"It is a pity to break off here," said Arthur. "Shall I come and finish it this afternoon?"

Ellen shook her head. In the afternoon she would have to drive out with Mrs. Cumberland.

Captain Bohun went home through the green lanes, and soon found himself amidst those other flowers—Mr. North's. That gentleman came forth from his room to meet him, apparently in some tribulation, a letter in hand.

"Oh, Arthur, I don't know what to say to you; I am so sorry," he exclaimed. "Look here. When the postman came this morning, I happened to be out on the lawn, and he gave me my two letters, as I thought, and as he must have thought too, going on to the hall-door with the rest. I put them into my pocket and forgot them, Arthur: my spectacles were indoors. When I remembered them only just now, I found one was directed to you in Sir Nash's handwriting. I am so sorry," repeated poor Mr. North in his helpless manner.

"Don't be sorry, sir," replied Arthur cheerily. "It's nothing; not of the least consequence at all," he added, opening the letter. Nevertheless, as his eyes fell on the contents, a rather startled expression crossed his face.

"There!" cried Mr. North. "Something's wrong, and the delay has done mischief."

"Indeed nothing's wrong—in the sense you are thinking," repeated Arthur—for he would not have added to the poor old man's troubles for the world. "My uncle says James is not as well as he could wish: he wants me to go up at once and stay with them. You can read it for yourself, sir."

Mr. North put on his glasses. "I see, Arthur. You might have gone the first thing this morning, but for my keeping the letter. It was very stupid of the postman to give it to me."

Arthur laughed. "Indeed, I should have made no such hurry. There's not the least necessity for that. I think I shall go up this afternoon, though."

"Yes, do, Arthur. And explain to Sir Nash that it was my fault. Tell him that I am growing forgetful and useless. Fit only to be cut down, Arthur; only to be cut down."

Arthur Bohun put the old man's arm affectionately within his, and took him back to his parlour. If Mr. North had grown old it was with worry, not with years: the worry dealt daily out to him by madam; and Arthur would have remedied it with his best blood had he known how.

"You had better go up with me, sir; for a little change. Sir Nash would be glad to see you."

"I go up with you! I couldn't, Arthur; I am not equal to it now. And the strike is on, you know, and my place ought to be here while it lasts. The men look upon me still as their master, though Dick—Dick acts. And there's another thing, Arthur—I couldn't leave my roses just as they have come into bloom."

Arthur Bohun smiled; the last reason was all powerful. Mr. North stayed behind, and he went up that same afternoon to London.

CHAPTER VIII

THE TONTINE

The tontine. If the reader only knew how important a share the tontine—with its results—holds in this little history, he would enter on it with interest.

Tontines may be of different arrangement. In fact they are so. This one was as follows. It had been instituted at Whitborough. Ten gentlemen put each an equal sum into a common fund, and invested the whole in the joint names of ten children all under a year old. This money was to accumulate at compound interest, until only one of these children should be living: the last survivor would then receive the whole of the money unconditionally.

Of these ten children whose names were inscribed on the parchment deed, Oliver Rane and Bessy North alone survived. Mr. North had been wont to call it an unlucky tontine, for its members had died off rapidly one after another. For several years only three had been left; and now one of them, George Massey, had followed in the wake of those who were gone. Under ordinary circumstances, the tontine would have excited no comment whatever, but have gone on smoothly to the end: that is, until one of the two survivors had collapsed. The other would have had the money paid him; and nothing would have been thought about it, except that he was a fortunate man.

But this case was exceptional. The two survivors were man and wife. For the good fortune to lapse to one of them, the other must die. It was certainly a curious position, and it excited a great deal of comment in the neighbourhood. Dallory, as prone to gossip as other places, made of it that oft-quoted thing, a nine-days' wonder. In the general stagnation caused by the strike, people took up the tontine as a source of relief.

Practically the tontine was of no further use to the two remaining members: that is, to the two combined. They were one, so to say; and so long as they continued to be so, the money could not lapse to either. If Bessy died, Dr. Rane would take it; if Dr. Rane died, she would take it. Nothing more could be made of it than this. It had been accumulating now just one-and-thirty years; how much longer it would be left to accumulate none could foresee. For one-and-thirty years to come, in all human probability; for Dr. Rane and his wife appeared to possess sound and healthy constitutions. Nay, they might survive ten or twenty years beyond that, and yet not be very aged. And so, there it was; and Dallory made the matter its own, with unceremonious freedom.

But not as Dr. and Mrs. Rane did. They had need of money, and this huge sum—huge to them—lying at the very threshold of their door, but forbidden to enter, was more tantalizing than pen can describe. Richard North had not been far wrong in his computation: and the amount, as it stood at present, was considerably over two thousand pounds. The round sum, however, was sufficient to reckon by, without counting the odds and ends. Two thousand pounds! Two thousand pounds theirs of right, and yet they might not touch it because both of them were living!

How many hours they spent discussing the matter with each other could never be told. As soon as twilight came on, wherever they might be and whatever the occupation, the theme was sure to be drifted into. In the dining-room when it grew too dark for Dr. Rane to pursue his writing; in the drawing-room, into which Bessy would wile him, and sing to him one of her simple songs; walking together, arm within arm, in the garden paths, the stars in the summer sky above them, the waving trees round about them, the subject of the tontine would be taken up: the tontine; nothing but the tontine. No wonder that they grew to form plans of what they would do if the money were theirs: we all know how apt we are to let imagination run away with us, and to indulge visions that seem to become almost realities. Dr.

Rane sketched a bright future, With two thousand pounds in hand, he could establish himself in a first-rate metropolitan locality, set up well, both professionally and socially; and there would be plenty of money for him and his wife to live upon whilst the practice was growing. Bessy entered into it all as eagerly as he. Having become accustomed to the idea of quitting Dallory, she never glanced at the possibility of remaining there. She thought his eager wish, his unalterable determination to leave it, was connected only with the interests of his profession; he knew that the dread of a certain possible discovery, ever haunting his conscience, made the place more intolerable to him day by day. At any cost he must get away from it: at any cost. There was a great happiness in these evening conversations, in the glowing hopes presented by plans and projects. But, where was the use of indulging in them, when the tontine money—the pivot on which all was to turn—could never be theirs? As often as this damping recollection brought them up with a check, Dr. Rane would fall into gloomy silence. Gradually, by the very force of thinking, he saw a way, or thought he saw a way, by which their hopes might be accomplished. And that was to induce the trustees to advance the money at once to him and his wife jointly.

Meanwhile the strike continued with unabated force. Not a man was at work; every one refused to do a stroke unless he could be paid for it what he thought right, and left off his daily labour! when he chose. One, might have supposed, by the independence of the demands, that the men were the masters, North and Gass the servants. Privation was beginning to reign, garments grow scanty, faces pale and pinched. There was not so much as a sixpence for superfluities: and under that head in troubled times must be classed the attendance of a medical man. It will readily be understood, therefore, that this state of affairs did not contribute to the income of Dr. Rane.

One day, Mr. North, sitting on the short green bench in front of his choicest carnation bed, found two loving hands put round his neck from behind. He had been three parts asleep, and woke up slightly bewildered.

"Bessy, child, is it you?"

It was Mrs. Rane. Her footfall on the grass had not been heard. She wore a cool print dress and a black silk mantle; and her plain straw bonnet looked charming, around the pretty falling curls. Bessy looked quiet and simple at all times: and always a lady.

"Did I startle you, papa?"

"No, my dear. When I felt the arms, I thought it was Mary Dallory. She comes upon me without warning sometimes. Here's room, Bessy."

She sat down beside him. It was a very hot morning, and Bessy unfastened the strings of her bonnet. There was a slight look of weariness on her face as if she were just a little worried with home cares. In truth she felt so: but all for Oliver's sake. If the money did not come in so freely as to make matters easy, she did not mind it for herself, but for him.

"Papa, I have come to talk to you," she began, laying one of her hands affectionately on his knee. "It is about the tontine money. Oliver thinks that it might be paid to us conjointly; that it ought to be."

"I know he does," replied Mr. North. "It can't be done, Bessy."

Her countenance fell a little. "Do you think not, papa?"

"I am sure not, child."

"Papa, I am here this morning to beg you to use your interest with Sir Thomas Ticknell. Oliver knows nothing about my coming. He said last night, when we were talking, that if you could be induced to throw your influence into the scale, the bank might listen to you. So I thought that I would come to you in the morning and ask."

"The bank won't listen to me, or to any one else, in this matter, Bessy. It's illegal to pay the tontine money over while two of you are living, and the Ticknells are too strict to risk it. I shouldn't do it myself in their places."

"What Oliver says is this, papa. The money must, in the course of events, come to either him or me, whichever of us survives the other. We have therefore an equal interest in it, and possess at present an equal chance of succeeding to it. No one else in the wide world, but our two selves, has the smallest claim to it, or ever can have. We are the only survivors of the ten; the rest are all dead. Why, then, should the trustees not stretch a point and let us have the money while it can be of use to us conjointly? Oliver says they ought to do it."

"I know he does," remarked Mr. North.

"Has Oliver spoken to you, papa?"

"No," said Mr. North. "I heard about it from Dick. Dick happened to be at the bank yesterday, and Thomas Ticknell mentioned to him that Dr. Rane had been urging this request upon them. Dick said Sir Thomas seemed quite horrified at the proposition; they had told Dr. Rane, in answer, that if they could consent to such a thing it would be no better than a fraud."

"So they did," replied Bessy. "When Oliver was relating it to me after he came home, he could not help laughing—in spite of his vexation. The money is virtually ours, so where would the fraud lie?"

"To be virtually yours is one thing, Bessy; to be legally yours is another. You young women can't be expected to understand business problems, my dear; but your husband understands them. Of course it would be a great boon to get the two thousand pounds whilst you are both together; but it would not be legal for the bankers to do it, and they are right in refusing it."

"Then—do you think there is no chance for us, papa?"

"Not the least chance, child."

A silence ensued. Mr. North sat watching his carnations, Bessy watching, with far-off gaze, the dark-blue summer sky. In spite of her father's opinion, she thought the brothers, Thomas and William Ticknell, unduly hard.

The Ticknells were the chief bankers of Whitborough. Upon the institution of the tontines, the two brothers, then in their early prime, had been made trustees to it, in conjunction with a gentleman named Wilson. In the course of time, Mr. Wilson died: and Thomas and William Ticknell grew into tolerably aged men; they wanted now not much of the allotted three score years and ten. The elder brother had gone up to court with some great local matter, and he came back Sir Thomas. These two gentlemen had full power over the funds of the tontine. They were straightforward, honourable men; of dispositions naturally cautious; and holding very strict opinions in business. Increasing years had not tended to lessen caution, or to soften strict tenets: and when Dr. Rane, soliciting a private interview with the brothers, presented himself before them with a proposition that they should pay over the tontine money to him and his wife conjointly, without waiting for the death of either, the few hairs remaining on the old gentlemen's white heads rose up on end.

Truly it had seemed to them, this singular application, as touching closely upon fraud. Dr. Rane argued the matter with them, putting it in the most feasible and favourable light: and it must be acknowledged that, to his mind, it appeared a thing not only that they might do, but that it would be perfectly right and honest to do. All in vain; they heard him with courtesy, but were harder than adamant. Richard North happened to go in upon some business soon after the conclusion of the interview, and the brothers— they were the bankers of North and Gass—told him confidentially of the application. Richard imparted it to his father: hence Mr. North heard Bessy without surprise.

Regarded from the narrow, legal point of view, of course the Messrs. Ticknell might be right; but, taking it broadly and comprehensively, there could be no doubt that it seemed hard upon Oliver Rane and his wife. The chief question that had presented itself to Richard North's mind was: if the money were handed over now, would the Messrs. Ticknell be quite secure from ulterior consequences? They said not. Upon Richard North's suggesting that a lawyer might be consulted on the point, Sir Thomas Ticknell answered that, no matter what a lawyer might say, they should never incur the responsibility of parting with the tontine money so long as two of its members were living. "And I think they must be right," Richard remarked afterwards to his father. Turning to Bessy, sitting by him on the bench, Mr. North repeated this. Bessy listened in dutiful silence, but shook her head.

"Papa, much as I respect Richard's judgment, clever as I know him to be, I am sure he is wrong here. It is very strange that he should go against me and Oliver."

"It is because of that same good judgment, my dear," replied Mr. North simply. "I'd trust it against the world, on account of his impartiality. When he has to decide between two opposite opinions, he invariably puts himself, or tries to put himself, in either place, weighs each side, and comes to an unbiassed conclusion. Look at this present strike: Dick has been reproached with leaning to the men's side, with holding familiar argument with them, for and against; a thing that few masters would do: but it is because he sees they really believe they have right on their side, and he would treat their opinions with respect, however mistaken he may know them to be."

"Richard cannot think the men are not to blame!" exclaimed Mrs. Rane.

"He lays the blame chiefly where, as he says, it is due—on the Trade Union. The men were deluded into listening to it at first; and they can't help obeying its dictates now. They have given themselves over to it, body and soul, Bessy, and can no more escape from it than a prisoner from a dungeon. That's Richard's view, mind; and it makes him lenient; I'd try and bring them to their senses in a different way, if I had the power and the means left me."

"In what way, papa?"

"Bessy, if I were what I once was—a wealthy man, independent of business—I'd close the works for good: break them up: burn them if necessary: anything but reopen them. The trade should go where it would, and the men after it; or stay here and starve, just as they chose. I would never have my peace of life worried out of me by these strikes; or let men that I have employed and always done liberally by dictate to me. They'll find it out, Bessy, to their cost, as sure as that we two are sitting here."

Mr. North seized the hoe that was resting beside the bench, and struck it lightly on the ground. Meaning no doubt to give emphasis to his words. Bessy Rane passed from the subject of the strike to that which more immediately concerned her.

"Richard is honest, papa; he would never say what he did not think; but he may be mistaken sometimes. I cannot understand how he can think the Ticknells right in refusing to let us have the money. If there were the slightest, smallest reason for their keeping it back, it would be different: but there is none."

"See here, Bessy. If they go by the strict letter of the law, they cannot do it. The tontine deed was drawn up as tightly as any deed can be: it expressly says that nine of the members must be dead, and only the tenth remaining, before the money can be withdrawn from its investment. The Ticknells can't get over this."

"Papa—forgive me—you should not say can't, but won't," spoke Mrs. Rane. "They can do it if they please; there is nothing to prevent it. All power lies with them; they are responsible to none. If they paid over the money to Oliver tomorrow, not an individual in the whole world could call them to account for it. The strictest judge on the bench could not say to them afterwards, You have paid away money that you had no right to pay."

"Stop, Bessy—that's just where the weak point lies. The Ticknells say that if they parted with the money now, they might be called upon again for it at some future time."

Bessy sat in amazement. "Why! How could that be?"

"Dick put it somehow in this way, my dear: that is, Thomas Ticknell put it to him. If you should die, Bessy, leaving your husband a widower with children: or, for the matter of that, if he should die, leaving you with some: those children might come upon the Ticknells for the money over again. Or Rane might come upon them, if he were the one left; or you, if you were. It was in that way, I think Dick said; but my memory is not as clear as it used to be."

"As if we should be so dishonourable! Besides—there could be no possibility of claiming the money twice over. Having received it once, the Ticknells would hold our receipt for it."

Mr. North shook his head. "The law is full of quips and quibbles, Bessy. If the trustees paid over this money to you and your husband now, contrary to the provisions of the tontine deed, I suppose it is at least a nice question whether the survivor could not compel them to pay it again."

Bessy held her breath. "Do you think they could be compelled, papa?"

"Well, I don't know, Bessy. I fancy perhaps they might be. Dick says they are right, as prudent men, to refuse. One thing you and Oliver may rest assured of, my dear—that, under the doubt, the Ticknells will never be persuaded to do it as long as oak and ash grow."

Bessy Rane sighed, and began to tie her bonnet. She had no idea that paying the money would involve the trustees in any liability, real or fancied, and hope went out of her from that moment. By nature she was as just as Richard; and she could not henceforth even wish that the bankers should incur the risk.

"Dick's indoors, my dear, if you'd like to ask him what Thomas Ticknell said; he would explain it to you better than I have. No hurry now, to be off in a morning: there are no works open to go to."

"I have heard enough, papa; I quite understand it now," was Mrs. Rane's answer. "It will be a dreadful disappointment to Oliver when he hears that no chance, or hope, is left. It would have been—oh such a help to us."

"He is not getting on very well, is he, Bessy?"

"No. Especially since the strike set in. The men can't pay."

"Seeley must feel it as well as Oliver."

"Not half as much; not a quarter. His practice chiefly lies amongst the richer classes. Well, we must have patience. As Oliver says, Fortune does not seem to smile upon us just now."

"If I could put a hundred-pound note, or so, into your hand, whilst these bad times are being tided over, I'd do it, Bessy, with all my heart. But I can't. Tell Oliver so. The strike is bringing us no end of embarrassment, and I don't know where it will end. It was bad enough before, as you remember, Bessy: but we always had Richard as a refuge."

"Richard will take care of you still, papa; don't be troubled; in some way or other, I am sure he will. As to ourselves, we are young, and can wait for the good time coming."

Very cheerily she spoke. And perhaps felt so. Bessy's gentle nature held a great deal of sunshine.

"I wonder Oliver's mother does not help him," remarked Mr. North.

"She would gladly do it, papa, but she lives up to every farthing of her income: beyond it, I fancy, sometimes. She is accustomed to luxuries, and her travelling about costs a good deal. Mrs. Cumberland is not one to economize, or to put up with small lodgings and discomforts on her different sojourns. Sometimes, as you know, she posts: it is easier, she says; and that is expensive."

"You'll come in, won't you, Bessy?" said Mr. North as she rose. "Miss Field and Matilda were sitting in the hall just now; it is the coolest place in the house."

She hesitated for a moment, and then walked on by his side. Mrs. Rane's visits to the Hall were rare. Madam had not been cordial with her since her marriage; and she had never once condescended to enter Bessy's home.

The hall was empty. Bessy was about to enter the drawing-room in search of Matilda, when the door opened and madam appeared. Madam started haughtily, stepped back, and shut the door in Bessy's face. Next moment, a hand was extended over Bessy's shoulder, and threw it wide.

"By your leave, madam," said Richard North calmly. "Room for my sister."

He marshalled her in as though she had been a duchess. Madam, drawing her lace shawl round her shoulders, swept majestically out, vouchsafing neither word nor look. It was nothing more than the contempt often dealt to Bessy: but Richard's blood went up in a boil.

That the trustees' refusal to part with the funds of the tontine was irrevocable, there could be no doubt about: nevertheless, Oliver Rane declined to see it. The matter got wind, as nearly everything else seemed to do in Dallory, and many people took his part. It was a frightful shame, they thought, that a man and his wife could not enjoy together the money that was their due, but must wait for one or the other's death before they received it. Jelly's tongue made itself particularly busy. Dr. Rane was not a favourite of hers on the whole, but she espoused his cause warmly in this.

"It's such a temptation," remarked Jelly to a select few, one night at Ketler's, whither she had betaken herself to blow up the man for continuing to keep out on strike, to which movement Jelly was a determined foe.

"A temptation?" rejoined Tim Wilks respectfully, who made one of her audience. "In what way, Miss Jelly?"

"In what way," retorted Jelly with scorn. "Why in the way of stealing the money, if it's to be got at; or of punching those two old bankers' heads. When a man's kept out of his own through nothing but some crotchet, it's enough to make him feel desperate, Tim Wilks."

"So it is," acquiesced meek Timothy.

"If my mistress withheld my wages from me—which is twenty pounds a-year, and her left-off silks—I should fight, I know: perhaps take them. And this is two thousand pounds."

"Two thousand pounds!" ejaculated honest Ketler in low tones of reverence, as he lifted his hands. "And for the doctor to be kept out of it because his wife's not dead! It is a shame."

"I wouldn't say, either, but it might bring another sort of temptation to some men, besides those mentioned by Miss Jelly," put in Timothy Wilks with hesitation.

"And pray what would that be?" demanded Jelly tartly—for she made it a point to keep Timothy under before company.

"The putting his wife out of the way on purpose to get the money, Miss Jelly," spoke Tim with deprecation. And the words caused a sudden pause.

"You—you don't mean murdering her!" shrieked Mrs. Ketler, who was a timid woman and given to being startled.

"Yes I did," replied Timothy Wilks. "Some might be found to do it. No offence to Dr. Rane. I'm putting the possible case of a bad man; not of him."

CHAPTER IX

AT THE SEASIDE

The summer was slowly passing. At a small and obscure seaside place on the East coast Mrs. Cumberland was located. She had engaged part of one of the few good houses there—houses that let at an enormous price in the season to visitors—and lived in it with Ellen Adair, and her maid to wait on her. Not Jelly this time, but the housemaid Ann. The interior of Mrs. Cumberland's own house at Dallory was being painted during her absence. She had deemed it well to leave Jelly in charge: and brought Ann instead.

They had been in this place, Eastsea, for some weeks now; and Ellen privately believed that this sojourn was never coming to an end. Any thing more wearisome than it was to her, could not have been found. Arthur Bohun was in London at his uncle's, where he had been staying for some time. It was several weeks since he and Ellen had met: to her it seemed as many months. James Bohun was still ill, but fluctuated much; at one time appearing to be beyond recovery, at another as if he were almost well again. He would not part with Arthur; Sir Nash said he must not think of leaving. Under the circumstances, Arthur did not see his way clear to getting away.

Another person was fluctuating. And that was Mrs. Cumberland. Her complaint, connected with the heart, was one of those that may snap life suddenly, or allow it to be prolonged for years. That she was gradually growing worse, was undoubted; but it was by almost imperceptible degrees. No change could be noted from day to day; it was only by comparing her present state with what it had been three, six, or twelve months before, that the change could be seen. Sometimes, for days together, she would feel very ill, be quite unable to quit her room; and again she would have an interval of ease, almost of seeming recovery, and walk and drive out daily. Dr. Rane had come over twice to see his mother: staying on each occasion only a few hours. His opinion was, that she might yet, with care, live for years; and probably many years. At the same time, he knew that there could be no certainty of it.

It was during this sojourn at Eastsea that Mrs. Cumberland received news from Mr. Adair. He wrote in answer to Mrs. Cumberland's letter—the first of the two letters already alluded to—wherein she had spoken of the probability of Ellen's being sought in marriage by a gentleman in every way desirable, but in which she had omitted, probably from inadvertence, to mention the gentleman's name. Mr. Adair's answer, now received, was to the effect that—fully relying on Mrs. Cumberland's judgment—he could not desire better for his daughter than that so suitable a marriage should be entered into; and accorded it his cordial consent.

But this involved a most unhappy contretemps: of which no one as yet was, or could be, conscious. That first letter of Mrs. Cumberland's had alluded to Mr. Graves: she imagined this consent to apply to Arthur Bohun. It takes time, as every one knows, for a letter to reach Australia from England and an answer to be returned. Whether, during those intervening weeks, Mrs. Cumberland actually forgot that her first letter had applied to Mr. Graves: or whether in her invalid state, memory had grown confused, and she remembered only the last letter, must ever remain a question. Certain it was, that she accepted this present approbation of Mr. Adair's as applying to Arthur Bohun. It might be, that she had altogether forgotten having written about Mr. Graves.

With her usual reticence, she said nothing to Ellen Adair. Not a word. Time enough for that when Arthur Bohun should speak—if he ever did speak. She held the consent ready for use if necessity ever required it: and was at ease.

"Ellen, how listless you seem!"

Ellen Adair looked up, faintly blushing at the abrupt charge, which came from Mrs. Cumberland.

"Listless!" exclaimed Ellen.

"My dear, it is nothing less. I don't think you care for Eastsea."

"Not very much. At least—it is rather dull."

"Well, I suppose you can only find it so; confined to the house half my time, as I am. At Niton you had often Captain Bohun to go out with; now you have to go out alone."

Ellen turned away, a soft blush rising to her face at the remembrance of Niton, "Shall you be going home soon, do you think, Mrs. Cumberland?" she asked.

"Oh dear no. I had a note from Jelly this morning, and she says the house is not half ready. Workpeople are so lazy! Once you get them into a place you can't get them out again. But if Jelly were ready for us I should still not go. This air is doing me good on the whole. Perhaps I shall remain the winter here."

Ellen's heart fell within her. All the autumn in this place, that verily seemed to her the fag end of the world, and all the winter! Should she ever again get the chance of seeing her heart's love, Arthur Bohun? And he?—perhaps he was forgetting her.

"Do you feel well enough to come out, Mrs. Cumberland?"

"No. I am sorry, Ellen, but you must go alone. Put on your things at once, child: the afternoon will be passing."

Ellen sighed. It was of no moment to her whether she went out or stayed in: she obeyed mechanically, and went forth. Quite alone. Generally speaking Ann attended her, but the servant was this afternoon wanted by her mistress.

The sunshine played on the clear blue sea, ever changing its lovely hues, as the light autumn clouds floated above it in the sky. Ellen Adair sat in a sheltered spot and watched it. It was her favourite seat: one hewn out of the rocks, and apparently frequented only by herself, as she had never yet been disturbed in it. Excepting the small strip of beach before her, nothing was to be seen from it but sea and sky. Overhead, she could hear the children's voices at play: the tide below was coming in with gentle monotony. Ellen had a book with her, and she had her diary; she had read a few pages in the one, she had written some lines in pencil in the other: and so the hours passed, and she was utterly dreary. The weary day was only the type of the other weary days that at present made up the sum total of her life.

"Will it ever come to an end?" she murmured, having watched a tiny pleasure-boat shoot past and disappear, leaving her to her silent solitude. "Shall we ever get back to Dallory Ham, and—the friends who live there? I suppose a winter might be got through and survived in this place, but—"

A gentleman in deep mourning walking on the strip of beach, looking to right and left. Ellen's thoughts were summarily ended, and she rose with a faint cry: the cry of intense joy that in its sound is so near akin to that of exquisite pain.

For it was no other than Captain Arthur Bohun. He had not heard it; but he saw her; it was for her he had been searching: and he turned with an outstretched hand. For a moment she felt utterly bewildered, half doubting the reality of the vision. But oh yes, it was he; it was he! The sea and sky, the rocks, and the monotony—all had changed into paradise.

"How do you do, Ellen?"

Nothing more than this commonplace greeting was spoken. They stood in silence, their hands clasped. His lips were quivering slightly, proving how ardent was the feeling that stirred him at their renewed meeting; Ellen, blushing and paling by turns, was agitated almost to pain. Sitting down quietly by her side on the ledge of rock he accounted for his unexpected appearance. On his arrival at Eastsea that afternoon, he had gone at once to call at Mrs. Cumberland's. Ann said her mistress was lying down, and that Miss Adair was on the beach.

"Did you think I was never coming to see you, Ellen? I thought so. I could not get away from my uncle's whilst James was so ill."

"Is he—dead?" hesitated Ellen, looking pointedly at the black clothes.

"Oh no. It is a cousin of Sir Nash's and of my father's who is dead: a very old man who has lived for years in the South of France. James Bohun is very much better."

"I thought, by the deep mourning, it must be."

"Is it deep? I suppose it looks so. I should not wish it otherwise in the present instance, for the good old man has been generous to me."

They fell into silence, each feeling the rapture of the other's presence, after the prolonged separation, as something more than human. So intense was it that Ellen, at least, might have been content to die in it there and then. The sea changed its beautiful colours, the sky seemed to smile on them, the children played overhead, a silvery flute from some unseen boat in the distance was softly playing. No: Eden could never have been sweeter than this.

"What have you been doing, all this time by yourself at Eastsea?" he at length asked her.

"Very much what I am doing now, I think—sitting here to watch the sea," she answered. "There has been nothing else to do. It was always dull."

"Has Mrs. Cumberland had any visitors?"

"Dr. Rane has been here twice. He gives a bad account of things at Dallory. The strike shows no signs of coming to an end; and the men are in want."

"So Dick says. I get a letter from him sometimes."

A great amount of talking, this. The tide turned; a big steamer went by in the distance.

"Do you hear that, Ellen?"

A man's soft tenor voice had struck up a love-song overhead: "Ellen Adair," Robin Adair, as the world more often has it. Arthur Bohun used to hear it sung as "Ellin Adair," when he was recovering from his wound in Ireland; the Irish insisted on it that so it was in the original song; and he had sometimes asked Ellen to sing it so for him since. The children ceased their play; the verses went on, and these two below the rocks, unseen, listened to the end, catching every word distinctly.

"Yet her I loved so well,
Still in my heart shall dwell.
Oh! I shall ne'er forget
Ellen Adair."

"Nor I," softly spoke Arthur, as the refrain died away.

Mrs. Cumberland was up when they got in. Ann had told her of Captain Bohun's appearance and that he had gone to find Miss Adair. Mrs. Cumberland took a few minutes for consideration, and then decided on her course of conduct, and that was to speak to Captain Bohun.

It might have been all very well, whilst she was armed with no authority, tacitly to countenance Captain Bohun's frequent visits; but now that she had authority, she deemed it right, in justice to Ellen, to take a different standing. If Captain Bohun had serious intentions, well and good; if not, she should request him to bring the intimacy to a close. Feeling the responsibility that lay upon her as the sole guardian in Europe of Ellen Adair, she thought she should be justified in saying so much, for, unless Arthur Bohun proposed to make the young lady his wife, it was cruel to allow her to fall in love with him.

When Mrs. Cumberland once made her mind up to any resolve, she did not usually lose time in putting it into practice, and she lost none here. Taking the opportunity this same evening, when Ellen was out of the room; sent from it by herself on some errand of excuse; she spoke to Captain Bohun.

But the most fastidious man living could not have taken exception to what she said. She spoke quite as a lady. Captain Bohun's appearance that day at Eastsea—coupled with the remembrance of his frequent sojourns at Niton when they were staying there, and his constant visits to her house at Dallory Ham— had revived a faint idea that had sometimes presented itself to her mind, namely, that he might be growing attached to Ellen Adair. Mrs. Cumberland did not wish to enlarge on this point; it might be, or it might not be; Captain Bohun si! one knew; perhaps she was wholly mistaken; all she wished to say was this—that if Captain Bohun had no future thoughts in regard to Miss Adair, she must request him to terminate his intimacy at once. When she returned to Dallory Ham she should be glad to see him at her house occasionally, just as any other visitor; but nothing more.

To this Arthur Bohun answered candidly enough. He did like Ellen Adair; if circumstances permitted he should be only too glad to make her his wife; but, as Mrs. Cumberland knew, he had hitherto been very poor. As he pleased, Mrs. Cumberland remarked; the matter was entirely for his own consideration; she did not attempt to press it, one way or the other; if he saw no chance of his circumstances improving, he should freely say so, and terminate his visits; she could not allow Ellen to be played with. And upon that, Arthur begged to have the night for reflection; he would see Mrs. Cumberland in the morning, and give her his decision.

So it was left. When Ellen returned to the room—unsuspicious of what had been said during her few minutes' absence from it—Captain Bohun took his departure. Arrived at the hotel where he had put up, he devoted himself to the consideration of the grave question, weighing it in all its bearings as fairly as his love for Ellen allowed him to do. Of course that biassed him.

He had sufficient to marry upon now. By the death of the relative for whom he was in mourning, he had come into about eight hundred a-year. With his own income, that made twelve. Quite sufficient to begin upon, though he was a Bohun. But—there were deterring considerations. In some way, as he suspected, his mother, in her fear of Ellen Adair, had contrived to instil a suspicion in the mind of Sir Nash, that Arthur, unless he were closely controlled, might be making a mésalliance. Sir Nash possessed all the pride of the Bohuns, and it frightened him. He spoke to Arthur, telling him that unless he married with the full approval of his family, he should never succeed to the estates. No, nor to the title if he could help it. If James died, he, Sir Nash, would marry first, and leave direct heirs.

This, it was, that now interfered with Arthur's decision. One fact was known to him—that James Bohun, since this illness set in, had joined his father in cutting off the entail, so that the threat of leaving the estates away from Arthur (even though he succeeded to the title) could be easily accomplished. What was to be done? Part with Ellen Adair he could not. Oh, if he might only make her his wife without the world knowing it; the world abroad, and the world at home! Might this be? Very slowly Arthur Bohun arrived at a conclusion—that the only plan, if Mrs. Cumberland and Ellen would accede to it, was to have a private marriage.

Arguments are so easy when inclination goes with them. The future looks very much as we ourselves paint it. They might be married at once, here at Eastsea. If James Bohun recovered and lived, why, there could be no question about the title or the estates lapsing to Arthur, and he might avow his marriage as soon as he pleased. If James died, he should not, as he really believed, have to conceal it long, for he thought Sir Nash's life quite as precarious as James's. A few months, perhaps a few weeks, and he might be able to tell the world that Ellen was his wife. He felt an inclination to whisper it beforehand to his good friend and aunt, Miss Bohun. But, he must first of all ascertain from Mrs. Cumberland what was the social standing of Mr. Adair. Unless he were undeniably a gentleman, Ellen could be no fit wife for a Bohun. Arthur, swayed by his love, had hitherto been content to take this fact for granted; now he saw the necessity of ascertaining it more certainly. It was not that he had any real doubt, but it was only right to make sure.

Mr. Adair held some post under the British Government, formerly in India, for a long time now in Australia. His wife had died young; his only child, Ellen, had been sent to a first-rate school in England for her education. Upon its completion, Mr. Adair had begged Mrs. Cumberland to receive her; he had some thought of returning home himself, so that he did not wish Ellen to go out to him. An impression was afloat in Dallory that Ellen Adair would inherit a fortune; also that Mrs. Cumberland received liberal remuneration for the expenses of the young lady. These generalities Arthur Bohun already knew; but he knew no more.

He paid the promised visit to Mrs. Cumberland in the morning. Ellen was on the beach with the maid; there was no interruption, and their conversation was long and confidential. Heaven alone knew how Arthur Bohun succeeded in making Mrs. Cumberland believe in the necessity for a private marriage. He did succeed. But he used no subterfuge. He frankly told of the prejudice his mother had taken against Ellen Adair, and that she had gained the ear of Sir Nash. In short, the same arguments he had used to himself the previous evening, he urged now. Mrs. Cumberland—naturally biassed against madam for the injury she had striven to work upon Dr. Rane—thought it a frightful shame that she should also strive to destroy the happiness and prospects of her own son Arthur, and sympathized with him warmly. It was this feeling that rendered her more easy than she would otherwise have been—in short, that made her give her consent to Arthur's plan. To counteract the bitter wrong contemplated by Mrs. North, she considered would be a merit on Arthur's part, instead of a sin. And then, when things were so far settled, and the speedy marriage determined on, Mrs. Cumberland astonished Captain Bohun by putting Mr. Adair's letter into his hands, explaining how it came to be received, and what she had written to that gentleman to call it forth. "So that her father's blessing will rest on the marriage," remarked Mrs. Cumberland; "but for that fact, I could not have consented to a private one."

This gave Arthur the opportunity to ask about the position of Mr. Adair, which, in the heat of argument, he had been forgetting. Certainly he was a gentleman, Mrs. Cumberland answered, and of very good Scotch family. Major Bohun, Mr. Adair, and her own husband, George Cumberland, had been firm friends in India at the time of Major Bohun's death. She could not help thinking, she added in conclusion, that it was the remembrance of that early friendship which induced Mr. Adair to give so ready and cordial a consent to his daughter's union with Major Bohun's son.

And so there the matter ended, all couleur-de-rose; Arthur believing that there could be no possible objection to his marrying Ellen Adair; nay, that the way had been most markedly paved for it through this letter of Mr. Adair's; Mrs. Cumberland deeming that she was not indiscreet in permitting the marriage to be a private one. Both were unsuspicious as the day. He, that there existed any real objection; she, that Mr. Adair's consent applied to a very different man from Arthur Bohun.

Captain Bohun went out from Mrs. Cumberland's in search of Ellen, with the light of love flushing his cheeks. He found her in the same sheltered spot, hedged in from the gaze of the world. Again alone. The servant had gone to the shops, to buy ribbon. Their salutations hitherto had been nothing but decorum and formality, as witness that of the previous day.

"Good-morning," said Ellen, rising and holding out her hand.

Instead of taking it, he took herself. Took her in his arms with a cry of long-repressed emotion, and laid her sweet face upon his breast, kissing it with impassioned kisses. Ellen, utterly astonished, could not escape.

"Do not shrink from me, Ellen. You are to be my wife."

CHAPTER X

A LAST PROPOSAL

Affairs grew more unsatisfactory at Dallory as the weeks went on. The strike continued; the men utterly refusing to return to work except on their own terms, or, rather, the Trades' Union refusing to allow them to do so. Supplies became more scanty. If not actual famine, something near to it began to reign. North Inlet, once so prosperous, looked like a half-starved place out at elbows. Oh, what senseless folly it was! What would it end in? Mrs. Gass had grown tired of going amongst the men to reason with them and try to bring them to their senses; but Miss Dallory still went. Miss Dallory could make no impression whatever. The men were moody, miserable, almost starved. They would gladly have gone back to work again almost on no pay at all, only as a relief to the present idleness; but they belonged to the famous Trades' Union now, and must obey its dictates. Mary Dallory grew angry sometimes, and asked whether they were men, or cravens, that they had no pity for their poor helpless children.

One day Mrs. Gass and Miss Dallory went forth together. Not of premeditation. One of Ketler's children was ill and weakly, incipient consumption, Dr. Rane said; she was a sweet little child, mild and gentle; and Miss Dallory would sometimes carry her strengthening things. It was a terrible shame, she would tell Ketler, that he should let even this poor sickly child starve: and Ketler humbly acknowledged to his own heart that the child was starving; and felt it keenly. The man was as well-meaning a man as Heaven ever sent into the world; anxious to do his duty: but he had signed himself a member of the Trades' Union, and was helpless.

Miss Dallory wore a print gown, and was altogether a great deal less fine than Jelly. She carried a small basket in her hand, containing fresh eggs. As she passed Mrs. Gass's that lady was standing at her open parlour window, in all the glory of a gorgeous green satin robe, and white bonnet with bird-of-paradise feather. She dearly loved fine clothes, and saw no reason why she should not wear them.

"Where be you bound to, my dear?" asked the grandly-dressed lady, as Mary stopped.

"I am taking these eggs to little Cissy Ketler. Mrs. Gass, what is to become of all the poor children if this state of things should last much longer?"

"I'm sure I don't know. It goes again' the grain to see 'em want; but when we give 'em food or helps it's just so much premium offered to the father's incorrigible obstinacy and idleness, my dear."

"But the child is ill," said Mary Dallory. "And so are many other children."

"They'll be worse before long. My dear, I was not talking at you, in saying that. But I don't see where it's all to end. We can't set up hospitals for the women and children, even with the best will to do it. And the will, I, for one, have not. Once get their wives and children took care of, and the men would lead the lives of gentlemen to the end o' the chapter. Here; I'll walk with you, my dear; and we can talk going along."

She came forth, drawing on her lemon-coloured gloves: and they went towards Ketler's. North Inlet looked deserted to-day. Not a man was lounging in it. The few stragglers to be seen were walking briskly in the direction of the works; as if they had business on hand, and were without their pipes. Mrs. Gass arrested one who was passing her.

"What's up, Dawson?"

"We've been called together, ma'am, to meet Mr. Richard North. He have som'at to say to us. Happen, maybe, he's a-going to give in at last."

"Is he!" retorted Mrs. Gass. "I don't think you need worrit your inside with that idea, Dawson. It's a deal more likely that he's going to warn you he'll sell the works out and out—if he can get any fool to buy 'em."

The man passed on. Mrs. Gass, as she turned to Miss Dallory, gave a flourish with her small white lace parasol and a toss to the bird-of-paradise.

"Had anybody told me men could be so obstinate, in regard to thinking themselves in the right, I'd never have believed it: but seeing's believing. My dear, suppose we just step on to the works, and learn what matter Mr. Richard has in hand."

The men, going in at the iron gates, branched round to their own entrance. Mrs. Gass took Miss Dallory to a private one. It led at once into what might now be called the audience chamber, for Richard North was already haranguing the men in it: a long and rather narrow room, with a counter running across it. It used to be the pay-room of the men: perhaps some of them, entering now, recalled those prosperous days with a sigh. Richard North did not see the ladies come in. He stood with his back to them, in his usual everyday attire, a plain black frock-coat and grey trousers. His hands rested on the counter as he talked to the men, who faced him on the other side; a crowd of them, all with attentive countenances. Mrs. Gass signed to Miss Dallory to halt; not to conceal themselves from Richard, but simply lest their advance should interrupt what he was saying. And so they remained listening, Richard unconscious that he had any other audience than his workpeople.

The matter was this. A contract had just been offered to North and Gass. It was a very large one, and would certainly, if accepted, keep the men employed for some time. It was offered at a certain price. Richard North made his calculations and found that he could accept it, provided the men would work on the former terms: but he could not if the rate of wages had to be raised. Considering the present hopeless condition of the men, imagining that they must have had very nearly sufficient experience of idleness and empty cupboards to bring them to reason, he determined to lay the proposal before them—that they might accept or reject it. In a clear and concise manner he stated this, and the men heard him respectfully to the end. One of them then advanced a few steps before the rest, and answered. Answered without the smallest deliberation; without so much as a pretence of inquiring what the feelings of his fellows might be.

"We can't do it, sir."

Richard North raised his hand for silence, as if the man had spoken before his time.

"Do you fully understand the case in all its bearings?" resumed Richard: "if not, take time to reflect until you do understand it. Look at it well; take into consideration the future as well as the present. Listen again. This contract has been offered me: it is a good one, as you must know. It will set our works going again; it will be the means of bringing back the business that seems to be drifting more hopelessly away from us day by day. It will provide you with, employment, with wages that you not so long ago thought liberal; and will place you again in what may be called prosperity—great prosperity as compared with what exists at present. Your homes may be homes of plenty again, your children have sufficient food. In short, both to you and to me, this contract offers just the turn of the tide. I wish to accept it: I see nothing but ruin before my father and myself if I cannot do so: what I see before you I do not care to speak of, if you are not wise enough to see it for yourselves. The decision lies with you, unfortunately; I wish it lay with myself. Shall I take it, or shall I not?"

"We couldn't return at them rate of wages, nohow," spoke up a voice from the crowd.

"It is the last chance that I shall offer you," proceeded Richard. "For your sakes I would strongly advise you to take it. Heaven is my witness that I am honest in saying 'for your sakes.' We have been associated together for many years, and I cannot see the breaking up of old ties without first using every effort to re-unite them. I must give my answer tomorrow, and accept this work or reject it. Little time is allowed me for decision, therefore I am unable to give much to you. Virtually the acceptance or rejection lies with you; for, without you, I could not fulfil it: but I cannot help a remark in passing, that for such a state of things to exist argues something rotten at the core in the relations between master and men. At six o'clock tomorrow morning the great bell shall be rung, calling you to work as formerly. My men, I hope you will all respond to it."

No, not at the terms offered, was the answer gathered by Richard North from the buzz that rose around.

"I cannot offer you better. I have said that this is the last chance," repeated Richard. "I shall never give you the option of working for me again."

The men couldn't help that. The fact was, they only half believed it. One ventured a supposition that if the works were sold, the new firm might give them work on new terms.

"No," said Richard North. "I am very different from you, my men. You see work at your very hand, and will not do it. You look forward to the future with, as I must suppose, easy apathy, giving neither care nor anxiety as to how you and your families are to live. I, on the contrary, am only anxious to work; at a reduced rate of profit, on a smaller scale if it must be; but, any way, to work. Night after night I lie awake, tormented with lively apprehensions for the future. What seemed, when you first turned out, to be a mere temporary stoppage, that reason and good sense on both our sides could not fail to rectify, has assumed gigantic proportions and a permanent aspect. After some time I gave way; offering to split the difference, as to wages, if you would return—"

"But we wanted the whole," came an interruption. "And you didn't give way as to time."

"I could not do either," said Richard North firmly. "I offered all I was able. That is a thing of the past: let it go. I now make you this last and final offer; and I think it only fair to tell you what my course will be if you reject it. I shall go over to Belgium and see if I cannot engage Belgian workmen to come here and take your places."

A dead silence fell on the room. Ketler broke it.

"You'd surely not do that, sir!"

"Not do it! Why, you force it upon me. I must either get a new set of men, or give up the works entirely. As I do not feel inclined to the latter course, the former alone is open to me."

"We'll have none o' them Belgiums here!" cried a threatening voice from the crowd.

"Allow me to tell you, Thoms, to tell you all, that the Belgians will not ask your leave to come," spoke Richard, raising his head to its full height. "Would you act the part of dogs-in-the-manger? I offer you the work; offer it now; and I heartily wish you to accept it; but if you do not, I shall certainly endeavour to get others here who will."

"Who be they Belgicks that they should snatch the bread out of honest Englishmen's mouths!"

"What are the honest Englishmen about, to give them the opportunity?" retorted Richard. "Listen, my men," he continued, as he leaned forward and raised his hand impressively. "If you (I speak of the country collectively) refuse to work, it can practically matter very little to you whether the work goes to Belgium or elsewhere to be done, or whether strangers come and do it here. It must end in one or the other."

"It shan't never end in them frogs o' foreigners coming here," spoke Thoms again, vexed that his voice should have been recognized by Richard North. And this second interruption was hissed down by his more sensible comrades; who sharply bade him hold his tongue, and hear the master. Richard put up his hand again.

"We will take it, for the moment's argument, at what Thoms says—that strangers would not, or should not, come here. In that case the other result must happen—the work of the country would pass away from it. It has already begun to pass; you know it, my men; and so do your rulers the Trades' Unions. How it affects their nerves I don't pretend to say; but, when once this tide of desolation has fairly set in as a settled result, there will not be much need of their agitation. As truly as that I live, and now stand here speaking to you, I believe this will come. In different parts of the country whole places are being dismantled—the work has left it. Do you suppose North Inlet is the only spot where the provision shops may as well be closed because the men have no longer money to spend in them? Any newspaper you take up will tell you the contrary. Read about the ship-building in the East of London; how it has gone away, and whole colonies of men are left behind starving. Gone to Scotland; to the banks of the Tyne; anywhere that men can be found to work. It is the same with other trades. Whose fault is this? Why, the men's own."

Murmurs. "No. No."

"No! Why, here's a present illustration of it. Whose fault is it that my works are shut up, and you are living in idleness—or, we'll say, starving in idleness, if you like the word better? If I am unable to take this contract now offered, and it goes elsewhere, whose doings will it be, but yours? Don't talk nonsense, my men. It is all very well to say that the Trades' Unions don't allow, you to take the work. I have nothing to do with that: you and the Unions may divide the responsibility between you."

"The fact is, sir, that we are not our own masters," said Ketler.

"Just so. And it seems that you cannot, or will not, emancipate yourselves from your new slavery and again become your own masters. However, I did not call you together to go over this old ground, but to lay before you the option of returning to work. You have the day to consider it. At six o'clock tomorrow the call-bell will ring—"

"'Twon't be of no use ringing it, sir," interrupted Ketler, some sadness in his tone.

"At six o'clock tomorrow morning the call-bell here will ring," authoritatively repeated Richard North. "You respond to it and I shall heartily welcome you back. If you do not, my refusal must go in, and the contract will lapse from me. If we part to-day it is our final parting, for I shall at once take measures to secure a fresh set of workpeople. Though I gather but ten together at first, and the work I undertake be insignificant in proportion, I'll get them. It will be something like beginning life again: and you will have forced it on me."

"And of all pig-headed idiotics that mortal master ever had to deal with, sure you men are the worst!"

The undignified interruption came from Mrs. Gass. Richard looked round, in great surprise; perhaps all the greater when he also saw Miss Dallory. Mrs. Gass came forward; talking volubly; her bird-of-paradise nodding time to her words. As usual she told the men some home truths; none the less forcibly because her language was homely as their own.

"Is this true?" asked Miss Dallory in a low tone, as Richard went back to shake hands with her. "Shall you really reopen the works again with another set of men?"

"Yes—if these do not return. It will be better, however quietly I may have to begin, than going out to seek my fortune in the world. At least, I have lately been thinking so."

"Do you think the men will return?"

"I am afraid to give you my true opinion. It might seem like a bad omen."

"And now you have given it me. It is also mine. They are blind to infatuation."

"Not so much blind, I think, as that they are—I have just said so to them—in a state of slavery from which they dare not emancipate themselves."

"And who would do so—under the specious promises of the Trades' Unions? Don't blame them too much, Mr. Richard North. If some strong body came down on you or me with, all sorts of agitation and golden promises for the future, we also might believe in them."

Richard shook his head. "Not if the strong body lived by the agitation: and took our hard-earned money to keep themselves and their golden promises going."

Mary Dallory laughed a little. "Shall you ring that great bell in the morning?"

"Yes; certainly."

"Ah, well—the men will only laugh at you. But I dare say you can stand that. Oh dear! What need there is that the next world should be great and good, when this is so foolish a one!"

The meeting had broken up. Richard North and a few of the more intelligent of the men—those who had filled the more important posts at the works—remained talking yet together. Mrs. Gass, and Miss Dallory with her basket of fresh eggs, went away together.

Women stood about with anxious faces, watching for the news. They were tired of the strike: heartsick, as some of them feelingly expressed it. Nothing teaches so well as experience: the women were as eager for the strike at one time as the men could be, believing it would bring them a tide of prosperity in its wake. They had not bargained for what it had really brought: misery, and dismantled homes, and semi-starvation. But for being obliged to keep up as others did—as we all have to do, whatever may be the life's struggles, the heart's bitter care—there were those amongst them who would have laid down to die in sheer hopelessness.

Mrs. Ketler stood at her door in a tattered black net cap—the once tidy woman. She was shading the sun from her eyes as she looked out for her husband. It prevented her noticing the approach of the ladies; and when they accosted her she backed into her house in her timid way, rather startled, attempting a few words by way of apology. The little girl who was sick—a wan child of seven years old—was being nursed by one somewhat older. Miss Dallory looked round to see that there was a chair left, and took the invalid on her own lap. Almost all the available things the house once contained had been parted with; either pledged or sold. Miss Dallory gave the eggs to the mother, and a half-pint bottle of beef-tea that lay at the bottom of the basket.

"How is Cissy to-day?" she asked tenderly of the child.

"Cissy tired," was the little one's answer.

"Has Cissy finished the strawberry-jam?"

Cissy nodded.

"Then let your big boy come to Ham Court for some more," said Miss Dallory, turning to the mother.

The "big boy" was the eldest. He had been employed at the works, but was of course condemned to idleness like the rest.

"Aren't you pretty tired of this sort o' thing?" demanded Mrs. Gass, who had come to an anchor on a wooden bucket turned upside-down.

The woman knew what she meant by "this sort o' thing," and gave a groan. It was very expressive, showing how tired she was of it, and how hopeless were any prospects of a change.

"I've heard about the master's offer, ma'am; but the men mean to reject it," she said. "Smith stopped to tell me as he went by. The Lord above knows what is to become of us!"

"If the men do reject it, they'll deserve to starve for the rest of their lives," retorted Mrs. Gass. "Any way, I hope they'll have it upon their consciences for ever."

"It's the Trades' Union," said the woman in a low tone, giving a frightened look around. "The men can't do as they would."

"Not do as they would!" echoed Mrs. Gass. "Don't you pick up their folly and retail it to me again, Susan Ketler. If the men was fools enough to be drawn into joining the Union at first—and I wouldn't blame 'em too much for that, for the best of us gets led away at times by fair promises that turn out in the end to be smoke, or worse—they ought not to be so obstinate as to keep there. Now that they've seen what good that precious Trades' Union is doing for 'em, and what it's likely to do, they should buckle on the armour of their common sense and leave it. Mr. Richard North has this day given them the opportunity of doing so. Every man Jack of 'em can go back to work tomorrow morning at the ringing of the bell: and take up again with good wages and comfort. If they refuse they'll not be so much fools as something worse, Susan Ketler: they'll be desperately wicked."

"They are afraid," murmured the woman. "They have yielded themselves by word and bond to the Union."

"Then let 'em break the bond. Don't tell me, Susan Ketler. Afraid? What of? Could the Union kill them for it? Could the men be hung, drawn and quartered for leaving it? Who is the Union? Giants that were born with thunderbolts and power from the Creator to control people's wills?—or just simple men like themselves: workmen too, once, some of 'em, if reports are true. You'd better not try to come over me with your fallacies. Facts is facts. If these men chose to do it, they could send the Trades' Union to the right about this very day, and return, with one accord, to work and their senses tomorrow. Who's to hinder them?"

Mrs. Ketler ventured to say no more. She only wished she dared say as much to her husband and the men. But, what with common sense, as Mrs. Gass called it, on the one side, and the Trades' Union sophistries on the other, the steering in North Inlet just now was difficult in the extreme. Mrs. Gass rose from her uncomfortable seat, and departed with Miss Dallory.

CHAPTER XI

UNDER THE CEDAR-TREE

There was commotion that day in Dallory. An offer such as this of Richard North's, coming as it did in the very midst of distress and prolonged privation, could not be rejected off-hand without dissenting voices. The few men who had not joined the Union, who only wished to get back to work, pleaded for acceptance as if they were pleading for life. Strangers also—that is, gentlemen who had no direct interest in the question—went about amongst the men, striving to impress upon them where their obligations lay, and what their course ought to be. One of these was Dr. Rane. There had been a good deal of sickness lately—when is there not where privation reigns?—and the doctor's services were in great requisition. Every house he visited that day, every workman with whom he came into contact, he spoke to forcibly and kindly: urging them all most strongly not to reject this opportunity of putting themselves right with the world. It was one, he said, that might never occur again, if neglected now. Dr. Rane, whilst blaming the men, was sorry for them; keenly sorry for their wives and children.

He had had a very fatiguing day. When the dusk of evening came on, he went and sat in the garden, tired and weary. Bessy had gone to spend the evening at Ham Court with Miss Dallory; and the doctor had promised to fetch her home. His ruminations still ran, as ever, on getting away from Dallory; but at present there seemed to be little chance of his doing it. Unless he could dispose of his practice here, he would not have the wherewithal to establish himself elsewhere. Had Oliver Rane been a less healthy man than he really was, he would long ago have thought and worried himself into a nervous fever.

It grew darker. Dr. Rane struck his repeater—for it was too dark to see the hands—wondering whether it was time to go for his wife. No; not quite, he found; he could delay another quarter-of-an-hour yet. And he lapsed into his musings.

The seat he had chosen was under the great cedar-tree at the extreme corner of the garden, close to the wire fence that divided his ground from Mrs. Cumberland's, and also close to that lady's back-door. Some foliage of clematis and woodbine would have hidden him from any one on the other side even in daylight, and Dr. Rane felt as solitary as he would have felt in an African desert. From his own troubles his thoughts went roaming off to other matters: to his mother's long sojourn at Eastsea; to wondering when she meant to return home; to speculating on what the workmen's answer to Richard North's call would be.

"Will they show the white feather still? it is nothing less, this cowardly grovelling to the dictates of the Union," soliloquized Dr. Rane; "or will they respond to Dick like men of sense, and go back to him? If it were not for those agitators—"

"I can tell you what it is, Mr. Tim Wilks—if you don't choose to keep to your time and your promises, you need not trouble yourself to come worrying after me later. A good two mortal hours by the clock have I been at Green's waiting for you."

The above, succeeding to the sound of footsteps in the lane, and uttered in Jelly's sharpest tones, cut short Dr. Rane's musings. A short squabble ensued: Jelly scolding; Tim Wilks breathlessly explaining. From what the doctor, sitting in silence, and unsuspected, could gather, it appeared that Jelly must have had some appointment with Tim—no doubt of her own imperious making—which he had failed to keep, and had come running after her, only to catch her up at the garden-door.

Jelly put the key in the lock, and stepped inside the garden: the servants sometimes chose that way of entrance in preference to the front. During the absence of Mrs. Cumberland Jelly acted as mistress, entertained her friends, and went in and out at will. Mr. Wilks meekly remained where he was, not daring to cross the threshold without permission.

"Is it too late to come in, Miss Jelly?" asked he.

"Yes, it is too late," retorted Jelly; the pair not having the slightest notion that any eavesdropper was near them. But the word could not justly be applied to Dr. Rane: he did not want to hear what was said; felt rather annoyed at the noise and interruption.

"I couldn't get home before," resumed Timothy, "though I ran all the way from Whitborough. When a young man has his day's work to finish, and that in a lawyer's office, he is obliged to stay beyond hours if necessary."

"Don't tell me," said Jelly, who stood with the half-closed door in her hand in the most inhospitable manner. "You could have come home if you'd chosen."

"But I couldn't, Miss Jelly."

"You are always stopping beyond hours now. That is, saying that you do."

"Because we have been so busy lately," answered Tim. "Our head clerk, Repton, is away through illness, and it puts more work on the others. Dale's as cranky as he can be, and works us like horses. If you'll believe me, Miss Jelly, I hadn't time to go out and get any tea. I've not had bit or drop inside me since one o'clock to-day."

This pitiful view of affairs a little pacified Jelly; and she dropped her sharp tone. Dr. Rane was wishing they would take their departure. He would have done so himself, but that he did not altogether care to betray his presence.

"Why does that old Dale not get another clerk?" demanded Jelly. "I should tell him plainly if I were you, Tim, that going without my regular meals did not suit me."

"We should not dare to say that. Much he'd listen if we did! As to getting another clerk, I believe he is doing it. Repton's doctor says he'll never be well again, so Dale thinks it's of no use waiting for him."

"You were to take Repton's place, if ever he left," said Jelly, quickly.

"I know I was"—and Timothy Wilks's voice became so rueful that it might have made Dr. Rane laugh under more open circumstances. "But when Dale made that promise, Miss Jelly, you see the affair of the anonymous letter had not taken place."

"What anonymous letter?"

"The one that killed Edmund North."

"Why, you don't mean to insinuate that Dale lays the blame of that on you?"

"I don't suppose he thinks I sent it. Indeed I'm sure he does not. But he was anything but pleasant over it to me at the time, and he has never been quite the same to me since."

"He is an unjust owl," said Jelly.

"One does not look for much else than injustice from lawyers."

"Does Dale say that letter is the reason of his not promoting you to Repton's place?"

"He doesn't say it: but I know that it is so, as if he did just as well."

Jelly struck the key two or three times against the door. She was thinking.

"That's through your foolish tongue, Timothy Wilks. You know you did talk of the matter out of the office."

"They say so," confessed Timothy. "But if I did, I'm sure I've been punished enough for it. It's hard that it should stick to me always. Why don't they find the writer of the letter, and punish him? He was the villain; not me."

"So he was," said Jelly. "Tim, what would you say if I told you I knew who it was?"

"I? Excuse me, Miss Jelly, but I should not quite believe it."

Jelly laughed. Not a loud laugh, but one rather derisive, and full of power. Its peculiar significance penetrated to him who was seated under the cedar-tree, betraying all too surely that Jelly knew his dangerous secret. Even the less sensitive Tim Wilks was impressed by the sound.

"Surely, Miss Jelly, you do not mean that you know who wrote the letter?"

"I could put my finger out from where I now stand, Tim, and lay it on the right person," she answered in low, impressive tones, little suspecting how literally true were her words.

Tim seemed overwhelmed. He drew a deep breath.

"Then, why don't you, Miss Jelly?"

"Because—" Jelly stopped short. "Well, because there are certain considerations that make it difficult to speak."

"But you ought to speak. Indeed you ought, Miss Jelly. If Lawyer Dale got to hear of this, he'd tell you he could compel you to speak."

Again there broke forth a laugh from Jelly. But quite a different laugh this time—one of mirth. Tim decided that she had only been making fun of him. He resented it, as much as he was capable of resenting anything.

"You shouldn't make game, of a young man in this way, Miss Jelly! I'm sure I thought you were in earnest. You'd make a fine play-actor."

"Shouldn't I?" assented Jelly, "and take in the audience nicely, as I take in you. Well," changing her tone, "you must be soft, Tim Wilks! The idea of believing that I could know who wrote the letter?"

The hint about Lawyer Dale had frightened Jelly, bringing back the prudence which her impulsive sympathy with Tim's wrongs had momentarily put to flight. All she could do, then, was to strive to efface the impression she had made. There existed certain considerations, that made it, as she had aptly said, difficult to speak. But she felt vexed with herself, and resented it on Tim.

"See here," cried she, "I can't stand at this gate all night, jabbering with you; so you can just betake yourself off again. And the next time you make a promise to be home by a certain hour to take a late cup of tea with friends at Mrs. Green's, I'll trouble you to keep it. Mind that, Mr. Wilks."

Mr. Wilks had his nose round the post, and was beginning some deprecatory rejoinder, but Jelly slammed the door, and nearly snapped the nose off. Locking it with a click, she put the key in her pocket, and marched on to the house.

Leaving Dr. Rane alone to the night dews under the heavy cedar-tree. Were the dews falling?—or was it that his own face gave out the damp moisture that lay on it? He sat still as death.

So, then, Jelly did know of it! As he had before half-suspected; and he had been living, was living, with a sword suspended over him. It mattered not to speculate as to how she acquired the terrible secret: she knew it, and that was sufficient. Dr. Rane had not felt very safe before; but now it seemed to him as though he were treading on the extreme edge of a precipice, and that his footing was crumbling from under him. There could be no certainty at any moment that Jelly would not declare what she knew: tomorrow—the next day—the day after: how could he tell what day or hour it might be? Oliver Rane passed his handkerchief over his face, his hand anything but a steady one.

The "certain considerations" to which Jelly had confessed, meant that she was in service with Mrs. Cumberland, and that he was Mrs. Cumberland's son. Whilst Jolly, retained her place, she would not perhaps be deliberately guilty of the bad faith of betraying, as it were, her mistress. Yet there were so many chances that might lead to it. Lawyer Dale's questioning might bring it about—and who could answer for it that this might not at once set in at a word from Wilks?—or she might be quitting Mrs. Cumberland's service—or taking upon herself to right Tim with the world—or speaking, as she had evidently spoken that night, upon impulse. Yes; there were a hundred-and-one chances now of his betrayal!

He must get away from Dallory without delay. "Out of sight, out of mind," runs the old proverb—and it certainly seemed to Dr. Rane that if he were out of sight the chances of betrayal would be wonderfully lessened. He could battle with it better, too, at a distance, if discovery came; perhaps keep it wholly from his wife. Never a cloud had come between him and Bessy: rather than let this disclosure come to her—he would have run away with her to the wilds of Africa. Or, perhaps from her.

Run away! The thought brought a circumstance to his mind. That self-same morning another letter had arrived from his friend in America, Dr. Jones. Dr. Jones had again urged on Oliver Rane his acceptance of the offer to join him in his practice there, saying it was an opportunity he might never have again throughout his lifetime. Dr. Rane fully believed it: it was, beyond doubt, a very excellent offer; but, alas! he had not the money to embrace it. Five hundred pounds—besides the expenses of the voyage and the removal: Dr. Rane had not five hundred shillings to spare. The tontine money came flashing through his brain. Oh, if he could only get it!

The air grew really damp; but he still sat in the dark under the shade of the cedar-tree, reviewing plans and projects, ways and means. To him it was growing as a very matter of life or death.

How long he sat, he knew not: but by-and-by the faint sound of Dallory Church clock was wafted to him through the clear air. He counted the strokes—ten. Ten? Dr. Rane started up: he ought to have gone for his wife long and long ago.

Six o'clock in the morning; and the great bell of the works of North and Gass was ringing out upon the morning air! It was a bell Dallory had not heard of late, and sleepy people turned in their beds. Many had been listening for it, knowing it was going to be rung; some got up and looked from their windows to see whether the street became lively with workmen, or whether it remained silent.

Richard North was within the works. He had come out thus early, hoping to welcome his men. Three or four entered with him. The bell rang its accustomed time, and then ceased; its sound dying away, and leaving a faint echo on the air. There was no other answer: the men had not responded to the call. Nothing more, than that faint vibration of sound remained to tell of the appeal made by Richard North.

Richard North threw up the proposed contract; and proceeded on a journey without loss of time. Some said he went to Scotland, some to Belgium; but the utmost known about it was that his departure had reference to business. But that he was a temperate man, and given to pity as much as to blame, he could have cursed the men's blind folly. What was to become of them? The work was there, and they drove it away from their doors, driving all chance with it of regaining prosperity. They were forcing him to supersede them: they were bringing despair, famine, death upon a place where content and comfort had once reigned. Yes, death: as you will find. Surely never did greater blindness than this fall on man!

Days went on, and grew into weeks: and Richard North was still absent. Prospects seemed to be looking gloomy on all sides. To make matters worse, some cases of fever began to manifest themselves at Dallory. Dr. Rane and his brother practitioner, Mr. Seeley, only wondered that something of the sort had not broken out before.

Amidst other places that wore an air of gloom was the interior of Dallory Hall. Madam's insatiable demands for money had been very partially responded to of late: not at all since the absence of Richard. Even she, with all her imperious scorn of whence supplies came, provided they did come, began to realize the fact that gold can no more be drawn from exhausted coffers than blood from a stone. It did not tend to improve her temper.

She sat one morning in what she was pleased to call her boudoir—a charming apartment opening from her dressing-room. Several letters lay before her, brought up by her maid: she had carelessly tossed them aside for some hours, but was getting to them now when it was nearing midday. Not very pleasant letters, any of them, to judge by madam's dark face. One was from Sidney at Homburg, piteously imploring for assistance—which had not recently been sent him; two or three were rather urgent demands for the payment of private accounts of madam's rather long delayed; one was a polite excuse from Frank Dallory and his sister for not accepting a dinner invitation. There was not a single pleasant letter amongst them all.

"I wonder what Dick North means by staying away like this!—and leaving orders at Ticknells' that no cheques are to be cashed!" growled madam in soliloquy. "He ought to be here. He ought to force those miserable men of his back to work, whether they will or not. He's away; Arthur's away; Sidney's away: and with this uncertain state of things out of doors and trouble within, the house is worse than a dungeon. People seem to be neglecting it: even Mary Dallory stays without the gates. That girl's an artful flirt: as Matilda said yesterday. If Arthur and Dick were back she'd come fast enough: I should like to know which of the two she most cares for. It is absurd, though, to speak of her in conjunction with Dick North! I think I'll go off somewhere for a time. Should this suspicion of fever prove correct, the place will not be safe. I shall want a hundred pounds or two. And Sidney must have money. He says he'll do something desperate if I don't send it—but he has said that before. Confound it all! Why does not gold grow upon trees?"

Madam's dress this morning was a striped lilac silk of amazing rustle and richness. Letting it all out behind her, she went down the stairs and through the hall, sweeping the dust along in a little cloud. Mr. North was not in his parlour; madam went about looking for him.

To her surprise she found him in the drawing-room; it was not often he ventured into that exclusive place. He had a shabby long coat on, and a straw hat. Madam's scornful head went up when she saw him there.

"What do you want?" she asked in a tone that plainly said he had about as much right in the room as an unwelcome stranger.

"I have come to beg some cotton of Matilda to tie up these flowers," was Mr. North's answer. "Thomas Hepburn's little boy is here, and I thought I'd give the child a posy."

"A posy!" repeated madam, scorning the homely term.

"I have no cotton," said Matilda, who lay back in a chair, reading. "What should bring cotton in a drawing-room?"

"Oh well—I can bind it with a piece of variegated grass," said Mr. North with resignation. "I'm sorry to have troubled you, Matilda."

"And when you have disposed of your 'posy,' I am coming to your parlour," said madam.

Mr. North groaned as he went out. He knew that his peace was about to be destroyed for the day. There were moments when he thought heart and brain must give way under home worries and madam's.

"When did this come?" enquired madam, pointing to a letter that was placed upright on the mantelpiece: one addressed to Richard North, in her son Arthur's writing.

"This morning," shortly answered Matilda, not looking up from her book.

"Yes, Arthur can write often enough to Dick. This is the second letter that has come for him within a week. What did you do with the other?" madam broke off to ask.

"Put it into Dick's room until he comes home."

"But Arthur does not trouble himself to write to us, or to let us know anything of his movements," resumed madam. "We have not had a syllable from him since he sent word that old Bohun was dead. Is he still in London?—or at his aunt's?—or where?"

"I'm sure I don't know where," retorted Matilda, irritated at being interrupted.

Neither did she care. Madam turned the letter over in idle curiosity: but the postmark was not to be deciphered. Leaving it on the mantelpiece, she went to look after Mr. North. He stood on the lawn, doing something to a dwarf-tree of small and beautiful roses. There was some wind to-day, and his long coat waved a little in the breeze.

"Did you hear what I said—that I was coming to your parlour?" demanded madam, swooping down upon him majestically. "Money must be had. I want it; Sidney wants it; the house wants it. I—"

Mr. North had straightened himself. Desperation gave him a little courage.

"I would give it you if I had it. I have always given it you. But what is to be done when I have it not? You must see that it is not my fault, madam."

"I see that when money is needed it is your place to find it," coolly returned madam. "Sidney cannot live upon air. He has—"

"It seems to me that he lives upon gold," Mr. North interrupted in querulous tones. "There's no end to it."

"Sidney must have money," equably went on madam. "I must have it, for I purpose going away for a time. You will therefore—"

"Goodness me! here's the telegraph man."

This second interruption was also from Mr. North. Telegraphic messages were somewhat rare at Dallory Hall; and its master went into a flutter. His fears flew to his well-beloved son, Dick. The messenger was coming up the broad walk, a despatch in his hand. Mr. North advanced to meet him; madam sailing behind.

"It is for Captain Bohun, sir," spoke up the man, perceiving something of Mr. North's agitation.

"For Captain Bohun!" interposed madam. "Where's it from?"

"London, madam."

Motioning the messenger to go to the house for his receipt, she tore it open without the smallest ceremony, and read its contents:

"Dr. Williams to Arthur Bohun, Esq.:

"James Bohun is dying. Sir Nash wishes you to come up without delay."

Looking to right and left, stood madam, her thoughts busy. Where could Arthur be? Why had he left London?

"Do you know?" she roughly asked of Mr. North.

"Know what, madam?"

"Where Arthur Bohun is."

Mr. North stared a little. "Why, how should I know?" he asked. "It's ever so long since Arthur wrote to me. He sends me messages when he writes to Dick."

Madam swept into the drawing-room. She took the letter from the mantelpiece, and coolly broke its black seal. Even Matilda's scruples were aroused at this.

"Oh, mamma, don't!" she exclaimed, starting up and putting her hand over the letter. "Don't open that. It would not be right."

Madam dexterously twitched the letter away, carried it to the window and read it from end to end. Matilda saw her face turn ghastly through its paint, as if with fright.

"Serves her right," thought the young lady. "Mamma, what is amiss?"

Madam crumpled the letter into a ball in her agitated hand: but no answer came from her white lips. Turning abruptly up the stairs, she locked herself into her chamber.

"She is in an agony of fright—whatever the cause may be," quoth Miss Matilda, in soliloquy.

Ere the day had closed, the household was called upon to witness madam's sudden departure by train. She went alone: and gave not the slightest clue as to where she might be going, or when she would return.

Matilda North had aptly worded the paroxysm: "an agony of fright." She might have added: a tempest of fury; for madam was in both. For that letter had given her the news of Arthur Bohun's present locality— and that he was by the side of Ellen Adair. What had become of Dick? the letter asked. He must hasten and come, or he would be too late. Madam did not understand at all. There followed a mysterious intimation to Dick; to Dick, whom Arthur so trusted and who was true as steel; it was more obscure even than the rest; but it seemed to hint at—yes, to hint at—marriage. Marriage? Madam felt her flesh creeping.

"A son of mine marry her!" she breathed. "Heaven help me to avert the danger."

About the last woman, one would think, who ought to call for help from Heaven.

CHAPTER XII

AN INTERRUPTION

The tide came rippling up on the sea-shore with a monotonous, soothing murmur. There were no waves to-day; the air was densely still; but in the western sky little black clouds were rising, no bigger yet than a man's hand; and as the weatherwise old fishermen glanced to the spot, they foretold a storm.

Two people, pacing the beach side by side, regarded neither the sea nor the threatened storm. Need you be told that they were Arthur Bohun and Ellen Adair. What were the winds and the waves to them in their happiness? Amidst the misery that was soon to set in for both, the recollection of this short time spent at Eastsea, these few weeks since their love had been declared, and their marriage was approaching, would seem as an impossible dream.

The private marriage, consented to by Mrs. Cumberland, must not be confounded with a secret marriage. It was to be kept from the world in general: but not from every friend they possessed. Mrs. Cumberland intended to be present as Ellen's guardian; and she very much urged that some friend of Arthur's should also attend. He acquiesced, and fixed on Richard North. Captain Bohun purposed to tell his aunt, Miss Bohun, his friend in every way: but not until the wedding was over: he would trust no one beforehand, he said, excepting Mrs. Cumberland and Dick. Even Dick he did not trust yet. He commanded Dick's presence at Eastsea, telling him that his coming was imperative: there must be no refusal. Finding Dick did not respond, Arthur wrote again; but still only mysteriously. The first letter was the one put aside by Miss Matilda North, the second was that opened by madam.

But there were moments when, in spite of his happiness, Arthur Bohun had qualms of conscience for his precipitation: more especially did they press upon him immediately after the marriage was decided upon. For, after all, he really knew nothing, or as good as nothing, of Mr. Adair's position: and the proud Bohun blood bubbled up a little, as a thought crossed him that it was just possible he might find too late that, in point of family, hers was not fitting to have mated with his.

The human heart is treacherous: given over to self-deception, and to sophistry. So long as a thing is coveted, when it seems almost unattainable, we see nothing but the advantages of gaining it, the happiness it must bring. But, let this desire be attained, and lo! we veer round, and repent our haste. Instantly every argument that could bear against it, true or false, rises up within us with mocking force, and we say, Oh that I had waited before doing this thing! It is that deceitful heart of ours that is in fault, nothing else; placing upon all things its own false colouring.

At first, as they sat together under cover of the rocks, or on the more open benches on the sands, or wandered to the inland walks and the rural lanes, his conversation would turn on Mr. Adair. But Ellen seemed to know as little of her father as he did.

"It is strange you don't remember more of him, Ellen!" he suddenly said on one occasion when he was alone with her at Mrs. Cumberland's.

"Strange! Do you think so?" returned Ellen, turning from the bay window where she was standing. "I was sent to Europe at eight years old, and children at that age so soon forget. I seem to recollect a gentleman in some sort of white coat, who cried over me and kissed me, and said mamma was gone to live in heaven. His face was a pleasant one, and he had bright hair; something the colour of yours."

She thought Arthur had alluded to personal appearance. But he had not meant that.

"I remember another thing—that papa used to say I was just like my mother, and should grow up like her," resumed Ellen. "It seems ages ago. Perhaps when I see him I shall find that my memory has given me an ideal father, and that he is quite different from what I have pictured him."

"You know none of your Scotch relatives, Ellen?"

"None."

"Or where they live?"

"No."

"Why does not Mr. Adair come home?"

"I don't know. He has been thinking of it for some years; and that's why I am with Mrs. Cumberland instead of going out to him again. I am sure he must have a very high opinion of Mrs. Cumberland," added Ellen, after a pause. "His letters prove it. And he often mentions her late husband as his dear friend and chaplain. I will show you some of his letters, if you like. Would you care to see them? I keep all papa's letters."

Arthur Bohun's face lighted up at the proposition. "Yes," he said with animation. "Yes. As many as you please."

She crossed the room to her desk, took out three or four letters indiscriminately from a bundle lying there, and brought them to him. He detained the pretty hands as well as the letters, and took some impassioned kisses from the blushing face, turned up unconsciously to his. Sweeter kisses than Arthur Bohun would ever impress upon any other face in afterlife. Ellen had almost learned not to shrink from them in her maiden modesty; he vowed to her that they were now his best right and privilege.

But the letters told him nothing. They were evidently a gentleman's letters; but of the writer's position or family they said not a word. Arthur returned them with a half-sigh: it was of no use, he thought, to trouble himself any more about the matter. After all, his own father and Mr. Adair had been close friends in India, and that was a sort of guarantee that all must be right. This decided, he delivered himself up to his ideal happiness: and the wedding day was finally settled.

This afternoon, when they were pacing the beach, unobservant of the little clouds rising in the west, was the marriage eve. It is the last day they need thus walk together as mere formal acquaintances: for at that little church whose spire is not a stone's-throw away, they will tomorrow be made man and wife. A strange light sits on Arthur Bohun's cheek; the light of intense happiness. The day and the hour are drawing near to its realization: and not so much as a thought has crossed his mind that any untoward fate can arise to mar it.

Ah, might not those dark clouds have read him a lesson? Just as the small circlets out there might gather into an overwhelming storm, before which both man and beast must bow their heads, so might be rising, even then, some threatening wave in the drama of his life. And it was so: though he suspected it not. Even now, as they walked, the clouds were increasing! just as the unseen thunderstorm was about to descend upon their lives and hearts. Suddenly, in turning to face the west, Arthur noticed the altered aspect of the sky.

"Look at those clouds, getting up! I hope the weather's not going to change for us tomorrow, Ellen. What does that mean?" he asked of a man who was doing something to his small boat, now high and dry upon the beach.

The sailor glanced up indifferently.

"It means a storm, master."

"Shall we get it here, do you think?"

"Ay, sir. Not till tomorrow, maybe. I fancy we shall, though"—giving a look round, as if he could see the storm in the air. "I knowed there was going to be a change."

"How did you know it?"

"Us fishermen sees a storm afore it comes, master. My foot tells it me besides. I got him jammed once, and he have had the weather in him ever since."

They walked on. "That will be two untoward events for us," remarked Captain Bohun; but he spoke with a smile, as if no untoward events could mar their happiness. "We want a third to complete it, don't we, Ellen?"

"What are the two?"

"The bad weather threatened for tomorrow; and Dick's non-arrival is the other. I am vexed at that."

For, on this same morning, Mrs. Cumberland had received a letter from her son. Amidst other items of news, Dr. Rane mentioned that Richard North was absent: it was supposed in Belgium, but no one knew positively where. This explained Richard's silence to Captain Bohun, and put an end to the hope that Richard would be at the wedding. Dr. Rane also stated another thing, which was anything but pleasant news: that beyond all doubt fever was breaking out at Dallory, though it was not yet publicly known. The doctor added that he feared it would prove of a malignant type, and he felt glad that his mother was away. Bessy was well, and sent her love.

"Will you rest a little before going in?"

They were passing the favourite old seat under the rocks. Ellen acquiesced, and they sat down. The black clouds grew larger and higher: but, absorbed in their own plans, their own happiness, had the heavens become altogether overshadowed it would have been as nothing to them. In low tones they conversed together of the future; beginning with the morrow, ending they knew not where. Their visions were of the sweetest rose-colour; they fully believed that bliss so great as their own had never been found on earth. His arm was round Ellen as they sat, her hand lay in his, her head seemed resting against his heart. To all intents and purposes they seemed as entirely alone in this sheltered nook as they could have been in the wilds of the desert. The beach was shingly; footsteps could not approach without being heard: had any one passed, they would have been seen sitting as decorously apart as though they had quarrelled: but the shore seemed deserted this afternoon.

The arrangement for the marriage was as follows:—At half-past eleven o'clock, Arthur, Ellen, and Mrs. Cumberland would enter the little church by a private door, and the ceremony would take place. Richard North was to have given her away, but that was over now. Arthur held the licence; he had made a friend of the clergyman, and all would be done quietly. He and Ellen were to go away for a few days; she would then return home with Mrs. Cumberland, and be to the world still as Miss Adair. After that, Arthur would take his own time, and be guided by circumstances for declaring the marriage: but he meant, if possible, to at once introduce Ellen to his aunt, Miss Bohun.

And Ellen Adair? Not a scruple rested on her mind, not a doubt or hesitation on her heart; her father had given his cordial approbation—as expressed in the letter to Mrs. Cumberland—and she was full of peace.

"Did you feel that, Ellen?"

A faint, quivering breeze had seemed to pass over them with sudden sharpness, and to die away in a moan.

Some white sails out at sea flapped a little, and the boats turned homewards.

"We had better be going, too, my love; or we may have it upon us."

She rose as he spoke, and they walked away. The sky was growing darker; the shades of evening were beginning to gather. Mrs. Cumberland had been lying down and was dressing, the maid said—if Captain Bohun would wait. Ellen took off her bonnet and mantle.

"Whilst we are alone, let me see that I have not made a mistake in the size, Ellen."

Taking from his pocket a bit of tissue-paper, he unfolded it and disclosed a wedding-ring. Ellen blushed vividly as he tried it on. "I—thought," she timidly began, "that you meant this to be my wedding-ring"— indicating the plain gold one she habitually wore on her right hand.

"No. Rane bought that one. This will be mine."

It fitted exactly. Captain Bohun had not allowed for the probability of those fragile fingers growing larger with years. As he held it on for a minute, their eyes met. Ellen suddenly recalled that long-past day in Dallory Church, when she had taken off Maria Warne's ring for Bessy North, the after-scene in the carriage, when Arthur Bohun put the other one on, and his sweet words: lastly, the scene in the garden when he put it on again. This was time the third.

"If this should ever become too small for me?" she murmured, as he took it off the finger.

"Oh, but that—if ever—won't be for ages and ages."

Not for ages, and ages! If, in their innocent unconsciousness, they could only have seen the cruel Fate that was already coiling its meshes around them!

The storm did not come that night. But whether, in revenge for the delay, it chose to expend itself with double violence, certain it was that such a storm had seldom been seen at Eastsea as raged in the morning. The sky was lurid and angry; the sea tossed itself in great waves; the wind whistled and shrieked; the rain dashed furiously down at intervals: all nature seemed at warfare.

In much distress lay Mrs. Cumberland. Exceedingly subject of late to outer influences, whether it might be the storm that affected her, she knew not, but she felt unable to rise from her bed. The hour for the marriage was drawing on. It had been fixed for half-past eleven. The clergyman had a funeral at half-past ten; and Mrs. Cumberland had said that she herself could not be ready before that time. At a little after eleven Arthur Bohun came up in the fly that was to convey them to church. Mrs. Cumberland sent to ask him to go upstairs to her; and he found her in tears. A curious eight in so self-contained a woman.

"I cannot help it, Captain Bohun: indeed I cannot. Had not the marriage better be put off for a day? I may be better tomorrow."

"Certainly not," he answered. "Why should it be put off? I am very sorry for Ellen's sake; she would have felt happier had you been in church. But your presence is not essential to the ceremony, Mrs. Cumberland."

"Her father and mother were my dear friends. It seems as though I should fail in my duty if I were to allow her to go to church without me."

Arthur Bohun laughed. He would not listen to a word—was it likely that he would do so? In less than an hour's time all responsibility in regard to Ellen would be transferred to himself, he answered, for he should be her husband.

"The marriage will be perfectly legal, dear Mrs. Cumberland, though you do not witness it," were his last words as he went downstairs.

Ellen was ready. She wore an ordinary silk dress of light quiet colour, and a plain white bonnet: such as she might have walked out in at Eastsea. There was nothing, save her pale face and quivering lips, to denote that she was a bride. To have to go to church alone was very unpalatable to her, and she could with difficulty suppress her tears.

"My dearest love, I am more grieved at it for your sake than you can be," he whispered. "Take a little courage, Ellen; it will soon be over. Once you are my wife, I will strive to shelter you from all vexation."

But this illness of Mrs. Cumberland's made a slight alteration in the programme. For Arthur Bohun to go out with Mrs. Cumberland and Ellen in a fly, was nothing; he sometimes accompanied them in their drives: but to go out alone with Ellen, and in that storm, would have excited the curiosity of Ann and the other servants. Arthur Bohun rapidly decided to walk to church, braving the rain: Ellen must follow in the fly. There was no time to be lost. It was twenty minutes past eleven.

"Shall I put you in the carriage first, Ellen?" he stayed to ask.

"No. I think you had better not."

"My darling, you will come?"

Did a doubt cross him, that he should say this? But she answered that she would: he saw she spoke sincerely. He wrung her hand and went out to the door.

Had the fly multiplied itself into two flies?—and were they squabbling for precedence? Certainly two were there: and the one wet driver was abusing the other wet driver for holding his place before the door, and not allowing him to draw up to it.

"Arthur! Good Heavens, how fortunate I am! Arthur Bohun! don't you see me?"

Every drop of blood in Arthur Bohun's veins seemed to stand still and turn to ice as he recognized his mother's voice and his mother's face. Madam, driven hastily from the railway-station, had come to bear him off bodily. That his wedding was over for that day, instinct at once told him: she would have gone to church and forbidden the banns. He stepped to the fly door.

In afterlife, he could never clearly recall these next few minutes. Madam spoke of the telegram that had been received at Dallory. She said—giving to matters her own colouring—that James Bohun was in extremity; that he only waited to see Arthur to die; that he was asking for him: not a moment was to be lost. She had hastened to London on receipt of the telegram, and had now come down to fetch him.

"Step in, Arthur. We must catch the quarter-to-twelve train."

"I—I cannot go," he answered.

"Not go!" screamed madam. "But I command you to go. Would you disobey the last wishes of a dying man?"

Well, no; he felt that he could not do that. "A quarter to twelve?" he said rather dreamily. "You must wait, madam, whilst I speak to Mrs. Cumberland. There's plenty of time."

He went in with his tale, and up to Mrs. Cumberland, as one in a dream. He was forced to go, he bewailed, but not for more than a day, when he should be back to complete the marriage. What could she answer? In her bewilderment, she scarcely understood what had happened. Leaping downstairs again, he closed the door of the sitting-room upon himself and Ellen, and clasped her to his heart.

"My darling! But for this, you would have been on your way to become my wife. Come what may, Ellen, I shall be down again within a few hours. God bless you, my love! Take care of these."

They were the ring and licence; he handed them to her lest he might lose them. Before Ellen could recover herself, whilst yet her face was glowing with his farewell kisses, he was being rattled away in the fly with madam to the station.

Crafty madam! Waiting in the fly at the door and making her observations, she had read what the signs meant almost as surely as though she had been told. The other fly waiting, and Ellen dressed; going out in it on that stormy day; Arthur out of mourning, his attire covered with a light overcoat. She guessed the truth (aided by the mysterious hint in the letter she had opened) and believed surely that nothing less than a MARRIAGE had she interrupted. Not a word said she on the way to the station. Getting him away was a great victory: it would not do to risk marring it. But when they were in the train, and the whistle had sounded, and they were fairly off, then madam spoke. They had the compartment to themselves.

"Arthur, you cannot deceive me: any attempt to do so would be useless. You were about to marry Ellen Adair."

She spoke quietly, almost affectionately; when the bosom is beating with a horrible dread, it produces calmness of manner rather than passion. For a single moment there wavered in Arthur Bohun's mind a doubt as to whether it should be avowal or evasion, but not for longer. As it had come to this, why he must take his standing, He raised his head proudly.

"Eight, mother. I am going to wed Ellen Adair."

Madam's pulses began to beat nineteen to the dozen. Her head grew hot, her hands cold.

"You were, you mean, Arthur."

"Yes. Put it as you like. What was interrupted to-day, will be concluded tomorrow. As soon as I have seen James, I shall return to Eastsea."

"Arthur! Arthur Bohun! It must never be concluded, Never."

"Pardon me, mother. I am my own master."

"A Bohun may not wed shame and disgrace."

"Shame and disgrace cannot attach to her. Madam, I must beg you to remember that in a few hours that young lady will be my wife. Do not try my temper too sorely."

"No, not to her, but to her father," panted madam—and Arthur felt frightened, he knew not why, at her strong emotion. "Would you wed the daughter of a—a—"

Madam paused. Arthur looked at her; his compressed lips trembled just a little.

"Of a what, mother? Pray go on."

"Of everything that is bad. A forger. A convict."

There was a dead pause. Nothing to be heard but the whirling train. "A—what?" gasped Captain Bohun, when he could get back his breath.

"A CONVICT," burst forth madam in a scream; for her agitation was becoming irrepressible. "Why do you make me repeat painful things?"

"Mother! Of whom do you speak?"

"Of her father: William Adair."

He fell back in the carriage as one who is shot. As one from whom life and all that can make it sweet, had suddenly gone out for ever.

CHAPTER XIII

PANIC

The funerals were going about in Dallory. Dr. Rane's prognostications had proved correct; the fever was severe. It spread, and a panic set in.

As yet it had been confined to the poor. To those who for some months now had been living in despair and poverty. Some called it a famine fever; some a relapsing fever; some typhus fever: but, whatever the name accorded to it, one thing was certain—it was of a malignant and fatal type.

It possessed a somewhat singular feature: it had seemed to break out all at once—in a single night. Before the doctors had well ascertained that anything of the kind was in the air, before most of the public had so much as heard of it, it came upon them. The probability of course was that it had been smouldering for some days. On the afternoon that witnessed madam's departure from Dallory Hall—after the receipt of the telegram and the reading of Dick's letter—there had not been one decided case: in the morning no less than seven cases had shown themselves. After that, it spread rapidly.

Madam remained away. James Bohun was dead, and she stayed with Sir Nash. Matilda North, taking French leave, went up to join her without an invitation; she did not care to stay in the midst of the sickness. So the master of Dallory Hall was alone, and enjoyed his liberty as much as trouble had left him any capacity for enjoyment.

A week or ten days had passed on since the outbreak, and the funerals were going about Dallory. The two medical men, Dr. Rane and Mr. Seeley, were worked nearly off their legs. The panic was at its height. Dallory had been an exceptionally healthy place: people were not used to this state of things, and grew frightened. Some of the better families took flight, for the seaside, or elsewhere. The long-continued distress, resulting on the strike, had predisposed the poorer classes for it. It was they whom it chiefly attacked, but there were now two or three cases amongst their betters. This was no time for the medical men to speculate whether they should or should not be paid; they put all such considerations aside, and gave the poor sufferers their best care. Dr. Rane in particular was tenderly assiduous with his patients. In spite of that fatal letter and the mistake—nay, the sin—it involved, he was a humane man. Were he a successful practitioner, making his hundreds or his thousands a-year, as might be, he would be one of the first and readiest to give away largely of his time and skill to any who could not afford to pay him.

The last person whom the fever had attacked was one of the brothers Hepburn, of Dallory, undertakers, carpenters, and coffin-makers. Both were sickly men, but very steady and respectable. The younger brother, Henry, was the one seized: it was universally assumed that he caught it in the discharge of certain of the duties of his calling, and the supposition did not tend to decrease the public panic. Dr. Rane thought him a bad subject for the illness, and did all he could for him.

Bessy Rane stood in her kitchen, making an apple pudding. It is rather a sudden transition of subject, from sickness to puddings, but only in accordance with life. Whatever calamity may be decimating society around, the domestic routine of existence goes on at home in its ordinary course. Molly Green was pudding-maker in general: but Molly was hastening over her other work that day, for she had obtained leave to go home in the evening to see her mother: a woman who had been ailing for years with chronic illness, and lived at Whitborough. So Bessy this morning took the pudding upon herself.

Mrs. Rane stood at the table; a brown holland apron tied over her light morning gown, her sleeves turned up to the middle of her delicate arms. Hands and wrists and arms were alike pretty and refined.

The apples were in a basin, ready pared, and she was rolling out the crust. Ever and anon she glanced at the kitchen clock. Her husband had been called out at four o'clock that morning, and she was growing a little anxious. Now it was close upon eleven. It cannot be said that Bessy was afraid of the fever for him: she shared in the popular belief that medical men are generally exempt from infection; but she was always glad to see him arrive home safe and well.

His latch-key was heard in the door whilst she was thinking of him. Dr. Rane went straight up to the unused top-room, changed his clothes, and washed his hands and face—a precaution he always took when he had been with fever patients. Bessy put the kitchen-door open, that he might see her when he came down.

"Pudding-making, Bessy!" he cried, looking in. "Why don't you let Molly do that?"

"Molly's busy. She wants to go home this evening, Oliver, as soon as we can spare her, and will not come back until tomorrow night. She received a letter this morning to say her mother has at last taken to her bed, and the doctor thinks her very ill. I have given her leave to go."

"But how shall you manage without her?"

"I shall have old Phillis in. Molly has been to her, and she says she'll be glad to come."

Dr. Rane said no more. It was quite the same to him whether Molly or Phillis did what was wanted. When men are harassed in spirit, they cannot concern themselves with the petty details of domestic life.

"I was thinking, Oliver, that—if you don't mind—as we can have Phillis, I would leave it to Molly whether to come back tomorrow night, or not. If her mother is really growing worse, the girl may like to stay a day longer with her."

"My dear, do just as you like about it," was the doctor's rather impatient answer.

"Your breakfast shall be ready in a moment, Oliver."

"I have taken breakfast. It was between eight and nine before I could get away from Ketler's, and I went and begged some of Mrs. Gass. After that I went the round of the patients."

Bessy was putting the crust into the basin. She lifted her hands and turned in some dismay.

"Surely, Oliver, they have not got the fever at Ketler's!"

Dr. Rane laughed slightly. "Not the fever, Bessy: something else. The baby. It was Ketler who called me up this morning."

"Oh dear," said Bessy, going on with her pudding. "I thought that poor baby was not expected for a month or two. How will they manage to keep it? It seems to me that the less food there is for them, the quicker the babies come."

"That's generally the case," observed Dr. Rane.

"Is the mother well?"

"Tolerably so."

"And—how are the other things going on, Oliver?"

He knew, by the tone of her voice, that she meant the fever. Bessy never spoke of that without a kind of timidity.

"Neither better nor worse. It's very bad still."

"And fatal?"

"Yes, and fatal. Henry Hepburn is in danger."

"But he will get over it?" rejoined Bessy quickly.

"I don't think so. His brother will have it next if he does not mind. He is as nervous over it as he can be. I am off now, Bessy, up the Ham."

"You will be in to dinner?"

"Before that, I hope."

Bessy settled to her pudding again, and the doctor departed. Not into danger this time, for the fever had not yet shown itself in Dallory Ham. Scarcely a minute had elapsed when the door-bell rang, and Molly went to answer it. Mrs. Rane, her hands all flour, peeped from the kitchen, and saw Mr. North.

"Oh papa! How glad I am to see you! Do you mind coming in here?"

Mind! Mr. North felt far more at home in Bessy's kitchen than in his wife's grand drawing-room. He had brought a small open basket of lovely hot-house flowers for Bessy. He put it on the table, and sat down on one of the wooden chairs in peace and comfort. Richard had not returned, and he was still alone.

"Go on with your pudding, my dear. Don't mind me. I like to see it."

"It's all but done, papa. Molly will tie it up. Oh, these beautiful flowers!" she added, bending down to them. "How kind of you to think of me!"

"I'm going to Ham Court about some seeds, child; the walk will do me good, this pleasant day. I feel stronger and better, Bessy, than I did."

"I am so glad of that, papa."

"And so I thought—as I intended to call in here—that I would cut a few blossoms, and bring them with me. How's the fever getting on, Bessy?"

"It is not any better, I am afraid, papa."

"So I hear. They say that Henry Hepburn's dying."

Bessy felt startled. "Oh, I trust not! Though I think—I fear—Oliver has not very much hope of him."

"Well, I've heard it. And I came here, Bessy, to ask if you would not like to come to the Hall for a week or two. It might be safer for you. Are you at all afraid of catching it, child?"

"N—o," answered Bessy. But it was spoken doubtfully, and Mr. North looked at her.

"Your husband has to be amongst it pretty well every hour of his life, and I can only think there must be some risk in it for you. You had better come to the Hall."

"Oliver is very careful to change his clothes when he comes in; hut still I know there must of course be some little risk," she said. "I try to be quite brave, and not think of it, papa: and I have a great piece of camphor here"—touching the bosom of her dress—"at which Oliver laughs."

"Which is as good as confessing that you are nervous about it, Bessy," said Mr. North.

"Not very, pupa. A doctor's wife, you know, must not have fancies."

"Well, come up to the Hall to-day, Bessy. It will be a change for you, and pleasant for me, now I'm alone; it will be like some of the old days come back again, you and me together. As to Oliver, I dare say he'll be glad to have the house to himself a bit, whilst he is so busy."

Bessy, wiping the flour off her hands, consented. In point of fact, her husband had proposed, some days ago, that she should go away: and she did feel half afraid of taking the fever through him.

"But it cannot be until tomorrow, papa," she said, as Mr. North rose to depart, and she accompanied him to the door, explaining that Molly was going home. "I should not like to leave Oliver alone in the house for the night. Phillis will be here tomorrow: she can stay and sleep, should Molly Green not return."

"Very well," said Mr. North.

So it was left. Bessy opened the door for her father, and watched him on his way up the Ham.

Dr. Rane came back to dinner; and found his patients allowed him an hour's peace for it. Bessy informed him of the arrangement she had made: and that he was to be a bachelor from the morrow for an indefinite period. The doctor laughed, making a jest of it: nevertheless he glanced keenly from under his eyelids at his wife.

"Bessy! I do believe you are afraid!"

"No, not exactly," was her answer: "I don't think 'afraid' is the right word. It is just this, Oliver: I do not get nervous about it; but I cannot help remembering rather often that you may bring it home to me."

"Then, my dear, go—go by all means where you will be out of harm's way, so far as I am concerned."

Dinner over, Dr. Rane hastened out again, on his way to see Mrs. Ketler. He had just reached that bench in the shady part of the road at the neck of the Ham, when he saw Jelly coming along. The doctor only wished there was some shelter to dart into, by which he might avoid her. Ever since the night when he had heard that agreeable conversation as he sat under the cedar-tree, Jelly's keen green eyes had been worse than poison to him. She stopped when she met him.

"So that child of Susan Ketler's is come, sir!"

"Ay," said Dr. Rane.

"What in the world brings it here now?"

"Well, I don't know," returned the doctor. "Children often come without giving their friends due notice. I am on my way there."

"And not as much as a bed gown to wrap it in," resentfully went on Jelly, "and not a bit of tea or oatmeal in the place for her! My faith! baby after baby coming into the world, and the men out on strike! This makes seven—if they'd all been alive: she'll be contented perhaps when she has seventeen."

"It is the way of the world, Jelly. Set up the children first, and consider what to do with them afterwards."

"What's this that's the matter with Tim Wilks, sir?" demanded Jelly, abruptly changing the subject.

"With Tim Wilks! I did not know that anything was the matter with him."

"Yes, there is," said Jelly. "I met old Green just now, and he said Timothy Wilks was in bed ill. They thought it might be a bilious attack, if it was not the fever."

"I'll call in and see him," said Dr. Rane. "Has he been drinking again?"

Jelly's eyes flashed with resentment. Considering that Tim had really kept sober and steady for the past year and a half, she looked on the question as a frightful aspersion. More especially so as proceeding from Dr. Rane.

"I can answer for it that he has not been drinking—and so, as I supposed, might everybody else," was her tart reply. "Timothy Wilks is worried, sir; that's what it is. He has never been at ease since people accused him of writing that anonymous letter: and he never will be till he is publicly cleared of it. Sir, I think he ought to be cleared."

Was it an ice-bolt that seemed to shoot through Oliver Rane's heart?—or only a spasm? Something took it: though he managed to keep his countenance, and to speak with quiet indifference.

"Cleared? Cleared of what? I fancied it had been ascertained that Wilks was the man who spoke of the affair out of Dale's office. He can't clear himself from that. As to any other suspicion, no one has cast it on him."

"Well, sir—of course you know best," answered Jelly, recollecting herself and cooling down: but she could not help emphasizing the words. "If Tim should become dangerously ill, it might have to be done to set his mind at rest."

"What might have to be done?" demanded Dr. Rane with authority.

And Jelly did not dare to answer the direct question. She could boast and talk at people in her gossiping way as long as she felt safe, but when it came to anything like proving her words, she was a very coward. Dr. Rane was looking at her, waiting for her to speak, his manner stern and uncompromising.

"Oh well, sir, I'm sure I don't know," she said, feeling as if her throat had dried up. "And I'm sure I hope poor Tim has not got the fever."

"I'll call and see him," repeated Dr. Rane, proceeding on his way. Jelly curtsied and went on hers.

When beyond her view, he took out his handkerchief and wiped his face, damp as with the dews of death. He must, he must get away from Jelly and Dallory! But for having a wife on his hands, he might have felt tempted to make a hasty flitting to America and join Dr. Jones. Join Dr. Jones? But how obtain the funds to do it with? His thoughts turned, as they ever did on these occasions, to that money of his locked up in the Tontine. Of his: that was how Dr. Rane had come to regard it. That money would bring him salvation. If he could only obtain it—

A bow from some white-haired old gentleman, passing in a carriage. Dr. Rane returned it, the singular coincidence of his appearance at that moment flashing through his mind. For it was Sir Thomas Ticknell. Yes: it truly seemed that that Tontine money would be nothing less than salvation to him. He went on with a great fear and pain in his throbbing heart, wondering for how long or how short a time Jelly would keep her counsel.

The next morning was Thursday. It brought news that almost struck people dumb: Henry Hepburn, the undertaker, was dead, and Mrs. Rane had been seized with the fever. Dr. Rane's account was, that his wife had been very restless all night; he gave her a composing draught, which seemed to be of use for the time: but upon attempting to get up she was attacked with nausea and faintness, and had to go back to bed. The symptoms that subsequently set in he feared were those of fever.

It was an awkward time for Bessy to be ill, as Molly Green had gone homo: but Phillis, an excellent substitute, was there. She attended on Mrs. Rane, and the doctor went abroad to his patients. Mr. North, disappointed at Bessy's non-arrival, hearing of her indisposition, came to the house; but Bessy sent down an urgent message by Phillis, begging him not to run any danger by coming up to her chamber. And Mr. North, docile and obedient—as madam in her imperiousness had trained him to be—left his best love, and went home again.

In the course of the morning Dr. Rane called in at Hepburn's. It was a double shop and house; in the one were sold articles of furniture, in the other the carpenter's work was carried on. Thomas Hepburn and his family lived in the former; Henry, now dead, had occupied the latter. He was a married man, but had no children. When Dr. Rane entered the second shop, he did not at first see Thomas Hepburn; the shutters up at the window made the place dark, coming in from the bright sunshine. Thomas Hepburn saw him, however, and came forward from the workshop behind, where he had been looking on at his men. Various articles seemed to be in the course of active construction, coffins amongst the rest.

"I am very sorry for this loss, Hepburn," began the doctor.

"Well, sir, I've not had any hope from the first," sighed Hepburn, his face looking careworn and unusually sickly in the half light. "I don't think poor Henry had."

"The fact is, Hepburn, he had not strength to carry him through the disorder; it did not attack him lightly. I did all I could."

"Yes, sir, I'm sure of that," returned Hepburn—and what with his naturally weak voice, and the hammering that was going on behind, Dr. Rane had to listen with all his ears to catch the words. "We've been an ailing family always: liable to take disorders, too, more than others."

Dr. Rane made no reply for the moment. He was looking at the speaker. Something in his aspect suggested the suspicion that the man was in actual fear himself.

"You must keep up a good heart, you know, Hepburn."

"I'd rather go a hundred miles, sir, than do what I've got to do just now amidst the dead," said Hepburn, glancing round, "That's how my brother took it."

"Let the workman go instead of you."

The undertaker shook his head. "One has to go with me; and the other is just as afraid as can be. No, I must go on myself. There'll be double work for me, now Henry's gone."

"Well, Hepburn, I begin to think the fever is on the turn," said the doctor cheerily, as he walked away.

The day wore on. Mrs. Rane's symptoms were decidedly those of fever, and the doctor went all the way to Whitborough himself: not far in point of distance, only that he could not well spare the time: to tell Molly Green she was to keep where she was, out of harm's way, and not return until sent for. When he returned home his wife was worse. Phillis met him at the door, and said her poor mistress's face was scarlet, and she rolled her head from side to side. Phillis wanted to remain the night, but the doctor would not have it: there was no necessity for it, he said, and she had better not be subjected to infection more than could be helped. So Phillis went away at ten o'clock.

Between eleven and twelve, just as Mr. Seeley was preparing for rest, Dr. Rane came in and asked him to go over to see his wife. The surgeon went at once. Bessy was lying in her comfortable chamber, just as Phillis had described—her face scarlet, her head turning uneasily on the pillow. A candle stood on the table, dimly lighting the room; Mr. Seeley took it close to inspect her face; but Bessy put up her hand and turned her head away, as if the light disturbed her.

"She seems slightly delirious," whispered Mr. Seeley apart, and Dr. Rane nodded. After that, the two doctors talked together a little on the stairs, and Mr. Seeley went away, saying he would come again in the morning.

In the morning, however, Dr. Rane went over to tell him that his wife, after a most restless night, had dropped into a quiet doze, and had better not be disturbed. He felt sure she was better. This was Friday.

Phillis arrived betimes. She found a wet sheet flapping in the grey ante-room, just outside the bedroom door, which Dr. Rane had saturated with disinfecting fluid. Jars of disinfectants stood on the wide landing, on the staircase, and in other parts of the house. Phillis had no fear, and went in behind the flapping sheet. She could make nothing of Mrs. Rane. Instead of the scarlet face and restless head, she now lay buried in her pillow, still, and pale, and intensely quiet. Phillis offered her some tea; Mrs. Rane just opened her eyes, and feebly motioned it away with her hand, just as she had motioned away the light the previous night. "It's a sudden change," thought Phillis. "I don't like it."

Later in the morning, Dr. Rane brought up Mr. Seeley. She lay in exactly the same position, deep in the pillow. What with that, and what with the large night-cap, the surgeon could get to see very little of her face.

"Don't disturb me," she faintly said, when he would have aroused her sufficiently to get a good look. "I am easy now."

"Do you know me?" questioned Mr. Seeley, bending over her.

"Yes," she answered, opening her eyes for a moment. "Let me sleep; I shall be better tomorrow."

"How do you feel?" he asked.

"Only tired. Let me sleep."

"Bessy," said her husband, in the persuasive voice he used to the sick, "won't you just turn to Mr. Seeley?"

"To-morrow. I want to sleep."

And so they did not disturb her further. After all, sleep does wonders, as Dr. Rane remarked.

It might have been that Mr. Seeley went away somewhat puzzled, scarcely thinking that the fever had been on her sufficiently long to leave her in this state of exhaustion.

As the day went on a rumour was whispered that Mrs. Rane was dying. Whence it arose none could trace, unless from a word or two dropped by Dr. Rane himself to Thomas Hepburn. They happened to meet in the street, and the undertaker stopped to inquire after Mrs. Rane. She was in a most critical state, was the doctor's answer; the night would decide it, one way or the other.

Phillis went up to her mistress several times. Dr. Rane kept the hanging sheet well saturated, and flapped it often. Mrs. Rane never seemed to rouse herself throughout the day: seemed, in fact, to sleep through it. Phillis began to hope that it was indeed comfortable, refreshing rest, and that she would wake from it better.

"You'll let me stay here to-night, sir?" she said, when there was nothing more to be done, as Dr. Rane—who had been out—came in, and passed by the kitchen.

"No need," he answered in his decisive manner. "Be here the first thing in the morning."

Phillis put on her shawl and bonnet, wished him goodnight, and departed. It was about ten o'clock. Dr. Rane saw her out and went up to the sick room. In less than five minutes he came down again with a white face, opened the front-door, and strode across the road to Mr. Seeley's. The latter was in his surgery, in the act of pouring some medicine into a small phial.

"Seeley! Seeley! My wife is gone!"

What with the suddenness of the interruption, and the words, the surgeon was so startled that he dropped the bottle.

"Gone!" he cried. "Do you mean dead?"

"I do."

"Why, when I saw you at dusk, you told me she was sleeping comfortably!" said the surgeon, staring at Dr. Rane. "Phillis also said it."

"And so she was. She was to all appearance. Heaven is my witness that I thought and believed the sleep then to be natural, and was refreshing her. She must have died in it. I went up now, and found her—found her—gone."

Oliver Rane put his arm on Mr. Seeley's counter and bent his face to hide his emotion. The surgeon in the midst of his surprise, had hardly ever felt so sorry for any one as he felt in that moment for his brother practitioner.

CHAPTER XIV

WHAT JELLY SAW

"It was too true; Mrs. Rane was dead," said sympathizing people one to the other; for even that same night the sad tidings went partially out to Dallory. What with the death of Hepburn the undertaker, and now the doctor's wife—both prominent people, as might be said, in connection with the sickness—something like consternation fell on those who heard it. Dr. Rane carried the news himself to Dallory Hall, catching Mr. North just as he was going to bed, and imparting it to him in the most gentle and soothing manner in his power. Fearing that if left until morning, it might reach him abruptly, the doctor had thus made haste. From thence he went on to Hepburn's. He had chanced to meet Francis Dallory in coming out of Seeley's; he met some one else he knew; these carried the tidings to others; so that many heard of it that night.

But now we come to a strange and singular thing that happened to Jelly. Jelly in her tart way was sufficiently good-hearted. There was sickness in Ketler's house: the wife had her three days' old infant: the little girl, Cissy, grew worse and weaker: and Jelly chose to sacrifice an afternoon to nursing them. Much as she disapproved of the man's joining the Trades' Union and upholding the strike, often as she had assured him that both starving and the workhouse, whichever he might prefer, were too good for him, now that misfortune lay upon the house, Jelly came-to a little. Susan Ketler was her cousin; and, after all, she was not to blame for her husband's wrong doings. Accordingly, in the afternoon of the last day of Mrs. Rane's illness, Jelly went forth to Ketler's, armed with some beef-tea, and a few scraps for the half-famished children, the whole enclosed in a reticule.

"I shall take the latch-key," she said, in starting, to the cook, who was commonly called Dinah, "so you can go to bed. If Susan Ketler's very ill I shall stop late. Mind you put a box of matches on the slab in the hall."

Susan Ketler was not very ill, Jelly found; but the child, Cissy, was. So ill, that Jelly hardly knew whether to leave her at all, or not. The mother could not attend to her; Ketler had gone tramping off beyond Whitborough after Union work, and had not returned. Only that she thought Mrs. Cumberland would not be pleased if she came to hear that Jelly, the confidential servant in charge, had stayed out for a night, leaving the house with only the cook in it, she had certainly remained. At past twelve poor Ketler arrived home, dead beat, sick, faint, having walked several miles without food. Jelly blew him up a little: she considered that the man who could refuse work when his children were starving, because he belonged to the Trades' Union, deserved nothing but blowing-up: bade him look to Cissy, told him ungraciously that there was a loaf in the pan, and departed. Ketler, ready to drop though he was, civilly offered to see her home; but all the thanks he received in return, was a recommendation to attend to his own concerns and not to meddle with hers.

It was a fine, still night, rather too warm for the illness that had fallen upon Dallory; and Jelly walked on at a swift pace, her reticule, empty now, on her arm. Some women might have felt timid at the midnight walk: Jelly was too strong-minded to feel anything of the sort. She certainly found it a little lonely on entering the Ham, as if the road under the overshadowing trees, beginning now to lose some of their leaves, had something weird about it. But this part was soon passed; and Jelly came to the houses, and within sight of home. Not a soul met she: it was as dreary, as far as human companionship went, as it could be. A black cat sprang suddenly from the hedge, and tore across the road almost touching Jelly's feet; and it made her start.

She began thinking about Mrs. Rane; quite unconscious of the death that had taken place. When Jelly left home in the afternoon Mrs. Rane was said to be in danger: at least such was Phillis's opinion, privately communicated: but, late in the evening, news had been brought to Keller's that all danger was over. Mrs. Rane was in a refreshing sleep, and going on safely to recovery.

"And I'm downright glad of it, poor young lady!" said Jelly, half aloud, as she turned in at her gate. "Doctors' wives are naturally more exposed to the chance of catching infectious illnesses. But on the other hand they have the best advice and care at hand."

It was striking one. Letting herself in with the latch-key, Jelly felt for the box of matches, passing her hand cautiously over the marble table. And passed it in vain: no matches were there.

"Forgetful hussy!" ejaculated Jelly, apostrophizing the unconscious Dinah. "Much good she's of!"

So Jelly crept quietly upstairs in the dark, knowing she had matches in her own chamber: and in a minute came upon another of the negligent Dinah's delinquencies. She had omitted to draw down the blind of the large window on the landing.

"She has been out at that back-door, talking to people," quoth Jelly in her wrath. "Just like her! Won't she catch it from me in the morning!"

Turning to draw the blind herself, she was suddenly arrested, with the cord in her hand, by something on the opposite landing, at Dr. Rane's. Standing there, dressed in something white, which Jelly at the time thought looked like a nightgown, was Mrs. Rane. The landing was faintly lighted, as if by some distant candle; but Mrs. Rane was perfectly visible, her features and even their expression quite clear. The first thought that crossed Jelly was, that Mrs. Rane was delirious: but she looked too still for that. She did not move; and the eyes gazed with a fixed stare, as it seemed to Jelly. But that she herself must have been invisible in the surrounding darkness, she would have thought Mrs. Rane was staring at her. For a full minute this lasted: Jelly watching, Mrs. Rane never moving.

"What in the world brings her standing there?" quoth Jelly in her amazement. "And what can she be staring at? It can't be at me."

But at that moment Jelly's bag slipped from her arm, and fell on the carpet. It caused her to remove her gaze from the opposite landing for a single second—it really did not seem longer. When she looked again, the place was in darkness: Mrs. Rane and the faint light had both disappeared.

"She has no business to be out of her bed—and the doctor ought to tell her so if he's at home," thought Jelly. "Anyway, she must be a great deal better: for I don't think it's delirium."

She waited a short time, but nothing more was seen. Drawing down the blind, Jelly picked up her bag, and passed on to her own chamber—one of the back rooms on this first floor. There she slept undisturbed until morning.

She did not get up until late. Being amenable to no one whilst Mrs. Cumberland was away, the house's mistress in fact, as well as Dinah's, Jelly did not hurry herself. She was not lazy in general, especially on a Saturday, but as she felt tired after her weary afternoon at Ketler's and from having gone so late to rest. Breakfast was ready in the kitchen when she went down; Dinah—a red-faced young woman in a brown-spotted cotton gown—being busy at the fire with the coffee.

"Now then!" began Jelly—her favourite phrase when she was angry. "What have you to say for yourself? Whereabouts on the slab did you put those matches last night?"

Dinah, taken-to, tilted the kettle back. Until that moment she had not thought of her negligence.

"I'm afraid I never put 'em at all," she said.

"No you didn't put 'em," retorted Jelly with sharp emphasis. "But for having matches and a candle in my room, I must have undressed in the dark. And I should like to know why you didn't put 'em; and what you were about not to do it?"

"I'm sure I'm sorry," said Dinah, who was a tractable sort of girl. "I forgot it, I suppose, in the upset about poor Mrs. Rane."

"In the upset about poor Mrs. Rane," scornfully repeated Jelly. "What upset you, pray, about her?—And you've never been out to fasten back the shutters!"

"She's dead," answered Dinah—and the tears came into the girl's eyes. "That's what I've got the shutters half-to for. I thought you'd most likely not have heard it."

A little confusion arose in Jelly's mind. Thought is rapid. Mrs. Rane's death, as she supposed, could not possibly have occurred before morning: the neglect, as to the matches, was last night. But, in the present shock she passed this over. Her sharp tone disappeared as by magic: her expression changed to sadness.

"Dead? When did she die, Dinah?"

"It was about nine o'clock last night, they think. And she lay an hour after that in her bed, Jelly, before it was found out."

On hearing this, Jelly's first impression was that Dinah must be trifling with her. The girl came from the fire with the coffee, the tears visible.

"Now what d'ye mean, girl? Mrs. Rane didn't die last night—as I can answer for."

"Oh but she did, Jelly. Dr. Rane went up to her at ten o'clock—he had been out till then—and found her dead. I can tell you, I didn't half like going all the way up to bed by myself to that top floor, and me alone in the house, knowing she was lying there at the very next door."

Jelly paused to take in the full sense of the words, staring the while at Dinah. What could it all mean?

"You must have taken leave of your senses," she said, as she began to pour out the coffee.

"I'm sure I've not," returned Dinah. "Why?"

"To tell me Mrs. Rane died last night. How did you pick up the tale?"

"Jelly, it's no tale. It's as true as you and me's here. I was standing at the front gate for a breath of air, before shutting-up, when Dr. Rane came out of his house in a hurry, and went across to Mr. Seeley's. It struck me that Mrs. Rane might be worse and that he had gone to fetch the other, so I stayed a bit to see. Presently—it wasn't long—he came back across the road again. Mr. Francis Dallory happened to be passing, and he asked after Mrs. Rane. She was dead, the doctor said; and went on to tell him how he had found her. You needn't look as if you thought I was making-up stories, Jelly. They stood close by the doctor's gate, and I heard every word."

Jelly did not precisely know how she looked. If this was true, why—what could be the meaning of what she had seen in the night?

"She can't be dead?"

"She is," said Dinah. "Why should you dispute it?"

Jelly did riot say why. She drank her hot coffee, and went out. She did not believe it. Dinah evidently did: but the girl might have caught up some wrong story.

The first thing that struck Jelly, when outside, was the appearance of the doctor's house. It was closely shut up, doors and windows, and the blinds were down. As Jelly stood, looking up, she saw Mr. Seeley standing at his door without his hat. She went over and accosted him.

"Is it true, sir, that Mrs. Rane is dead?"

"Quite true," was the answer. "She died yesterday evening, poor lady. It was terribly sudden."

Jelly felt a very queer sensation come over her. But she was still full of disbelief. Mr. Seeley was called from within, and Jelly returned and knocked softly at Dr. Rane's door. Phillis opened it, her eyes red with crying.

"Phillis, what is all this?" demanded Jelly, in low tones. "When did she die?"

"Stop," interposed Phillis, barring her entrance. "You'd better not come in. I am not afraid: and, for the matter of that, somebody must be here: but it isn't well for those to run risks that needn't. The doctor says it was the quickest and most malignant case of them all."

"I never caught any disorder in my life, and I don't fear that I ever shall," answered Jelly, quietly making her way to the kitchen. "When did she die, Phillis?"

"About nine o'clock last evening, as is thought. The minute and hour will never be known for sure: at ten, when the doctor found her, she was getting cold. And for us below to have thought her quietly sleeping!" wound up Phillis with a sob.

The queer sensation increased. Jelly had never experienced anything like it in her whole life. She stood against the dresser, staring helplessly at Phillis.

"I don't think she could have died last evening," whispered Jelly presently.

"And I'm sure I as little thought she was dying," returned Phillis. "The last time I went up was about half-after seven: she was asleep then; that I'm positive of; and it seemed a good healthy sleep, for the breathing was as regular as could be. Sometime after eight o'clock, master went up: he came down and said she was still sleeping, and he hoped she'd sleep till morning, and I'd better not go up again for fear of disturbing her. I didn't go up, Jelly. I knew if she woke and wanted anything she'd ring: the bell-rope was to her hand. Master went out to a patient, and I cleared up the kitchen here. He came in at ten o'clock. I was ready to go, but asked him if I should stay all night. There was no need, he answered, missis being better; and I went. I never heard nothing more till I came this morning. The milkman got to the door just as I did; and he began saying what a sad thing it was that she had died. 'Who had died,' I asked him, and he said, 'Why, my missis.' Jelly, you might have knocked me down with a breath of wind."

By Jelly's looks at this moment, it seemed as if a breath of wind might have done the same for her. Her face and lips had turned livid.

"The master opened the door to me: and told me all about it: about his finding her dead close upon my going out," continued Phillis. "He's frightfully cut up, poor man. Not that there's any tears, but his face is heavy and sad, like one who has never been in bed all night—as he hasn't been. I found a blanket on the dining-room sofa, so he must have lain down there."

"Where is he now?" asked Jelly.

"Out. He was fetched to somebody at Dallory. I must stir up the pots," added Phillis, alluding to the earthen jars that stood about with disinfectants. "Master charged me to do it every hour. It's safer for the undertaker's men and others that have to come to the house."

Armed with a piece of stick, she went into the hall, and gave the contents of each jar a good stir. The dining-room door was open: Dr. Rane's solitary breakfast was spread there, waiting for him. From thence, Phillis went up the staircase to the other jars. Jelly followed.

"Nasty stuff! I do hate the smell of it," muttered Phillis. "I wouldn't come up if I were you," she added to Jelly, in the low, hushed voice that we are all apt to use when near the dead.

Jelly disregarded the injunction. She believed herself safe: and was not given to following advice at the best of times. "What's that?" she exclaimed when she reached the landing.

The sheet that had been flapping for two days outside the bedroom door, now flapped, wet as ever, on the landing before the door of the ante-room. Dr. Rane considered this the better place for it now. Phillis knocked it a little with the stick to bring out its properties.

Compared with the gloom of the rest of the house, with its drawn blinds, this landing, with its wide, staring, uncovered window, was especially bright. Jelly glanced round, it might have been thought nervously, only that she was not a nervous woman. Here, in the middle of the floor, at one o'clock in the morning, her face turned to that window, had stood Mrs. Rane. If not Mrs. Rane—who?—or what?

"Phillis," whispered Jelly, "I should like to see her."

"You can't," answered Phillis.

"Nonsense. I am not afraid."

"But you can't, Jelly. She is fastened down."

"She is— Why what do you mean?" broke off Jelly.

Phillis took up a corner of the sheet, unlocked the door—in which the key was left—and opened it half an inch for Jelly to peep in. There, in the middle of the grey room stood a closed coffin, supported on trestles. In the shock of surprise Jelly fell back against the wall, and began to tremble.

The idea that came over her—as she said to some one afterwards—was, that Mrs. Rane had been put into the coffin alive. What with the sight of the previous night (and Jelly did not yet fully admit to herself what that sight might have been), and what with this, she felt in a sort of hopeless horror and bewilderment. Recovering a little, she pushed past the sheet into the room, but with creeping, timid steps.

"Jelly, I wouldn't go in! The master charged me not to do so."

But Jelly heard not. Or, if she heard, did not heed. It was a common deal shell: nailed down. Jelly touched it with her finger.

"When was she put in here, Phillis?"

"Sometime during the night."

"And fastened down at once?"

"To be sure. I found it like this when I came this morning."

"But—why need there have been so much haste?"

"Because it was safest so. Safest for us that are living, as my master said. The leaden one will be here to-day."

Well—of course it was safer. Jelly could but acknowledge it, and recovered somewhat. She wished she had not seen—that—in the night. It was that sight, so unaccountable, that was now troubling her mind so strangely.

With her usual want of ceremony, Jelly opened the bedroom door and looked in. It had not been put straight: Phillis said her master would not let her go in to do anything to it until the two rooms should have been disinfected. Medicine bottles stood about; the bed-clothes lay over the foot of the bed, just as Hepburn's men must have placed them when they removed the dead. On the dressing-table lay a bow of blue ribbon that poor Bessy had worn in her gown the last day she had one on, a waistband with his buckle, and other trifles. Jelly began to feel oppressed, as if her breath were growing short, and came away hastily. Phillis stood on the landing beyond the sheet.

"It seems like a dream, Phillis."

"I wish we could awake and find it one," answered Phillis, practically, as she turned the key in the lock; and they went downstairs.

Not a minute too soon. Before they had well reached the kitchen, Dr. Rane's latch-key was heard.

"There's the master," cried Phillis under her breath, as he turned into his consulting-room. "It's a good thing he didn't find us up there."

"I want to say a word to him, Phillis; I think I'll go in," said Jelly, taking a sudden resolution to acquaint Dr. Rane with what she had seen. The truth was, her mind felt so unhinged, knowing not what to believe or disbelieve, that she thought she must speak, or die.

"Need you bother him now?—what's it about?" asked Phillis. "I'd let him get his breakfast first."

But Jelly went on to the consulting-room; and found herself very nearly knocked down by the doctor—who was turning quickly out of it. She asked if she could speak to him: he said Yes, if she made haste; but he wanted to catch Mr. Seeley before the latter went out.

"And your breakfast, sir?" called out Phillis in compassionate tones.

"I'll take some presently," was the answer. "What is it you want, Jelly?"

Jelly carefully closed the door before speaking. She then entered on her tale. At first the doctor supposed, by all this caution, that she was about to consult him on some private ailment of her own; St. Anthony's fire in the face, for instance, or St. Vitus's dance in the legs; and thought she might have chosen a more fitting moment. But he soon found it was nothing of the sort. With her hands pressing heavily the back of the patients' chair, Jelly told her tale. The doctor stood facing her, his arms folded, his back to the drawn blind. At first he did not appear to understand her.

"Saw my wife upon the landing in her nightgown?" he exclaimed—and Jelly thought he looked startled. "Surely she was not so imprudent as to get out of bed and go there!"

"But, sir, it is said that she was then dead!"

"Dead when? She did not die until nine o'clock. She could not have known what she was doing," continued Dr. Rane, passing his hand over his forehead. "Perhaps she may then have caught a chill. Perhaps—"

"You are misunderstanding me, sir," interrupted Jelly. "It was in the night I saw this; some hours after Mrs. Rane's death."

Dr. Rane looked bewildered. He gazed narrowly at Jelly, as if wondering what it was she would infer.

"Not last night?"

"Yes, sir. Or, I'd rather say this morning; for it was one o'clock. I saw her standing there as plainly as I see you at this moment."

"Why, Jelly, you must have been dreaming?"

"I was as wide awake, sir, as I am now. I had just got home from Ketler's. I can't think what it was I did see," added Jolly, dropping her voice.

"You saw nothing," was the decisive answer—and in the doctor's tone there was some slight touch of anger. "Fancy plays tricks with the best of us: it must have played you one last night."

"I have been thinking whether it was possible that—that—she was not really dead, sir," persisted Jelly. "Whether she could have got up, and—"

"Be silent, Jelly. I cannot listen to this folly," came the stern interruption. "You have no right to let your imagination run away with you, and then talk of it as reality. I desire that you will never speak another word upon the subject to me; or to any one."

Jelly's green eyes seem to have borrowed the doctor's bewildered look. She gazed into his face. This was a most curious business: she could not see as yet the faintest gleam of a solution to it.

"It was surely her I saw on the landing, sir, dead or alive. I could swear to it. Such things have been heard of before now as swoons being mistaken for death. When poor Mrs. Rane was left alone after her death—that is, her supposed death—if she revived; and got up; and came out upon the landing—"

"Hold your tongue," interposed the doctor, sharply. "How dare you persist in this nonsense, woman! You must be mad or dreaming. An hour before the time you speak of, my poor wife, dead and cold, was where she is now—fastened down in her shell."

He abruptly left the room with an indignant movement; leaving Jelly speechless with horror.

"Fastened down," ran her thoughts, "at twelve o'clock—dead and cold—and I saw her on the landing at one! Oh, my goodness, what does it mean?"

CHAPTER XV

DESOLATION

At the front-parlour window at Eastsea, sat Ellen Adair—looking for one who did not come. Whatever troubles, trials, mysteries might be passing elsewhere, Eastsea was going through its usual monotonous routine. How monotonous, Ellen Adair could have told: and yet, even here, something like mystery seemed to be looming in the air.

"Come what may, Ellen, I shall be down again within a few hours," had been Arthur Bohun's parting words to her. But the hours and the days passed on, and he came not.

To have one's marriage suddenly interrupted, and the bridegroom borne off from, as may be said, the very church-door, was not more agreeable to Ellen Adair than it would be to any other young lady. She watched him away in the fly, whilst his kisses were yet warm upon her lips. All that remained, was to make the best of the situation. She took off her bonnet and dress, and locked up the ring and licence he had begged her to take care of. Until the morrow she supposed; only until the morrow. Mrs. Cumberland sent out a message to her own flyman to the effect that, finding herself unable to get up, she could not take her drive, but he was to bring the fly at the same hour on the morrow. Mrs. Cumberland also wrote a line to the clergyman.

The morrow came; and went. Ellen scarcely stirred from the window, which commanded a view of the road from the station; but she did not see Captain Bohun. "Sir Nash's son must be worse, and he cannot leave," she said to herself, striving to account for the delay, whilst at the same time a vague undercurrent of uneasiness lay within her, which she did her best not to recognize or listen to. "There will be a letter tomorrow morning—or he himself will come."

But on the morrow there was no letter. Ellen watched the postman pass the house, and she turned sick and white. Mrs. Cumberland—who was better and had risen early, expecting Captain Bohun, and that the marriage would certainly take place that day—took the absence of letters with philosophy.

"He might as well have written a line, of course, Ellen; but it only shows that he is coming in by the first train. That will be due in twenty minutes."

Ellen stood at the window, watching: her spirit faint, her heart beating. That vague undercurrent of uneasiness had grown into a recognized fear now—but a fear she knew not of what. She made no pretence to eating any breakfast; she could not have swallowed a morsel had it been to save her life: Mrs. Cumberland said nothing, except that she must take some after Captain Bohun had arrived.

"There's the train, Ellen. I hear the whistle."

Ellen sat behind the Venetian blind at the window, glancing through it. Three or four straggling passengers were at length perceived, making their way down the street. But not one of them was Captain Bohun. The disappointment was turning her heart to sickness, when a station fly came careering gaily up the street.

Ah, how hope rose again! She might have known he would take a fly, and not walk up. The driver seemed making for their house. Ellen's eyes grew bright; her pale cheeks changed to rose-colour.

"Is that fly coming here, my dear?"

"I think so, Mrs. Cumberland."

"Then it is Captain Bohun. We must let the clergyman know at once, Ellen."

The fly stopped at their house, and Ellen turned away; she would not seem to be looking for him, though he was so soon to be her husband. But—something was shrilly called out from the inside; upon which the driver started on again, and pulled up at the next door. A lady and child got out. It was not Captain Bohun.

I wonder whether disappointment so great ever fell on woman? Great emotions, whether of joy or sorrow, are always silent. The heart alone knoweth its own bitterness, says the wise King, and a stranger may not intermeddle with its joy. Ellen laid her hands for a minute or two on her bosom; but she never spoke.

"He will be here by the next train," said Mrs. Cumberland. "He must come, you know, Ellen."

She watched through the livelong day. How its hours dragged themselves along she knew not. Imagination pictured all sorts of probabilities that might bring him at any moment. He might post down: he might have alighted by mistake at the wrong station, and walk on: he might have arrived by the last train, and be changing his dress at the hotel after travelling. Five hundred ideas, alternating with despair, presented themselves to her. And thus the weary day went on. Towards night the same delusive hope of the morning again rose; the same farce, of the possible arrival of Captain Bohun, was gone through.

It was almost dark: for Ellen, watching ever, had not thought about lights; and Mrs. Cumberland, tired with her long day, had gone into the small back dining-room to lie undisturbed on the sofa. The last train for the night was steaming in: Ellen heard the whistle. If it did not bring Captain Bohun she thought she could only give him up for ever.

A short interval of suspense; and then—surely he was coming! A fly or two came rattling through the street from the station: and one of them—yes—one of them drew up at the door. Ellen, thinking she had learnt wisdom, said to herself that she would not get up any undue expectation in regard to this. Foolish girl! when her whole heart was throbbing and beating.

One of the house servants had gone out, and was opening the fly door. A gentleman's hand threw out a light overcoat; a gentleman himself leaped out after it, and turned to get something from the seat. Tall and slender, Ellen thought it was Captain Bohun: the light coat was exactly like his.

And the terrible suspense was over! She should now know what the mystery had been. He had written most likely, and the letter had miscarried: how stupid she was not to have thought of that before! She heard his footsteps in the passage: in another instant she should be in his arms, feel his kisses on her lips. It was a moment's delirium of happiness: neither more nor less. Ellen stood gazing at the door, her colour coming and going, her nervous hands clasped one within the other.

But the footsteps passed the sitting-room. There seemed to be some talking, and then the house subsided into silence. Where was he? Whither had he gone? Not into the dining-room, as Ellen knew, for Mrs. Cumberland might not be awakened. Gradually the idea came creeping in, and then bounded onwards with a flash that, after all, it might not have been Captain Bohun. A faint cry of despair escaped her, and she put her hands up as if to ward off some approaching evil.

But the suspense at least must be put an end to; it was too great to bear; and she rang the bell. Ann, who chiefly waited on them, answered it.

"For lights, Miss Ellen?"

"Yes. Who has just come here in a fly?"

"It's the landlady's son, miss. A fine, handsome man as ever was seen!"

When Mrs. Cumberland entered, Ellen sat, pale and quiet, on the low chair. In truth the inward burden was becoming hard to bear. Mrs. Cumberland remarked that Captain Bohun had neither come nor written, and she thought it was not good behaviour on his part. And, with that, she settled to her evening newspaper.

"Why, Ellen! Here's the death of James Bohun," she presently exclaimed. "He died the day after Arthur left us. This accounts for the delay, I suppose."

"Yes," murmured Ellen.

"But not for his not writing," resumed Mrs. Cumberland. "That is very strange. I hope," she added, smiling, "that he does not intend to give you up because he is now heir-presumptive to a baronetcy."

Mrs. Cumberland, as she spoke, happened to look at Ellen, and was struck by her expression. Her face was pale as death; her eyes had a sort of wild fear, the lips trembled.

"My dear child, you surely did not take what I said in earnest! I spoke in jest. Captain Bohun is not a man to behave dishonourably; you may quite rely upon that. Had he come into a dukedom, you would still be made his duchess."

"I think I will go to bed, if you don't mind my leaving you," said Ellen, faintly. "My head aches."

"I think you had better, then. But you have tormented yourself into that headache, Ellen."

To bed! It was a mere figure of speech. Ellen sat up in her room, knowing that neither bed nor sleep could bring her ease—for her dreams the past two nights had been worse than reality. She watched for hours the tossing sea; it had never properly calmed down since the storm.

The morning brought a letter from Captain Bohun. To Mrs. Cumberland; not to Ellen. Or, rather a note, for it was not long enough to be called a letter. It stated that urgent circumstances had prevented his returning to Eastsea—and he would write further shortly. He added that he was very unwell, and begged to be remembered to Miss Adair.

To Miss Adair! The very formality of the message told its tale. Something was wrong: it was evident even to Mrs. Cumberland. The letter was short, constrained, abrupt; and she turned it about in haughty wonder.

"What can the man mean? This is not the way to write when things are at their present crisis. Here the ring and licence are waiting; here the clergyman is holding himself in readiness from day to day; here you are fretting your heart out, Ellen, and he writes such a note as this! But for being his own handwriting, I know what I should think."

"What?" asked Ellen, hastily.

"Why, that he is worse than he says. Delirious. Out of his senses."

"No, no; it is not that."

"I think if it is not, it ought to he," sharply retorted Mrs. Cumberland. "We must wait for his next letter, I suppose; there is nothing else to be done."

And they waited. And the weary days dragged their slow length along.

Any position more cruelly difficult than that of Captain Bohun cannot well be conceived. Madam's communication was not confined to the one first revelation; she added another to it. At first there had been no opportunity for more; the train stopped at a branch station just beyond Eastsea, and the carriage became filled with passengers. Arthur, in his torment, would have further questioned his mother, praying for elucidation; but madam demanded in a whisper whether he was mad, and then turned her back upon him. The people went all the way to London, but as soon as Arthur had handed his mother into a cab, on their way to Sir Nash Bohun's, he began again. The storm that raged at Eastsea had apparently extended its fury to London; the rain beat, the wind blew, the streets were as deserted as London streets at a busy hour of the afternoon can be. Arthur shuddered a little as he glanced out; the elements just now seemed as dark and warring as his fate.

"Mother, things cannot rest here," he said. "You evaded my questions in the train; you must answer them now. Cannot you see how dreadful this suspense must be to me? I am engaged to marry Ellen Adair: if not to-day, some other day. And now you tell me that, which—which—"

Which ought to break it off, he was about to say: but emotion stopped him. He raised his hand and wiped the moisture from his forehead. Madam bent down, and kissed his hand. He did not remember to have been kissed by her since he was a child. Her voice assumed a soft, tender tone; something like tears stood in her eyes.

"I can see how you suffer, Arthur; I am sure you must love her, poor young lady; and I would give anything not to have to inflict pain or disappointment on you. But what else can I do? You are my son: your interests are dear to me: and I must speak. Don't you remember how I have always warned you against Miss Adair? But I never suspected there would be cause for it so great as this."

He did remember it. This new soft mode of madam's became her well. In the midst of his own trouble Arthur spared a moment to think that perhaps he had in a degree misjudged her.

"I cannot understand how so frightful a charge can be brought against Mr. Adair," spoke Arthur. "What you tell me sounds like a fable. I had been given to understand that he and my father were close friends."

"As they were, once."

"And yet you say that he, Mr. Adair, was a—a—"

"A convict," spoke madam, supplying the words. "I cannot give you details, Arthur: only facts. He was tried, out there, and convicted. He obtained a ticket-of-leave—which I dare say may not have expired yet."

"And his crime?—What was it?"

"I told you. Forgery."

"Did you ever know him?"

"Of course I did: at the time when he was intimate with your father. We never quite knew who he was, Arthur; or who his people were at home, or what had taken him originally to India; but Major Bohun was unsuspicious as the day, as you yourself. There arose great trouble, Arthur; gambling and wickedness, and I can't tell you what: and through it all, nearly up to the last, your father believed in Adair."

"Was he a convict then?"

"No, no; all that came afterwards: not the crime, perhaps, but discovery, trial, and conviction. Arthur—how sorry I am to say it, I can never tell you—your father's son had better go and marry that miserable drab, than a daughter of William Adair."

She pointed to a poor wretch that was passing. A gaunt skeleton of a woman, with paint on her hollow cheeks, and a tawdry gown trailing in the mud.

Arthur pressed his hands to his temples; all sorts of confused thoughts were fighting together within his breast.

"Did Mrs. Cumberland know of this?" he asked.

"I cannot say. Her husband did. At the time it all happened, Mrs. Cumberland was away in ill-health. I should think she would hear it from her husband afterwards."

"Then—how could she encourage me to enter into this contract with Miss Adair?" returned Arthur, in a flash of resentment.

"You must never see her again, Arthur; you must never see her again. Go abroad for a time if need be: it may be the better plan."

"What am I to say to them?" he cried in self-commune. "After all, Ellen is not responsible for her father's sins."

A spasm caught madam. Was this information not sufficient?—would he carry out the marriage yet?

"Arthur, there's worse behind," she breathed. "Why can't you be satisfied?—why do you force me to tell you all?—I would have spared you the rest."

"What rest?" he asked, his lips turning white.

"About that man—William Adair."

"What rest?"

"He killed your father."

"Killed—my father?"

"Yes. He forged his name; he ruined him: and in the shock—in the shock—he—"

Madam stopped. "What?" gasped Arthur.

"Well, the shock killed your father."

"Do you mean that he died of it?"

"He could not bear the trouble; and he—shot himself."

Madam's face was white now: white with emotion. Arthur, in his emotion, seized her hand, and gazed at her.

"It is true," she whispered. "He shot himself in the trouble and disgrace that Adair brought upon him. And you, his son, would have married the man's daughter!"

With a horrible fear of what he had all but done—with a remorse that nearly turned him mad—with a sort of unformed vow never again to see Mrs. Cumberland or Ellen Adair, Arthur Bohun dropped his mother's hand with a suppressed groan, and kept silence until they stopped before the house of Sir Nash Bohun.

Mechanically he looked up at the windows, and saw that the shutters were open. So James was not dead. Arthur gave his hand to madam, to help her in.

But James Bohun was as ill as he could be: very palpably nearer death than when madam had started from the house at break of dawn. In fact there had then been some hope, for he had rallied in the night. Arthur never knew that. He supposed his mother had really come off to fetch him, in order that he should be present at the close: he suspected not that she had frantically hastened down to disturb him in his paradise.

And this was Arthur Bohun's present position. It is not possible, as was just remarked, to imagine one more cruelly difficult. Bound by every tie of honour to Ellen Adair, only not married to her through a mere chance, she waiting for him now—each hour as it passed—to return and complete the ceremony; and loving her as he should never love any other in this world. And—in the very midst of these obligations—to have made the sudden and astounding discovery that Ellen Adair was the only woman living who must be barred to him; whom, of all others, of all the numbers that walked the earth, he must alone not make his wife. The position would have been bewildering to a man without honour; to Arthur Bohun, with his fastidiously high standard, it was simply terrible.

For the few hours that James Bohun lasted, Arthur did nothing. It may almost be said that he thought nothing, for his mind was in a chaos. On the day following his arrival James died: and he, Arthur, had then become heir-presumptive. To many, it might have seemed that he was quite as secure of the succession as though he were heir-apparent; for Sir Nash was old and ailing. A twelvemonth ago Sir Nash Bohun had been full of life; upright, energetic, to all appearance strong, hearty, and likely to outlive his son. But since then he had changed rapidly; and the once healthy man seemed to have little health in him now. Medical men told him that if he would go abroad and for some months take certain medicinal springs, he might—and in all probability would—regain health and strength. Sir Nash would have tried it but for the declining health of his son. James could not leave home; Sir Nash would not be separated from him.

What though Arthur Bohun was the heir? In his present misery, it seemed worse than a mockery to him. A Bohun could not live dishonoured: and he must be dishonoured to the end of his days. To abandon Ellen Adair would bring the red stain of undying shame to his cheek; to marry her would be, of the two, only the greater disgrace. What, then, could anticipated rank and wealth be to him?—better that he should depart for some far-off land and become an exile for ever.

He knew not what to do; even at this passing moment, he knew it not. What ought he to do? Torn with conflicting emotion, he could not see where lay his duty in this very present dilemma. What was he to say to Ellen?—what to Mrs. Cumberland? Where seek an excuse for his conduct? They were expecting him, no doubt, by every train, and he did not go to them. He did not mean to go. What could he write?—what say? On the day of James Bohun's death, he took pen in hand and sat down: but he never wrote a word. The true reason he could not urge. He could not say to Ellen, Your father was a convict; he caused my father's death; and so our union must not take place. That Ellen knew nothing of any disgrace attaching to her father was as clear as day. "I tell you these dreadful truths in confidence," madam had said to Arthur, "you must not repeat them. You might be called upon to prove them—and proof would be very difficult to obtain at this distance of time. The Reverend George Cumberland knew all, even more than I; but he is dead: and it may be that Mrs. Cumberland knows nothing. I should almost think she does not: or she would never have wished to marry you to Adair's daughter. You can only be silent, Arthur; you must be so, for the poor girl's sake. By giving a mere hint as to what her father was, you would blight her prospects for life. Let her have her fair chance: though she may not marry you, she may be chosen by someone else: do nothing to hinder it. If the story ever comes out through others, why—you will be thankful, I dare say, that at least it was not through you."

He sat with the pen in his hand, and did not write a word. No word or phrase in the whole English language would have served him. "My darling, Fate has parted us, but I would a great deal rather die than have to write it, and I shall hold you in my heart for ever." Something like that he would have said, had it been practicable. But he had no longer to deal with romance, but with stern reality.

He put ink and pens away for the day, and lay back in his chair with a face almost as white as that of his dead cousin; and almost felt as though he were dying himself. Man has rarely gone through a keener mental conflict than this. He saw no way out of his dilemma; no possible means of escape.

On the third day he spoke to Sir Nash. It was not that a suspicion of his mother's veracity crossed his mind: it did not do so: for she had betrayed too much agitation to permit him to doubt the genuineness of her revelation. Therefore, he spoke not to hear the tale confirmed, but in the fulness of his stricken heart.

They were alone in the library. Sir Nash began talking of different things; of Arthur's probable succession; of his lost son. James, never strong, had worn himself out between philanthropy and close reading, he said. Arthur, he hoped, would take a lesson, embrace rational pursuits, and marry. He, Sir Nash, understood there was a charming young lady waiting to be asked by him; a young lady of family and fortune, possessing everything in her favour: he alluded to Miss Dallory.

"Did you know anything of the cause of my father's death, sir?" questioned Arthur, who had stood listening, in silence, his elbow on the mantelpiece, his hand supporting his brow.

"Do you know?" returned Sir Nash, glancing keenly at Arthur.

"I always understood that he died of sunstroke. But my mother has at length disclosed the truth to me. He—died in a different way."

"He shot himself," said Sir Nash, in hushed tones. "My brother was suddenly overwhelmed with trouble, and—he was unable to face it. Poor Tom!"

Arthur asked for some of the particulars: he was anxious to hear them. But Sir Nash could not tell him a syllable more than he already knew: in fact, the baronet seemed very hazy about it altogether.

"Of course I never learned the details as clearly as if I had been on the spot, Arthur," he said, "Your poor father fell into the meshes of a scoundrel, one Adair, who had somehow forged his way by false pretences into society—which I suppose is not difficult to manage, out there. And this Adair brought some disgrace on him from which there was no escape: and—and Tom, poor fellow, could not survive it. He was honour and integrity itself, believing all men to be as upright as he, until he found them otherwise. If he had a failing, it was on the side of pride—but I'm afraid most of us Bohuns have too much of that. A less proud man might have got over it. Tom could not. He died, rather than live with dishonoured name."

Arthur Bohun, standing there and looking more like a ghost than a living man, thought of the blow his own honour had just received—the slur that would rest on it for ever.

"And you know nothing of the details, uncle?" he resumed. "I wonder you did not stir in it at the time— bring Adair to justice."

"On the contrary, we hushed it up. We have never spoken of it, Arthur. Tom was gone; and it was as well to let it die out. It took place in some out-of-the-way district of India; and the real truth was not known to half-a-dozen people. The report there was that Major Bohun had died of sunstroke; it spread to Europe, and we let it go uncontradicted. Better, we thought, for Tom's little son—you,—Arthur—that the real facts should be allowed to rest, if rest they would."

There ensued a pause. Presently Arthur lifted his face; and spoke, as Sir Nash supposed, in derision. In truth, it was in desperation.

"It would not do, I suppose, for a gentleman to marry Adair's daughter?"

Sir Nash turned quickly. "Why do you ask this? I have heard that you know the girl."

"I will tell you, sir. No one could have been nearer marriage than I was with Ellen Adair. Of course it is all at an end: I cannot do it now."

Sir Nash Bohun stared for a moment, as if unable to take in the wildness of the words. He then drew up his fine old head with dignity.

"Arthur Bohun! a gentleman had rather do as your poor father did—shoot himself—than marry Ellen Adair."

And Arthur Bohun in his misery, wondered whether he had not better do it, rather than live the life that remained to him now.

CHAPTER XVI

IN THE CHURCHYARD

Nothing of late years had affected Mr. North so much as the death of Bessy Rane. His son Edmund's death, surrounded by all the doubt and trouble connected with the anonymous letter, did not touch him as did this. Perhaps he had never realized until now how very dear Bessy was to his heart.

"Why should Bessy have died?" he asked over and over again in his deep distress. "They have called it a famine fever, some of them, but why should a famine fever attack Bessy? I knew she was exposed to danger, through her husband; but if she did take it, why should she not have recovered from it? Others recovered who had not half Bessy's constitution. And why, why did she die so suddenly?"

No one could answer him. Not even Dr. Rane. Fever was capricious, the latter said. And death was capricious, he added in lower tones, often taking those we most cared to save.

Dallory echoed Mr. North's sentiments. The death of Mrs. Rane was the greatest shock that had fallen on them since the outbreak of the fever. Mrs. Gass, braving infection—though, like Jelly, she did not fear it—went down to Dr. Rane's house on the Monday morning to tender her sympathy, and relieve herself of some of her surprise. She felt much grieved, she was truly shocked: Bessy had always been a favourite of hers; it seemed impossible to realize that she was dead. Her mental arguments ran very much as did Mr. North's—Why should Bessy have died, when so many of the poor and the half starved recovered? But the point that pressed most forcibly on Mrs. Gass was the rapidity of the death. None had died so soon as Bessy, or anything like so soon; it seemed unaccountable that she should not have battled longer for life.

Phillis received Mrs. Gass in the darkened drawing-room; her master was out. Dr. Rane could not stay indoors to indulge his grief and play propriety, as most men can. Danger and death were abroad, and the physician had to go forth and try to avert both from others, in accordance with his duty to Heaven and to man. That he felt his loss keenly, was evident; there was no outward demonstration; neither sighs nor tears; but he seemed as a man upon whom some heavy weight had fallen; his manner preoccupied, his bearing almost unnaturally still and calm. Phillis and Mrs. Gass were talking, and, if truth must be told, shedding tears together, when the doctor came in. Phillis, standing near the centre table, had been giving particulars of the death, as far as she knew them, just as she had given them to Jelly the morning after the sad event. Mrs. Gass, seated in the green velvet chair, had untied the strings of her bonnet—she had not come down in satins and birds-of-paradise to-day, but in subdued attire—and was wiping away the tears with her broad-hemmed handkerchief while she listened.

The old servant retired at the entrance of her master. He sat down, and prepared to go through the interview with equanimity, though he heartily wished Mrs. Gass anywhere else. His house was desolate; infected also; he thought that visitors, for their own sake and his, had better keep away. They had not met since the death, and Mrs. Gass, though the least exacting woman in the world, took it a little unkindly that he had not been in, knowing that he passed her house several times in the day.

In subdued tones, Oliver Rane gave Mrs. Gass a summary of Bessy's illness and death. He had done all he could to keep her, he said; all he could. Seeley had come over once or twice, and knew that nothing more had remained in his power.

"But, doctor, I heard that on the Friday you told people she was getting better and the danger was over," urged Mrs. Gass, her tears flowing afresh.

"And I thought it was so," he answered. "What I mistook for sleepiness from exhaustion, and what Seeley mistook for the same, must have been the exhaustion of approaching death. We are deceived thus sometimes."

"But, doctor, she never had more than a day's fever. Was that enough to cause death from exhaustion?"

"She had a day and a night of fever. And consider how intense it was: I never before saw anything like it. We must not always estimate the fatality of a fever by its duration, Mrs. Gass. The terrible suddenness of the blow has been worse to me than it could have been to any one else."

Yes, Mrs. Gass believed that, and warmly sympathized with him. She then expressed a wish to see the coffin. "Would it be well for her to go up?" he asked. "Oh dear, yes," Mrs. Gass answered; "she was not afraid of anything." And the doctor took her up without further hesitation. There was little if any danger now, he observed, as he raised the sheet, which still hung there, to enable her to enter the grey room.

Everything was completed. Hepburn's men had been to and fro, and all was ended. The outer coffin was of oak, its lid bearing the inscription. Mrs. Gass's tears fairly gushed out as site read it.

"BESSY RANE.
AGED 31."

"But you have not put the date of the death, doctor!" cried Mrs. Gass, surprised at the omission.

"No? True. That's Thomas Hepburn's fault; I left it to him. The man is half-crazed just now, between grief for his brother and fear for himself. It will be put on the grave."

From Dr. Rane's Mrs. Gass went to Dallory Hall, knowing that madam was absent. Otherwise she would not have ventured there. And never was guest more welcome to its master. Poor Mr. North spoke out to her all his grief for Bessy without reservation.

But of all who felt this death, none were so affected by it as Jelly. She could not rest for the wild thoughts that tormented her day and night. The idea at first taken up kept floating through her head, and sometimes she could not get rid of it for hours: an idea that Mrs. Rane had been put into her coffin alive; that what she saw was Mrs. Rane herself, and not her spirit. Yet Jelly knew that this could not be, and her imagination would turn to another wild improbability, though she dared not follow it—that the poor lady had not died a natural death. One night there came surging into Jelly's brain the suggestive case put by Timothy Wilks, that some men might be found who would put their wives out of the way for the sake of the tontine money. Jelly tossed from side to side in her uneasy bed, and stared at the candle—for she no longer cared to sleep in the dark—and tried to get rid of the wicked notion. But she never got rid of it again; and when she rose in the morning, pale, and trembling, and weary, she believed that the dread mystery had solved itself to her, and would be found in this.

What ought she to do? Going about that day as one in a dream, the question continually presented itself to her. Jelly was at her wits' end with indecision: at night resolving to tell of the apparition, and of her suspicion of Dr. Rane; in the morning putting the thoughts from her, and call herself a fool for yielding to them. Dinah could not make out what ailed her, she was so strange and silent, but privately supposed it might be the condition of Mr. Timothy Wilks. For that gentleman was confined to his bed with some attack connected with the liver.

Wednesday, the day of the funeral, drew on. It had been a little retarded to allow of the return of Richard North. News had been received of him the morning after Bessy's death. It may readily be imagined what Richard's consternation and grief must have been to hear of his sister's death; whom he so recently left well, happy, and as likely to live as he himself.

The funeral was fixed for twelve o'clock. Richard only arrived the same morning at ten. He had been delayed twelve hours by the state of the sea, the Ostend boat not having been able to put out. Jelly, in her superstition, thought the elements had been conspiring to keep Richard North from following one to the grave who had not been sent to it by Heaven.

Long before twelve o'clock struck, groups had formed about the churchyard. The men, out on strike, and their wives, were there in full force: partly because it was a break to their monotonous idleness, partly out of respect to their master. The whole neighbourhood sincerely regretted Bessy Rane, who had never made an enemy in her life.

In the church people of the better class assembled, all in mourning. Mrs. Gass was in her pew, in an upright bonnet and crape flowers. Seeing Jelly come in looking very woebegone, she hospitably opened the pew door to her. And this was close upon the arrival of the funeral.

The first to make his appearance was Thomas Hepburn in his official capacity; quite as woebegone as Jelly, and far more sickly. The rest followed. The coffin, which Mrs. Gass had seen the other day, was placed on its stand; for the few last words of this world to be read over it. Dr. Rane, as white as a sheet; and Mr. North, leaning on his son Richard's arm, comprised the followers. No strangers were invited: Dr. Rane thought, considering what Bessy had died of, that they might not care to attend. People wondered whether Captain Bohun had been bidden to it. If so, he certainly had not come.

It seemed only a few minutes before they were moving out of the church again. The grave had been dug in the corner of the churchyard, near to Edmund North's: and he, as may be remembered, lay next to his mother. Mrs. Gass and Jelly took their seats on a remote bench, equally removed from the ceremony and the crowd. The latter stood at a respectful distance, not caring, from various considerations, to approach too near. Not a word had the two women as yet spoken to each other. The bench they sat on was low, and overshadowed by the trees that bordered the narrow walks. Not ten people in the churchyard were aware that any one sat there. Jelly was the first to break the silence.

"How white he looks!"

It was rather abrupt, as Mrs. Gass thought. They could see the clergyman in his surplice through the intervening trees, and the others standing bare-headed around him.

"Do you mean the doctor, Jelly?"

"Yes," said Jelly, "I mean him."

"And enough to make him, poor berefted man, when the one nearest and dearest to him is suddenly cut off by fever," gravely rejoined Mrs. Gass. "In the midst of life we are in death."

Now, or never. Sitting there alone with Mrs. Gass, surrounded by these solemn influences, Jelly thought the hour and the opportunity had come. Bear with the secret much longer, she could not; it would wear her to a skeleton, worry her into a fever perhaps; and she had said to herself several times that Mrs. Gass, with her plain common sense, would be the best person to confide in. Yes, she mentally repeated, now or never.

"Was it the fever that cut her off?" began Jelly, significantly.

"Was it the fever that cut her off?" echoed Mrs. Gass. "What d'you mean, Jelly?"

Jelly turned to the speaker, and plunged into her tale. Beginning, first of all, with the apparition she had certainly seen, and how it was—staying late at Ketler's, and Dinah's having left the blind undrawn—that she had come to see it. There she paused.

"Why, what on earth d'you mean?" sharply demanded Mrs. Gass. "Saw Mrs. Rane's ghost! Don't be an idiot, Jelly."

"Yes, I saw it," repeated Jelly, with quiet emphasis. "Saw it as sure as I see them standing there now to bury her. There could be no mistake. I never saw her plainer in life. It was at one o'clock in the morning, I say, Mrs. Gass; and she was screwed down at twelve: an hour before it."

"Had you taken a little too much beer?" asked Mrs. Gass, after a pause, staring at Jelly to make sure the question would not also apply to the present time. But the face that met hers was strangely earnest: too much so even to resent the insinuation.

"It was her ghost, poor thing: and I'm afraid it'll walk till justice lays it. I never knew but one ghost walk in all my life, Mrs. Gass: and he had been murdered."

Mrs. Gass made no rejoinder. She was absorbed in looking at Jelly. Jelly went on—

"It's said there's many that walk: the world's full of such tales; but I never knew but that one. When people are put to an untimely end, and buried away out of sight, and their secrets with 'em, it stands to reason that they can't rest quiet in their graves. She won't."

Mrs. Gass put her hand impressively on Jelly's black shawl, and kept it there. "Tell me why you are saying this?"

"It's what I want to do. If I don't tell it to some one, I shall soon be in the grave myself. Fancy me living at the very next door, and nobody in the house just now but Dinah!"

Jelly spoke out all: that she believed Dr. Rane might have "put his wife out of the way." Mrs. Gass was horrified. Not at the charge: she didn't believe a word of it; but at Jelly's presuming to imagine it. She gave Jelly a serious reprimand.

"It was him that wrote that anonymous letter, you know," whispered Jelly.

"Hush! Hold your tongue, girl. I've warned you before to let that alone."

"And I'm willing to do so."

"That is downright wicked of you, Jelly. Dr. Rane loved his wife. What motive do you suppose he could have had for killing her?"

"To get the tontine money," replied Jelly, in a whisper.

The two women gazed at each other; gaze meeting gaze. And then Mrs. Gass suddenly grew whiter than Dr. Rane, and began to shiver as though some strange chill had struck her.

CHAPTER XVII

AT SIR NASH BOHUN'S

Reclining on the pillows of an invalid chair was Arthur Bohun, looking as yellow as gold, recovering from an attack of jaundice. The day of James Bohun's funeral it had poured with rain; and Arthur, standing at the grave, had caught a chill. This had terminated in the jaundice—his unhappy state of mind no doubt doing its part towards bringing on the malady. He was recovering now. Sir Nash, at whose house he lay, was everything that was kind.

Madam was kind also: at least she made a great profession of being so. Her object in life just now was to get her son to marry Miss Dallory. Madam cared no more for her son Arthur or his welfare than she did for Richard North; but she was shrewd enough to foresee that the source, whence her large supplies of money had hitherto been drawn, was now dried up: and she hoped to get supplies out of Arthur for the future. Marrying an heiress, wealthy as Miss Dallory, would wonderfully increase his power to help her. Moreover, she wished to be effectually relieved from that horrible nightmare that haunted her still—the possibility of his marrying Ellen Adair.

So madam laid her plans—as it was in her scheming nature ever to be laying them—and contrived to bring Miss Dallory, at that time in London with her aunt, to Sir Nash Bohun's for a few days' visit when Arthur was recovering. The young lady was there now: and Matilda North was there; and they both spent a good part of every day with Arthur; and Sir Nash made much of Mary Dallory, partly because he really liked her, and partly because he thought there was a probability that she would become Arthur's wife. During his illness, Captain Bohun had had time for reflection: not only time, but calmness, in the lassitude it brought to him mentally and physically: and he began to see his immediate way somewhat clearer. To give no explanation to the two ladies at Eastsea, to whom he was acting, as he felt, so base a part, was the very worst form of cowardice; and, though he could not explain to Ellen Adair, he was now anxious to do so to Mrs. Cumberland. Accordingly the first use he made of his partially-recovered health, was to ask for writing materials and write her a note in very shaky characters. He spoke of his serious illness, stated that certain "untoward circumstances" had occurred to intercept his plans, but that as soon as he was sufficiently well to travel he should beg of her to appoint a time when she could allow him a private conference.

The return post brought him a letter from Ellen. Rather to his consternation. Ellen assumed—not unnaturally, as the reader will find—that the sole cause of his mysterious absence was illness; that he had been ill from the first, and unable to travel. It ran as follows:—

"My Dearest Arthur,

"I cannot express to you what my feelings are this morning; so full of joy, yet full of pain. Oh I cannot tell you what the past two or three weeks have been to me; looking back, it almost seems a wonder that I lived through them. For I thought—I will not say here what I thought, and perhaps I could not say, only that you were never coming again; and that it was agony to me, worse than death. And to hear now that you could not come: that the cause of your silence and absence has been dangerous illness, brings to me a great sorrow and shame. Oh Arthur, my dearest, forgive me! Forgive also my writing to you thus freely; but it almost seems to me as though you were already my husband. Had you been called away only half-an-hour later you would have been, and perhaps even might have had me with you in your illness.

"I should like to write pages and pages, but you may be too ill yet to read very much, and so I will say no more. May God watch over you and bring you to health again.

"Ever yours, Arthur, yours only, with the great love of my heart,

"Ellen Adair."

And Captain Arthur Bohun, in spite of the cruel fate that had parted them, pressed the letter to his heart, and the sweet name, Ellen Adair—sweeter than any he would ever hear again—to his lips, and shed tears of anguish over it in the feebleness induced by illness.

They might take Mary Dallory to his room as much as they pleased; and Matilda might exert her little wiles in praising her, and madam hers to leave them "accidentally" together; but his heart was too full of another, and of its own bitter pain, to have room for as much as a responsive thought to Mary Dallory.

"Arthur is frightfully languid and apathetical!" spoke Miss North one day in a burst of resentment. "I'm sure he is quite rude to me and Mary: he lets us sit by him for an hour at a time, and never speaks."

"Consider how ill he has been—and is," remonstrated Sir Nash.

Mrs. Cumberland's span of life was drawing into a very narrow space: and it might be that she was beginning to suspect this. For some months she had been growing inwardly weaker; but the weakness had for a week or two been visibly and rapidly increasing. Captain Bohun's unaccountable behaviour had tried her—for Ellen's sake. She was responsible to Mr. Adair for the welfare of his daughter, and the matter was a source of daily and hourly annoyance to her. When this second tardy note arrived, she considered it, in one sense, a satisfactory explanation; in another, not so: since, if Captain Bohun had been too ill to write himself, why did he not get some one else to write to her and say so? However, she was willing to persuade herself that all would be right: and she told Ellen, without showing her the note, that Captain Bohun had been dangerously ill, unable to come or write. Hence Ellen's return letter.

But, apart from the progress of the illness in itself, nothing had done Mrs. Cumberland so much harm as the news of her daughter-in-law's death. It had been allowed to reach her abruptly, without the smallest warning. I suppose there is something in our common nature that urges us to impart sad tidings to others. Dinah, Jelly's friend and underling, was no exception to this rule. On the day after the death, she sat down and indited a letter to her fellow-servant, Ann, at Eastsea, in which she detailed the short progress of Mrs. Rane's illness, and her strangely sudden death. Ann, before she had well mastered the cramped lines, ran with white face to her mistress; and Miss Adair afterwards told her that she ought to have known better. That it was too great a shock for Mrs. Cumberland in her critical state, the girl in her repentance very soon saw. Mrs. Cumberland asked for the letter, and scarcely had it out of her hand for many hours. Dead! apparently from no sufficient cause; for the fever had lasted only a day, Dinah said, and had gone again. Mrs. Cumberland, in her bewilderment, began actually to think the whole thing was a fable.

Not for two or three days did she receive confirmation from Dr. Rane. Of course the doctor did not know or suppose that any one else would be writing to Eastsea; and he was perhaps willing to spare his mother the news as long as he could do so. He shortly described the illness—saying that he, himself, had entertained very little hope from the first, from the severity of the fever. But all this did not help to soothe Mrs. Cumberland; and in the two or three weeks that afterwards went on, she faded palpably. Little wonder the impression, that she was growing worse, made its way to Dallory.

CHAPTER XVIII

JELLY'S TROUBLES

With the same rapidity that the sickness had appeared, so did it subside in Dallory. Mrs. Rane's was the last serious case: the last death; the very few cases afterwards were of the mildest description; and within a fortnight of the time that ill-fated lady was laid in the ground, people were restoring their houses and throwing their rooms open to the renewed air.

The inhabitants in general, rallying their courage, thought the sooner they forgot the episode the better. Excepting perhaps by the inmates of those houses from which some one had been taken, they did soon forget it. It was surprising—now that fear was at an end and matters could be summed up dispassionately—how few the losses were. With the exception of Henry Hepburn the undertaker and Mrs. Rane, they were entirely amongst the poor working people out on strike, and, even here, were principally amongst the children. Mrs. Gass told men to their faces that the fever had come of nothing but famine and poverty, and that they had only themselves to thank for it. She was in the habit, as the reader knows, of dealing some home truths out to them: but she had dealt out something else during the sickness, and that was wholesome food. She continued to do so still to those who had been weakened by it: but she gave them due warning that it was only temporary help, which, but for the fever, they would never have received from her. And so the visitation grew into a thing of the past, and Dallory was itself again.

One, there was, however, who could not forget: with whom that unhappy past was present night and day. Jelly. That Dr. Rane had in some way wilfully caused the death of his wife, Jelly was as sure of as though she had seen it done. Her suspicion pointed to laudanum; or to some equally fatal preparation. Suspicion? Nay, with her it had become a certainty. In that last day of Bessy Rane's life, when she was described as sleeping, sleeping, always sleeping; when her sole cry had been—"I am easy, only let me sleep," Jelly now felt that Dr. Rane knew she had been quietly sleeping away to death. Unerringly as though it had been written with the pen of truth, lay the conviction upon her heart. About that, there could be neither doubt nor hesitation: the difficulty was—what ought to be her own course in the matter?

In all Jelly's past life she had never been actually superstitious; if told that she was so now, she would have replied that it was because circumstances had forced it upon her. That Mrs. Rane's spirit had appeared to her that memorable night for one sole purpose—that she, Jelly, should avenge her dreadful end by publicly disclosing it, Jelly believed as implicitly as she believed in the Gospel. Not a soul in the whole wide world but herself (saving of course Dr. Rane) had the faintest idea that the death was not a natural one. Jelly moaned and groaned, and thought her fate unjustly hard that she should have been signalled out by Heaven—for so she solemnly put it—for the revelation, when there were so many others in the community of Dallory who might have done it better than herself. Jelly had periods of despondency, when she did not quite know whether her head was on or off, or whether her mind wouldn't "go." Why couldn't the ghost have appeared to some one else, she would mentally ask at these moments: to Phillis, say; or to Dinah; or to Seeley the surgeon? Just because she had been performing an act of charity in sitting up with Keller's sick child, it must show itself to her! And then Jelly's brain would go off into problems, that it might have puzzled one wiser than she to answer. Supposing she had not been at Ketler's that night, the staircase blind would have been drawn at dusk as usual, she would have gone to bed at her ordinary hour, have seen, nothing, and been spared all this misery. But no. It was not to be. And although Jelly, in her temper, might wish to throw the blame on Ketler for staying out, and on Dinah for her negligence, she recognized the finger of Destiny in all this, and knew she could not have turned aside from it.

What was she to do? Living in constant dread of again seeing the apparition, feeling a certainty within herself that she should see it, Jelly pondered the question every hour of the day. Things could not rest as they were. On the one hand, there was her natural repugnance to denounce Dr. Rane: just as there had been in the case of the anonymous letter: not only because she was in the service of his mother, but for his own sake; for Jelly, with all her faults, as to gossip and curiosity, had by no means a bad heart. On the other hand, there was the weighty secret revealed to her by the departed woman, and the obligation laid upon her in consequence. Yet—how could she speak?—when the faintest breath of such an accusation against her son, would assuredly kill Mrs. Cumberland in her present critical state! and to Jelly she was a good and kind mistress. No, she could never do it. With all this conflict going on within her, no wonder Jelly fell away: she had been thin enough before, she was like a veritable skeleton now. As to the revelation to Mrs. Gass, Jelly might just as well have made it to the moon. For that lady, after the first shock had passed, absolutely refused to put any faith in the tale: and had appeared ever since, by her manner, to ignore it as completely as though it had never been uttered.

Gradually Jelly grew disturbed by another fear: might she not be taken up as an accomplice after the fact? She was sure she had heard of such cases: and she tormented Tim Wilks almost out of patience—that gentleman having recovered from his temporary indisposition—by asking endless questions as to what the law might do to a person who found out that another had committed some crime, and kept back the knowledge: say stolen a purse, for instance, and appropriated the money.

One night, when Jelly, by some fortunate chance, had really got to sleep early—for she more often lay awake until morning—a ring at the door-bell suddenly roused her. Mrs. Cumberland had caused a night-bell to be put to the door: in case of fire, she had said. It hung on this first landing, not very far from Jelly's head, and it awoke her instantly. Dinah, sleeping above, might have heard it just as well as Jelly; but Dinah was a sound sleeper, and the bell, as Jelly knew, might ring for an hour before it awoke her. However, Jelly lay still, not caring to get up herself, hoping against hope, and wondering who in the world could be ringing, unless it was some one mistaking their house for Dr. Rane's. Such a thing had happened before.

Ring; ring; ring. Not a loud ring by any means; but a gentle peal, as if the applicant did it reluctantly. Jelly lay on. She was not afraid that it was connected with the sight she was always in dread of again seeing, since ghosts are not in the habit of ringing to announce their visits. In fact, surprise, and speculating as to who it could be, put all fear for the time being out of Jelly's head.

Ring; ring; ring. Rather a louder peal this time, as if a little impatience now mingled with the reluctance.

Flinging on a warm shawl, and putting her feet into her shoes, Jelly proceeded to the front-room—Mrs. Cumberland's chamber when she was at homo—threw up the window, and called to know who was there. A little man, stepping back from the door into the bright moonlight, looked up to answer—and Jelly recognized the form and voice of Ketler.

"It's me," said he.

"You!" interrupted Jelly, not allowing the man to continue. "What on earth do you want here at this hour?"

"I came to tell you the news about poor Cissy. She's dead."

"Couldn't it wait?" tartly returned Jelly, overlooking the sad nature of the tidings in her anger at having been disturbed. "Would it have run away, that you must come and knock folks up to tell it, as if you'd been the telegraph?"

"It was my wife made me come," spoke Ketler, with much humility. "She's in a peck o' grief, Jelly, and nothing would do but I must come right off and tell you; she thought, mayhap, you'd not be gone to bed."

"Not gone to bed at midnight!" retorted Jelly. "And there it is, striking: if you've any ears to hear. You must be a fool, Ketler."

"Well, I'm sorry to have disturbed you," said the man, with a sigh. "I wouldn't have done it myself; but poor Susan was taking on so, I couldn't deny her. We was all so fond of the child; and—and—"

Ketler broke down. The man had loved his child: and he was weak and faint with hunger. It a little appeased Jelly.

"I suppose you don't expect me to dress myself and come off to Susan at this hour?" she exclaimed, her tone, however, not quite so sharp as it had been.

"Law, bless you, no," answered Ketler. "What good would that do? It couldn't bring Cissy back to life again."

"Ketler, it's just this—instead of being upset with grief, you and Susan might be thankful the child's taken out of the trouble of this world. She won't be crying for food where she's gone, and find none."

The man's grief was renewed at the last suggestion. But Jelly had really meant it in the light of consolation.

"She was your god-child, Jelly."

"You needn't tell me that," answered Jelly. "Could I have saved her life at any trouble or cost, I would have done it. If I had a home of my own I'd have taken her to it, but I'm only in service, as you know. Ketler, it is the strike that has killed that child."

Ketler was silent.

"Cissy was a weakly child and required extra comforts; as long as you were in work she had them, but when that dropped off, of course the child suffered. And now she's gone. She is better off, Ketler."

"Yes," assented the man as if he were heartbroken. "If it wasn't for the thought of the rest, I should wish it was me that was gone instead."

"Well, give my love to Susan and say I'm sorry for it altogether, and I'll come down some time in the morning. And, look here, Ketler—what about the money for the burial? You've nothing towards it, I expect."

"Not a penny," moaned Ketler.

"Well, I know you wouldn't like the poor little thing to be buried by the parish, so I'll see what's to be done, tell Susan. Goodnight."

Jelly shut down the window sharply. She really looked upon the strike as having led to the child's death—and remotely possibly it had done so; so what with that, and the untimely disturbance, her anger was somewhat excusable.

In passing across the landing to her own chamber, the large window became suddenly illuminated. Jelly stopped. Her heart, as she would herself have expressed it, leaped into her mouth. The light came from the outside; no doubt from Dr. Rane's. Jelly stood motionless. And then—what desperate courage impelled her she never knew, but believed afterwards it must have been something akin to the fascination of the basilisk—she advanced to the window, and drew aside the white blind.

But she did not see Bessy Rane this time, as perhaps she had expected; only her husband. Dr. Rane had a candle in his hand, and was apparently picking up something he had dropped quite close to his own window. In another moment he lodged the candle on a chair that stood there, so as to have both hands at liberty. Jelly watched. What he had dropped appeared to be several articles of his deceased wife's clothing, some of which had unfolded in the fall. He soon had them within his arm again, caught up the candle, and went downstairs. Jelly saw and recognized one beautiful Indian shawl, which had been a present from her own mistress to Bessy.

"He is going to pack them up and sell them, the wicked man!" spoke Jelly in her conviction. And her ire grew very great against Dr. Rane. "I'd almost rather have seen the spirit of his poor wife again than this," was her comment, as she finally went into her room.

Putting aside all the solemn doubts and fears that were making havoc with Jelly's mind, her curiosity was insatiable. Perhaps no woman in all Dallory had so great a propensity for prying into other people's affairs as she. Not, it must be again acknowledged, to harm them, but simply to gratify her inquisitiveness.

On the following morning, when Jelly attired herself to go to Ketler's after breakfast—the meal being seasoned throughout with reproaches to Dinah for not hearing the night-bell—she bethought herself that she would first of all step into the next door. Ostensibly with the neighbourly object of informing Phillis of the death of the child; really, to pick up any items of information that might be floating about. Dr. Rane, it may be here remarked, had given Molly Green a character to get herself another situation, preferring to retain the elder servant, Phillis, who, however, only went to him by day. The doctor was alone in his house at night, and Jelly believed he dared not have even old Phillis in, knowing it was haunted. He made no secret now of his intention of quitting Dallory. As soon as his practice should be disposed of, and the tontine money paid over to him, away he would go.

Jelly coolly walked out of the window of Mrs. Cumberland's dining-room, and through that of the doctor's. She had seen him go out some little time before. Phillis was upstairs, putting her master's chamber to rights, and Jelly sought her there. She described the fright Ketler had given her by coming at midnight to bring the news about Cissy; and Phillis, whose heart was tender, dropped a tear or two to the child's memory. Cissy had been loved by every one.

"Miss Dallory will be sorry to hear this when she comes back," remarked Phillis.

"I say, Phillis, what does your master mean to do with Mrs. Rane's clothes?" abruptly asked Jelly.

Phillis, dusting the looking-glass at the moment, paused in her occupation, as if considering.

"I'm sure I don't know, Jelly, He pointed out a few of the plain things to me one day, and said I might divide them between myself and Molly Green, but that he wouldn't like to see us wear them till he was gone away. As of course we shouldn't, being in black for her."

"She had lots of beautiful clothes. I'm sure the shawls, and scarfs, and embroidered robes, and worked petticoats, and other valuable Indian things that my mistress was always giving her, would have set up any lady's wardrobe. What will he do with them?"

Phillis shook her head, and pointed to a high chest of drawers. Her heart was full yet when she spoke of her late mistress.

"They are all in there, Jelly."

Are they, thought Jelly. But Phillis was going down now, her occupation ended. Jelly lingered behind, and put her black bonnet out at the window, as if looking at something up the road. When Phillis had descended the stairs, Jelly tried the drawers. All were locked except one. That one, which Jelly softly drew open, was filled with articles belonging to the late Mrs. Rane; none of them, as far as Jelly could gather by the cursory glance, of much value.

"Yes," she said bitterly. "He keeps these open for show, but he is sending away the best. Those other drawers, if they could be looked into, are empty."

If ever Jelly had been startled in all her life at human footstep, it was to hear that of Dr. Rane on the stairs. How she closed the drawer, how she got her bonnet stretched out at the window again as far as it would stretch, she hardly knew. The doctor came in. Jelly, bringing in her head, apparently as much surprised as if a rhinoceros had walked into the room, apologized and explained rather lamely. She supposed Phillis must have gone down, she said, while she was watching that impudent butcher's boy; she had made bold to step up to tell Phillis about Ketler's little girl.

"Ah, she is gone," observed Dr. Rane, as Jelly was walking out. "There has been no hope of her for some time."

"No, sir, I know there hasn't," replied Jelly, somewhat recovering her equanimity. "I told Ketler that he may thank the strike for it."

Jelly got out with this, and was passing through the grey room, when the doctor spoke again.

"Have you heard from your mistress this morning, Jelly?"

"No, sir."

"Well, I have. I am very much afraid that she is exceedingly ill, Jelly?"

"Dinah had a letter from Ann a day or two ago, sir; she said that her missis was looking worse, and seemed lower than she had ever known her."

"Ay, I wish she would come home. Eastsea is far away, and I cannot be running there everlastingly," added the doctor, as he closed the chamber-door in Jelly's face.

CHAPTER XIX

COMING HOME TO DIE

Time went on again; nearly a fortnight. Dallory had relapsed into its old routine; the fever was forgotten. Houses had recovered from the aroma of soap and scrubbing: their inhabitants were back again; and amongst them were Mrs. North and her daughter Matilda.

The principal news madam found to interest her was, that Richard North had opened the works again. The glow of hope it raised within her was very bright; for she considered it as an earnest that supplies would spring up again in the future as they had in the past. That she would find herself mistaken was exceedingly probable; Richard himself could have said a certainty. Madam had the grace to express some calm regret for the untimely death of Bessy Rane, in the hearing of Mr. North and Richard; she had put herself and Matilda into deeper mourning than they had assumed for James Bohun. It was all of the most fashionable and costly description; and the master of Dallory Hall, poor helpless man, had the pleasure of receiving the bills for it from the London court-milliners and dressmakers. But madam never inquired into the particulars of Bessy's illness and death; in her opinion the less fevers were talked about the better.

Yes: the North works were reopened. Or, to be quite correct, they were on the point of being reopened. Upon how small a scale he must begin again, Richard, remembering the extent of past operations, felt almost ashamed to contemplate. But, as he good-humouredly remarked, half a loaf was better than no bread. He must earn a living; he had no fortune to fly to; and he preferred doing this to seeking employment under other firms, if indeed anything worth having could have been found; but the trade of the country was in a most depressed state, and hundreds of gentlemen, like himself, had been thrown on their beam ends. It was the same thing as beginning life over again; a little venture, that might succeed or might fail; one in which he must plod on carefully and cautiously, even to keep it going.

The whole staff of operatives would at first number less than twenty. The old workmen, idly airing themselves still in North Inlet, laughed derisively when they heard this. They were pleasantly sarcastic over it, thinking perhaps to conceal their real bitterness of heart. The new measure did not find favour with them. How should it, when they stood out in the light of exclusion? Some eight or ten, who had never willingly upheld the strike, had all along been ready to return to work, would be taken on again; the rest were foreigners that Richard North was bringing over from abroad. And the anger of the disaffected may be imagined.

Mrs. Gass entered cordially into Richard's plans. She would have put unlimited money into his new undertaking; but Richard would not have it. Some portion of her capital that had been embarked in the firm of North and Gass, of necessity remained in it—all, in fact, that was not lost—but this she counted as nothing, and wanted to help Richard yet further. "It's of no good crying over spilt milk, Mr. Richard," she said to him, philosophically; "and I've still a great deal more than I shall ever want." But Richard was firm: he would receive no further help: it was a risk that he preferred to incur alone.

Perhaps there were few people living that Richard North liked better than Mrs. Gass. He even liked her homely language; it was honest and genuine; far more to be respected than if she had made a show of attempting what she could not have kept up. Richard had learned to know her worth: he recognized it more certainly day by day. In the discomfort of his home at Dallory Hall—which had long been anything but a home to him—he had fallen into the habit of almost making a second home with Mrs. Gass. Never a day passed but he spent an hour or two of it with her; and she would persuade him to remain for a meal as often as she could.

He sat one afternoon at her well-spread tea-table. His arrangements were very nearly organized now; and in a day the works would open. The foreign workmen had arrived, and were lodging with their families in the places appointed for them. Two policemen, employed by Richard, had also taken up their position in Dallory, purposely to protect them. Of course their mission was not known: Richard North would not be the one to provoke hostilities; but he was quite aware of the ill-feeling obtaining amongst his former workmen.

"Downright idiots, they be," said Mrs. Gass, confidentially, as she handed Richard a cup of tea. "They want a lesson read to 'em, Mr. Richard; that's what it is."

"I don't know about that," dissented Richard. "It seems to me they could hardly receive a better lesson than these last few months must have taught them."

"Ah, you don't know 'em as I do. I'm almost double your age, sir; and there's nothing gives experience like years."

Richard laughed. "Not double my age yet, Mrs. Gass."

"Anyway, I might have been your mother—if you'll excuse my saying it," she contended. "You're hard upon thirty-three, and I'm two years turned fifty."

In this homely manner Mrs. Gass usually liked to make her propositions undeniable. Certainly she might, in point of age, have been Richard's mother.

"I know the men better than you do, Mr. Richard; and I say they want a lesson read to 'em yet. And they'll get it, sir. But we'll leave the subject for a bit, if you please. I've been tired of it for some time past, and I'm sure you have. To watch once sensible men acting like fools, and persisting in doing it, in spite of everybody and everything, wearies one's patience. Is it tomorrow that you open?"

"The day after."

"Well, now, Mr. Richard, I should like to say another word upon a matter that you and me don't agree on—and it's not often our opinions differ, is it, sir? It's touching your capital. I know you'll want more than you can command: it would give me a real pleasure if you'll let me find it."

Richard smiled, and shook his head, "I cannot say more than I have said before," was his reply. "You know all I have urged."

"Promise me this, then," returned Mrs. Gass. "If ever you find yourself at a pinch as things go on, you'll come to me. I don't ask this, should the concern turn out a losing one, for in that case I know cords wouldn't draw you to me for help. But when you are getting on, and money would be useful, and its investment safe and sure, I shall expect you to come to me. Now, that's enough. I want to put a question, Mr. Richard, that delicacy has kept me from worrying you about before. What about the expenses at Dallory Hall? You can't pretend to keep 'em up yourself."

"Ah," said Richard, "that has been my nightmare. But I think I see a way through it at last. First of all, I have given notice to Miss Dallory that we shall not renew the lease: it will expire, you know, next March."

"Good," observed Mrs. Gass.

"My father knows nothing about it—it is of no use troubling him earlier than is necessary; and of course madam knows nothing. She imagines that the lease will be renewed as a matter of course. Miss Dallory will, at my request, keep counsel—or, rather, her brother Francis for her, for it is he who transacts her business."

"They know then that you are the real lessee of Dallory Hall? Lawk a mercy, what a simpleton I am!" broke off Mrs. Gass. "Of course they must have known it when the transfer was made."

Richard nodded. "As soon as Christmas is turned I shall look out for a moderate house in lieu of the Hall; one that I shall hope to be able to keep up. It shall have a good garden for my father's sake. There will be rebellion on the part of madam and Matilda, but I can't help that. I cannot do more than my means will allow me."

"See here, Mr. Richard; don't worry yourself about not being able to keep up a house for Mr. North. I'll do my part in that: do it all, if need be. He and my husband were partners and friends, and grew rich together. Mr. North has lost his savings, but I have kept mine; and I will never see him wanting comfort while he lives. We'll look out for a pretty villa with a lovely garden; and he'll be happier in it than he has ever been in that grand Hall. If madam doesn't like to bring her pride down to it, let her go off elsewhere—and a good riddance of bad rubbish.—Mr. Richard, have you heard the news about Mary Dallory?"

"What news?" he asked.

"That she's going to be married to Captain Bohun."

Richard North drank his tea to the dregs. His face had flushed a little.

"I hear that madam wishes it, and is working for it," he answered. "Miss Dallory was staying with them when they were at Sir Nash Bohun's."

"I know madam has given it out that they're going to marry," rejoined Mrs. Gass. "By the way, Mr. Richard, how is Captain Bohun getting on, after his illness?"

"He is better. Almost well."

Mrs. Gass helped herself to some buttered toast. "I shall believe in that marriage when it has taken place, Mr. Richard; not before. Unless I am uncommonly out, Captain Bohun cares for another young lady too well to think of Mary Dallory. Folks mayn't suspect it; and I believe don't. But I have had my eyes about me."

Richard knew that she alluded to Ellen Adair.

"They are both as sweet and good girls as ever lived, and a gentleman may think himself lucky to get either of 'em. Mr. Richard, your coat-sleeve is coming into contact with the potted-ham."

Richard smiled a little as he attended to his cuff. Mourning was always bad wearing, he remarked, and showed every little stain. And then he said a few words about her for whom it was worn. He had rarely alluded to the subject since she died.

"I cannot grow reconciled to her loss," he said in low tones. "At times can scarcely believe in it. To have been carried off after only a day's fever seems to me incredible."

And Mrs. Gass felt that the words startled her to pallor. She turned away lest he should see the change in her countenance.

Bad news arrived from Mrs. Cumberland. Only a morning or two later, a loud knock at the front-door disturbed Jelly and Dinah at their breakfast. Upon its being opened by the latter, Dr. Rane walked straight into the kitchen without ceremony, an open letter in his hand. Jelly rose and curtsied. She had been markedly respectful to the doctor of late, perhaps in very fear lest he should suspect the curious things that were troubling her mind.

"My mother will be home to-night, Jelly."

"To-night, sir!" exclaimed Jelly in her surprise.

"She is much worse. Very ill indeed. She says she is coming home to die."

Jelly was startled out of her equanimity.

"It is only three lines, and she writes herself," continued Dr. Rane, just showing the letter in his hand, as if in confirmation. "They were to go to London yesterday, remain there the night, and will come home to-day. Of course you will have everything in readiness."

"Yes, sir. And what about meeting my mistress at the station?"

"I shall go myself," said Dr. Rane.

He went away with the last words. Jelly sat still for a few minutes to digest the news, and came to the conclusion that "coming home to die" was a mere figure of speech of Mrs. Cumberland's. Then she rose up to begin her preparations, and overwhelmed and bewildered Dinah with a multitude of orders.

During the day, Jelly, in pursuance of something or other she wanted, was walking quickly towards Dallory, when in passing the Hall gates she found herself accosted by Mrs. North. Madam was taking her usual promenade in the grounds, and had extended it to the gates. Jelly stood still in sheer amazement; it was the first time within her recollection that madam had condescended to address her or any other inhabitant of the neighbourhood.

How was Mrs. Cumberland?—and where was she? madam graciously asked. And Jelly in the moment's haste, answered that she was at Eastsea.

"To stay the winter, I believe," went on madam. "And Miss Adair—is she with her?"

"I ought to have said was at Eastsea," corrected Jelly, who did not like madam well enough to be more than barely civil to her. "My mistress is worse, and is coming home to-day. Miss Adair is with her of course. I must wish you good-morning, madam; I've all my work before me to-day." And away went Jelly, leaving madam a mental compliment:

"Nasty proud cat! she had some sly motive for asking, I know."

And so the day went on.

The early twilight of the autumn evening was beginning to fall, together with a heavy shower of rain, when the carriage containing Mrs. Cumberland stopped at her door. Jelly ran out; and was met by Ellen Adair, who spoke in a startled whisper.

"Oh, Jelly, she is so ill! too ill to speak."

The doctor stood helping his mother out. Ann was gathering up small articles from beside the driver. Jelly caught one glimpse of her mistress's face and fell back in alarm. Surely that look was the look of death!

"She ought not to have come," murmured Dr. Rane in Jelly's ear. "Go and ask Seeley to step over—whilst I get my mother upstairs."

There was bustle and confusion for the moment. Mrs. Cumberland was placed in the easy-chair in her room, and her bonnet and travelling wraps were removed. She refused to go to bed. In half-an-hour or so, when she had somewhat recovered the fatigue, she looked and seemed much better, and spoke a little, expressing a wish for some tea. The doctors left her to take it, enjoining strict quiet. Jelly was near her mistress, holding the cup and saucer.

"What did she die of, Jelly?" came the unexpected question.

"Who?" asked Jelly, wonderingly.

Mrs. Cumberland motioned in the direction of her son's house: and her voice was subdued to faintness: "Bessy Rane."

Jelly gave a start that almost upset the teacup. She felt her face grow white; but she could not move to conceal it.

"Why don't you reply? What did she die of?"

"Ma'am, don't you know? She caught the fever."

"It troubles me, Jelly; it troubles me. I've done nothing but dream about her ever since. And what will Oliver do without her?"

The best he can, Jelly had a great mind to answer. But all she said, was, to beg her mistress to leave these questions until the morning.

"I don't think any morning will dawn for me," was Mrs. Cumberland's remark. "I sent you word I was coming home to die. I wanted to come for many reasons. I knew the journey would do me harm; I had put it off too long. But I had to come home: I could not die away from it."

Every consoling thing that Jelly could think of, she said, assuring her mistress it was nothing but the journey that had brought her into this state of depression.

"I want to see Mr. North," resumed Mrs. Cumberland. "You must bring him to me."

"Not to-night," said Jelly.

"To-night. At once. There is no time to be lost. To see him was one of the things I had to come home for."

And Mrs. Cumberland, ill though she was, was as resolute in being obeyed as she had ever been in the days of her health. Jelly had the sense to know that refusal would excite her more than any result from compliance, and prepared to obey. As she passed out of the presence of Mrs. Cumberland, she saw Ellen Adair sitting on the stairs, anxiously listening for any sound from the sick-room that might tell how all was going on within it.

"Oh, Miss Ellen! You should not be there."

"I cannot rest anywhere, Jelly. I want to know how she is. She is my only friend on this side of the wide world."

"Well now, Miss Ellen, look here—you may come in and stay with her, whilst I am away: I was going to call Ann. But mind you don't talk to her."

Hastily throwing on a shawl, Jelly started for Dallory Hall. It was an inclement night, pouring with rain. And Ellen Adair took up her place in silence by the side of the dying woman—for she was dying, however ignorant they might be of the fact. Apart from Ellen's natural grief for Mrs. Cumberland, thoughts of what her own situation would be, if she lost her, could but intrude on her mind, bringing all sorts of perplexity with them. It seemed to her that she would be left without home or protector in the wide world.

CHAPTER XX

RICHARD NORTH'S REVELATION

For a wonder, the dinner-table at Dallory Hall included only the family-party. Madam headed it; Mr. North was at the foot; Richard on one side; Matilda on the other. Scarcely a word was being spoken. Madam was in one of her imperious humours—when, indeed, was she out of them?—the servants waited in silence.

Suddenly there rang out a loud peal from the hall-bell. Richard, who was already beginning to be disturbed by vague fears as to what his ex-workmen's hostilities might make them do, sat back in his chair absently, and turned his head.

"Are you expecting any one, Dick?" asked his father.

"No, sir. Unless it be a message to call me out."

It was, however, a message for Mr. North; not for Richard. Mrs. Cumberland wanted to see him. "On the instant," the servant added: for so Jelly had imperatively put it.

Mr. North laid down his knife and fork and looked at the man. He did not understand.

"Mrs. Cumberland is at Eastsea," he cried.

"No, sir, she has just got home, and she wants to see you very particular. It's the lady's maid who has brought the message."

"Mr. North cannot go," broke forth madam to the servant. "Go and say so."

But Jelly, to whom the words penetrated as she stood in the hall, had no notion of her mistress's wishes being set at nought by madam. Jelly had a great deal of calm moral and physical courage—in spite of the supernatural terrors that had recently influenced her—some persons might have said her share of calm impudence also: and she made no ceremony of putting her black bonnet inside the room.

"My mistress is dying, sir; I don't think there can be a doubt of it," she said, advancing to Mr. North. "She wishes to say a few last words to you, if you'll please to come. There's no time to be lost, sir."

"Bless me!—poor Fanny!" cried Mr. North, rising: his hands beginning to tremble a little. "I'll come at once, Jelly."

"You will not go," spoke madam, as if she were issuing an imperial edict.

"I must go," said Mr. North. "Don't you hear, madam, that she is dying?"

"I say you shall not go."

"The wishes of the dying must be respected by the living," interposed Jelly, still addressing Mr. North. "Otherwise there's no telling what ghosts might haunt 'em after."

The words were somewhat obscure, but their meaning was sufficiently plain. Mr. North took a step or two towards the door: madam came quickly round and placed herself before him.

"My will is law in this house, and out of it you do not go."

For a minute or two Mr. North looked utterly helpless; then cast an appealing look at his son. Richard rose, laying down his table-napkin.

"Leave the room for an instant," he quietly said to the servants, including Jelly. And they filed out.

"My dear father, is it your wish to see Mrs. Cumberland?"

"Oh, Dick, you know it is," spoke the poor brow-beaten man. "There's little left to me in life to care for now; but if I let her die without going to her there'll be less."

"Then you shall go," said Richard. Madam turned to him in furious anger.

"How dare you attempt to oppose me, Richard North? I say your father shall not go forth at the beck and call of this crazy woman."

"Madam, I say he shall," calmly spoke Richard.

"Do you defy me? Has it come to that?"

"Why yes, if you force it upon me: it is not my fault. Pardon me if I speak plainly—if I set you right upon one point, madam," he added. "You have just said your will is law in the house and out of it: in future it must, on some occasions, yield to mine. This is one of them. My father will go to Mrs. Cumberland's. Say no more, madam: it will be useless; and I am about to admit the servants."

From sheer amazement madam was silent. The resolution born of conscious power to will and to execute lay in every tone and glance of Richard North. Before she could rally her energies, the door was opened to the servants, and she heard Richard's order to make ready and bring round the close carriage. Instantly.

"Mr. North will be with your mistress as soon as you are, Jelly," said he. And Jelly curtsied as she took her departure.

But a scene ensued. Madam had called Mrs. Cumberland a crazy woman: she seemed nothing less herself. Whatever her private objection might have been to her husband's holding an interview with Mrs. Cumberland—and there could be no doubt that she had one—Richard fairly thought she was going mad in her frenzied attempts to prevent it. She stamped, she raved, she threatened Mr. North, she violently pushed him into his chair, she ordered the servants to bar the house doors against him; she was in fact as nearly mad, as a woman out of an asylum could be. Matilda cried: indifferent as that young lady remained in general to her mother's ordinary fits of temper, she was frightened now. The servants collected in dark nooks of the hall, and stood peeping; Mr. North stole into his parlour, and thence, by the window, to a bench in the garden, where he sat in the dark and the rain, trembling from head to foot. Of his own accord he had surely never dared to go, after this: but Richard was his sheet anchor. Richard alone maintained his calm equanimity, and carried matters through. The servants obeyed his slightest word; with sure instinct they saw who could be, and was, the Hall's real master: and the carriage came to the door.

But all this had caused delay. And yet more might have been caused—for what will an unrestrained and determined woman not do—but that just as the wheels, grating on the wet gravel struck on madam's ear, her violence culminated in a species of fainting-fit. For the time at least she could not move, and Richard took the opportunity to conduct his father to the carriage. It was astonishing how confidingly the old man trusted to Richard's protection.

"Won't you come also, Dick? I hardly dare go alone. She'd be capable of coming after me, you know."

Richard's answer was to step in beside his father. It was eight o'clock when they reached Mrs. Cumberland's. Jelly, with a reproachful face, showed them into a sitting-room.

"You can't go up now, sir; you will have to wait!" said she.

"Is she any better?" asked Richard.

"She's worse," replied Jelly; "getting weaker and weaker with every quarter-of-an-hour. Dr. Rane thinks she'll last till morning. I don't. The clergyman's up there now."

And when the time came for Mr. North to be introduced into the room, Mrs. Cumberland was almost beyond speaking to him. They were alone—for she motioned others away. Mr. North never afterwards settled with himself what the especial point could have been that she had wished to see him upon; unless it was the request that he should take charge of Ellen Adair.

Her words were faint and few, and apparently disjointed, at times seeming to have no connection one with another. Mr. North—sitting on a chair in front of her, holding one of her hands, bending down his ear to catch what fell from her white lips—thought her mind wandered a little. She asked him to protect Ellen Adair—to take her home to the Hall until she should be claimed by her husband or her father. It might be only a few days, she added, before the former came, and he would probably wish the marriage to take place at once; if so, it had better be done. Then she went on to say something about Arthur Bohun, which Mr. North could not catch at all. And then she passed abruptly to the matter of the anonymous letter.

"John, you will forgive it! You will forgive it!" she implored, feebly clasping the hand in which hers lay.

"Forgive it?" returned Mr. North, not in dissent but in surprise that she should allude to the subject.

"For my sake, John. We were friends and playfellows in the old days—though you were older than I. You will forgive it, John, for my sake; because I am dying, and because I ask it of you?"

"Yes, I will," said John North. "I don't think as much about it as I did," he added. "I should like to forgive every one and everything before I go, Fanny; and my turn mayn't be long now. I forgive it heartily; heartily," he repeated, thinking to content her. "Fanny, I never thought you'd go before me."

"God bless you! God reward you," she murmured. "There was no ill intention, you know, John."

John North did not see why he merited reward, neither could he follow what she was talking about. It might be, he supposed, one of the hallucinations that sometimes attend the dying.

"I'll take every care of Ellen Adair: she shall come to the Hall and stay there," he said, for that he could understand, "I promise it faithfully, Fanny."

"Then that is one of the weights off my mind," murmured the dying woman. "There were so many on it. I have left a document, John, naming you and Richard her guardians for the time being. She's of good family, and very precious to her father. There has been so short a time to act in: it was only three or four days ago that I knew the end was coming. I did not expect it would be quite so soon."

"It mostly come when it's not expected," murmured poor John North: "many of us seem to be going very near together. Edmund first; then Bessy; now you, Fanny: and the next will be me. God in His mercy grant that we may all meet in a happier world, and be together for ever!"

Richard North had remained below in the dining-room with Ellen Adair. The heavy crimson curtains were drawn before the large garden window, a bright fire blazed in the grate. Ellen in her black dress, worn for Bessy, sat in the warmth: she felt very chilly after her journey, was nervous at the turn the illness seemed to be taking; and every now and then a tear stole silently down her sweet face. Richard walked about a little as he glanced at her. He thought her looking, apart from the present sorrow, pale and ill. Richard North was deliberating whether to say a word or two upon a matter that puzzled him. He thought he would do so.

"I have been across the Channel, you know, Ellen, since you left for Eastsea," he began. He had grown sufficiently intimate at Mrs. Cumberland's since his enforced term of idleness, to drop the formal "Miss Adair" for her Christian name.

"Yes, we heard of it. You went to engage workmen, did you not?"

"For one thing. When I returned home, I found a letter or two awaiting me from Arthur Bohun, who was then at Eastsea. Madam had opened one of them."

Ellen looked up, and then looked down again immediately. Richard North saw a change pass over her face, as though she were startled.

"I could not quite understand the letters; I think Arthur intended me not to fully understand them. They spoke of some—some event that was coming off, at which he wished me to be present."

Ellen saw that he did understand: at least, that he believed he did. She rose from her seat and went close to him, speaking in agitation.

"Will you grant me a request, Richard? I know you can be a firm friend; you are very true. Do not ever think of it again—do not speak of it to living man or woman."

"I presume it did not take place, Ellen."

"No. And the sooner it is altogether forgotten, the better."

He took her hand between his, and drew her to the fire. They stood before it side by side.

"I am glad you know that I am your firm and true friend, Ellen; you may trust me always. It is neither idle curiosity nor impertinence that makes me speak. Madam stopped it, I conclude."

"I suppose so. She came and fetched him away; James Bohun was dying and wanted him. Since then I—I hardly know. He never came down again. He has been ill."

"Yes, very ill. Let him regain his health, and it will be all right. That's all, my dear. I should like to take care of you as though you were my sister."

"Care!" she replied. "Oh, Richard, I don't see what will become of me, or where I shall go. They say Mrs. Cumberland will not live till morning; and papa, you know, is so far away."

Jelly appeared with some coffee; and stayed for a minute or two to gossip, after the bent of her own heart. The carriage and the horses were waiting outside in the rain. Dr. Rane came in and out, in his restlessness. It was an anxious night for him. He would—how willingly!—have restored his mother for a time, had human skill alone been able to do it.

Before the interview with Mr. North was over—and it did not last twenty minutes—Mrs. Cumberland had changed considerably. Her son went into the room as Mr. North left it; and he saw at once how fallacious was the hope he had entertained of her lasting until morning.

Poor Mr. North, broken alike in health and heart, weak in spirit almost as a child, burst into tears as soon as he entered the dining-room. Richard spoke a few soothing words to him: Ellen Adair, who had rarely, if ever, seen a man shed tears, stood aghast.

"They are all going, Dick," he sobbed; "all going one by one. Fanny and I were almost boy and girl together. I loved the child; she was as pretty a little thing as you'd ever wish to see. She was younger than me by a good deal, and I never thought she'd go before me. There'll be only you left, Dick; only you."

Ellen touched Richard's arm: she held a cup of coffee in her hand. "If he can take it, it may do him good," she whispered.

Mr. North drank the coffee. Then he sat awhile, breaking out ever and anon with reminiscences of the old days. Presently Richard reminded him that the carriage was waiting; upon which Mr. North, who had quite forgotten the fact, rose in nervous agitation.

"I should like to know how she is before I go, Dick," he said. "Whether there's any change."

A change indeed. Even as the words left his lips, some slight commotion was heard in the house, following upon Dr. Rane's voice, who had come out of the chamber. The last moment was at hand. Ellen Adair went up, and Jelly went up. Mr. North said he must wait a little longer.

In five minutes all was over. Ellen Adair, brought down by Dr. Rane, was overcome with grief. Mr. North said she should go back with them to the Hall, and bade Jelly put up what she might immediately require. At first Ellen refused: it seemed strangely sudden, almost unseemly, to go out of the house thus hurriedly; but when she came to reflect how lonely and undesirable would be her position if she remained there, she grew eager to go. To tell the truth, she felt half afraid to remain: she had never been in personal contact with death, and the feeling lay upon her as a dread.

So a small portmanteau was hastily repacked—not an hour had elapsed since it was unpacked—and taken out to the carriage, Jelly undertaking to send the larger box in the morning. And Ellen was driven to the Hall with Mr. North and Richard.

"I am glad to come," she said to them, in her emotion. "It is so very kind of you to receive me in this extremity."

"Not at all, my dear," answered Mr. North. "The Hall will be your home until we receive instructions from your father. Mrs. Cumberland has appointed me and Richard as your temporary guardians: I was telling Dick so when you were upstairs."

Ellen broke down afresh, and said again and again how kind it was of them. Richard North felt that he loved her as dearly as a sister.

But there would be words to the bargain: they had not taken madam into consideration. The idea that she would object to it never occurred to Mr. North or Richard; madam was so very fond of having company at Dallory Hall. When the coachman, tired of being in the wet, dashed up to the door, and they descended and entered into the blaze of light, and madam, standing a little back, saw the young lady and the luggage, her face was a picture.

"What does this intrusion mean?" she demanded, slowly advancing.

"It means, madam, that Mrs. Cumberland is dead, and that she has left Miss Adair in my charge and in Dick's for a bit," answered Mr. North with trembling courtesy, remembering the frightful mood he had escaped from. Whilst Richard, catching madam's ominous expression, hastily took Ellen into the drawing-room, introduced her to Matilda, and closed the door on them.

"You say Mrs. Cumberland is dead!" had been madam's next words to Mr. North.

"Yes, she's dead. It has been terribly sudden."

"What did she want with you?" resumed madam, her voice lowered almost to a whisper; and, but that Mr. North was not an observant man, he might have seen her very lips grow white with some dread suspense.

"I don't know what she wanted," he replied—"unless it was a promise that I would take care of Miss Adair. She was almost past speaking when I went up to her; things had made me late, madam."

"Did she—did she— By the commotion that woman, Jelly, made, one would have supposed her mistress had some great secret to impart," broke off madam. "Had she?"

"Had who?" asked Mr. North, rather losing the thread of the dialogue.

"Mrs. Cumberland," said madam, with a slight stamp. And, in spite of her assumed carelessness, she watched her husband's face for the answer as if she were watching for one of life or death. "Did she impart to you any—any private matter?"

"She had none to impart, madam, that I am aware of. I shouldn't think she had. She rambled in her talk a bit, as the dying will do; about our old days, and about the anonymous letter that killed Edmund. There was nothing else, except that she wanted me to take temporary charge of Miss Ellen Adair, until we can hear from her father."

Mr. North was too simply honest to deceive, and madam believed him. Her old arrogance resumed its sway as fear died out.

"What did she tell you about the father?"

"Nothing; not a word, madam: what should she? I tell you mind and speech were both all but gone. She rambled on about the old days and the anonymous letter and I couldn't follow her even in that, but she said nothing else."

All was right then. The old will and the old arrogance reasserted themselves; madam was herself again.

"Miss Adair goes back to Mrs. Cumberland's to-night," said she. "I do not receive her, or permit her to remain here."

"What?" cried Mr. North; and Richard, who had just entered, stood still to listen. "Why not, madam?"

"Because I do not choose to," said madam. "That's why."

"Madam, I wouldn't do it for the world. Send her back to the house with the dead lying in it, and where she'd have no protector! I couldn't do it. She's but a young thing. The neighbours would cry shame upon me."

"She goes back at once," spoke madam in her most decisive tones. "The carriage may take her, as it rains; but back she goes."

"It can't be, madam, it can't, indeed. I'm her guardian, now, and responsible for her. I promised that she should stay at Dallory Hall."

And madam went forth with into another of her furious rages; she stamped and shook with passion. Not at being thwarted: her will was always law, and she intended it to be so now; but at Mr. North's attempting to oppose it.

"You were a fool for bringing her at all, knowing as you might that I should not allow her to stay here," raved madam. "The hall is mine: so long as I am mistress of it, no girl that I don't choose to receive shall find admittance here. She goes lack at once."

Mr. North seemed ready to fall. The look of despair, piteous in its utter helplessness, came into his face. Richard drew nearer, and caught his expression. All this had taken place in the hall under the great lamp.

"Dick, what's to be done?" wailed Mr. North. "I should die of the shame of turning her out again. I wish I could die; I've been wishing it many times to-night. It's time I was gone, Dick, when I've no longer a roof to offer a poor young lady for a week or two's shelter."

"But you have one, my dear father. At least I have, which comes to the same thing," added Richard, composed as usual. "Madam"—politely, but nevertheless authoritatively, taking madam's hand to lead her into the dining-room—"will you pardon me if I interfere in this?"

"It is no business of yours," said madam.

"Excuse me, madam, but it is. I think I had better take it on myself exclusively, and relieve my father of all trouble—for really, what with one thing and another, he is not capable of bearing much more."

"Oh, Dick, do; do!" interposed poor Mr. North, timidly following them into the dining-room. "You are strong, Dick, and I am weak. But I was strong once."

"Madam," said Richard, "this young lady, Miss Adair, will remain at the Hall until we receive instructions from her father."

Madam was turning livid. Richard had never assumed such a tone until to-night. And this was the second time! She would have been glad to strike him. Had he been some worthless animal, her manner could not have expressed more gratuitous contempt.

"By what right, pray, do you interfere?"

"Well, madam, Mrs. Cumberland expressed a wish that I, as well as my father, should act as Miss Adair's guardian."

"There's a document left to that effect," eagerly put in Mr. North.

"And what though you were appointed fifty times over and and fifty to that; do you suppose it would give you the right to bring her here—to thrust her into my home?" shrieked madam. "Do not believe it, Richard North."

"Madam," said Richard, quietly, "the home is mine."

"On sufferance," was the scornful rejoinder. "But I think the sufferance has been allowed too long."

"You have known me now many years, madam: I do not think in all those years you have found me advance a proposition that I could not substantiate. In saying the home here was mine I spoke what is literally true. I am the lessee of Dallory Hall. You and my father—My dear father"—turning to him—"I know you will pardon me for the few plain words I must speak—are here on sufferance. My guests, as it were."

"It is every word Gospel truth," spoke up poor Mr. North, glad that the moment of enlightenment had at length come. "Dick holds the lease of Dallory Hall, and he is its real master. For several years now we have all been pensioners on his bounty. He has worked to keep us, madam, in this his own house; and he has done it nobly and generously."

It seemed to madam that her brain suddenly reeled, for the words brought conviction with them. Richard the master! Richard's money that they had been living upon!

"I am grieved to have been obliged to state this, madam," Richard resumed. "I shall wish never to allude to it again, and I will continue to do the best I can for all. But—in regard to Miss Ellen Adair, she must remain here, and she shall be made welcome."

CHAPTER XXI

UNDER THE SAME ROOF

A crafty and worldly-wise woman, like Mrs. North, can change her tactics as readily as the wind changes its quarters. The avowal of Richard, that he was the master of Dallory Hall, so far as holding all power went—had been the greatest blow to her of any she had experienced in all these later years. It signed, as she perceived, the death-warrant of her own power; for she knew that she should never be allowed to rule again with an unjust and iron hand, as it had been her cruel pleasure to do. In all essential things, where it was needful to interfere, she felt that Richard's will and Richard's policy would henceforth outweigh her own.

Madam sat in her dressing-room that night, mentally looking into the future. It was very dim and misty. The sources whence she had drawn her exorbitant supplies were gone; her power was gone. Would it be worth while to remain at the Hall, she questioned, under the altered circumstances. Since the death of James Bohun, and her short sojourn with Sir Nash, an idea had occasionally crossed her mind that it might be desirable to take up her residence with the baronet—if she could only accomplish it. From some cause or other she had formerly not felt at ease when with Sir Nash; but that was wearing off. At any rate, a home in his well-appointed establishment would be far preferable to Dallory if its show and luxury could not be kept up; and all considerations gave way before madam's own selfish interest.

Already madam tasted of deposed power. Ellen Adair was to remain at the Hall, and—as Richard had emphatically enjoined—was to be made welcome. Madam gnashed her teeth as she thought of it. Ellen Adair, whom she so hated and dreaded! She lost herself in a speculation of what Richard might have done had she persisted in her refusal.

But as madam sat there, a doubt slowly loomed into her mind, whether it might not, after all, be the better policy for Ellen Adair to be at the Hall. The dread that Arthur Bohun might possibly renew his wish to marry her, in spite of all that had been said and done, occasionally troubled madam. In fact it had never left her. She could not make a child again of Arthur and keep him at her apron-string: he was free to go where he would; no matter in what spot of the habitable globe Ellen might be located, no earthly power could prevent his going to her if he wished to do so. Why then, surely it was better that the girl should be under her own eye, and in her own immediate presence. Madam laughed a little as she rose from her musings; she could have found it in her heart to thank Richard North for bringing this about.

And so, with the morning, madam was quite prepared to be gracious to Ellen Adair. Madam was one of those accommodating people who are ready, as we are told, to hold a candle to a certain nameless personage, if they think their interest may be served by doing it. Matilda North, who knew nothing whatever of madam's special reasons for disliking Miss Adair—saving that she had heard her mother once scornfully speak of her as a nameless young woman, a nobody—was coldly civil to her on Richard's introduction. But the sweet face, the gentle voice, the refined bearing, won even on her; and when the morning came Matilda felt rather glad that the monotony of the Hall was to be relieved by such an inmate, and asked her all about the death of Mrs. Cumberland.

And thus Ellen Adair became an inmate of Dallory Hall. But Mrs. North had not bargained for a cruel perplexity that was to fall upon her ere the day was over: no less than the return of Captain Bohun.

It has been mentioned that Sir Nash was ailing. In madam's new scheme, undefined though it was at present—that of possibly taking up her residence in his house—she had judged it well to inaugurate it by trying to ingratiate herself into his favour so far as she knew how. She would have liked to make herself necessary to him. Madam had heard a whisper of his going over to certain springs in Germany, and as she knew she should never get taken with him there, though Arthur might, she schemed a little to keep him in England. During the concluding days of her stay, Sir Nash had been overwhelmed with persuasions that he should come down to Dallory Hall, and get up his health there. To hear madam, never had so salubrious a spot been discovered on earth as Dallory; its water was pure, its air a tonic in itself; for rural quiet, for simple delight, it possessed attractions never before realized saving in Arcadia. Sir Nash, in answer to all this, had not given the least hope of trying its virtues; and madam had finally departed believing that Dallory would never see him.

But on the morning after Ellen Adair's arrival, madam, amongst other letters, received one addressed in her son Arthur's handwriting. According to her frequent habit of late—though why she had fallen into it she could not have told—she let her letters lie, unheeded, until very late in the morning. Just before luncheon she opened them; Arthur's the last: she never cared to hear from him. And then madam opened her eyes as well as her letter. She read, that Sir Nash had come to a sudden resolution to accept her hospitality for a short time, and that he and Arthur would be with her that day. At this very moment of reading, they were absolutely on their road to Dallory Hall.

Madam sat staring. Could she prevent it, was her first thought. It was very undesirable that they should come. Ellen Adair was there; and besides, after this new and startling revelation of Richard's, madam was not quite sure that she might continue to crowd the house with guests. But there was no help for it; ransack her fertile brain as she would, there seemed no possible chance of preventing the travellers' arrival. Had she known where a message would reach them, she might have telegraphed that the Hall was on fire, or that fever had broken out in it.

Mrs. North was not the first who has had to make the best of an unlucky combination of circumstances. She gave orders to her servants to prepare for the reception of the guests: and descended to the luncheon-table with a smooth face, saying not a word. Richard was out, or she might have told him: he was so busy over the reopening of those works of his, that he was now only at home night and morning. It happened, however that on this day he had occasion to come home for some deed that lay in his desk.

It was about four o'clock in the afternoon—a showery one—and Richard North was quickly approaching the gates of the Hall, when he saw some one approaching them more leisurely from the other side. It was Mary Dallory. He did not know she had returned; and his face had certainly a flush of surprise on it, as he lifted his hat to her.

"I arrived home yesterday evening," she said, smilingly. "Forced into it. Dear old Frank wrote the most woebegone letters imaginable, saying he could not get on without me."

"Did you come from Sir Nash Bohun's?" asked Richard.

"Sir Nash Bohun's! No. What put that into your head? I was at Sir Nash Bohun's for a few days some ages ago—weeks, at any rate, as it seems to me—but not lately. I have been with my aunt in South Audley Street."

"London must be lively at this time," remarked Richard rather sarcastically; as if, like Francis Dallory, he resented her having stayed there.

"Very. It is, for the tourists and people have all come back to it. I suppose you would have liked me to remain here and catch the fever. Very kind of you! I was going in to see your father."

He glanced at her with a half smile, and held out his arm after passing the gates.

"I am not sure that I shall take it. You have been quite rude, Mr. Richard."

Richard dropped it at once, begging her pardon. His air was that of a man who has received a disagreeable check. But Miss Dallory had only been joking; she glanced up at him, and a hot flush of vexation overspread her face. Richard held it out once more, and they began talking as they went along. Rain was beginning to fall, and he put up his umbrella.

He told her of Mrs. Cumberland's death. She had not heard of it, and expressed her sorrow. But she had had no acquaintance with Mrs. Cumberland, could not remember to have seen her more than once, and that was more than three years ago: and the subject passed.

"I hear you have begun business again," she said.

"Well—I might answer you as Green, my old timekeeper, answered me to-day. I happened to say to him, 'We have begun once more, Green.' 'Yes, in a sort of way, sir,' said he, gruffly. I have begun 'in a sort of way,' Miss Dallory."

"And what 'sort of way,' is it?"

"In as cautious and quiet a way as it is well possible for a poor man to begin," answered Richard. "I have no capital, as you must be aware; or at least, as good as none."

"I dare say you could get enough of that if you wanted it. Some of your friends have plenty of it, Mr. Richard."

"I know that. Mrs. Gass quarrels with me every day, because I will not take hers, and run the risk of making ducks and drakes of it. No. I prefer to feel my way; to stand or fall alone, Miss Dallory."

"I have heard Richard North called obstinate," remarked the young lady, looking into the air.

"When he believes he is in the right. I don't think it is a bad quality, Miss Dallory. My dear sister Bessy used to say—"

"Oh! Richard—what of Bessy?" interrupted Miss Dallory, all ceremony thrown to the winds. "I never was so painfully shocked in my life as when I opened Frank's letter telling me she was dead. What could have killed her?"

"It was the fever, you know," answered Richard, sadly. "I shall never forget what I felt when I heard it. I was in Belgium."

"It seemed very strange that she should die so quickly."

"It seems strange to me still. I have not cared to talk about her since: she was my only sister and very dear to me. Rane says it was a most violent attack: and I suppose she succumbed to it quickly, without much struggle."

"That poor little Cissy Ketler is gone, too."

"Yes."

"Is Ketler one of the few men who have gone back to work?"

"Oh dear, no!"

The rain had ceased: but they were walking on, unconsciously, under the umbrella. By-and-by the fact was discovered, and the umbrella put down.

"Who's this?" exclaimed Richard. "Visitors for madam, I suppose."

Richard alluded to the sound of carriage-wheels behind. He and Miss Dallory had certainly not walked as though they were winning a wager, but they were close to the house now; and reached its door as the carriage drew up. Richard stood in very amazement, when he saw its inmates—Arthur, thin and sallow: and Sir Nash Bohun.

There was a hasty greeting, a welcome, and then they all entered together. Madam, Matilda, and Miss Adair were in the drawing-room. Arthur came in side by side with Miss Dallory; they were talking together, and a slight flush illumined his thin face. Ellen, feeling shy amongst them all, remained in the background: she would not press forward: but a general change of position brought her and Arthur close to each other; and she held out her hand timidly, with a rosy blush.

He turned white as death. He staggered back as though he had seen a spectre. Just for a minute he was utterly unnerved; and then, some sort of presence of mind returning to him, he looked another way without further notice, and began talking again to Miss Dallory. But Miss Dallory had no longer leisure to waste on him. She had caught sight of Ellen, whom she had never seen, and was wonderfully struck by her. Never in her whole life had she found a face so unutterably lovely.

"Mr. Richard"—touching his arm, as he stood by Arthur Bohun—"who is that young lady?"

"Ellen Adair."

"Is that Ellen Adair? What a sweet face! I never saw one so lovely. Do take me to her, Richard."

Richard introduced them. Arthur Bohun, his bosom beating with shame and pain, turned to the window: a faintness was stealing over him; he was very weak still. How he loved her!—how he loved her! More; ay, ten times more, as it seemed to him, than of yore. And yet, he must only treat her with coldness; worse than if she and he were strangers. What untoward mystery could have brought her to Dallory Hall? He stole away, on the plea of looking for Mr. North. Madam, who had all her eyes about her and had been using them, followed him out.

There was a hasty colloquy. He asked why Miss Adair was there. Madam replied by telling (for once in her life) the simple truth. She favoured him with a short history of the previous night's events that had culminated in Richard's assertion of will. The girl was there, as he saw, concluded madam, and she could not help it.

"Did Mrs. Cumberland before she died reveal to Miss Adair what you told me about—about her father?" inquired Arthur, from between his dry and feverish lips.

"I have no means of knowing. I should think not, for the girl betrays no consciousness of it in her manner. Listen, Arthur," added madam, impressively laying her hand on his arm. "It is unfortunate that you are subjected to being in the same house with her; but I cannot, you perceive, send her away. All you have to do is to avoid her; never allow yourself to enter into conversation with her; never for a moment remain alone with her. You will be safe then."

"Yes, it will be the only plan," he mechanically answered, as he quitted madam, and went on his way.

Meanwhile Ellen Adair little thought what cruelty was in store for her. Shocked though she had been in the first moment by Arthur Bohun's apparent want of recognition, it was so improbable a rudeness from him, even to a stranger, that she soon decided he had purposely not greeted her until they should be alone, or else had really not recognized her.

In crossing the Hall an hour later, Ellen met him face to face. He was coming out of Mr. North's parlour as she was passing it. No one was about; they were quite alone.

"Arthur," she softly said, smiling at him and putting out her hand.

He went red and white, and hot and cold. He lifted his hat, which he was wearing, having come in through the glass-doors, and politely murmured some words that sounded like "I beg your pardon:" but he did not attempt to touch her offered hand. And then he turned and traversed the room back to the garden.

It seemed as though she had received her death-blow. There could no longer be any doubt or misapprehension after this, as to what the future was to be. And Ellen Adair crept into the empty drawing-room, and leaned her aching brow against the window frame.

Presently Matilda North entered. The young lady had her curiosity even as her mother, and fancied some one was in sight.

"What are you looking at, Miss Adair?"

"Nothing," answered Ellen, lifting her head. And in truth she had not been looking out at all.

"Ah! I see," significantly spoke Miss North.

Walking slowly side by side along a distant path, went Captain Bohun and Miss Dallory. Matilda, acting on a hint from madam, would not lose the opportunity.

"Captain Bohun is losing no time, is he?"

"In what way?" inquired Ellen.

"Don't you know that they are engaged? He is to marry Miss Dallory. We had all kinds of love passages, I assure you, when he was ill at my uncle's, and she was there helping me to nurse him."

It was a wicked and gratuitous lie: there had been no "love passages" or any semblance of them. But Ellen believed it.

"Do you say they are engaged?" she murmured.

"Of course they are. It will be a love match too, for he is very fond of her—and she of him. I think Richard was once a little bit touched in that quarter; but Arthur has won. Sir Nash is very pleased at Arthur's choice; and mamma is delighted. They are both very fond of Mary Dallory."

And that ceremony, all but completed, only a few weeks ago in the church at Eastsea!—and the ring and licence she held still!—and the deep, deep love they had owned to each other, and vowed to keep for ever—what did it all mean? Ellen Adair asked the question of herself in her agony. And as her heart returned the common-sense answer—fickleness: faithlessness—she felt as if a great sea were sweeping away hope and peace and happiness. The iron had entered into her soul.

CHAPTER XXII

TANGLED THREADS

It was a curious position, that of some of the present inmates of Dallory Hall. Sir Nash Bohun, who went down to accompany Arthur more than anything else, and who had not intended to remain above a day or two, stayed on. The quiet life after the bustle of London was grateful to him; the sweet country air really seemed to possess some of the properties madam had ascribed to it. Sir Nash was to go abroad when the genial springtime should set in, and try the effect of some medicinal waters. Until then, he was grateful for any change, any society that served to pass away the time.

Sir Nash had been as much struck with the wonderful beauty of Ellen Adair as strangers generally were. That she was one of those unusually sweet girls, made specially to be loved, he could not fail to see. In the moment of their first arrival, he had not noticed her: there were so many besides her to be greeted; and the appearance of Miss Dallory amongst them was a most unexpected surprise. Not until they were assembling for dinner, did Sir Nash observe her. His eyes suddenly rested on a most beautiful girl in a simple black silk evening dress, its low body and sleeves edged with white tulle, and a black necklace on her pretty neck. He was wondering who she could be, when he heard Richard North speak of her as Ellen Adair. Sir Nash drew Arthur Bohun to the far end of the drawing-room, ostensibly to look at a rare Turner hanging on the walls.

"Arthur, who is she? It cannot be Adair's daughter?"

"Yes, sir, it is."

"Mercy be good to her!" cried Sir Nash in dismay. "What a calamity! She looks absolutely charming; fitted to mate with a prince of the blood-royal."

"And she is so."

"To have been born to an inheritance of shame!" continued Sir Nash. "Poor thing! Does she know about it?"

"No, I am sure she does not," replied Arthur warmly, his tone one of intense pain. "She believes her father to be as honourable and good as you are yourself, sir."

For the very fact of Ellen's having put out her hand to him in the hall with that bright and confiding smile, had convinced Arthur Bohun that at present she knew nothing.

It made his own position all the worse: for, to her, his behaviour must appear simply infamous. Yet, how tell her? Here they were, living in the same house; and yet they could only be to each other as strangers. An explanation was due to Ellen Adair; but from the very nature of the subject, he could not give it. If he had possessed the slightest idea that she was attributing his behaviour to a wrong cause—an engagement with Miss Dallory—he would at least have set that right. But who was likely to tell him? No one. Madam and Matilda, be very sure, would not do so: still less would Ellen herself. And so the complication would, and must, go on; just as unhappy complications do sometimes go on. But there is this much to be said—that to have set straight the only point on which they were at cross purposes would not have healed the true breach by which the two were hopelessly separated.

And Sir Nash Bohun never once entered into any sort of intercourse with Ellen Adair. He would not, had he known it beforehand, have taken up his sojourn under the same roof with one whose father had played so fatal a part with his long-deceased brother: but circumstances had brought it about. In herself the young lady was so unobjectionable—nay, so deserving of respect and homage—that Sir Nash was won out of his intended coldness; and he would smile pleasantly upon her when paying her the slight, unavoidable courtesies of everyday life. But he never lingered near her, never entered into prolonged conversation: a bow or two, a good-morning and goodnight, comprised their acquaintanceship. He grew to pity her; almost to love her; and he relieved his feelings at least once a day in private by sending sundry unorthodox epithets after the man, William Adair, for blighting the name held by this fair and sweet young lady.

It was not a very sociable party, taken on the whole. Sir Nash had a sitting-room assigned him, and remained much in it: his grief for his son was not over, and perhaps never would be. Mr. North was often shut up in his parlour, or walking with bent head about the garden paths. Madam kept very much aloof, no one knew where; Matilda was buried in her French and English novels, or chattering above to madam's French maid. Richard was at the works all day. Ellen Adair, feeling herself a sort of interloper, kept her chamber, or went to remote parts of the garden and sat there in solitude. As to Arthur Bohun, he was still an invalid, weak and ill, and would often not be seen until luncheon or dinner-time. There was a general meeting at meals, and a sociable evening closed the day.

Madam had not allowed matters to take their course without a word from herself. On the day after Sir Nash and Arthur arrived, she came, all smiles and suavity, knocking at Ellen's chamber-door. She found that young lady weeping bitter tears—who stammered out, as she strove for composure, some excuse about feeling so greatly the sudden death of Mrs. Cumberland. Madam was gracious and considerate; as she could be when it pleased her: she poured some scent on her own white handkerchief, and passed it over Miss Adair's forehead. Ellen thanked her and smoothed her hair back, and dried her tears, and rose up out of the emotion as a thing of the past.

"I am sorry it should have happened that Sir Nash chose this time for his visit," spoke madam; "you might just now have preferred to be alone with us. Captain Bohun is still so very unwell that Sir Nash says he could but bring him."

"Yes," mechanically replied Ellen, really not knowing what she was assenting to.

"And Arthur—of course he was anxious to come; he knew Miss Dallory would be at home again," went on madam, with candour, like a woman without guile. "We are all delighted at the prospect of his marrying her. Before he was heir to the baronetcy, of course it did not so much matter how he married, provided it was a gentlewoman of family equal to the Bohuns. But now that he has come into the succession through poor James's death, things have changed. Did you know that Sir Nash has cut off the entail?" abruptly broke off madam.

Ellen thought she did. The fact was, Arthur had told Mrs. Cumberland of it at Eastsea: but Ellen did not understand much about entails, so the matter had passed from her mind.

"Cutting off the entail has placed Arthur quite in his uncle's hands," continued madam. "If Arthur were to offend him, Sir Nash might not leave him a farthing. It is fortunate for us all that Mary is so charming: Sir Nash is almost as fond of her as is Arthur. And she is a great heiress, you know: she must have at the very least three or four thousand a-year. Some people say it is more; the minority of the Dallory children was a long one."

"It is a great deal," murmured Ellen.

"Yes. But it will be very acceptable. I'm sure, by the way affairs seem to be going on with Mr. North and Richard, it seems as though Arthur would have us all on his hands. It has been a great happiness to us, his choosing Miss Dallory. I don't believe he thought much of her before his illness. She was staying with us in town during that time, and so—so the love came, and Arthur made up his mind. He had the sense to see the responsibility that James Bohun's death has thrown upon him, the necessity for making a suitable choice in a wife."

Ellen had learnt a lesson lately in self-control, and maintained her calmness. She did not know madam—except by reputation—quite as well as some people did, and believed she spoke in all sincerity. One thing she could not decide—whether madam had known of the projected marriage at Eastsea. She felt inclined to fancy that she had not done so, and Ellen hoped it with her whole heart. Madam lingered yet to say a few more words. She drew an affecting picture of the consolation this projected union brought her; and—as if she were addressing an imaginary audience—turned up her eyes and clasped her hands, and declared she must put it to the honour and good feeling of the world in general not to attempt anything by word or deed that might tend to mar this happy state of things. With that she kissed Ellen Adair, and said, now that she had apologized for their not being quite alone at the Hall and had explained how it happened that Sir Nash had come, she would leave her to dress.

The days went on, and Mary Dallory came on a visit to the Hall. Her brother Frances left home to join a shooting party, and madam seized the occasion to invite his sister. She came, apparently nothing loth; and with her a great trunkful of paraphernalia. Matilda North had once said, when calling Mary Dallory a flirt, that she would come fast enough to the Hall when Richard and Arthur were there. At any rate, she came now. After this, Arthur Bohun would be more downstairs than he was before; and he and she would be often together in the grounds; sitting on benches under the evergreens or strolling about the walks side by side. Sometimes Arthur would take her arm with an invalid's privilege; his limp at the present time more perceptible than it ever had been; and sometimes she would take his. Ellen Adair would watch them through the windows, and press her trembling fingers on her aching heart. She saw it all: or thought she did. Arthur Bohun had found that his future prospects in life depended very much upon his wedding Miss Dallory, or some equally eligible young lady; and so he had resolved to forget the sweet romance of the past, and accept reality.

She thought he might have spoken to her. So much was certainly due to her, who had all but been made his wife. His present treatment of her was simply despicable; almost wicked. Better that he had explained only as madam had done: what was there to prevent his telling her the truth? He might have said, ever so briefly: "Such and such things have arisen, and my former plans are frustrated, and I cannot help myself." But no; all he did was to avoid her: he never attempted to touch her hand; his eyes never met hers if he could help it. It was as though he had grown to despise her, and sought to show it. Had he done so? When Ellen's fears suggested the question—and it was in her mind pretty often now—she would turn sick with despair, and wish to die.

The truth was really this. Arthur Bohun, fearing he should betray his still ardent love, was more studiously cold to Ellen than he need have been. A strange yearning would come over him to clasp her to his heart and sob out his grief and tenderness: and the very fear lest he might really do this some day, lest passion and nature should become too strong for prudence, made him shun her and seem to behave, as Ellen felt and thought, despicably. He knew this himself; and he called himself far harder names than Ellen could have called him: a coward, a knave, a miserably-dishonoured man. And so, in this way things went on at Dallory Hall: and were likely to continue.

One afternoon, a few days after Mrs. Cumberland had been interred, Ellen went to see her grave. Madam, Miss Dallory, Matilda, and Sir Nash had gone out driving: Arthur had been away somewhere since the morning, Mr. North was busy at the celery-bed with his head gardener. There was only Ellen: she was alone and lonely, and she put her things on and walked through Dallory to the churchyard. She happened to meet three or four people she knew, and stayed to talk to them. Mrs. Gass was one; the widow of Henry Hepburn was another. But she made way at last, feeling a little shy at being out alone. When walking as far as Dallory Mrs. Cumberland had always caused a servant to attend her.

The grave was not far from Bessy Rane's. Ellen had no difficulty in distinguishing the one from the other, though as yet there was no stone to mark either. Mrs. Cumberland's was near that of the late Thomas Gass; Bessy's was close to Edmund North's. A large winter tree, an evergreen, overshadowed this corner of the churchyard, and she sat down on the bench that encircled the trunk. Bessy's grave was only a very few yards away.

She leaned her face on her hand, and was still. The past, the present, the future; Mrs. Cumberland, Bessy Rane, Edmund North; her own bitter trouble, and other things—all seemed to be crowding together tumultuously in her brain. But, as she sat on, the tumult cleared a little, and she lost herself in imaginative thoughts of that heaven where pain and care shall be no more. Could they see her? Could Mrs. Cumberland look down and see her, Ellen Adair, sitting there in her sorrow? A fanciful idea came to her that perhaps the dead were the guardian angels appointed to watch the living: to be "in charge over them, to keep them in all their ways." If so, who then was watching her?—It must be her own mother, Mary Adair. Could these guardian angels pray for them?—intercede with the mighty God and the Saviour that their sins here might be blotted out? How long Ellen was lost in these thoughts she never knew: but she wound up by crying quietly to herself, and she wondered how long it would be before she joined them all in heaven.

Some one, approaching from behind the tree, came round with a slow step and sat down on the bench. It was a gentleman in mourning; she could see so much, though he was almost on the other side of the tree, and had his back to her. Ellen found she had not been observed, and prepared to leave. Twilight had fallen on the dull evening. As she stooped to pick up her handkerchief, which had fallen, the intruder turned and saw her. Saw as well the tears on her face. It was Captain Bohun. He got up more quickly than he had sat down, intending no doubt to move away. But in his haste he dropped the stick that he had used for support in walking since his illness—and it fell close to Ellen's feet. She stooped in some confusion to pick it up, and so did he.

"Thank you—I beg your pardon," he said, with an air of humiliation so great that it might have wrung a tender heart to witness. And then he felt that he could not for very shame go off without some notice, as he had been attempting to do. Though why he stayed to speak and what he said, it might have puzzled him at the moment to tell. Instinct, more than reason, prompted the words.

"She was taken off very suddenly."

Though standing close to Bessy's grave, Ellen thought he looked across at Mrs. Cumberland's. And the latter had been last in her thoughts.

"Yes. I feared we should not get her home in time. And I feel sure that the journey was fatal to her. If she had remained quiet, she would not have died quite so soon."

"It was of Bessy I spoke."

"Oh—I thought you alluded to Mrs. Cumberland. Mrs. Cumberland's death has made so much difference to me, that I suppose my mind is much occupied with thoughts of her. This is the first time I have been here."

Both were agitated to pain: both could fain have pressed their hearts tightly to still the frightful beating there.

"Ellen, I should like to say a word to you," he suddenly exclaimed, turning his face to her for a moment, and then turning it away again. "I am aware that nothing can excuse the deep shame of my conduct in not having attempted any explanation before. To you I cannot attempt it. I should have given it to Mrs. Cumberland if she had not died."

Ellen made no answer. Her eyes were bent on the ground.

"The subject was so intensely painful and—and awkward—that at first I did not think I could have mentioned it even to Mrs. Cumberland. Then came my illness. After that, whilst I lay day after day, left to my own reflections, things began to present themselves in rather a different light; and I saw that to maintain silence would be the most wretched shame of all. I resolved to disclose everything to Mrs. Cumberland, and leave her to repeat it to you if she thought it well to do so—as much of it, at least, as would give you some clue to my strange and apparently unjustifiable conduct."

Ellen's eyes were still lowered, but her hands trembled with the violence of her emotion. She did not speak.

"Mrs. Cumberland's death, I say, prevented this," continued Captain Bohun, who had gathered a little courage now that the matter was opened: "and I have felt since in a frightful dilemma, from which I see no escape. To you I cannot enter on any explanation: nor yet am I able to tell you why I cannot. The subject is altogether so very painful—"

Ellen lifted her head suddenly. Every drop of blood had deserted her face, leaving it of an ashen whiteness. The movement caused him to pause.

"I know what it is," she managed to say from between her white and trembling lips.

"You—know it?"

"Yes. All."

Alas for the misapprehensions of this world. He was thinking only of the strange disclosure made to him concerning Mr. Adair; she only of his engagement to Miss Dallory. At her avowal a multitude of thoughts came surging through his brain. All! She knew all!

"Have you known it long?" he questioned in low tones.

"The time may be counted by days."

He jumped to the conclusion that Mrs. Cumberland had disclosed it to her on her death-bed. And Ellen's knowledge of it improved his position just a little. But, looking at her, at her pale sweet face and downcast eyes, at the anguish betrayed in every line of her countenance, and which she could not conceal, Arthur Bohun's heart was filled to overflowing with a strange pity, that seemed almost to reach the point of breaking. He drew nearer to her.

"Thank God that you understand, Ellen—that at least you do not think me the shameless scoundrel I must otherwise have appeared," he whispered, his voice trembling with its deep emotion. "I cannot help myself: you must see that I cannot, as you know all. The blow nearly killed me. My fate—our fate, if I may dare still so far to couple your name with mine—is a very bitter one."

Ellen had begun to shiver. Something in his words grated terribly on her ear: and pride enabled her to keep down outward emotion.

"You left the ring and licence with me," she abruptly said, in perhaps a sudden bitterness of temper. "What am I to do with them?"

"Burn them—destroy them," he fiercely replied. "They are worthless to us now."

But he so spoke only in his anguish. Ellen interpreted it differently.

"God help us both, Ellen! A cruel fate has parted us for this world: but we may be permitted to be together in the next. It is all my hope now. Heaven bless you, Ellen! Our paths in life must lie apart, but I pray always that yours may be a happy one."

Without further word, without touching her hand, thus he left her. Limping on to the broad path, and then down it towards the churchyard gate.

There are moments into which a whole lifetime of agony seems to be compressed. Such a moment was this for Ellen Adair. Darkness was coming on rapidly now, but she sat on, her head bent low on her hands. They were, then, separated for ever; there was no further hope for her!—he himself had confirmed it. She wondered whether the pain would kill her; whether she should be able to battle with it, or must die of the humiliation it brought. The pain and the humiliation were strong and sharp now— now as she sat there. By-and-by there stole again into her mind those thoughts which Captain Bohun's appearance had interrupted—the heavenly place of rest to which Bessy and Mrs. Cumberland had passed. Insensibly it soothed her: and imagination went roving away unchecked. She seemed to see the white robes of the Redeemed; she saw the golden harps in their hands, the soft sweet light around them, the love and peace. The thoughts served to show her how poor and worthless, as compared with the joys of that Better Land, were the trials and pains of this world: how short a moment, even at the longest, they had to be endured: how quickly and surely all here must pass away! Yes, she might endure with patience for the time! And when she lifted her head, it was to break into a flood of violent yet soothing tears, that she could not have shed before.

"Father in heaven, Thou seest all my trouble and my agony. I have no one in the world to turn to for shelter—and the blast is strong. Vouchsafe to guide and cover me!"

But night was falling, and she rose to make her way out of the churchyard. In a sheltered nook that she passed, sat a man: and Ellen started a little, and quickened her pace. It was Captain Bohun. Instead of going away, he had turned back to wait. She understood it at once: at that hour he would not leave her alone. He wished to be chivalrous to her still, for all his utter faithlessness. In the very teeth of his avowed desertion, his words and manner had proved that he loved her yet. Loved her, and not another. It brought its own comfort to Ellen Adair. Of course it ought not to have done so, but it did: for the human heart at best is frail and faulty.

Captain Bohun followed her out of the churchyard, and kept her in sight all the way home, every feeling he possessed aching for her. He had seen the signs and traces of her weeping; he knew what must be the amount of her anguish. He might have been ready to shoot himself could it have restored her to peace; he felt that he should very much like to shoot Mr. Adair, whose bad deeds had entailed this misery upon them.

At the Hall gates he was overtaken by Richard, striding home hastily to dinner. Richard, passing his arm through Arthur's, began telling him that he feared he was going to have some trouble with his ex-workmen.

And as they, the once fond lovers, sat together afterwards at table, and in the lighted drawing-room, Arthur as far from her as he could place himself, none present suspected the scene that had taken place in the churchyard. Ellen Adair's eyes looked heavy; but that was nothing unusual now. It was known that she grieved much for Mrs. Cumberland.

CHAPTER XXIII

JELLY'S TWO EVENING VISITS

Jelly—to whom we are obliged to refer rather frequently, as she holds some important threads of the story in her hands—found times went very hard with her. A death within the house in addition to the death close without it, was almost more than Jelly could well put up with in her present state of mind.

The startling circumstances that had characterized Mrs. Rane's demise did not attend Mrs. Cumberland's: but it had been very sudden at last, and Jelly was sincerely attached to her mistress.

Dr. Rane was left sole executor to his mother's will. It was a very simple one: she bequeathed to him all she had. That was not much; for a portion of her income died with her. He found that he had two hundred a-year—as he had always known that he should have—and her household furniture. Of ready money there was little. When he should have discharged trifling claims and paid the funeral expenses, some twenty or thirty pounds would remain over, that was all.

Dr. Rane acted promptly. He discharged two of the servants, Ann and Dinah, retaining Jelly for the present to look after the house. He wished, if he could, to get the furniture taken with the house; so he advertised it in the local papers. He had been advertising his practice—I think this has been already said—but nothing satisfactory had come of it. Inquiries had been made, but they all dropped through. Perhaps Dr. Rane was too honest to say his practice was worth much, or to conceal the fact that Mr. Seeley had the best of it in Dallory. Neither was the tontine money as yet paid over to him; and, putting out of consideration all other business, the doctor must have waited for that.

Now, of all things that could have happened, Jelly most disliked and dreaded being left alone in the house. From having been as physically brave as a woman can be, she had latterly become one of the most timid. She started at her own shadow; she would not for the world have entered alone at night the room in which Mrs. Cumberland died. Having seen one ghost, Jelly could not feel sure that she should not see two. Some people hold a theory that to a very few persons in this world—and not to others—is given the faculty, or whatever you may please to call it, of discerning supernatural sights or visions. Jelly had heard this: and she became possessed of the idea that for some wise purpose she had been suddenly endowed with it. To remain in the house alone was more than her brain would bear; and she selected Ketler's eldest girl, a starved damsel of thirteen, called "Riah," to come and keep her company. As it was one less to feed, and they had tried in vain to get Riah a place—for the strike and badness of trade had affected all classes, and less servants seemed to be wanted everywhere—Ketler and his wife were very glad to let her go.

How do rumours get about? Can any one tell? How did a certain rumour get about and begin to be whispered in Dallory? Certainly no one there could have told. Jelly could have been upon her Bible oath if necessary (or thought she could) that she had not set it floating. It was a very ugly one, whoever had done it.

Late one afternoon Jelly received a call from Mrs. Gass's smart housemaid. The girl brought a letter from her mistress; Mrs. Gass wanted very particularly to see Jelly, and had sent to say that Jelly was to go there as soon as she could. Jelly made no sort of objection. She had been confined to the house much more closely of late than she approved of: partly because Dr. Rane had charged her to be in the way in case people called to look over it: partly because she had found out that Miss Riah had a tendency to walk off, herself, if she could get Jelly's back turned.

"Now, mind you sit still in the kitchen and attend to the fire, and listen to the door; and perhaps I'll bring you home a pair of strings for that bonnet of yours," said Jelly to the girl, when she was ready to start. "The doctor will be in by-and-by, so don't attempt to get out of the way."

With these injunctions, Jelly began her walk. She had on her best new mourning—and was in a complaisant mood. It looked inclined to rain—the weather had been uncertain of late—but Jelly had her umbrella: a silk one that had belonged to her mistress, and that Dr. Rane had given, with many other things, to Jelly. She rather wondered what Mrs. Gass wanted with her, but supposed it was to tell her of a situation. It had been arranged that if an eligible one offered, Jelly should be at liberty to depart, and a woman might be placed in the house to take care of it. Mrs. Gass had said she would let Jelly know if she heard of anything desirable. So away went Jelly with a fleet foot, little thinking what was in store for her.

Mrs. Gass, wearing mourning also, was in her usual sitting-room, the dining-room. As Jelly entered, the smart maid was carrying out the tea-tray. Mrs. Gass stirred up her fire, and bade Jelly to a chair near it, drawing her own pretty closely to her.

"Just see whether that girl have shut the door fast before I begin," suggested Mrs. Gass. "It won't do to have ears listening to me."

Jelly went, saw the door was closed, came back and sat down again. She noticed that Mrs. Gass looked keenly at her, as if studying her face before speaking.

"Jelly, what is it that you have been saying about Dr. Rane?"

The question was so unexpected that Jelly did not immediately answer it. Quite a change, this, from an offer of a nice situation.

"I've said nothing," she replied.

"Now don't you repeat that to me. You have. And it would have been a'most as well for you that you had cut your tongue out before doing it."

"I said—what I did—to you, Mrs. Gass. To nobody else."

"Look here, Jelly—the mischiefs done, and you'd a great deal better look it full in the face than deny it. There's reports getting up about Dr. Rane, in regard to his wife's death, and no mortal woman or man can have set 'em afloat but you. This morning I was in North Inlet, looking a bit after them scamps of workmen that won't work, and won't let others work if they can help it: and after I had given a taste of my mind to as many of 'em as was standing about, I stepped into Mother Green's. She has the rheumatics—and he has a touch of 'em. Talking with her of one thing and another, we got on to the subject of Dr. Rane and the tontine; and she said two or three words that frightened me; frightened me, Jelly; for they pointed to a suspicion that the doctor had sacrificed his wife to get it. I pretended to understand nothing—she didn't speak out broad enough for me to take it up and answer her—and it was the best plan not to understand—"

"For an old woman, Mother Green has the longest tongue I know," interrupted Jelly.

"You've a longer," retorted Mrs. Gass. "Just wait till I've finished, girl. 'Twas a tolerable fine morning, and after that I went walking on, and struck off down by the Wheatsheaf. Packerton's wife was standing at the door with cherry ribbons in her cap, and I stopped to talk to her. She brought up Dr. Rane; and lowered her voice as if it was high treason; asking me if I'd heard what was being said about his wife's not having died a natural death. I did give it the woman; and I think I frightened her. She acknowledged that she only spoke from a hint dropped by Timothy Wilks, and said she had thought at the time it couldn't have anything in it. But what I have to say to you is this," continued Mrs. Gass to Jelly more emphatically, "whether it's Tim Wilks that's spreading the report, or whether it's Mother Green, they both had it in the first place from you."

Jelly sat in discomfort. She did not like this. It is nothing to be charged with a fault when you are wholly innocent; but when conscience says you are partly guilty it is another thing. Jelly was aware that one night at Mother Green's, taking supper with that old matron and Timothy, she had so far yielded to the seductions of social gossip as to forget her usual reticence; and had said rather more than she ought. Still, at the worst, it had been only a word or two: a hint, not a specific charge.

"I may have let fall an incautious word there," confessed Jelly. "But it was nothing anybody can take hold of."

"Don't you make sure of that," reprimanded Mrs. Gass. "We are told in the sacred writings—which it's not well to mention in ordinary talk, and I'd only do it with reverence—of a grain of mustard seed, that's the least of all seeds when it's sown, and grows into the greatest tree. You remember Who it is says that, Jelly, so it's not for me to enlarge upon it. But I may say this much, girl, that that's an apt exemplification of gossip. You drop one word, or maybe only half a one, and it goes spreading out pretty nigh over the world."

"I'm sure, what with the weight and worry this dreadful secret has been on my mind, almost driving me mad, the wonder is that I've been able to keep as silent as I have," put in Jelly, who was growing cross. Mrs. Gass resumed.

"If the thing is what you think it to be—-a dreadful secret, and it is brought to light through you, why, I don't know that you'd get blamed—though there's many a one will say you might have spared your mistress's son and left it for others to charge him. But suppose it turns out to be no dreadful secret; suppose poor Bessy Rane died a natural death of the fever, what then?—where would you be?"

Jelly took off her black gloves as if they had grown suddenly hot for her hands. She said nothing.

"Look here, girl. My belief is that you've just set a brand on fire! one that won't be put out until it's burnt out. My firm belief also is, that you be altogether mistaken. I have thought the matter over with myself hour after hour; and, except at the first moment when you whispered it to me in the churchyard, and I own I was startled, I have never been able to bring my common sense to believe in it. Oliver Rane loved his wife too well to hurt a hair of her head."

"There was that anonymous letter," cried Jelly.

"Whatever hand he might have had in that anonymous letter—and nobody knows the truth of it whether he had or whether he hadn't—I don't believe he was the man to hurt a hair of his wife's head," repeated Mrs. Gass. "And for you to be spreading it about that he murdered her!"

"The circumstances all point to it," said Jelly.

"They don't."

"Why, Mrs. Gass, they do."

"Let's go over 'em, and see," said Mrs. Gass, who had a plain way of convincing people. "Let's begin at the beginning. Hear me out, Jelly."

She went over the past minutely. Jelly listened, growing more uncomfortable every moment. There was absolutely not one fact inconsistent with a natural death. It is true the demise had been speedy, but the cause assigned, exhaustion, might have been the real one; and the hasty fastening down of the coffin was no doubt a simple measure of precaution, taken out of regard for the living. No; as Mrs. Gass put it in her sensible way, there was positively not a single fact that could be urged for supposing that Mrs. Rane came to an untimely end. Jelly twirled her gloves, and twisted her hands, and grew hot and uncomfortable.

"There was what I saw—the ghost," she said.

But Mrs. Gass ridiculed the ghost—that is, the idea of it—beyond everything earthly. Jelly, however, would not give way there; and they had some sparring.

"Ghost, indeed! and you come to this age! It was the beer, girl; the beer."

"I hadn't had a drop of beer," protested Jelly, almost crying. "How was I to get beer at Ketler's? They've none for themselves. I had had nothing inside my lips but tea."

"Well; beer or no beer, ghost or no ghost, it strikes me, Jelly, that you have done a pretty thing. This story is as sure to get wind now as them geraniums of mine will have air when I open the window tomorrow morning. You'll be called upon to substantiate your story; and when you can't—and I'm sure you know that you can't—the law may have you up to answer for it. I once knew a man that rose a bad charge against another; he was tried for it, and got seven years' transportation. You may come to the same."

A very agreeable prospect! If Jelly's bonnet had not been on, her hair might have risen up on end with horror. There could be no doubt that it was she who had started the report; and in this moment of repentance she sat really wishing she had first cut her foolish tongue out.

"Nothing can be done now," concluded Mrs. Gass. "There's just one chance for you—that the rumour may die away. If it will, let it; and take warning to be more cautious in future. The probability is that Mother Green and Tim Wilks have mentioned it to others besides me and Packerton's wife: if so, nothing will keep it under. You have been a great fool, Jelly."

Jelly went away in terrible fright. Mrs. Gass had laid the matter before her in its true light. Suspect as she might, she had no proof; and if questioned by authority could not have advanced one.

"Dr. Rane have been in here three times after you," was young Riah's salutation when Jelly reached home.

"Dr. Rane has?"

"And he said the last time you oughtn't to be away from the house so long with only me in it," added the damsel, who felt aggrieved, on her own score, at having been left.

"Oh, did he!" carelessly returned Jelly.

But she began considering what Dr. Rane could want. For her parting charge to Riah, that Dr. Rane was coming in, had been a slight invention of her own, meant to keep that young person up to her duty. Just as she had decided that it might refer to this same report, which he might have heard, and Jelly was growing more and more ill at ease in consequence, he came in. She went to him in the dining-room.

"Jelly," said the doctor, "I think I have let the house."

"Have you, sir?" returned Jelly, blithely, in the agreeable revulsion of feeling. "I'm sure I am glad."

"But only for a short time," continued Dr. Rane. "Two ladies of Whitborough are wanting temporary change of air, and will take it if it suits them. They are coming tomorrow to look at it."

"Very well, sir."

"They will occupy the house for a month, and perhaps take it for longer. This will give me time to let it for a permanency. If you feel inclined to take service with them, I believe there will be room for you."

"Who are they?" asked Jelly.

"Mrs. and Miss Beverage. Quakers."

She knew the name. Very respectable people; plenty of money.

"You'll show them over it tomorrow when they come: I may or may not be in the way at the time," concluded Dr. Rane.

Jelly attended him to the door. It was evident he had not heard the rumour that had reached Mrs. Gass; or, at least, did not connect Jelly in any way with it. But how was he likely to hear it? The probability was, that all Dallory would be full of it before it reached him.

Jelly could not eat her supper. Mrs. Gass's communication had left no room for appetite. Neither did she get any sleep. Tossing and turning on her bed, lay she: the past doubt and present dread troubling her brain until morning.

But, when Jelly had thus tormented herself and regarded the matter in all its aspects, the result was, that she still believed her own version of the tale—namely, that Mrs. Rane had not come fairly by her death. True, she had no proof: but she began wondering whether proof might not be found. At any rate, she resolved to search for it. Not openly; not to be used; but quietly and cautiously: to hold, as it were, in case of need. She could not tell how to look for this, or where to begin. No one had seen Mrs. Rane after death—excepting of course the undertakers. Jelly resolved to question them: perhaps something might be gleaned in this way.

It was afternoon before the expected ladies arrived. Two pleasant women, dressed after the sober fashion of their sect. Mrs. Beverage, a widow, was sixty; her daughter nearly forty. They liked the house, and said they should take it; and they liked Jelly, and engaged her as upper maid, intending to bring two servants of their own. After their departure, Jelly had to wait for Dr. Rane: it would not do for him to find only Riah again. He came in whilst Jelly was at tea. She told him the ladies wished to enter as soon as convenient; and the doctor said he would at once go over to Whitborough and see them.

This left Jelly at liberty. It was growing late when she set out on her expedition, and she started at the hedge shadows as she went along. Jelly's thoughts were full of all kinds of uncanny and unpleasant things. Jelly's disposition was not a secretive one; rather the contrary; and she hated to have to do with anything that might not be discussed in the broad light of day.

The commencement of her task was at any rate not difficult: she could enter the Hepburns' house without excuse or apology, knowing them sufficiently well to do so. When they were young, Thomas Hepburn, his wife, and Jelly had all been companions at the same day-school. Walking through the shop without ceremony, saving a nod to young Charley, who was minding it, Jelly turned into the little parlour: a narrow room with the fireplace in the corner surmounted by a high old-fashioned wainscoting of wood, painted stone-colour. Thomas Hepburn, who seemed to be always ailing with something or other, had an inflammation on his left arm, and his wife was binding bruised lily leaves round it. Jelly, drawing near, at once expressed her disapprobation of the treatment.

"I can't think how it should have come, or what it is," he observed. "I don't remember to have hurt it in any way."

Jelly took the seat on the other side the fireplace, and Mrs. Hepburn, a stout healthy woman, sat down at the small round table and began working by lamplight. Thomas Hepburn, nursing his arm, which pained him, led all unconsciously to the subject Jelly had come to speak about. Saying that if his arm was not better in the morning, he should show it to Dr. Rane, he thence went on to express his sorrow that the doctor should talk of leaving Dallory, for they liked him so much both as a gentleman and a doctor.

"But after such a loss as he has experienced in his wife, poor lady, no wonder the place is distasteful to him," went on Hepburn. And Jelly felt silently obliged for the words that helped her in her task.

"Ah, that was a dreadful thing," she observed. "I shall never forget the morning I heard of it, and the shock it gave me."

"I'm sure I can never forget the night he came down here, and said she was dead," rejoined the undertaker. "It was like a blow. Although I was in a degree prepared for it, for the doctor had told me in the afternoon what a dangerous state she was in—and I didn't like his manner when he spoke: it seemed to say more than his words. I came home and told Martha here that I feared it was all over with Mrs. Rane. Poor Henry was lying dead at the same time."

"And the answer I made to Thomas was, that she'd get over it," said Mrs. Hepburn, looking up from her sewing at Jelly. "I thought she would: Bessy North was always hearty and healthy. You might have taken a lease of her life."

"We had shut up the shops for the night, though the men were at work still next door, when the doctor came," resumed Thomas Hepburn, as if he found satisfaction in recalling the circumstances for Jelly's benefit. "It was past eleven o'clock; but we had to work late during that sad time; and Henry's illness and death seemed to make a difference of nearly as much as two hands to us. I was in the yard with the men when there came a knocking at the shop-door: I went to open it, and there stood the doctor. 'Hepburn,' said he, 'my poor wife is gone.' Well, I did feel it."

Jelly gave a groan by way of sympathy. She was inwardly deliberating how she could best lead on to what she wanted to ask. But she was never at fault long.

"I have heard you express distaste to some of the things that make up your trade, Thomas Hepburn, but at least they give you the opportunity of taking last looks at people," began Jelly. "I'd have given I don't know how much out of my pocket to have had a farewell look at Mrs. Rane."

"That doesn't always bring the pleasure you might suppose," was the answer of the undertaker.

"Did you go to her?" asked Jelly.

"No. I sent the two men: Clark and Dobson. They took the coffin at once: the doctor had brought the measure."

"And they screwed her down at once," retorted Jelly, more eagerly than she had intended to speak.

"Ay! It was best. We did it in some other cases that died of the same."

"Did the men notice how she looked—whether there was much change in her?" resumed Jelly, in a low tone. "Some faces are very sweet and placid after death: so much so that one can't help thinking they are happy. Was Mrs. Rane's so?"

"The men didn't see her," said Hepburn.

"Didn't see her!"

"No. The doctor managed that they should not. It was very kind of him. Dobson had had an awful dread all along of catching the fever; and Clark was beginning to fear it a little: Dr. Rane knew this, and said he'd not expose them to more risk than could be helped. The men carried the coffin up to the ante-room, and he said he would manage all the rest."

Jelly sat with open mouth and eyes staring. The undertaker put it down to surprise.

"Medical men are used to these things, Jelly. It comes as natural to them as to us. Dr. Rane said to Clark that he would call Seeley over if he found he wanted help. I don't suppose he would want it: she was small and light, poor young lady."

Jelly found her speech. "Then they—Clark and Dobson—never saw her at all!"

"Not at all. She was in the far room. The door was close shut, and well covered besides with a sheet wet with disinfecting fluid. There was no danger, Dr. Rane assured them, so long as they did not go into the room where she lay. The men came away wishing other people would take these precautions; but then, you see, doctors understand things. He gave them each a glass of brandy-and-water too."

"And—then—nobody saw her!" persisted Jelly, as if she could not get over the fact.

"I dare say not," replied Thomas Hepburn.

"He must have hammered her down himself!" cried the amazed Jelly.

"He could do it as well as the men could. They left the nails and hammer."

"Well—it—it—seems dreadful work for a man to have to do for his wife," observed Jelly, after a pause, staring over Mr. Hepburn's head into vacancy.

"He did violence to his own feelings out of consideration to the men," said the undertaker. "And I must say it was very good of him. But, as I've observed, doctors know what's what, and how necessary it is to keep away from danger in perilous times."

"Did he manage the lead coffin as well as the first one?" continued Jelly, in a hard, sarcastic tone, which she found it impossible to suppress. "And then there was the third coffin, after that?"

"I went and soldered down the lead myself. The men took up the last one and made all ready."

"Were you not afraid to run the risk, Thomas Hepburn?" asked Jelly, tauntingly, for she despised the man for being so unsuspicious.

"The rooms had been well disinfected then, the doctor said. Any way, we took no harm."

That Thomas Hepburn had never discerned cause for the slightest suspicion of unfair play on the part of Dr. Rane was evident. Jelly, in her superior knowledge, could have shaken him for it. In his place she felt sure she should not have been so obtuse. Jelly forgot that it was only that superior knowledge that enabled her to see what was hidden from others: and that whilst matters, from Hepburn's point of view, looked all right; from her own, they were all wrong.

"Well, I must be wishing you good-evening, I suppose," she said. "I've left only Riah in the house—and she's of no mortal use to anybody, except for company. With people dying about one like this, one gets to feel dull, all alone."

"So one does," answered the undertaker. "Don't go yet."

Jelly had not risen. She sat looking at the fire, evidently deep in thought. Presently she turned her keen eyes on the man again.

"Thomas Hepburn, did you ever see a ghost?"

He received the question as calmly and seriously as though she had said, Did you ever see a funeral? And shook his head negatively.

"I can't say I ever saw one myself. I've known those who have. That is, who say and believe they have. And I'm sure I've no reason to say they haven't. One hears curious tales now and then."

"They are not pleasant things to see," remarked Jelly a little dreamily.

"Well, no; I dare say not."

"For my part, I don't put faith in ghosts," said hearty Mrs. Hepburn, looking up with a laugh. "None will ever come near me, I'll answer for it. I've too many children about me, and too much work to do, for pastime of that sort. Ghosts come from nothing but nervous fancies."

Jelly could not contradict this as positively as she would have liked, so it was best to say nothing at all. She finally rose up to go—Riah might be falling asleep with her head in the candle.

And in spite of the suggested attractions of a supper of toasted cheese and ale, Jelly departed. Things had become as clear as daylight to her.

"I don't so much care now if it does come out," she said to herself as she hastened along. "What Thomas Hepburn can tell as good as proves the doctor's guilt. I knew it was so. And I wish that old Dame Gass had been smothered before she sent me into that doubt and fright last night!"

But the road seemed terribly lonely now; and Jelly more nervous than ever of the shadows.

CHAPTER XXIV

MISCHIEF BREWING IN NORTH INLET

Morning, noon and night, whenever the small body of fresh workmen had to pass to and from the works, they were accompanied by the two policemen specially engaged to protect them, whilst others hovered within call. North Inlet, the ill-feeling of its old inhabitants increasing day by day, had become dangerous. It was not that all the men would have done violence. Ketler, for instance, and others, well-disposed men by nature, sensible and quiet, would not have lifted a hand against those who had, in one sense of the word, displaced them. But they did this: they stood tamely by, knowing quite well that some of their comrades only waited their opportunity to kill, or disable—as might be—Richard North's new followers. North Inlet was not quite so full as it used to be: for some of the old inhabitants, weary and out of patience with hope deferred: hope they hardly knew of what, unless for the good time promised by the Trades' Union: had departed on the tramp, with their wives and little ones, seeking a corner of the earth where work sufficient to give them a crust of bread and a roof, might be found. Others had decamped without their wives and children: and were in consequence being sought by the parish. North Inlet, taken on the whole, was in a sore plight. The men and women, reduced by want and despair to apply for parish relief, found none accorded them. They had brought themselves to this condition; had refused work when work was to be had; and to come and ask to be supported in idleness by the parish was a procedure not to be tolerated or entertained; as one resolute guardian, sitting at the head of a table, fiercely told them. Not as much as a loaf of bread would be given them, added another. If it came to the pass that they were in danger of dying of hunger—as the applicants urged—why they must come into the house with their wives and families: and a humiliating shame that would be for able-bodied men, the guardian added: but they would receive no relief out-of-doors. So North Inlet, not choosing to go into that unpopular refuge for the destitute, kept out of it. And to terrible straits were they reduced!

Looking back upon their past life of plenty, and their present empty homes and famished faces, little wonder that this misguided body of men grew to find that something of the old Satan was in them yet. A great deal of it, too. Perhaps remorse held its full share with them. They had intended that it should be so entirely for the better when they threw up work; and it had turned out so surprisingly for the worse. They had meant to return to work on their own terms; earning more and toiling less: they had been led to believe that this result lay in their own hands, and was as safe and certain as that the sun shone overhead at noonday. Instead of that—here they were, in as deplorable a condition as human beings could well be; Time had been, not very long ago either, that the false step might have been redeemed; Richard North had offered them work again on the old terms. Ay, and he had once conceded a portion of their demands—as they remembered well. But that time and that offer had gone by for ever. Fresh men (few though they were) had taken their places, and they themselves were starving and helpless.

The feeling against these new men was bitter enough; it was far more bitter against the small number of old workmen who had gone back again. We are told that the heart of man is desperately wicked: our own experience shows us that it is desperately selfish. They saw the employed men doing the work which once was theirs; they saw them wearing good coats, eating good food. They themselves had neither one nor the other; and work they had rejected. It would not have seemed quite so hard had the work altogether left the place: but to see these others doing it and living in comfort was more than mortal temper could brook.

This was not all. The men unreasonably held to it that these others having taken work again, was the cause why they themselves were kept out of it. Richard North would ha' come-to, they said, if these curs hadn't went sneaking back again to lick his hand. If all had held out, Dick North must ha' given in. And this they repeated so constantly, in their ire, one to another, that at last they grew to believe it. It was quite wrong, and they were wholly mistaken: for had Richard North not begun again cautiously as he did, and on the old terms, he would not have recommenced at all: but the men refused to see this, and held to their idea, making it a greater grievance than the want of food. It is so convenient to have something substantial on which to throw blame: and unlimited power and permission to punch the obnoxious head would have afforded intense gratification. Oh, it was very hard to bear. To see this small knot of men re-established in work, and to know that it was their own work once, and might have been theirs still! Peeping through hedges, hiding within doorways, standing sulkily or derisively in the open ground, they would watch the men going to and fro, guarded by the two policemen. Many a bitter word, many a silent threat was levelled at the small band. Murder had been done from a state of mind not half as bad as they were cherishing.

"What be you looking at, with those evil frowns on your faces?"

A group of malcontents, gazing from a corner of North Inlet at the daily procession, found this question suddenly sounding on their ears. Mrs. Gass had stepped out of a dwelling close by, and put it to them. Their eyes were following the escorted men coming home to their twelve-o'clock dinner, so that they had not observed her.

They turned to her, and dropped their threatening expression. A man named Poole, not too much respected in the most prosperous times, and one of the worst of the malcontents, answered boldly too.

"We was taking the measure o' that small lot o' convic's. Wishing we could brand 'em."

"Ah," said Mrs. Gass. "It strikes me some of you have been wishing it before to-day. I should like to give you a bit of advice, my men; and you, especially, Poole. Take care you don't become convicts yourselves."

"For two pins, I'd do what 'ud make me one," was the rejoinder of Poole, who was in a more defiant mood than even he often dared exhibit. He was a large, thick-set man, with shaggy light hair and a brick-dust complexion. His clothes, originally fustian, had been worn and torn and patched until they now hardly held together.

"You are a nice jail-bird, Poole! I don't think you ever were much better than one," added Mrs. Gass. To which candid avowal Poole only replied by a growl.

"These hard times be enough to make jail-birds of all of us," interposed another, Foster; but speaking civilly. "Why don't the Government come down and interfere, and prevent our work being took out of our hands by these rascals?"

"You put the work out of your own hands," said Mrs. Gass. "As to interference, I should have thought you'd had about enough of that, by this time. If you had not suffered them fine Trades' Unionists to interfere with you, my men, you'd have been in full work now, happy and contented as the day's long."

"What we did, we did for the best."

"What you did, you did in defiance of common sense, and of the best counsels of your best friends," she said. "How many times did your master show you what the upshot would be if you persisted in throwing up your work?—how much breath did I waste upon you, as I'm doing now, asking you all to avoid a strike—and after the strike had come, day after day begging you to end it?—could any picture be truer than mine when I said what you'd bring yourselves to?—rags, and famine, and desolate homes. Could any plight be worse than this that you've dropped into now?"

"No, it couldn't," answered Foster. "It's so bad that I say Government ought to interfere for us."

"If I was Government, I should interfere on one point—and that's with them agitating Unionists," bravely spoke Mrs. Gass. "I should put them down a bit."

"This is a free country, ma'am," struck in Ketler, who made one of the group.

"Well, I used to think it was, Ketler," she said; "but old ways seem to be turned upside down. What sort of freedom do you enjoy just now?—how much have you had of it since you bound yourselves sworn members of the Trades' Unions? You have wanted to work and they haven't let you: you'd like to be clothed and fed as you used to be and to clothe and feed your folks at home, and they prevent your exercising the means by which you may do it. What freedom or liberty is there in that?—Come, Ketler, tell me, as a reasonable man."

"If the Trades' Unions could do as they wish, there'd be work and comfort for all of us."

"I doubt that, Ketler."

"But they can't do it," added Ketler. "The masters be obstinate and won't let 'em."

"That's just it," said Mrs. Gass. "If the Trades' Unions held the world in their hands, and there were no such things as masters and capital, why then they might have their own way. But the masters have their own interests to look after, their business and capital to defend: and the two sides are totally opposed one to the other, and squabbling is all that comes of it, or that ever will come of it. You lose your work, the masters lose their trade, the Unionists fight it out fiercer than ever—and, between it all, the commerce of the country is coming to an end. Now, my men, that is the bare truth; and you can't deny it if you talk till midnight."

"'Twouldn't be no longer much of a free country, if the Government put down the Trades' Unions," spoke a man satirically; one Cattleton.

"But it ought to put down their arbitrary way of preventing others working that want to work," maintained Mrs. Gass. "The Unionists be your worst enemies. I'm speaking, as you know I have been all along, of the heads among 'em who make laws for the rest; not of poor sheep like yourselves who have joined the society in innocence. If the heads like to live without work themselves, and can point out a way by which others can live without it, well and good; there's no law against that, nor oughtn't to be; but what I say Government ought to put down is this—their forcing you men to reject work when it's offered you. It's a sin and a shame that, through them, the country should be brought to imbecility, and you, its once free and brave workmen, to beggary."

"The thought has come over me at times that under the new state of things we are no better than slaves," confessed Ketler, his eyes wearing an excited look.

"Now you've just said it, Ketler," cried Mrs. Gass, triumphantly. "Slaves. That's exactly what you are; and I wish to my heart all the workmen in England could open their eyes to the truth of it. You took a vow to obey the dictates of the Trades' Union; it has bound you hand and foot, body and soul. If a job of work lay to your hand, you dare not take it up; no, not though you saw your little ones dying of famine before your eyes. It's the worst kind of slavery that ever fell on the land. Press-gangs used to be bad enough, but this beats 'em hollow."

There was no reply from any of the men. Mrs. Gass had been a good friend to their families even recently; and the old habits of respect to her, their mistress, still held sway. Perhaps some of them, too, silently assented to her reasoning.

"It's that that I'd have put down," she resumed. "Let every workman be free to act on his own judgment, to take work or to leave it. Not but what it's too late to say so: as far as I believe, the mischief has gone too far to be remedied."

"It be mighty fine for the masters to cry out and say the Trades' Unions is our enemies! Suppose we choose to call 'em our friends?" spoke Poole.

"Put it so, Poole, if you like," said Mrs. Gass equably. "The society's your friend, let's say. How has it showed its friendship? what has it done for you?"

Mr. Poole did not condescend to say.

"It's not hard to answer, Poole. The proofs, lie on the surface; not one of you but may read 'em off-hand. It threw you all out of good work that you had held for years under a good master, that you might probably have held, to the last day of your lives. It dismantled your homes and sent your things to the pawnshop. It has reduced you to a crust of bread, where you used to have good joints of beef; it has taken your warm shoes and coats, and sent you abroad half naked. Your children are starving, some of them are dead; your wives are worn out with trouble and discontent. And this not for a time, but for good: for, there's no prospect open to you. No prospect, that I can see, as I am a living woman. That's what your friends, as you call 'em, have done for you; and for thousands and thousands beside you. I don't care what they meant: let it be that they meant well by you, and that you meant well—as I'm sure you did—in listening to 'em: the result is as I've said. And you are standing here this day, ruined men."

Mr. Poole looked fierce.

"What is to become of you, and of others ruined like you, the Lord in heaven only knows. It's a solemn question. When the best trade of the country's driven from it, there's no longer any place for workmen. Emigration, suggest some of the newspapers. Others say emigration's overdone for the present. We don't know what to believe. Any way, it's a hard thing that a good workman should find no employment in his native land, but must be packed off, very much as if he was transported, to be an exile for ever."

Poole, not liking the picture, broke into an oath or two. The other men looked sad enough.

"You have been drinking, Poole," said Mrs. Gass with dignity, "Keep a civil tongue in your head before me if, you please."

"I've not had no more than half-a-pint," growled Poole.

"And that was half-a-pint too much," said Mrs. Gass. "When people's insides are reduced by famine, half-a-pint is enough to upset their brains in a morning."

"What business have Richard North to go and engage them frogs o' Frenchmen?" demanded Poole who had in truth taken too much for his good. "What business have them other fellows, as ought to have stuck by us, to go back to him? It's Richard North as wants to be transported."

"Richard North was a good master to you. The world never saw a better."

"He's a rank bad man now."

"No, no—hold th' tongue!" put in Ketler. "No good to abuse him."

"If you men had had a spark of gratitude, you'd have listened to Mr. Richard North, when he prayed you to go back to him," said Mrs. Gass. "No, you wouldn't; and what has it done for him? Why, just ruined him, my men: almost as bare as you are ruined. It has took his hopes from him; wasted what little money he had; played the very dickens with his prospects. The business he once had never will and never can come back. If once you break a mirror to pieces, you can't put it together again. Mr. Richard has a life of work to look forward to; he may earn a living, but he won't do much more. You men have at least the satisfaction of knowing that whilst you ruined your own prosperity, you also ruined his."

They had talked so long—for all that passed cannot be recorded—that it was close upon one o'clock, and the small band of workmen and the two policemen were seen coming back again towards the works. The malignant look rose again on Poole's face: and he gave forth a savage growl.

"There'll be mischief yet," thought Mrs. Gass, as she turned away.

Sounds of a woman's sobbing were proceeding from an open door as she went down North Inlet, and Mrs. Gass stepped in to see what might be the matter. They came from Dawson's wife. Dawson had been beating her. The unhappy state to which they were reduced tried the tempers of the men—of the women also, for that matter—rendering some of them little better than ferocious beasts. In the old days, when Dawson could keep himself and his family in comfort, never a cross word had been heard from him: but all that was changed; and under the new order of things, it often came to blows. The wife had now been struck in the eye. Smarting under ills of body and ills of mind, the woman enlarged on her wrongs to Mrs. Gass, and displayed the mark; all of which at another time she would certainly have concealed. The home was miserably bare; the children, wan and thin, were in tatters like their mother; it was a comprehensive picture of wretchedness.

"And all through those idiots having thrown up their work at the dictates of the Trades' Union!" was the wrathful comment of Mrs. Gass, as she departed. "They've done for themselves in this world: and, to judge by the unchristian lives they are living, seem to be in a fair way of doing for themselves in the next."

As she reached her own house, the smart housemaid was showing Miss Dallory out of it. That young lady, making a call on Mrs. Gass, had waited for her a short time, and was departing. They now went in together. Mrs. Gass, entering her handsome drawing-room, began recounting the events of the morning; what she had heard and seen.

"There'll be mischief, as sure as a gun," she concluded. "My belief is, that some of them would kill Mr. Richard if they had only got the chance."

Mary Dallory looked startled. "Kill him!" she cried. "Why, he has always been their friend. He would have been so still, had they only been willing."

"He's a better friend to them still than they are aware of," said Mrs. Gass, nodding her head wisely. "Miss Mary, if ever there was a Christian man on earth, it is Richard North. His whole life has been one long thought for others. Who else has kept up Dallory Hall? Who would have worked and slaved on, and on, not for himself, but to maintain his father's home, finding money for madam's wicked extravagance, to save his poor father pain, knowing that the old man had already more than he could bear. At Mr. Richard's age, he ought, before this, to have been making a home and marrying: he would have done so under happier circumstances: but he has had to sacrifice himself to others. He has done more for the men than they think for; ay, even at the time that they were bringing ruin upon him—as they have done—and ever since. Richard North is worth his weight in gold. Heaven, that sees all, knows that he is; and he will sometime surely be rewarded for it. It may not be in this world, my dear; for a great many of God's own best people go down to their very graves in nothing but disappointment and sorrow: but he'll find it in the next."

Miss Dallory made no reply. All she said was, that she must go. And Mrs. Gass escorted her to the front-door. They had almost reached it, when Miss Dallory stopped to ask a question, lowering her voice as she did so.

"Have you heard any rumour about Dr. Rane?"

Mrs. Gass knew what must be meant as certainly as though it had been spoken. She turned cold, and hot, and cold again. For once language failed her.

"It is something very dreadful," continued Miss Dallory. "I do not like to give utterance to it. It—it has frightened me."

"Law, my dear, don't pay no attention to such rubbish as rumours," returned Mrs. Gass, heartily. "I don't. Folk say all sorts of things of me, I make little doubt; just as they are ready to do of other people. Let 'em! We shan't sleep none the worse for it. Goodbye. I wish you'd have stayed and taken some dinner with me—as lovely a turkey-poult as ever you saw, and a jam dumpling."

CHAPTER XXV

DAYS OF PAIN

Pacing the shrubbery walk at Dallory Hall, a grey woollen shawl wrapped closely round her flowing black silk dress, her pale, sweet, sad face turned up to the lowering sky, was Ellen Adair. The weather, cold and dull, gave signs of approaching winter. The last leaves left on the trees fell fluttering to the earth; the wind, sighing through the bare branches, bore a melancholy sound. All things seemed to speak of death and decay.

This ungenial weather had brought complication with it. Just as Sir Nash Bohun was about to quit Dallory Hall, taking Arthur with him, the wind caught him in an unguarded moment, and laid him up with inflammation of the chest. Sir Nash took to his bed. One of the results was, that Arthur Bohun must remain at the Hall, and knew not how long he might be a fixture there. Sir Nash would not part with him. He had come to regard him quite as his son.

Ellen Adair thought Fate was cruel to her, taking one thing with another. And so it was; very cruel. Whilst they were together, she could not begin to forget him: and, to see him so continually with Mary Dallory, brought her the keenest pain. She was but human: jealousy swayed her just as it sways other people.

Another thing was beginning to trouble her—she did not hear from Mr. Adair. It was very strange. Not a letter had come from him since that containing the permission to marry Arthur Bohun;—as Mrs. Cumberland had interpreted it—received at Eastsea. Ellen could not understand the silence at all. Her father had always written so regularly.

"He ought not to remain here," she murmured passionately as she walked, alluding to Arthur Bohun. "I cannot help myself; I have nowhere else to go: but he ought to leave, in spite of Sir Nash."

A greyer tinge seemed to creep over the sky. The shrubbery seemed to grow darker. It was only the first advent of twilight, falling early that melancholy evening.

"Will there ever be any brightness in my life again?" she continued, clasping her hands in pain. "Is this misery to last for ever? Did any one, I wonder, ever go through such a trial and live? Scarcely. I am afraid I am not very strong to bear things. But oh—who could bear it?"

She sat down on one of the benches, and bent her aching brow on her hands. What with the surrounding gloom, and her dark dress, some one who had turned into the walk, came sauntering on without observing her. It was Arthur Bohun. He started when she raised her head: his face was every whit as pale and sad as hers; but he could not help seeing how ill and woebegone she looked.

"I fear you are not well," he stopped to say.

"Oh—thank you—not very," was the confused answer.

"This is a trying time. Heaven knows I would save you from it, if I could. I would have died to spare you. I would die still, if by that means things for you could be made right. But it may not be. Time alone must be the healer."

He had said this in a somewhat hard tone, as if he were angry with some one or other; perhaps with Fate; and went on his way with a quicker step, leaving never a touch of the hand, never a loving word, never a tender look behind him; just as it had been that day in Dallory Churchyard. Poor girl! her heart felt as though it were breaking there and then.

When the echo of his footsteps had died away, she drew her shawl closer round her slender throat and passed out of the shrubbery. Hovering in a side walk, unseen and unsuspected, was madam. Not often did madam allow herself to be off the watch. She had seen the exit of Captain Bohun; she now saw Ellen's; and madam's evil spirit rose up within her, and she advanced with a dark frown.

"Have you been walking with Captain Bohun, Miss Adair?"

"No, madam."

"I—thought—I heard him talking to you."

"He came through the shrubbery when I was sitting there, and spoke to me in passing."

"Ah," said madam. "It is well to be careful. Captain Bohun is to marry Miss Dallory: the less any other young woman has to say to him, the better."

To this speech—remarkable as coming from one who professed to be a gentlewoman—Ellen made no reply, saving a bow as she passed onwards, with erect head and self-possessed step, leaving madam to her devices.

She seemed to be tormented on every side. There was no comfort, no solace anywhere. Ellen could have envied Bessy Rane in her grave.

And the farce that had to be kept up before the world. That very evening, as fate had it, Captain Bohun took Miss Adair in to dinner and sat next her, through some well-intentioned blundering of Richard's. It had pleased madam to invite seven or eight people; it did not please Mr. North to come in to dinner as he had been expected to do. Richard had to be host, and to take in a stout lady in green velvet, who was to have fallen to his father. There was a moment's confusion; madam had gone on; Richard mixed up the wrong people together, and finally said aloud, "Arthur, will you take in Miss Adair?" And so they sat, side by side, and no one observed that they did not converse together, or that anything was wrong. It is curious how long two people may have lived estranged from each other in a household, and the rest suspect it not. Have you over noticed this?—or tried it? It is remarkable, but very true.

After dinner came the drawing-room; and the evening was a more social one than had been known of late. Music, cards, conversation. Young Mr. Ticknell, a relative of the old bankers' at Whitborough, was there; he had one of the sweetest voices ever given to man, and delighted them with his unaffected singing. One song, that he chose after a few jesting words with Ellen, in allusion to her name, two of them at least had not bargained for. "Ellen Adair." Neither had heard it since that evening at Eastsea; so long past now, in the events that had followed, that it seemed to be removed from them by ages.

They had to listen. They could not do otherwise. Ellen sat at the corner of the sofa in her black net dress with its one white flower, that Mr. North had given her, in the middle of the corsage, and nothing, as usual, in her smooth brown hair; he was leaning against the wall, not far from her, his arms folded. And the verses went on to the last one.

"But now thou art cold to me,
Ellen Adair:
But now thou art cold to me,
Ellen my dear.
Yet her I loved so well,
Still in my heart shall dwell,
Oh! I shall ne'er forget
Ellen Adair."

She could not help it. Had it been to save her life, she could not have helped lifting her face and glancing at him as the refrain died away. His eyes were fixed on her, a wistful, yearning expression in their depths; an expression so sad that in itself it was all that can be conceived of pain. Ellen bent her face again; her agitation at that moment seeming greater than she knew how to suppress. Lifting her hand to shade her eyes, the plain gold ring, still worn on it, was conspicuously visible.

"You look as though you had all the cares of the nation on your shoulders, Arthur."

He started at the address, which came from Miss Dallory. She had gone close up to him. Rallying his senses, he smiled and answered carelessly. The next minute Ellen saw them walking across the room together, her hand within his arm.

The next morning, Jelly made her appearance at the Hall, with two letters. They were from Australia, and from Mr. Adair. One was addressed to Mrs. Cumberland, the other to Ellen. Dr. Rane had desired Jelly to take both of them to Miss Adair, whom he now considered the most proper person to open Mrs. Cumberland's. Ellen carried it to Mr. North, asking if she ought to open it. Certainly, Mr. North answered, confirming Dr. Rane's view of the matter.

Ellen carried the letters to a remote and solitary spot in the garden, one that she was fond of frequenting, and in which she had never yet been intruded upon. She opened her own first: and there read what astonished her.

It appeared that after despatching his last letter to Mrs. Cumberland: the one already alluded to, that she had read with so much satisfaction to Arthur Bohun at Eastsea: Mr. Adair had been called from his station on business, and had remained absent some two or three months. Upon his return he found other letters awaiting him from Mrs. Cumberland, and learnt, to his astonishment, that the gentleman proposing for Ellen was Arthur Bohun, son of the Major Bohun with whom Mr. Adair had once been intimate. (The reader has not forgotten how Mrs. Cumberland confused matters in her mind, or that in her first letter she omitted to mention any name.) In a few peremptory lines written to Ellen—these that she was now reading—Mr. Adair retracted his former consent. He absolutely forbade her to marry, or ever think of marrying, Arthur Bohun: a union between them would be nothing less than a calamity for both, he wrote, and also for himself. He added that in consequence of an unexpected death he had become the head of his family, and was making preparations to return to Europe.

Wondering, agitated, Ellen dropped the letter, and opened Mrs. Cumberland's. An enclosure fell from it: a draft for a sum of money, which, as it appeared, Mrs. Cumberland was in the habit of receiving every half-year for her charge of Ellen. Mr. Adair wrote in still more explicit terms on the subject of the proposed marriage to Mrs. Cumberland—almost in angry terms. She, of all people, he said, ought to know that a marriage between his daughter and the late Major Bohun's son would be unsuitable, improper, and most distasteful to himself. He did not understand how Mrs. Cumberland could have laid such a proposal before him, or have permitted herself to entertain it for a moment: unless indeed she had never been made acquainted with certain facts of the past, connected with himself and Major Bohun and Major Bohun's wife, which Cumberland had known well. He concluded by saying, as he had said to Ellen, that he hoped shortly to be in England. Both letters had evidently been written in haste and in agitation: all minor matters being accounted as nothing, compared with the distinct and stern embargo laid upon the marriage.

"So it has happened for the best," murmured Ellen to her breaking heart, as she folded the letters and put them away.

She took the draft to Mr. North's parlour. He put on his spectacles, and mastered its meaning by the help of some questions to Ellen.

"A hundred and fifty pounds!" exclaimed he. "But surely, my dear, Mrs. Cumberland did not receive three hundred a-year with you! It's a large sum—for so small a service."

"She had two hundred, I think," said Ellen. "I did not know the exact sum until to-day: Mrs. Cumberland never talked to me about these matters. Papa allows me for my own purse fifty pounds every half-year. Mrs. Cumberland always gave me that."

"Ah," said Mr. North. "That's a good deal, too."

"Will you take the draft, sir; and let me have the fifty pounds at your convenience?"

Mr. North looked up as one who does not understand.

"The money is not for me, child."

"But I am staying here," she said, deprecatingly.

He shook his head as he put back the paper.

"Give it to Richard, my dear. He will know what to do about it, and what's right to be done. And so your father is coming home! We shall be sorry to lose you, Ellen. I am getting to love you, child. It seems as if you had come in the place of my poor lost Bessy."

But Ellen was not sorry. The arrival of Mr. Adair would at least remove her from her present position, where every hour, as it passed, could only bring fresh pain to her.

CHAPTER XXVI

MRS GASS AT HOME

It was a warm and sunny day in Dallory. Mrs. Gass threw open her window and sat behind the geraniums enjoying the sunshine, exchanging salutations and gossip with as many of her acquaintances as happened to pass her windows.

"How d'ye do, doctor? Isn't this a lovely day?"

It was Dr. Rane who was hurrying past now. He turned for an instant to the window, his brow clearing. For some time now a curious look of care and perplexity had sat upon it.

"Indeed it is," he answered. "I hope it will last. Are you pretty well, Mrs. Gass?"

"I'm first-rate," said that lady. "A fine day, with the wind in the north, always sets me up. Doctor, have they paid you the tontine money yet?"

"No," said Dr. Rane, somewhat angrily. "There are all sorts of forms to be gone through, apparently; and the Brothers Ticknell do not hurry for any one. The two old men are past business, in my opinion. They were always slow and tiresome; it is something more than that now."

"Do you stir 'em well up?" questioned Mrs. Gass.

"When I have the chance of doing it; but that's very rarely. Go when I will, I can scarcely ever see any one except the confidential clerk, old Latham; and he is as slow and methodical as his master. I suppose the money will come sometime, but I am tired of waiting for it."

"And what about your plans when you get it, doctor? Are they all cut and dried?"

"Time enough to decide on them when I do get the money," replied the doctor, shortly.

"But you still intend to leave Dallory Ham?"

"Oh yes, I shall do that."

"You won't be going to America?"

"I think I shall. It is more than likely."

"Well, I wouldn't banish myself from my native country for the best practice that ever shoes dropped into. You might be getting nothing but Red Indians for patients."

Dr. Rane laughed a little; and there was an eager sort of light in his eyes that seemed to speak of anticipation and hope. Only he knew how thankful he would be to get to another country and find himself clear of this.

"I wonder," soliloquized Mrs. Gass, as he walked on his way, "whether it is all straight-for'ard about that tontine money? Have the Ticknells heard any of these ugly rumours that's flying about; and are they keeping it back in consequence? If not, why it ought to have been paid over to him before this. The delay is odd—say the least of it. How d'ye do, sir? A nice day."

A gentleman, passing, had raised his hat to Mrs. Gass. She resumed her reflections.

"The rumours be spreading wider and getting uglier. They'll go up presently, like a bomb-shell. I'm heartily sorry for him; for I don't believe—no, I don't—that he'd do such a frightful thing. If it should turn out that he did—why, then I shall blame myself ever after for having procrastinated my intentions."

Mrs. Gass paused, and began to go over those intentions, with a view, possibly, to seeing whether she was very much to blame.

"Finding Oliver and his wife couldn't get the tontine money paid to them—and a hard case it was!—I had it in my mind to say, 'I'll advance it to you. You'll both be the better for something in my will when I'm gone—the doctor being my late husband's own nephew, and the nearest relation left of him—and if two thousand pounds of it will be of real good to you now, you shall have it. But I didn't say it at once— who was to suppose there was such need for hurry—and then she died. If the man's innocent—and I believe he is—that Jelly ought to have her mouth sewn up for good. She— Why, there you are! Talk of the dickens and he's sure to appear."

"Were you talking of me?" asked Jelly: for Mrs. Gass had raised her voice with surprise and brought it within Jelly's hearing. She carried a small basket on her arm, under her black shawl, and turned to the window.

"I was thinking of you," responded Mrs. Gass. "Be you come out marketing?"

"I'm taking a few scraps to Ketler's," replied Jelly, just showing the basket. "My mistress has given me general leave to give them any trifles not likely to be wanted at home. The cook's good-natured too. This is a jar of dripping, and some bones and bread."

"And how do you like the Beverages, Jelly?"

"Oh, very well. They are good ladies; but so serious and particular."

Mrs. Gass rose from her seat, pushed the geraniums aside, and leaning her arms upon the window-sill, brought her good-natured red face very near to Jelly's bonnet.

"I'll tell you what I was thinking of, girl: it was about these awful whispers that's flying round. Go where you will, you may hear 'em. Within dwelling-houses or at street corners, people's tongues are cackling secretly about Dr. Rane's wife, and asking what she died of. I knew it would be so, Jelly."

Jelly turned a little paler. "They'll die away again, perhaps," she said.

"Perhaps," repeated Mrs. Gass, sarcastically. "It's to be hoped they will, for your sake. Jelly, I wouldn't stand in your shoes to be made a queen tomorrow."

"I wouldn't stand in somebody else's," returned Jelly, irritated into the avowal. "I shall have pretty good proof at hand, if I'm forced to bring it out."

"What proof?"

"Well, I'd rather not say. You'd only ridicule it, Mrs. Gass, and blow me up into the bargain. I must be going."

"I guess it's moonshine, Jelly—like the ghost you saw. Good-morning."

Jelly went away with a hard and anything but a happy look, and Mrs. Gass resumed her seat again. Very shortly there came creeping by, following the same direction as Jelly, a poor shivering woman, with a ragged shawl on her thin shoulders, and a white, pinched, hopeless face.

"Is that you, Susan Ketler?"

Susan Ketler turned and dropped a curtsy. Some of the women of North Inlet were even worse off than she was. She did have help now and then from Jelly.

"Yes, ma'am, it's me."

"How long do you think you North Inlet people will be able to keep going—as things be at present?" demanded Mrs. Gass.

"The Lord above only knows," said the woman, looking upwards with a pitiful shiver. "Here's the winter a-coming on."

"What does Ketler think of affairs now?"

Ketler's wife shook her head. The men were not fond of disclosing what they might think, unless it was to one another. Ketler had never told her what he thought.

"Is he still in love with the Trades' Unions, and what they've done for him? My opinion is this, Susan Ketler," continued Mrs. Gass, after a pause: "that in every place where distress reigns, as it does here, and where it can be proved that the men have lost their work through the dictates of the society, the parish ought to go upon the society and make it keep the men and the families. If a law was passed to that effect, we should hear less of the doings of the Trades' Union people than we do now. They'd draw in a bit, Susan; they'd not give the gaping public quite so many of their procession-shows, and their flags, and their speeches. It would be a downright good law to make, mind you. A just one, too. If the society forbids men to work, and so takes the bread necessary for life out of their mouths, it is only fair they should find them bread to replace it."

An almost hopeful look came into the woman's eyes. "Ma'am, I said as good as this to Ketler only yesterday. Seeing that it was the society that had took the bread from us, and that the consequences had been bad instead of good, for we were starving, the society ought to put us into work again. It might bestir itself to do that: or else support us while we got into something."

Mrs. Gass smiled pityingly. "You must be credulous, Susan Ketler, to fancy the society can put 'em into work again. Where's the work to come from? Well, it's not your fault, my poor woman, and there's more people than me sorry for you all. And now, tell me," Mrs. Gass lowered her voice, "be any of the men talking treason still? You know what I mean."

Mrs. Ketler glanced over both her shoulders to see that no one was within hearing, before she whispered in answer.

"They be always a-talking it. I can see it in their faces as they stand together. Not Ketler, ma'am; he'd stop it if he could: he don't wish harm to none."

"Ah. I wish to goodness they'd all betake themselves off from the place. Though it's hard to say so, for there's no other open to them that I see. Well, you go on home, Susan. Jelly has just gone there with a basket of scraps for you. Stay a minute, though."

Mrs. Gass quitted the room, calling to one of her servants. When she returned she produced a half-pint physic bottle corked up.

"It's a drop of beer," she said. "For yourself, mind, not for Ketler. You want it, I know. Put it under your shawl. It will help down Jelly's scraps."

The woman went away with grateful tears in her eyes. And Mrs. Gass sat on and enjoyed the sunshine. Just then Mary Dallory came by in her little low pony-carriage. She often drove about in it alone. Seeing Mrs. Gass, she drew up. That lady, without any ceremony, went out in her cap and stood talking.

"I hear you have left the Hall, my dear," she said, when the gossip was coming to an end.

"Ages ago," replied Miss Dallory. "Frank is at home again, and wanted me."

"How did you enjoy your visit on the whole?"

"Pretty well. It was not very lively, especially after Sir Nash was taken ill."

"He is better, Mr. Richard tells me," said the elder lady.

"Yes; he sits up now. I went to see him yesterday."

"Captain Bohun looks but poorly still."

"His illness was a bad one. Fancy his having jaundice. I thought it was only old people who had that."

"My dear, it attacks young and old. Once the liver gets out of order, there's no telling. Captain Bohun was born in India; and they are more liable to liver complaint, it's said, than others. You are driving alone to-day, as usual," continued Mrs. Gass.

"I like to be independent. Frank won't show himself in this little chaise; he says it is no better than a respectable wheelbarrow; and I'm sure I am not going to be troubled with a groom at my side."

"If all tales told are true, you'll soon run a chance of losing your independence," rejoined Mrs. Gass. "People say a certain young lady, not a hundred miles at this moment from, my elbow, is likely to give her heart away."

Instead of replying, Mary Dallory blushed violently. Observant Mrs. Gass saw and noticed it.

"Then it is true!" she exclaimed.

"What's true?" asked Mary.

"That you are likely to be married."

"No, it is not."

"My dear, you may as well tell me. You know me well; I'll keep good counsel."

"But I have nothing to tell you. How can I imagine what you mean?"

"'Twasn't more than a hint I had: that Captain Bohun—Sir Arthur as he will be—was making up his mind to have Miss Dallory, and she to have him. Miss Mary, is it so?"

"Did madam tell you that?"

"Madam wouldn't be likely to tell me—all of us in Dallory are so much dust under her feet; quite beneath being spoken to. No: 'twas her maid, Parrit, dropped it to me. She had heard it through madam, though."

Mary Dallory laughed a little and flicked the ear of the rough Welsh pony. "I fancy madam would like it," she said.

"Who wouldn't?" rejoined Mrs. Gass. "I put the question to Richard North—Whether there was anything in it? He answered there might be; he knew it was wished for."

"Richard North said that, did he? Of course, so it might be—and may be—for anything he can tell."

"But, my dear Miss Mary, is it so?"

"Well—to tell you the truth, the offer has not yet been made. When it comes, why then—I dare say it will be all right."

"Meaning that you'll accept him."

"Meaning that—oh, but it is not right to tell tales beforehand, even to you, Mrs. Gass," she broke off, with a laugh. "Let the offer come. I wish it would."

"You would like it to come, child?"

"Yes, I think I should."

"Then be sure it will come. And God bless you, my dear, and bring you happiness whatever turns out. Though it is not just the marriage I had carved out in my own mind for one of the two of you."

She meant Arthur Bohun. Mary Dallory thought she meant herself; and laughed again as the pony trotted away.

The next friend to pass the window after Mrs. Gass had again resumed her seat, was Richard North. He did not stop at the window, but went in. Certain matters connected with the winding-up of the old firm of North and Gass, had arisen, rendering it necessary that he should see Mrs. Gass.

"Do as you think best, Mr. Richard," she said, after they had talked together for a few minutes. "Please yourself, sir, and you'll please me. We'll leave it at that: I know it's all safe in your hands."

"Then I will do as I propose," said Richard.

"I've had Miss Dallory here—that is, in her pony-chay before the door," observed Mrs. Gass. "I taxed her with what I'd heard about her and Captain Bohun; She didn't say it was, and she didn't say it wasn't: but Mr. Richard, I think there's truth in it. She as good as said she'd like him to make her an offer: and she did say madam wished it. So I suppose we shall have wedding cards before a year's gone over our heads. In their case—he next step to a baronet, and she rolling in money—there's nothing, to wait for."

"Nothing," mechanically-answered Richard North.

"But I did think, as to him, that it would have been Ellen Adair. Talking of that, Mr. Richard, what is it that's amiss with her?"

"With her?—with whom?" cried Richard, starting out of a reverie.

"With that sweet young lady, Ellen Adair?"

"There's nothing amiss with her that I know of."

"Isn't there! There is, Mr. Richard, if my judgment and eyes are to be trusted. Each time I see her, she strikes me as looking worse and worse. You notice her, sir. Perhaps now the clue has been given you'll see it too. I once knew a young girl, Mr. Richard, that was dying quietly under her friends' very eyes, and they never saw it. Never saw it at all, till an aunt came over from another country. She started back when she saw the child, and says: 'Why, what have yon been doing with her? She's dying.' They were took aback at that, and called in the first doctor: but it was too late. I don't say Ellen Adair is dying, Mr.

Richard; 'tisn't likely; but I'm sure she is not all right. Whether it's the mind, or whether it's the body, or whether it's the nerves, I'm not prepared to say; but it's something."

"I will find out," said Richard.

"Anything fresh about the men, Mr. Richard?"

"Nothing. Except that my workmen are getting afraid to stir out at night, and the disaffection increases amongst the others. I cannot see what is to be the end of it," he continued. "I do not mean of this rivalry, but of the sad state to which the men and their families are reduced. I often wish I did not think of it so much: it is like a chain about me from which I cannot escape. I wish I could help them to find work elsewhere."

"Ah!" said Mrs. Gass, "work elsewhere is very nice to think about in dreamland; but I'm afraid it'll never be seen for them in reality. It's not as if work was going a-begging: it has broken up everywhere, Mr. Richard; and shoals and shoals of men, destitute as our own, are tramping about at this minute, like so many old ravens with their mouths open, ready to pick up anything that may fall."

Richard North went home, his mind full of what Mrs. Gass had said about Ellen Adair. Was she indeed looking so ill? He found her sitting in the open seat near what would be in spring the tulip bed. Mr. North had just left her and gone in. Yes: Richard saw that she looked very ill; the face was wan, the eyes were sad and weary. She was coughing as he went up to her: a short, hacking cough. Some time ago she had caught cold, and it seemed to hang about her still.

"Are you well, Ellen?" he asked, as he sat down beside her.

"Yes, I believe so," was her reply. "Why?"

"Because I don't think you look well."

A soft colour, like the pink on a sea-shell, stole over her face as Richard said this. But she kept silence.

"You know, Ellen, we agreed to be as brother and sister. I wish to take care of you as such: to shield you from all ill as far as I possibly can. Are you happy here?"

A moment's pause, and then Ellen took courage to say that she was not happy.

"I should like to go elsewhere," she said. "Oh, Richard, if it could only be managed!"

"But it cannot," he answered.

"I have sufficient money, Richard."

"My dear, it is not that. Of course you have sufficient. I fancy, by sundry signs, that you will be a very rich young lady," he added, slightly laughing. "But you have no near friends in England, and we could not entrust you to strangers."

"If I could go for a time into some clergyman's family, or something of that sort."

"Ellen!"

She raised her hand from beneath the grey shawl—her favourite outdoor covering, for the shawl was warm—and passed it across her brow. In every movement there was a languor that spoke weariness of body or of spirit.

"When Mr. Adair comes home, if he found you had gone into 'some clergyman's family,' what would he think and say of us, Ellen?"

"I would tell him I went of my own accord."

"But, my dear, you cannot be allowed to do things of your own accord, if they are not wise. I and my father are appointed to take charge of you, and you must remain with us, Ellen, until Mr. Adair returns to England."

It was even so. Ellen's better judgment acknowledged it, in the midst of her great wish to be away. A wish: and not a wish. To be where Arthur Bohun was, still brought her the most intense happiness; and this, in spite of the pain surrounding it, she would not willingly have relinquished: but the cruelty of his conduct—of their estrangement—was more than she knew how to bear. It was making her ill, and she felt that it was. There was, however, no help for it. As Richard said, she had no friends to whom they could entrust her. The lady in whose house she was educated had recently died, and the establishment was being broken up.

Ten times a-day she longed to say to Arthur Bohun, "You are ungenerous to remain here. I cannot help myself, but you might." But pride withheld her.

"It may be months before papa arrives, Richard."

"And if it should be! We must try to make you happier with us."

"I think I must go in," she said, after a pause. "The day has been very fine, but it is growing cold now."

Folding the shawl closer to her throat, as if she felt chilly, and coughing a little as she walked, Ellen went round to the hall-door and entered. Richard, occupied in watching her and busy with his own thoughts, did not perceive the almost silent approach of Arthur Bohun, who came slowly up from behind.

"Well, Dick, old fellow!"

"Why, where did you spring from?" asked Richard, as Arthur flung himself down in the place vacated by Ellen.

"I have been under yonder tree, smoking a cigar. It has a good broad trunk to lean against."

"I thought the doctors had forbidden you to smoke."

"So they have. Until I grew stronger. One can't strictly obey orders. I don't suppose it matters much one way or the other. You have been enjoying a confidential chat, Dick."

"Yes," replied Richard. He had not felt very friendly in his heart towards Arthur for some time past. What was the meaning of his changed behaviour to Ellen Adair?—what of the new friendship with Mary Dallory? Richard North could not forgive dishonour; and he believed Arthur Bohun was steeping himself in it to the backbone.

"Were you making love, Dick?"

Richard turned his eyes in silence on the questioner.

"She and I have had to part, Dick. I always thought you admired and esteemed her almost more, perhaps quite more, than you do any other woman. So if you are thinking of her—"

"Be silent," sternly interrupted Richard, rising in anger. "Are you a man?—are you a gentleman? Or are you what I have been thinking you lately—a false-hearted, despicable knave?"

Whatever Arthur Bohun might be, he was just then in desperate agitation. Rising too, he seized Richard's hands.

"Don't you see that it was but sorry jesting, Richard? Pretending to a bit of pleasantry, to wile away for a moment my weight of torment. I am all that you say of me; and I cannot help myself."

"Not help yourself?"

"As Heaven is my witness, No! If I could take you into my confidence—and perhaps I may do so one of these days, for I long to do it—you would see that I tell you the truth."

"Why have you parted from Ellen Adair?—she and you have parted? You have just said so."

"We have parted for life. For ever."

"You were on the point of marriage with her only a short time ago?"

"No two people could have been nearer marriage than she and I were. We were within half-an-hour of it, Dick; and yet we have parted."

"By your doing, or hers?"

"By mine."

"I thought so."

"Dick, I have been compelled to do it. When you shall know all, you will acknowledge that I could not do otherwise. And yet, in spite of this, I feel that to her I have been but a false-hearted knave, as you aptly style me: a despicable, dishonourable man. My father fell into dishonour—or rather had it forced upon him by another—and he could not survive it; he shot himself. Did you know it, Dick?"

"Shot himself!" repeated Richard, in his surprise. "No, I never knew that. I thought he died of sunstroke."

"My father shot himself," cried Arthur. "He could not live dishonoured. Dick, old fellow, there are moments when I feel tempted to do as he did."

"What—because you have parted from Ellen?"

"No. That's bitter enough to bear; but I can battle with it. It is the other thing, the dishonour. That is always present with me, always haunting me night and day; I know not how to live under it."

"I do not understand at all," said Richard. "You are master of your own actions."

"In this case I have not been: my line of conduct was forced upon me. I cannot explain. Don't judge me too harshly, my friend. I am bad enough, Heaven knows, but not quite as bad, perhaps, as you have been thinking me."

And Arthur Bohun turned and went limping away, leaving Richard lost in wonder.

He limped away to indulge his pain where no mortal eye could see him. Parted from Ellen Adair, the whole world was to him as nothing. A sense of dishonour lay ever upon him, the shame of his conduct towards her was present to him night and day. With all his heart he wished James Bohun had not died, that there might have been no question of his succession. He would then have gone somewhere away with her, have changed his name, and been happy in obscurity. But there was no place unfrequented by man; he could not change his wife's face; and she might be recognized as the daughter of Adair the convict. Besides, would it not be an offence against Heaven if he wedded the daughter of the man who had caused the death of his father? No; happiness could never be his. Look where he would, there was nothing around him but pain and misery.

CHAPTER XXVII

ONCE AGAIN

Jelly lived, so to say, on a volcano. She felt that, figuratively speaking, there was not an hour of the day or night but she might be blown into fragments. The rumours as to the death of Mrs. Rane were becoming more terrible. They stole up and down Dallory like a scorching tongue of fire, and Jelly had the satisfaction of knowing that it was she who had first set light to the flame. It was all very well to say that she had made herself safe by securing the evidence of Thomas Hepburn: in her secret conscience she knew that she was not safe; and that, even in spite of that evidence, Dr. Rane might chance to be innocent. If so, why, a pretty dilemma she would find herself in. There was no help for it; she could do nothing. The creeping, scorching tongue went twisting itself in and out, and she could not quench it.

One night Jelly was lying awake, according to custom now, buried deep in some horrible visions that had lately begun to haunt her: now of working in chains; now of stepping incessantly up a treadmill; now of picking oakum and living upon gruel. Turning in the bed, to escape, if possible, these imaginary pictures, she suddenly heard a knock at her door. A loud hasty knock; and now a louder. Jelly turned hot then cold as ice. Had the officers of the law come to arrest her?

"Who's there?—what is it?" she asked faintly, not daring to sit up in bed.

"Art thee awake, Jelly?" came the gentle response, as her door was opened a few inches. "I am very sorry to have to ask thee to get up, but my mother is worse. Make haste, please."

Had Miss Beverage's voice been that of an angel, it could not have sounded sweeter to Jelly just then. The relief was great.

"I'll get up instantly, ma'am," was the ready answer—and Miss Beverage wondered it should have in it a tone as of gratitude. "I'll be with you at once."

Mrs. Beverage was subject to violent but rare attacks of spasms. She had felt ill before going to bed, but hoped it would pass off. Jelly and her own two servants were soon at her bedside. She was very ill indeed. Some of them ran to get hot water ready; Jelly thought it would be well to call in Dr. Rane.

"I should like the doctor to see her; at the same time, I grieve to arouse him from sleep," said Miss Beverage.

"Law, ma'am, that's nothing to doctors; they are used to it," cried Jelly.

"Mother, would thee like Oliver Rane sent for?" asked Miss Beverage, bending over the suffering lady. "Yes—yes," was the feeble answer. "I am very ill, Sarah."

"Thee go, then, Jelly."

Away went Jelly. Unbarring their own front-door, she passed out of it, and approached Dr. Rane's. The doctor's professional lamp burnt clearly, and, to her great surprise, Jelly saw that the door was not closed.

"He cannot have gone to bed to-night," she thought, as she walked in without ringing. It was past three o'clock.

But the house seemed to be still and dark. Jelly left the front-door open, and the light shone a little way into the passage. She tried the surgery-door; it was locked; she tried the dining-room; the key of that was also turned; the kitchen-door stood open, but it was all in darkness.

"He has gone to bed and forgotten to shut up," was the conclusion Jelly now arrived at. "I'll go up and call him."

Groping her way upstairs, she had almost reached the top, when a pale white light suddenly illumined the landing—just the same faint sort of light that Jelly had seen once before, and remembered all too well. Raising her head hastily, there stood—what?

Not quite at the moment did Jelly know what. Not in the first access of terror did she clearly recognize the features of Bessy Rane. It was she, all too surely; that is, the image of what she had been. She seemed to stand almost face to face with Jelly: Jelly nearly at the top of the staircase, she facing it before her. The light was even more faint before the figure than behind: but there was no mistaking it. What it was dressed in or whence it came, Jelly never knew: there it was—the form and face of Bessy

Rane. With a cry of agony, that echoed to the ends of the empty house in the night's silence, Jelly turned and flew down again.

She never looked behind. Out at the front-door went she, slamming it, in her terror, to keep in what might be following her; and she almost gave forth another scream when she found herself touched by some one coming in at the gate, and saw that it was Dr. Rane.

"I am called out to a country patient," he quietly said. "Whilst I was putting the horse to the gig, an impression came over me that I had left my house-door open, so I thought I had better come back and see. What are you doing here at this hour, Jelly? Any one ill?"

Jelly was in terrible distress and confusion of mind. Clutching his arm as if for protection, she sobbed for an instant or two hysterically. Dr. Rane stared at her, not knowing what to make of it. He began to think she must require his services herself.

"Sir—do you know—do you know who is in the house?"

"Nobody's there: unless they've come in these last few minutes—for I suppose I did leave the door open," was Dr. Rane's rejoinder, and his composure contrasted strongly with Jelly's emotion. "When I leave my house at night, I carry my household with me, Jelly."

"Your wife's there," she whispered, with a burst of agony. "Sir, it's as true as that I am living to tell it."

"What do you say?"

Jelly's answer was to relate what she had seen. When Dr. Rane had gathered in her full meaning, he grew very angry.

"Why, you must be mad, woman," he cried in a low concentrated voice. "This is the second time. How dare you invent such folly?"

"I swear that her ghost walks, and that it is in there now," exclaimed Jelly, almost beside herself. "It is on the landing, exactly where I saw it before. Why should she come again?—why should she haunt that one particular spot? Sir, don't look at me like that. You know I would not invent such a thing."

"Your fancy invents it, and then you speak of it as if were fact. How dare you do so?"

"But he could not appease Jelly: he could not persuade her out of her belief. And the doctor saw that it was useless to attempt it.

"Why, why should her poor ghost walk?" wailed Jelly, wringing her hands in distress.

"I'm sure I don't know why it should walk," returned the doctor, as if he would humour Jelly and at the same time ridicule her words. "It never walks when I am in the house." But the ridicule was lost on Jelly.

"She can't lie quiet in her grave. What reason is there for it?—oh, what dreadful mystery is in it?"

Dr. Rane looked as though he would have liked to annihilate Jelly. "I begin to think that you are either a fool or a knave," he cried. "What brought you in my house at three o'clock in the morning?"

The question, together with his unconcealed anger, recalled Jelly's scattered senses. She told him about the illness of Mrs. Beverage, and asked if he would come in.

"No, I cannot come," said Dr. Rane quite savagely, for it seemed that he could not get the better of his anger. "I am called out to a case of emergency, and have no time to waste over Mrs. Beverage. If she wants a doctor, send for Seeley."

He opened his door with his latch-key, and shut it loudly after him. However, it seemed that he reconsidered the matter, for when Jelly was slowly walking across the road towards Mr. Seeley's, Dr. Rane came out again, called her back, and said he would spare a minute or two.

With a stern caution to Jelly not to make the same foolish exhibition of herself to others that she had to him, he went up to Mrs. Beverage—who was then easier, and had dozed off to sleep. Giving a few general directions in case the paroxysm should return, Dr. Rane departed. About ten minutes afterwards, Jelly was in her room, which looked towards the lane, when she heard his gig come driving down and stop at his garden-door. After waiting there a short time—he had probably come in for some case of instruments—it went away quickly across country.

The horse and gig used by the doctor belonged to the neighbouring public-house. Dr. Rane had a key to the stables, so that if he wanted to go out during the night, he could harness the horse to the gig without disturbing any one.

"If he had not said beforehand that he was putting the horse to, I should have thought he'd gone out because he daredn't stay in the house," muttered Jelly, as she glued her face to the window pane, to look after the doctor and the gig. She could see neither; the night was very dark.

Jelly's mind was in a chaos. What she had witnessed caused her still to shiver and tremble as though she had an ague; and she fully believed that she was really in danger of becoming what the doctor had told her she was already—mad.

Suddenly, a cry arose in the house. Mrs. Beverage was worse again. The paroxysm had returned so violently that it seemed to the frightened beholders as though she would die. Dr. Rane was not attainable, and Miss Beverage sent one of the under-servants for Mr. Seeley. He came promptly.

In about an hour the danger had passed; the house was quiet again, and Mr. Seeley was at liberty to return to his rest. He had crossed the road to his own door when he heard a step following him. Turning he saw Jelly.

"Surely she is not ill again!" he hastily exclaimed.

"No, sir, she is all right I think now. Mr. Seeley," added Jelly in agitation so marked that he could not help noticing it, "I want to speak to you: I want to tell you something. I must tell somebody, or I shall never live till morning."

"Are you ill?" questioned Mr. Seeley.

"When I was holding the flannels just now, and otherwise helping you, sir, you might have seen that I hadn't all my wits about me. Miss Beverage looked at me once or twice, as much as to ask what had become of them. Mr. Seeley, I have the weight of a most awful secret upon me, and I can't any longer bear with it."

"A secret!" repeated Mr. Seeley.

Jelly drew near to him. She pointed to the house of Dr. Rane, and lowered her voice to a whisper.

"Mrs. Rane's there."

He looked across at the house—so apparently still and peaceful behind its white blinds; he turned and looked at Jelly. Not a syllable did he understand of her assertion.

"Mrs. Rane comes again, sir. She haunts the house. I have seen her twice with my own eyes. Once, the night of her death, just after she had been put into her coffin; and again this very night."

"Why, what on earth do you mean?" questioned Mr. Seeley in amazement. "Mrs. Rane haunts the house?—I don't understand you."

"Her ghost does, sir. It is there now."

The surgeon leaned against his door-post, and stared at Jelly as if he thought her mind was wandering. A minute or two passed in utter silence.

"My good woman, you need a composing draught as badly as Friend Beverage did just now. What is the matter with you, Jelly?"

In reply, Jelly told her story—as to the appearance of Mrs. Rane—from the beginning. But she cautiously avoided all mention of suspicion as to unfair play: in fact she did not mention Dr. Rane's name at all. Mr. Seeley listened quietly, as though he were hearing a fairy tale.

"Have you spoken of this to Dr. Rane?" was his first question.

"Yes, sir: both times. To-night I met him as I was rushing out of the house in my terror."

"What does he say to it?"

"He ridicules it. He says it's my fancy, and is in a towering rage with me. Mrs. Gass asked whether I had been taking too much beer. People are hard of belief as to such things."

"You told Mrs. Gass, then?"

"I told her the first time. I was in great distress and perplexity, and I mentioned it to her as we sat together in the churchyard looking at Mrs. Rane's funeral."

"What did Mrs. Gass say?"

"She cautioned me never to speak of it again to living soul. Neither of that, nor of—of anything. But this very night, sir, I have seen it again: and if it is to go on like this, I shall soon be in a lunatic asylum."

Mr. Seeley had no faith in ghosts. At the same time he saw how implicit was Jelly's belief in what she fancied she had seen, and the distressed state of mind it had induced. What to answer for the best, he did not know. If he threw ridicule on the story, it would make no impression upon her: if he pretended to receive it as truth, it could bring her no relief.

"Jelly," said he, "I should not believe in a ghost if I saw one."

"I didn't believe in them once," answered Jelly. "But seeing brings belief."

"I'm sure I don't know what to say to you," was his candid avowal. "You are evidently so imbued with your own view of the matter, that any argument to the contrary would be useless."

"What troubles me is this," resumed Jelly, as if she had not heard him. "Why is she unable to rest, poor thing? What's the reason for it?"

"I should say there was no reason," observed Mr. Seeley.

"Should you, sir?"

Jelly spoke significantly, and he looked at her keenly. There was a professional lamp over the door, as there was over Dr. Rane's; and their faces were visible to each other. The significant tone had slipped out in the heat of argument, and Jelly grew cautious again.

"What am I to do, sir?"

"Indeed I cannot tell you, Jelly. There is only one thing to be done, I should say—get rid of the fancy again as quickly as you can."

"You think I did not see it!"

"I think all ghost-stories proceed purely from an excited imagination," said the surgeon.

"You have not lived here very long, sir, but you have been here quite long enough to know that I've not much imagination. I don't remember that, before this happened, I ever felt excited in my whole life. My nature's not that way. The first time I saw her, I had come in, as I say, from Ketler's; and all I was thinking of was Dinah's negligence in not putting out the matches for me. I declare that when I saw her, poor thing, that night, I was as cool as a cucumber. She stood there some time, looking at me with a fixed stare, as it seemed, and I stood in the dark, looking at her. I thought it was herself, Mr. Seeley, and felt glad that she was able to be out of bed. In the morning, when I heard she was dead and shut up in her coffin, I thought she must have been shut in alive. You were the first I asked whether it was true that she was dead," added Jelly, warming with the sudden recollection, "I saw you standing here at the door after Dinah had told me, and I stepped over to you."

The surgeon nodded. He remembered it

"To-night when I went for Dr. Rane, there was not a thought or particle of superstition in my mind. I was troubled about Mrs. Beverage, and wondering what carelessness brought the doctor's front-door open. And there she stood!—facing me as I went up the stairs—just in the same identical spot that she had stood in the time before. Ugh!" broke off Jelly, with a shudder. "But don't say again, sir, please, that it was my excited imagination."

"I could tell you stories of the imagination that would surprise you, Jelly."

"If it was not Mrs. Rane—that is, her apparition—that appeared to me to-night, sir, and that appeared to me the other night, I wish these eyes may never behold anything again," spoke Jelly solemnly. And Mr. Seeley saw how worse than useless would be any further contention.

"Jelly, why have you told me this? I do not see how I can help you."

"I've told you because the weight of keeping it to myself was greater than I could bear," she replied. "It's an awful thing, and a cruel thing, that it should be just me that's singled out for it. I think I know why: and I am nearly torn to pieces with the responsibility. As to helping me, sir, I don't think that you or anybody else can do that. Did you see Mrs. Rane after she died?"

The question was put abruptly, but in a tone that Jelly meant to be indifferent. Mr. Seeley replied in a very matter-of-fact manner.

"No."

"Well, I'll wish you goodnight, sir. Keeping you talking here will do no good."

"Good-morning, I should say," returned the surgeon.

Jelly had reached her own gate, when she paused for a moment and then turned back across the road. The surgeon had not moved. He was still leaning against his door-post, apparently gazing at Dr. Rane's house. Jelly said what she had returned to say.

"You will please not speak of this again to any one, Mr. Seeley. There are reasons why."

"Not I, Jelly," was the hearty rejoinder. "I don't want to be laughed at in Dallory as a retailer of a ghost-story."

"Thank you, sir."

With that, the surgeon passed into his dwelling, and Jelly went over to hers. And the winter's night wore on to its close.

In the favourable reaction that had fallen on Mrs. Beverage, Jelly might have gone to rest again had she so chosen. But she did not do so. There could be neither rest nor sleep for her. She sat by the kitchen-fire, and drank sundry cups of tea: and rather thought, what with one perplexity and another, that it was not sinful to wish herself dead.

In the morning about seven o'clock, when she was upstairs in her chamber, she heard the sound of a gig in the lane, and looked out. It was Dr. Rane, returning from his visit to his patient. His face was white and troubled. An ordinary passer-by would have said the doctor was cold: Jelly drew a different conclusion.

"It's his conscience," she mentally whispered. "It's the thought of having to live in his house now that he knows what's in it. He might have set it down to my fancy the first time: he can't this. Who knows, either, but what she appears to him?—who knows? but it strikes me his nerves are made of iron. He must have been driving like mad, too, by the way the gig's splashed!" added Jelly, catching a glimpse of the state of the vehicle as it whirled round the corner towards the stables. "Good Heavens! what is to be done?—what is to be done about this dreadful secret? Why should it have fallen on ME of all people in the world?"

CHAPTER XXVIII

COMING VERY NEAR

When rumours of this grave character arise, they do not come suddenly to a climax. Time must be given them to grow and settle down. It came at length, however, here. Doubts ripened into convictions: suppressed breathings widened into broad assertions: Oliver Rane had certainly murdered his wife for the sake of the tontine money. People affirmed it one to another as they met in the street—or rather, to avoid compromising themselves, said that others affirmed it. Old Phillis heard it one day, and almost fell down in a fit. She did not altogether believe it: nevertheless from that time she could not speak to her master without visibly trembling. The doctor thought she must be suffering from nervous derangement. At length it penetrated to Dallory Hall and the ears of madam; and upon madam it produced an extraordinary effect.

It has been stated throughout that Mrs. North had conceived a violent dislike to Dr. Rane; or at least, that she persistently acted in a manner that produced the impression that she had done so. As if she had only waited for this rumour to accuse him of something tangible, madam made the cause her own. She never appeared to doubt the truth of the report, or to inquire as to its grounds; she drove about, here, there, and everywhere, unequivocally asserting that Bessy Rane had been poisoned, and that her husband, Oliver Rane, had done the deed.

In truth Mrs. North had been in a state of mental ferment ever since she had become cognizant of the expected return of Mr. Adair to England. Why she should dread this, and why it should excite her in no measured degree she alone knew. No one around her had the least idea that the home-coming of Mr. Adair would be more to her than the arrival of any stranger might be. Restless, nervous, anxious, with an evil and crafty look in her eyes, with ears that were ever open, with hands that could never be still, waited madam. The household saw nothing—only that her tyranny became more unbearable day by day.

It almost seemed as though she took up the whispered accusation against Dr. Rane as a vent for some of her other and terrible uneasiness. He must be brought to the bar of justice to answer for his crime, avowed madam. She drove to the houses of the different county magistrates, urging this view upon them; she besieged the county coroner in his office, and bade him get the necessary authority and issue his orders for the exhumation of the body.

The coroner was Mr. Dale. There had recently been a sharp contest for the coronership, which had become vacant, between a doctor and a lawyer: the latter was Dale, of Whitborough, and he had gained the day. To say that madam, swooping down upon him with this command, startled him, would be saying little, as describing his state of astonishment. Occupied very much just now with the proceedings attaching to his new honour, Lawyer Dale had found less time for gossiping about his neighbours' affairs than usual; and not a syllable of the flying rumour had reached him. So little did he at first believe it, and so badly did he think of madam for the part she was playing, that, had she been a man, he would have given her the lie direct. But she was persistent, repeating the charge over and over to him in the most obnoxious and least delicate manner possible: Oliver Rane had poisoned his wife during her attack of fever, and he had done it to get possession of the tontine money. She went over the grounds of suspicion, dwelling on them one by one; and perhaps the lawyer's belief in Dr. Rane's innocence was just a trifle shaken—which, however, he did not acknowledge. After some sparring between them—Mr. Dale holding back from interference, she pressing it on—the coroner was obliged to admit that if a demand for an inquest were formally made to him he should have no resource but to call one. Finally he undertook to institute some private inquiries into the matter, and see whether there were sufficient grounds to justify so extreme a course. Madam sharply replied that if he showed the smallest disposition to stifle the inquiry, she should at once cause the Home Secretary to be communicated with. And with that she swept down to her carriage.

Perhaps, of all classes of men, lawyers are most brought into contact with the crimes and follies committed by the human race. Mr. Dale had not been at all scrupulous as to what he undertook; and many curious matters had come under his experience. Leaning back in his chair after madam's visit, revolving the various points of the story, his opinion changed, and he came to the conclusion that, on the face of things, it did look very much as though Dr. Rane had been guilty. Lawyer Dale had no reason to wish the doctor harm; especially the fearful harm a public investigation might entail upon him: had the choice lain with him, he would have remained quiescent, and left the doctor to his conscience. But he saw clearly that Mrs. North would not suffer this, and that it was more than probable he would have to act.

The first move he made, in his undertaking to institute some private inquiry, was to seek an interview with Mr. Seeley. He went himself; the matter was of too delicate a nature to be confided to a clerk. In his questions he was reticent, after the custom of a man of law, giving no clue, and intending to give none, as to why he put them; but Mr. Seeley had heard of the rumoured accusation, and spoke out freely.

"I confess that I could not quite understand the death," he avowed: "but I do not suspect that Dr. Rane, or any one else had any hand in it. She died naturally, as I believe. Mr. Dale, this is a horrible thing for you to bring against him."

"I bring it!" cried Mr. Dale. "I don't bring it; I'd rather let the doubt die out. It is forced upon me."

"Who by? These confounded scandalmongers?"

"By Mrs. North."

"Mrs. North!" echoed the surgeon, in surprise. "You don't mean to say the North family are taking it up."

"I don't know about the family. Madam is, with a vengeance. She won't let it rest. There is an evident animus in her mind against Dr. Rane, and she means to pursue the charge to its extremity."

Mr. Seeley felt vexed to hear it. When these rare and grave charges are brought against one of the medical body, the rest, as a rule, would rather resent than entertain it. And, besides, the surgeon liked Dr. Rane.

"Come; you may as well tell me the truth," cried the lawyer, breaking the silence. "You'll have to do it publicly, I fancy."

"Mr. Dale," was the answer, "I have told you the truth according to my belief. Never a suspicion of foul play crossed my mind in regard to Mrs. Rane's death. I saw nothing to give rise to it."

"You did not see her after she died: nor for some hours before it?"

"No."

"You think she went off naturally."

"Most certainly I think so."

"But, see here—we lawyers have to probe opinions, you know, so excuse me. If it were to be proved that she went off in—in a different way, you would not be surprised; eh, Seeley?"

"I should be very much surprised."

"From your recollection of the facts, you would not be able to bring forth any proof to the contrary?"

"Well, no; I should not be able."

"There's the difficulty, you see," resumed the lawyer; "there's where it will lie. You believe Rane was innocent, I may believe him innocent; but no one can furnish sufficient proof to stop the inquiry. It will have to go on as sure as fate."

"Cannot you stop it, Mr. Dale?"

"I promise you this: that I will throw as many difficulties in the way of it as I possibly can. But when once I am publicly called upon to act, I shall have to obey."

That was the end of the interview. It had a little strengthened the lawyer's doubts, if anything. Mr. Seeley had not seen her after death. What he was going to do next Mr. Dale did not say.

By the day following this, perhaps the only two people accustomed to walk up and down the streets of Dallory who still remained in blissful ignorance of the trouble afloat, were Dr. Rane himself, and Richard North. No one had dared to mention it to either of them. Richard, however, was soon to be enlightened.

Business took him to his bankers' in Whitborough. It was of a private nature, requiring to be transacted between himself and one of the old brothers at the head of the firm. After it was over they began talking about things in general, and Richard asked incidentally whether much further delay would take place in paying the tontine money to Dr. Rane.

"I am not sure that we shall be able to pay it at all," replied Sir Thomas Ticknell.

"Why not?" asked Richard, in surprise.

For answer, the old gentleman looked significantly at Richard for a moment, and then demanded whether he was still in ignorance of what had become the chief topic of the place.

Bit by bit, it all came out. The Brothers Ticknell, it appeared, had heard the report quite at the first: friends are always to be found when there is an opportunity of doing a fellow-man an injury; and some one had hastened to the bankers with the news. Richard North sat aghast as he listened. His sister was supposed to have come by her death unfairly! For once in his life he changed to the hue of the grave, and his strong frame trembled.

"We hear the new coroner, Dale, has the matter in hand now," remarked Sir Thomas. "I fear it will be a terrible scandal."

Recovering the shock in some degree, Richard North took his departure, and went over to Dale's, whose offices were nearly opposite the bank. The lawyer was there, and made no scruple of disclosing what he knew to Richard.

"It's a pity that I have to take the matter up," said Dale. "Considering the uncertainty at present attending it—considering that also it cannot bring the dead to life, and that it will be a most painful thing for old Mr. North—and for you too, Mr. Richard—I think it would be as well to let it alone."

"But who is stirring in it?" asked Richard.

"Madam."

"Madam! Do you mean Mrs. North?"

"To be sure I do. I don't say that public commotion and officious people would not soon have brought it to the same issue; but, any way, Mrs. North has forestalled them." And he told Richard of madam's visit to him.

"You say you have been making some private inquiries," observed Richard.

Mr. Dale nodded.

"And what is your candid opinion? Tell me, Dale."

But the lawyer hesitated to say he feared Dr. Rane might have been guilty. Not only because it was an unpleasant assertion to make to Dr. Rane's brother-in-law, but also because he really had doubts as to whether it was so or not.

"I hold no decided opinion as yet," he said. "I may not be able to form one until the post-mortem examination has taken place—"

"You do not mean to say that they will—that they will disturb my sister!" interrupted Richard North, his eyes full of horror.

"Why, that's the first thing they will do—if the investigation goes on at all," cried the lawyer. "That's always the preliminary step in these cases. You are forgetting."

"I suppose I am," groaned Richard. "This has been a great shock to me. Dale, you cannot believe him guilty!"

"Well, I can't tell; and that's the fact," candidly avowed the lawyer. "There are certainly some suspicious circumstances attending the case: but at the same time, they are only what Dr. Rane may be able to explain satisfactorily away."

"How have the doubts arisen?" questioned Richard. "There were none—I suppose—at the time."

"As far as I can at present ascertain, they have sprung from some words incautiously dropped by Jelly, the late Mrs. Cumberland's maid. Whether Jelly saw anything at the time of Mrs. Rane's illness to give rise to suspicion I don't know. I have not yet seen her. It is necessary to go about this business cautiously; and Jelly, I expect, will not prove a willing witness."

"Did madam tell you this arose from Jelly?"

"Oh dear, no. Madam does not concern herself as to the source of the suspicions; she said to me: 'There they are, and you must deal with them.' I had the information from my clerk, Timothy Wilks. In striving to trace the rumours to their source, I traced them to him. Carpeting him before me in this room, I insisted upon his telling me where he obtained them from. He answered readily enough, 'From Jelly.' It seems Jelly was spending an evening at his aunt's, or cousin's, or grandmother's—whatever it is. I mean the wife of your timekeeper, Mr. Richard North. Wilks was present: only those three; the conversation turned upon Mrs. Rane's death, and Jelly said a few words that startled them. I quite believe that was the beginning of the scandal."

"What can Jelly know?" exclaimed Richard, dreamily.

"I can't tell. The report is, that Mrs. Rane had something wrong given to her by her husband the last day of her life: and that his object was to get the tontine money, which he could not touch whilst she lived. A curious thing that the husband and wife should be the two last left in that tontine!" added the lawyer. "I've often said so."

"But even"—Richard paused—"if this had been so, how could Jelly have learnt it?"

"Well, things come out in strange ways sometimes; especially if they are things that ought to be kept secret. I've noticed it. Jelly's mistress was away, and she may have gone in to help nurse Mrs. Rane in her illness: we don't yet know how it was."

Richard North rose to depart. "At any rate, I do not see that it was madam's place to take it up," he remarked. "She should have left that to the discretion of my father and myself."

"She was in a perfect fever over it," cried Mr. Dale. "She talked of sending an application to the Home Secretary. I shouldn't wonder but what it has already gone up."

From the lawyer's house, Richard went direct to that of the late Mrs. Cumberland. The darkness of evening was then drawing on. As he reached the door, Miss Beverage, in her dove-coloured Quaker's bonnet, approached it from an opposite direction. Raising his hat, he asked whether he could be allowed a five minutes' interview with Jelly. Miss Beverage, who knew Richard by sight, was very chatty and pleasant: she took him into the drawing-room and sent Jelly to him. And Jelly felt half inclined to faint as she shut the door, for she well knew what must be coming.

But, after some fencing with Richard's questions, Jelly gave in. He was resolute in hearing all she could tell, and at length she made a clean breast of it. She related what she knew, and what she suspected, from beginning to end; and before she had finished, a strange relief, that Richard should know it, grew upon her.

"For I shall consider that the responsibility is now taken off my shoulders, sir," she said. "And perhaps it has been nothing but this that the ill-fated lady has wanted me to do, in coming again."

In the whole narrative, the part that most struck Richard North was Jelly's positive assertion that she had since twice seen Mrs. Rane. He was simply astounded. And, to tell the truth, he did not attempt to cast ridicule or disbelief on it. Richard North was an educated and practical man, possessed of an abundance of good common sense, with no more tendency to believe in supernatural appearances than men have in general; but his mind had been so unhinged since the interview with Sir Thomas Ticknell, that he almost felt inclined to admit the possibility of his sister's not resting in her grave.

He sat with his head leaning on his hand. Collecting in some degree his scattered senses, he strove to go over the grounds of suspicion. But he could make nothing more of them than Dale had said. Grounds there certainly were, but none that Dr. Rane might not be able to explain away. Jelly drew her own deductions, and called them proofs: but Richard saw that of proofs as yet there were none.

"Ever since that first night, I've lived in mortal horror of seeing it again," said Jelly, interrupting his reverie. "Nobody can imagine, sir, what a dreadful time it has been. And when I was least thinking of it, it came the second time."

"To whom have you repeated this story of having seen her?" asked Richard.

"The first time I told Dr. Rane and Mrs. Gass. This last time I told the doctor and Mr. Seeley."

"Jelly," said Richard quietly, "there is no proof that anything was wrong, except in your fancy."

"And the hasty manner that she was hid out of the way, sir—no woman called in to do anything for her; no soul allowed to see her!" urged Jelly. "If it wanted proof positive before, it can't want it since what Thomas Hepburn related to me."

"All that may have been done out of regard to the welfare of the living," said Richard.

Jelly shook her head. To her mind it was clearer than daylight.

But at this juncture, a servant came in to know if she should bring lights. Richard took the opportunity to depart. Of what use to prolong his stay? As he went out he saw Mr. Seeley standing at his door. Richard crossed over and asked to speak with him: he knew of Dale's interview with the surgeon.

"Can Rane have been guilty of this thing, or not?" questioned Richard, when they were closeted together.

But not even here could Richard get at any decided opinion. It might have been so, or it might not, Seeley replied. For himself, he was inclined to think it was not so: that Mrs. Rane's death was natural.

Leaving again, Richard paced up and down the dark road. His mind was in a tumult. He, with Seeley, could not think Dr. Rane guilty. And, even though he were so, he began to question whether it would not be better for his father's sake, for all their sakes, to let the matter lie. Richard put the two aspects together, and compared them. On the one side there would be the merited punishment of Oliver Rane and vengeance on Bessy's wrongs; the other would bring a terrible amount of pain, exposure, almost disgrace. And Richard feared for the effect it might have on Mr. North. Before his walk was over, he decided that it would be infinitely best to hush up the scandal, should that still be possible.

But, for his own satisfaction, he wished to get at the truth. It seemed to him that he could hardly live in the uncertainty. Taking a rapid resolution, he approached Dr. Rane's; knocked at the door, and asked old Phillis if he could see her master.

She at once showed him into the dining-room. Dr. Rane, weary, perhaps, with the cares of the day, had fallen asleep in his chair. He sprang up at the interruption; a startled, almost frightened expression appeared in his face. Richard North could but notice it, and his heart failed him, for it seemed to speak of guilt. Phillis shut them in together.

How Richard opened the interview, he scarcely knew, and could never afterwards recall. He soon found that Dr. Rane remained as yet in ignorance of the stir that was abroad; and this rendered his task all the more difficult. Richard entered on the communication in the most delicate manner that the subject admitted of. Dr. Rane did not receive it kindly. He first swore a great oath, and then—his anger checked suddenly as if by some latent thought or fear—he sank back in his chair and bent his head on his hands, as a man struck dumb with tribulation.

"I think you need not have given credit to this report against me, Richard North," he presently spoke in reproachful accents. "But I believe you lost confidence in me a year and a half ago."

He so evidently alluded to the anonymous letter that Richard did not affect to misunderstand him. It might be better to speak openly.

"I believe you wrote that, Rane."

"True. I did. But not to injure your brother. I thought Alexander must be a bad man—that he must be leading Edmund North into difficulties to serve himself. I had no cause to spare him, but the contrary, for he had injured me, was injuring me daily; and I wrote what I did to Mr. North, hoping it might expose

Alexander and damage him. There: you have it. I would rather have had my hand cut off than have hurt your brother. I wished afterwards that it had been cut off first. But it was too late then."

And because of that anonymous letter Dr. Rane knew, and Richard felt, that the accusation, now made, gathered weight. When a man has been guilty of one thing, we think it a reason why he may be guilty of another.

A silence ensued. They sat, the table between them. The room was rather dark. The lamp was shaded, the fire had burned low; before the large window wore stretched the sombre curtains. Richard North would have given some years of his life for this most distressing business never to have come into it.

He went on with what he had to say. Dr. Rane, motionless now, kept his hand over his face whilst he listened. Richard told of the public commotion; of the unparalleled shock it had been to himself, of the worse shock he feared it might be to his father. Again there was an interruption: but Dr. Rane in speaking did not raise his face.

"Is my liberty in danger?"

"Not yet—in one sense of the word. I believe you are under the surveillance of the police."

"Watched by them?"

"Yes. But only to see that you do not get away."

"That is—they track me out and home, I am to understand? I am watched in and out of my patients' houses. If I have occasion to pay country visits, these stealthy bloodhounds are at my heels, night or day?"

"I conclude it is so," answered Richard.

"Since when has this been?"

"Since—I think since the day before yesterday. There is a probability, as I hear, that the Home Secretary will be applied to. If—"

"For what purpose?"

"For authority to disturb the grave," said Richard, in low tones.

Dr. Rane started up, a frenzy of terror apparent in his face.

"They—they—surely they are not talking of doing that?" he cried, turning white as death.

"Yes they are. To have her disturbed will be to us the most painful of all."

"Stop it, for Heaven's sake!" came the imploring cry. "Stop it, Richard North! Stop it!"

But at that moment there broke upon their ears a frightful commotion outside the door. Richard opened it. Dr. Rane, who had sunk on to his seat again, never stirred. Old Phillis, coming in from the scullery after a cleaning excursion, had accidentally dropped a small cartload of pots and pans.

CHAPTER XXIX

IN THE SHRUBBERY

Wintry weather set in again. The past few days had been intensely cold and bleak. Ellen Adair sat in one of her favourite outdoor seats. Sheltered from the wind by artificial rocks and clustering evergreens, and well wrapped-up besides, she did not seem to feel the frost.

Her later days had been one long trial. Compelled constantly to meet Arthur Bohun, yet shunned by him as far as it was possible without attracting the observation of others, there were times when she felt as though her position at the Hall were killing her. Something, in fact, was killing her. Her state of mind was a mixture of despair, shame, and self-reproach. Captain Bohun's conduct brought her the bitterest humiliation. Looking back on the past, she thought he despised her for her ready acquiescence in his wish for a private marriage: and the repentance, the humiliation it entailed on her was of all things the hardest to bear. She almost felt that she could die of the memory—just as other poor creatures, whose sin has been different, have died of their shame. The thought embittered her peace by night and by day: it was doing her more harm than all the rest. To one so sensitively organized as Ellen Adair, reared in all the graces of refined feeling, this enforced sojourn at Dallory Hall could indeed be nothing less than a fiery ordeal, from which there might be no escape to former health and strength.

Very still she sat to-day, nursing her pain. Her face was wan, her breathing laboured: that past cold she had caught seemed to hang about her strangely. No further news had been received from Mr. Adair, and Ellen supposed he was on his way home. After to-day her position would not be quite so trying, for Arthur Bohun was quitting Dallory. Sir Nash had decided that he was strong enough now to travel, and they were to depart together at two o'clock. It was past twelve now. And so—the sunshine of Ellen Adair's life had gone out. Never, as she believed, would a gleam come into it again.

In spite of the commotion beyond the walls of the Hall now increasing daily and hourly to a climax, in spite of madam's unceasing exertions to urge it on, and to crush Oliver Rane, no word of the dreadful accusation had as yet transpired within to its chief inmates. Mr. North, his daughter Matilda, Ellen Adair, Sir Nash Bohun, and Arthur; all were alike in ignorance. The servants of course knew of it, going out to Dallory, as they often did: but madam had issued her sharp orders that they should keep silence; and Richard had begged them not to speak of it for their master's sake. As to Sir Nash and Arthur Bohun, Richard was only too glad that they should depart without hearing the scandal.

He himself was doing all he could to stop proceedings and allay excitement. Since the night of his interviews with Jelly, Mr. Seeley, and Dr. Rane, Richard had devoted his best energies to the work of suppression. He did not venture to see any official person, the coroner excepted, or impress his views on the magistrates; but he went about amongst the populace, and poured oil on the troubled waters. "For my father's sake, do not press this on," he said to them; "let my sister's grave rest in peace."

He said the same in effect to the coroner; begging of him, if possible, to hush it up; and he implied to all, though not absolutely asserting it, that Dr. Rane could not be guilty. So that Ellen Adair, sitting there, had not the knowledge of this to give her additional trouble.

A little blue flower suddenly caught her eye, peeping from a mossy nook at the foot of the rocks. She rose, and stooped. It was a winter violet. Plucking it, she sat down again, and fell into thought.

For it had brought vividly before her memory that long-past day when she had played with her violets in the garden at Mrs. Cumberland's. "Est-ce qu'il m'aime? Oui. Non. Un peu. Beaucoup. Pas du tout. Passionnément. Il m'aime passionnément." False augurs, those flowers had been! Deceitful blossoms which had combined to mock and sting her. The contrast between that time and this brought to Ellen Adair a whole flood-tide of misery. And those foolish violets were hidden away still! Should she take this indoors and add it to them?

By-and-by she began to walk towards the house. Turning a corner presently she came suddenly upon three excited people: Captain Bohun, Miss Dallory, and Matilda North. The two former had met accidentally in the walk. Miss Dallory's morning errand at the Hall was to say goodbye to Sir Nash; and before she and Captain Bohun had well exchanged greetings, Matilda bore down upon them in a state of agitation, calling wildly to Arthur to stay and hear the tidings she had just heard.

The tidings were those that had been so marvellously kept from her and from others at the Hall—the accusation against Dr. Rane. Matilda North had just learnt them accidentally, and in her horror and surprise she hurried to her half-brother, Arthur, to repeat the story. Ellen Adair found her talking in wild excitement. Arthur turned pale as he listened; to Mary Dallory the rumour was not new.

But Arthur Bohun and Matilda North were strong enough to bear the shock. Ellen Adair was not so. As she drank in the meaning of the dreadful words—that Bessy had been murdered—a deadly sickness seized upon her heart; and she had only time to sit down on a garden-bench before she fainted away.

"You should not have told it so abruptly, Matilda," cried Arthur, almost passionately. "It has made even me feel ill. Get some water: you'll go quicker than I should."

Alarmed at Ellen's state, and eager to be of service, both Matilda and Miss Dallory ran in search of the water. Arthur Bohun sat down on the bench to support her.

Her head lay on his breast, as he placed it. She was without consciousness. His arm encircled her waist; he took one of her lifeless hands between his. Thus he sat, gazing down at the pale, thin face so near to his; the face which he had helped to rob of its bloom.

Yet he loved her still! loved her better than he did all the rest of the world put together! Holding her to his beating heart, he knew it. He knew that he only loved her the more truly for their estrangement. His pulses were thrilling with the rapture this momentary contact brought him. If he might but embrace her, as of old! An irrepressible yearning to press her lips to his, came into his heart. He slightly lifted the pale sweet face, and bent down his own.

"Oh, my darling! My lost darling!"

Lips, cheeks, brow were kissed again and again, with impassioned tenderness. It was so long since he had touched them! A sigh escaped him; and he knew not whether it contained most of bliss or of agony.

This treatment was more effective than the water could have been. Ellen drew a deep breath, and stirred uneasily. As soon as she began really to revive, he managed to get his coat off and fold it across the head and arm of the bench. When Ellen awoke to consciousness, she had her head leaning on it; and Captain Bohun stood at a very respectful distance from her. Never a suspicion crossed her mind of what he had been doing.

"You are better," he said. "I am glad!"

The words, the voice, aroused her fully. She lifted her head and opened her eyes and gazed around her in bewilderment. Then what Matilda had said came back with a rush.

"Is it true?" she exclaimed, looking piteously at him. "It never can be true!"

"I don't know," he answered. "If false, it is almost as dreadful to us who hear it. Poor Bessy! I loved her as a sister."

Ellen, exhausted by the fainting-fit, her nerves unstrung by the news, burst into tears. Matilda and Miss Dallory came hastening up with water, wine, and smelling-salts. But she soon recovered her equanimity, so far as outward calmness went, without the aid of remedies, which she declined. Rising from the bench, she turned towards the house, her steps a little uncertain.

"Pray give your arm to Miss Adair, Captain Bohun," spoke Mary Dallory in sharp, quick tones, surprised perhaps that he did not do so. And upon that, Captain Bohun went to Ellen's side, and held it out.

"Thank you," she answered, and refused it with a slight movement of the head.

They walked on at first all together, as it were. But Matilda and Miss Dallory were soon far ahead, the former talking excitedly about Bessy Rane and the terrible accusation regarding her. Ellen's steps were slower; she could not help it; and Captain Bohun kept by her side.

"May I wish you goodbye here, Ellen?" he suddenly asked, stopping towards the end of the shrubbery, through which they had been passing.

"Goodbye," she faintly answered.

He took her hand. That is, he held out his own, and Ellen almost mechanically put hers into it. To have made a scene by refusing, would have wounded her pride more than all. He kept it within his own, clasping his other hand upon it. For a moment his eyes met hers.

"It may be, that we shall never again cross each other's path in life, Ellen. God bless you, my love, and keep you always! I wish to Heaven, for both our sakes, that we had never met!"

"Goodbye," she coldly repeated as he dropped her hand. And they walked on in silence and gained the lawn, where the two in advance had turned to wait for them.

But this was destined to be an eventful day: to others, at least, if not to them. At the appointed time, Sir Nash Bohun and Arthur took their departure; Richard North, who had paid the baronet the attention of coming home to luncheon—for there was no longer any concealment now as to the true host of Dallory Hall—seeing them into their carriage.

"You have promised to come and stay with me, Richard," said the baronet, at the farewell hand-shake.

"Conditionally. When my work allows me leisure," answered Richard, laughing.

"Can't you go with us to the station, Dick?" put in Arthur.

"Not to-day, I fear. I must hold an immediate interview with madam; it is important. If you waited for me you might lose the train."

Arthur bent his face—one of pain now—to Dick's, and whispered.

"Is it money-trouble again, Richard?"

"No; not this time."

"If she brings anything of that sort on you in future, refer her to me. Yes, Richard: I must deal with it now."

Farewells were exchanged, and the carriage drove away. Richard, stepping backwards, came into contact with Miss Dallory.

"I beg your pardon!" he exclaimed. "Have I hurt you? I did not know you were there."

"Of course you have not hurt me: and I had no business to be there. I stood to wave to them. Good-afternoon, Mr. Richard."

"Are you going?" he asked.

"I have promised to spend the afternoon and take tea with Mrs. Gass. Luncheon was my dinner. I saw you looking at me as if you thought my appetite remarkable."

"Miss Dallory!"

She laughed slightly.

"To confess the truth, I don't think I noticed whether you took anything or nothing," said Richard. "I have a great deal to trouble me just now. Good-afternoon."

He would be returning to Dallory himself in perhaps a few minutes, but he never said to her, "Stay, and I will walk with you." Miss Dallory thought of it as she went away. It had indeed crossed Richard's mind to say so: but he arrested the words as they were about to leave his lips. If she was to be Arthur Bohun's wife, the less Richard saw of her the better.

Inquiring for madam when he went indoors, he found she was ensconced in her boudoir. Richard went up, knocked at the door, and opened it. Madam appeared not to approve of the procedure; she bore down on him with a swoop, and would have bade him retire.

"What do you want here, Richard North? I am not at liberty. I cannot admit you."

"Pardon me, madam, I must speak with you for five minutes," he answered, passing quietly in.

By something he had heard that morning from Dale, Richard had reason to suppose that Mrs. North was still actively pursuing the charge against Dr. Rane; was urging in high quarters the necessity for an investigation. Richard had come to ask her whether this was the case, and to beg her, once for all, to be still. He sat down uninvited whilst he put the question.

But madam would acknowledge nothing. In fact, she led him to believe that it was altogether untrue; that she had not stirred in it at all since the caution Richard had given her, not to do so, some days ago. It was simply impossible to know whether what she said might be depended on—for she was habitually more false than true. Richard could only hope she was true on this occasion.

"It would be a terrible exposure," he urged. "Madam, I beg you; I beg you for all our sakes, to be still. You know not what you would do."

She nodded an ungracious acquiescence: and Richard departed for his works, casually mentioning to Mr. North, as he passed him in the garden, that he should not return home until night. Like Miss Dallory, he had intended the midday meal to be his dinner.

"Dick," cried Mr. North, arresting him, "what's the matter with Matilda? She seems to be in a great commotion over something or other."

Richard know not what to answer. If his father had to be told, why, better that he himself should break it to him. There was still a chance that it might be kept from him.

"Something or other gone wrong, I suppose, sir. Never mind. How well those new borders look!"

"Don't they, Dick! I'm glad I decided upon them."

And Richard went on to his works.

CHAPTER XXX

LYING IN WAIT

Night had fallen: not a bright or pleasant night.

A few skulkers had gathered behind the dwarf hedge, that skirted the piece of waste land near the North Works. An ill-looking set of men, as seen at present: for they had knelt so as to bring themselves almost on a level with the top of the hedge. Poole was in the middle; his face savage, a pistol in his right hand.

Of all the men who had returned to work, the most obnoxious to the old hands was one named Ralley. It was not so much because he had been a turn-coat—that is, after holding out to the eleventh moment, had finally gone back at the twelfth—that the men hated him, as because they believed him to be treacherous. Ralley had been red-hot for the strike; had done more by his agitation than any one man to bring it about. He had resolutely refused all the overtures made by Richard North: and yet—he had gone back when the works were finally reopened. For this the men heartily despised him—far more than they did those who had been ready to go back from the first. In addition to this, they had been suspecting— and lately had felt sure—that he was a snake in the grass. That he had laid himself out to pick up, fairly or stealthily, as might be, bits of information about them, their doings and sayings, their wretched condition and threats of revenge, and had carried them to the works and to Richard North. And so—the contents of the pistol that Poole held in his hand were meant for Ralley.

For a long time the malcontents of North Inlet had been burning to take vengeance on some one: some new treachery on Ralley's part, or suspected treachery, had come to light, and they determined to shoot him. Poor, misguided, foolish men! As if it would improve things for them! Suppose they killed Ralley, how would it better their condition? Ralley had not suffered half what they suffered. He was unmarried; and, during the strike, he had been helped by his relatives, who were pretty well off, so that he had known neither starvation nor tattered clothing, as they had: and this made his returning to work all the worse in their eyes. Ralley was about the age of Richard North, and not unlike him in height and figure: so much like him, indeed, that since their evil act had been determined on, one of the others had bade Poole take care he did not mistake the master for him in the dark. Poole's sullen rejoinder was, that it would not much matter if he did.

The night was dark; a drizzling rain had come on, and the part where they were was not too well lighted. The small band, about to issue from the gates of the works, would pass this waste land within some fifteen yards of them. Poole had been a famous marksman in his day, and felt sure of his aim. John Allen knelt on his right, one Denton on his left, and one on either side beyond: five in all.

Five o'clock struck. Almost simultaneously the bell at the works was heard, giving warning that it was time for the men to go to tea. Three or four sharp, quick strokes: nothing more.

"That's Green, I'll swear," cried Denton, alluding to the ringer. "I didn't know he was back again: his rheumatics must be better."

"Hush—sh—sh!" was all Denton received in answer. And a death-like silence ensued. Poole broke it.

"Where the devil are they? Why don't they come?"

Ay, why did they not come? Simply because there had been scarcely sufficient time for them to do so. But every moment, to these would-be murderers, kneeling there, seemed like a long-drawn-out period.

"Here they are," whispered Denton.

It was so. The men were coming out at the gate, about twenty of them; two and two; the policemen to-night heading the string. Sometimes the officers were behind, at other times at the side of the men.

Poole rose cautiously and prepared to take aim. They were crossing from the gates, and presently would pass the hedge. This was the second night the men had thus lain in ambush. The previous night they had waited in like manner; but Ralley happened to be then on the other side his companion in the march, and so for the time was saved.

Allen stretched up his head. His sight was keen as a sailor's.

"Which side's he on, Jack?" whispered Poole. "I don't see him yet."

For answer John Allen put his hand quickly on Poole's arm to lower the pistol. "No good again, mates," said he. "Ralley ain't there."

"Not there!" retorted Poole with a strong oath.

"I'm as nigh sure of it as I can be," said Allen. "Wait till they come nearer."

It proved to be so. Ralley for some reason or other was not with the men. Denton again gave vent to a furious oath.

Tramp, tramp, tramp; their regular tread sounded in the stillness of the night as they passed. Poole had crouched down again.

The steps died away in the distance, and the conspirators ventured to raise their heads. Allen happened to look in the direction of the gates.

"Here he is!" burst forth Allen, with almost a suppressed scream. "Something must have kept him back. Now's our time, mates. Here's Ralley."

"That ain't his hat, Jack Allen," dissented one.

"Hat be smothered! it's himself," said John Allen.

Ralley was coming on quickly, a dark, low-crowned hat somewhat drawn over his brows. A minute's silence, during which you might have heard their hearts beat, and then—

Poole fired. Ralley gave a cry: staggered, and walked on. He was struck, no doubt, but not killed.

"Your boasted aim has failed, Poole," cried Denton with a savage oath.

Not more savage than Poole's, though, as he broke through the low hedge. What the bullet had not done, the pistol itself should. Suddenly, with a startled cry, Allen broke after him, shouting to him to stay his hand.

"It's the master, Poole; it's not Ralley. Stop, you fool!—it's the master."

Too late. It was, indeed, Richard North. And Mr. Poole had felled him by a wicked blow on the temple.

Mrs. Gass and Mary Dallory were seated at tea in a sad and sorrowful mood—for the conversation had turned on those dreadful rumours that, in spite of Richard North, would not be hushed. Mrs. Gass was stoutly asserting that she had more faith in Dr. Rane than to believe them, when some commotion in the street dawned on their ears. Mrs. Gass stopped in the midst of an emphatic sentence.

"What's that?" she cried.

Fleet steps seemed to be running to and fro; voices were raised in excitement. They distinctly heard the words, "Mr. Richard," "Richard North." Mrs. Gass drew aside her crimson curtains, and opened the window.

"Smith—is it you?" she said, arresting a man who was running in the wake of others. "What's the matter?"

"I don't rightly know, ma'am," he answered. "They are saying that Mr. Richard North has been shot dead."

"Lord help us!" cried Mrs. Gass. She shut down the window and brought her face round to the light again. Every vestige of colour had left it. Mary Dallory stood rigidly upright, her hands clasped, as one who had been turned to stone.

"Did you hear what he said, child?"

"I heard," was the scarcely murmured answer.

Mrs. Gass caught up a bonnet, which happened to lie on a chair, and went into the street. At the entrance to North Inlet a crowd of men and women had gathered. As in all similar cases, reports varied. Some said it had taken place in the high-road to Whitborough, some at the works, others near Dallory Hall. So the mob was puzzled which way to go and not miss the excitement. Thoms was talking at the top of his voice as Mrs. Gass arrived, anxious, perhaps, to disclaim complicity on his own score.

"They've had it in their heads to do it, some o' them bad uns have. I could name names, but I won't. If the master had knowed all, he'd ha' went about in fear of his life this long while past."

This was enough for Mrs. Gass. Gathering her black silk skirts in her hands, and her face paler than the assemblage had ever seen it, she stood, unmindful of the rain, and told them what she thought.

"If you've shot Richard North, you have shot the best and bravest man you'll ever know in this life. You'll never find such a friend again. Ay, he was brave. Brave for good in the midst of difficulties, brave to forbear. Don't you boast, Thoms, with your ready tongue. None of you men round me now may be the one that's shot him, but you've been all rowing in the same boat. Yes, you have. You mayn't have planned out murder yourselves—I wouldn't answer for it that you've not—but, any way, you knew that others was a-planning it, and you winked at it and kept silence. Who has been the friend to you that Richard North has been? Since you've been half starving, and your wives and children's been half starving, where has all the help come from, d'you suppose, that has kept you from starving outright? Why, from him. The most has come from him. The money I gave was his, the things I bought was mostly paid for by him. A little came from me; not much; I was too angry with your folly; but he couldn't see you quite clam, and he took care you shouldn't. Look at how you were all helped through the fever; and meat, and bread, and beer given you to get up your strength a bit, after it! Who did all that? Why, Richard North. You thought it was me; but it was him; only he wouldn't have it known. That was his return for all the black ingratitude you'd showed, in refusing to work for him and bringing him to ruin. Pray God he may not be dead! but if he is, a good man has gone to his reward.—Is that you, Ketler?"

"Yes, it's me," answered Ketler, who was standing in shadow, his face wearing a deeper gloom than the night could cast.

"When that child of yours died, Cissy—and many a little help did she have in life from him—who but Richard North took care that she shouldn't be buried by the parish? He met Fanny Jelly, and he put some money into her hand, and charged her to let it be thought it was hers. 'They are in distress and trouble, I know, Jelly,' he said; 'let this be used in the way that's best for them.' Go and ask Jelly, if you don't believe me: I had it from her. And that's the master you've been conspiring together to kill, Ketler!"

Ketler swallowed down a groan. "I'd never have raised a hand again the master; no, nor countenanced it. If anybody has said I would, it's a lie."

"There's not one of you but knew what mischief was in the wind, or might have known it; and you've countenanced it by keeping silence," retorted Mrs. Gass. "You are a pack of cowards. First of all you ruin him by throwing up his work, and when you find yourselves all clamming together, or nigh upon it, you turn round on him and kill him. May the Lord forgive you! I never will."

Some disturbance. A tramping of feet, and a shouting of running boys. Poole, Denton, John Allen, and one more were marching by in handcuffs, marshalled by some policemen. A hiss greeted them.

"'Twas a mistake," said Jack Allen, in answer to the hiss, reckless under his untoward fate. "'Twas meant for Ralley, not for the master."

"Is he dead?" called out Mrs. Gass.

But amidst the confusion she received no answer. And at that moment she became aware of a pale countenance near her, peeping out from a cloud of wool.

"Good gracious, Miss Mary, child! You shouldn't be out here."

"I have been with you all the time."

"Then, my dear, you just betake yourself home again. I'll come in as soon as I can learn the truth of it all."

Mrs. Gass had not long to wait. Almost as she spoke, Richard North appeared: and thereupon ensued more excitement than ever. Blood was trickling from his temple, but he appeared quite sensible, and was walking slowly, helped by two men.

"Thank God!" said Mrs. Gass aloud: and the words were heartily echoed. "To my house, men. Mr. Richard, sir, it is but a few steps more, and we'll soon have the doctor. A fine night's work, this is!" she concluded, leading the way to her home.

Little Barrington, the druggist, came out of his shop, and helped to place Richard on Mrs. Gass's sofa. They managed to get off his coat. The left arm was injured, as well as the temple. Barrington staunched the blood trickling from the latter; but preferred not to meddle with the arm. "He had better be kept quite quiet, until the surgeon comes," said the druggist to Mrs. Gass.

Mrs. Gass cleared the room. A dozen excited messengers had run to the Ham for Mr. Seeley or Dr. Rane, or both if they should be found at home. She stood at the front-door, watching and waiting.

Richard North, weak and faint, lay with his eyes closed. Opening them in the quiet room, he saw Mary Dallory kneeling by the sofa, pale and sad.

"Don't be alarmed," he whispered. "It might have been worse."

"I would have given my life to save yours, Richard," she impetuously exclaimed in the sorrow and terror of the moment.

His right hand went out a little and met hers.

"Richard, I wish I might stay and nurse you. You have no sister. Matilda is useless in a sick-room."

Richard North nervously pressed her fingers. "Don't try me too much, Mary. I care for you already more than is good for my peace. Don't tempt me."

"And if I were to tempt you? Though I don't quite know what you mean," she rejoined softly and nervously. "What then?"

"I might say what I ought not to say."

He paused.

"It would make it all the harder for me," he continued, after a moment's silence. "I am a man of the people; a man of work. You will belong to—to one of a different order."

She knew he alluded to Arthur Bohun, and laughed slightly.

But, though she said no more, she left her hand in his. Richard thought it was done solely out of compassion.

And now there was a bustle heard, and in came Mr. Seeley, warm with hastening. The hands parted, and Mary Dallory went round to the other side of the table, and stood there in all due decorum.

CHAPTER XXXI

DISTURBING THE GRAVE

By twos and threes, by fours and fives and tens, the curious and excited groups were wending their way towards Dallory churchyard. For a certain work was going on there, which had never been performed in it within the memory of the oldest inhabitant.

Richard North was lying incapacitated at Dallory Hall. When Mr. Seeley—assisted by Dr. Rane, who had come in—examined into his injuries at Mrs. Gass's, he pronounced them not to be of a grave character. The bullet had struck a fleshy part of the arm, and passed off from it, inflicting a wound. Care and rest only would be necessary to heal it; and the same might be said with regard to the blow on the temple. Perfect rest was essential to guard against any after consequences. Mrs. Gass wished Richard to remain at her house and be nursed there; but he thought of the trouble it would cause her regular household, and said he preferred to be taken home. Mr. Seeley continued to attend him by Richard's own wish; not Dr. Rane. The public thought the rejection of the latter significant, in spite of Richard's recent exertions to do away with any impression of his guilt.

"Absolute quiet both of body and mind," enjoined Mr. Seeley, not only to Richard himself but to the family and servants. "If you have it, Mr. Richard, you will be about again in a short time: if you do not have it, I cannot answer for the result."

But Richard North, with his good common sense, was an obedient patient. He knew how necessary it was for his business, that he should not long be laid by, and he kept as quiet as Mr. Seeley could desire. No stranger was allowed to disturb him; none of the household presumed to carry him the smallest item of public or domestic news. It was during this confinement of Richard's that Ellen Adair received her summons for departure. Her father had arrived in London, and wrote to Mrs. Cumberland—unconscious of that lady's death—begging that she and Ellen would at once join him there. He apologized for not coming to Dallory, but said that family business required his presence in London. Mr. North at first proposed to take Ellen up herself: but he was really not able to do it: and it was decided that madam's maid should attend her thither.

Ellen was allowed to go in and bid goodbye to Richard before her departure. She burst into tears as she strove to thank him for his kindness.

"You must come and see papa as soon as you are well enough, Richard. When I tell him how kind you have been, he will want to see and thank you."

"Goodbye, my dear," said Richard, releasing her hand. "I trust you will soon get up all your spirits again, now your father has come."

She smiled faintly. It was not on her father—so imperfectly, if at all, remembered—that her spirits depended. As Ellen was passing through the hall to enter the carriage that would take her to the station, she found herself touched by madam, and drawn into the dining-room.

"You have not seemed very happy with us, Miss Adair. But I have tried to make you so."

"Yes, madam, I am sure you have; and I thank you," returned Ellen gratefully—for madam really did appear to have been very kind to her of late. "I trust papa will have an opportunity of thanking you and Mr. North personally."

Madam coughed. "If you think I deserve thanks, I wish you would do me a slight favour in return."

"If I can. Certainly."

"Some years ago, when we were in India," proceeded madam, "my late husband, Major Bohun, and your father were acquainted with each other. Some unpleasant circumstances took place between them: a quarrel in fact. Major Bohun considered he was injured; Mr. Adair thought it was himself who was so. It was altogether very painful, and I would not for the world have that old matter raked up again; it would cost me too much pain. Will you, then, guard from Mr. Adair's knowledge that I, Mrs. North, am she who was once Mrs. Bohun?"

"Yes, I will," said Ellen, in the impulse of the moment, without pausing to consider whether circumstances would allow her to do so.

"You promise me this?"

"Yes, certainly. I will never speak of it to him, madam."

"Thank you, my dear." And madam kissed her, and led her out to the carriage.

Day by day Richard North never failed to question the surgeon as to whether anything fresh was arising in regard to the accusation against Dr. Rane. The answer was invariably No. In point of fact, Mr. Seeley, not hearing more of it himself, supposed there was not; and at length, partly in good faith, partly to calm his patient, who was restless on the subject, he said it had dropped through altogether.

But the surgeon was wrong. During Richard's active opposition, madam had found her power somewhat crippled; she scarcely deemed it might be altogether to her own interest at the Hall to set him at defiance; but the moment he was laid up, she was at work again more actively than ever. It was nothing but providential, madam considered, that Richard had been put out of the way for a time: and could madam have released Poole from the consequences of his act, and sent him on his road rewarded, she had certainly done it. She gained her point. Poor Mrs. Rane was to be taken up from her grave.

Dale, who had it in hand, went about the proceedings as quietly and secretly as possible. He was sorry to have to do it, for he bore no ill-will to Richard North, but the contrary, and he knew how anxious he was that this should not be done; whilst at the same time the lawyer hated madam. But, he had no alternative: he had received his orders, as coroner, to call an inquest, and could not evade it. He issued his instructions in private, strictly charging the few who must act, to keep silence abroad. And not a syllable transpired beforehand.

The work was commenced in the darkness of the winter's morning. By ten o'clock, however, the men had been seen in the churchyard, and secrecy was no longer possible. The news ran like wildfire to all parts of Dallory—Mrs. Rane was being taken up. Never had there been such excitement as this. The street was in an uproar, windows were alive with heads: had Dallory suddenly found itself invaded by a destroying army, the commotion could not have been greater.

Then began the exodus to the churchyard. Mr. Dale had foreseen this probability, and was prepared for it. A body of police appeared in the churchyard, and the people found they could only approach the actual spot within a very respectful distance. Resenting this, they relieved their feelings by talking the louder.

Jelly was there. Never nearer losing her reason than now. Between dismay at what she had set afloat, and horror at the crime about to be revealed, Jelly was not clear whether she stood on her head or her heels. When the news was carried to her of what was going on, Jelly very nearly fainted. Now that it had come to the point, she felt that she would have given the world never to have meddled with it. It was not so much the responsibility to herself that she thought of, as the dreadful aspect of the thing altogether. She went into a violent fit of trembling, and sought her chamber to hide it. When somewhat recovered, she asked leave of Mrs. Beverage to be allowed to go out for a few hours. To have been compelled to remain indoors would have driven her quite mad. The morning was growing late when Jelly arrived at the scene, and the first person she specially noticed there was Mrs. Gass.

But Mrs. Gass had not come forth in idle curiosity as most others had done—and there were some of the better classes amongst the mob. Mrs. Gass was inexpressibly shocked and dismayed that it should really have come to this. Oliver Rane was her late husband's nephew; she did not think he could have been guilty: and she had hastened to see whether any argument or persuasion might avail at the twelfth hour, to arrest proceedings and spare disgrace to the North and Gass families.

But no. Stepping over the barrier-line the police had drawn, without the smallest regard to the remonstrance of a red-faced inspector, who was directing things, Mrs. Gass approached the small throng around the grave. She might have spared herself the pains. In answer to her urgent appeal she was told that no one here had any power now; it had passed out of their hands. In returning, Mrs. Gass encountered Jelly.

"Well," said she, regarding Jelly sternly, "be you satisfied with your work?"

Jelly never answered. In her shame, her regret, her humiliation at what she had done, she could almost have wished herself labouring at the treadmill that had so long haunted her dreams.

"Anyway, you might have had the decency to keep away," went on Mrs. Gass.

"I couldn't," said Jelly, meekly. "I couldn't stop at home and bear it."

"Then I'd have gone a mile or two the other way," retorted Mrs. Gass. "You must be quite brazen, to show your face here. And you must have a conscience too."

A frightful noise interrupted them: a suppressed shout of horror. The heavy coffin was at length deposited on the ground with the pick-axes beside it, and the populace were expressing their mixed sentiments at the sight: some in applause at this great advance in the show: others in a groan meant for Dr. Rane, who had caused it all. Mrs. Gass, what with the yelling, the coffin and pick-axes, and the crush, had never felt so humiliated in all her days; and she retired behind a remote tree to hide her emotion.

At that moment Thomas Hepburn appeared in sight, his face sad and pale.

"Hepburn," said Mrs. Gass, "I can't think they'll find anything wrong there. My belief is she died naturally. Unless there were better grounds to go upon than I know of, they ought not to have gone to this shameful length."

"Ma'am, I don't think it, either," assented the man. "I'm sure it has been more like a dream to me than anything else, since I heard it. Folks say it is madam at the Hall that has forced it on."

Had Mrs. Gass been a man, she might have felt tempted to give madam a very strong word. What right had she, in her wicked malice, to inflict this pain on others?

"Whatever may be the upshot of this, Thomas Hepburn, it will come home to her as sure as that we two are talking here. What are you going there for?" added Mrs. Gass, for he was preparing to make his way towards the grave.

"I've had orders to be here, ma'am. Some of those law officials don't understand this sort of work as well as I do."

He crossed over, the police making way for him, Inspector Jekyll giving him a nod. Jelly was standing against a tree not far from Mrs. Gass, straining her eyes upon the scene. By the eagerness displayed by the crowd, it might have been supposed they thought that they had only to see the face of the dead, lying within, to have all suspicion of Dr. Rane turned into fact.

The work went on. The leaden covering came off amidst a tumult, and the common deal shell alone remained.

It was at this juncture that another spectator came slowly up. The mob, their excited faces turned to the grave and to Thomas Hepburn, who was already at his work, did not see his approach. Perhaps it was as well: for the new arrival was Dr. Rane.

Even from him had these proceedings been kept secret; perhaps especially from him: and it was only now, upon coming forth to visit a patient in Dallory, that he learnt what was taking place in the churchyard. He came to it at once: his countenance stern, his face white as death.

Mrs. Gass saw him; Jelly also. Mrs. Gass silently moved to prevent his further approach, spreading her portly black silk skirts. Her intentions were good.

"Go back," she whispered. "Steal away before you are seen. Look at this unruly mob. They might tear you to pieces, doctor, in the humour they are in."

"Let them—when I have stopped that," he recklessly answered, pointing to what Thomas Hepburn was doing.

"You are mad," cried Mrs. Gass in excitement. "Stop that! Why, sir, how impossible it would be, even with the best wish, to stop it now. A nail or two more, sir, and the lid's off."

It was as she said. Dr. Rane saw it. He took out his handkerchief, and passed it over his damp face.

"Richard North gave me his word that he would stop it, if it came to this," he murmured more to himself than to Mrs. Gass.

"Richard North knows no more of this than it seems, you knew of it," she said. "He is shut up in his room at the Hall, and hears nothing. Doctor, take advice and get away," she whispered imploringly. "There's still time."

"No," he doggedly said. "As it has gone so far, I'll stand my ground now."

Mrs. Gass groaned. The sound was lost in a rush—police contending against King Mob, King Mob against the police. Even Mrs. Gass turned pale. Dr. Rane voluntarily arrested his advancing steps. Jelly's troubled face was peering out from the distant tree.

The lid had been lifted, and the open shell stood exposed. It was more than the excited numbers could witness, and be quiet. Inspector Jekyll and his fellows keep them back from looking into it? Never. A short, sharp struggle, and the police and their staves were nowhere. With a triumphant whoop the crowd advanced.

But a strange hush, apparently of consternation, had fallen on those who stood at the grave; a hush fell on these interlopers as they reached it. The coffin was empty.

Of all unexpected stoppages to proceedings, official or otherwise, one more complete than this had never fallen. An old magistrate who was present, the coroner—who had just come striding over the ground, to see how things were going on—Thomas Hepburn, and others generally, stared at the empty coffin in profound perplexity.

And the mob, when it had duly stared also, elbowing each other in the process,18 and fighting ruefully for precedence, burst out into a howl. Not at all a complimentary one to Dr. Rane.

He had sold her for dissection! He had never put her in at all! He had had a sham funeral! 'Twasn't enough to poison of her, but he must sell her afterwards!

To accuse a man of those heinous offences behind his back, is one thing, but it is not felt to be quite so convenient to do it in his presence. The sight of Dr. Rane walking calmly, not to say impudently, across the churchyard into their very midst, struck a certain timidity on the spirits of the roarers. Silence ensued. They even parted to allow him to pass. Dr. Rane threw his glance on the empty coffin, and then on those who stood around it.

"Well," said he, "why don't you take me?"

And not a soul ventured to reply.

"I have murdered my wife, have I? If I have done so, why, you know I deserve no quarter. Come, Mr. Coroner, why don't you issue your orders to arrest me? You have your officers at hand."

The independence with which this was spoken, the freedom of Dr. Rane's demeanour, the mockery of his tone, could not be surpassed. He had the best of it now; might say what he pleased, and laugh derisively at them at will: and they knew it. Even Dale, the coroner, felt small—which is saying a good deal of a lawyer.

Turning round, the doctor walked slowly back again, his head in the air. Mrs. Gass met him.

"Tell me the truth for the love of goodness, doctor. I have never believed it of you. You did not help her to her death?"

"Help her to her death?" he retorted. "No: my wife was too dear to me for that. I'd have killed the whole world rather than her—if it must have come to killing at all."

"And I believe you," was the hearty response. "And I have told everybody, from the first, that the charge was wicked and preposterous."

"Thank you, Mrs. Gass."

He broke away from any further questions she might have put, and stalked on towards Dallory, coolly saying that he had a patient to see.

As to the crowd, they really did not know what to make of it: it was a shameful cheat. The small staff of officials, including the police, seemed to know as little. To be enabled to take Oliver Rane into custody for poisoning his wife they must first find the wife, and ascertain whether she really had been poisoned. Lawyer Dale had never met with so bewildering a check in the long course of his practice; the red-faced Inspector stroked his chin, and the old magistrate clearly had not recovered his proper mind yet.

By the appearance of the shell, it seemed evident that the body had never been there at all. What had he done with it?—where could he have hidden it? A thought crossed Mr. Jekyll, experienced in crime, that the doctor might have concealed it in his house—or buried it in his garden.

"How was it you did not feel the lightness of the shell when you put it into the lead, you and your men?" asked the Inspector, turning sharply upon Thomas Hepburn.

"We did not do it," was the undertaker's answer. "Dr. Rane undertook that himself, on account of the danger of infection. We went and soldered the lead down, but it was all ready for us."

A clearer proof of guilt, than this fact conveyed, could not well be found: as they all murmured one to another. The old magistrate rubbed up his hair, as if by that means he could also rub up his intellect.

"I don't understand," he said, still bewildered. "Why should he have kept her out of the coffin? If he did what was wrong—surely to bury her out of sight would be the safest place to hide away his crime. What do you think about it, Jekyll?"

"Well, your worship, I can only think that he might have feared some such proceeding as this, and so secured himself against it," was the Inspector's answer. "I don't know, of course: it is only an idea."

"But where is the body, Jekyll?" persisted the magistrate. "What could he have done with it?"

"It must be our business to find out, your worship."

"Did he cut her up?" demanded the mob. For which interruption they were chased backwards by the army of discomfited policemen.

"She may be about his premises still, your worship," said the Inspector, hazarding the opinion. "If so, I should say she is lying a few feet below the surface somewhere in the garden."

"Bless my heart, what a frightful thing!" cried his worship. "And about this? What is going to be done?"

He pointed to the coffins and the open grave. Yes: what was to be done? Lawyer Dale searched his legal memory and could not remember any precedent to guide him. A short counsel was held.

"When her bones is found, poor lady, they'll want Chris'an bur'al: as good let the grave lie open," interposed one of the grave-diggers respectfully—who no doubt wished to be spared the present labour of filling-in the earth. To which opinion the gentlemen, consulting there, condescended to listen.

And, finally, that course was decided upon: Thomas Hepburn being requested to have the coffins removed to his place, pending inquiry. And the gentlemen dispersed, and the mob after them.

A very dissatisfied mob tramping out of the churchyard. They seldom had much pleasure now, poor things, in their enforced idleness and starvation: and to be balked in this way was about as mortifying a termination to the day as could have happened. Only one greater evil could be imagined—and that was a possibility not to be glanced at: that it should have been discovered that poor Mrs. Rane had died a natural death.

The last person left in the churchyard—excepting a man or two who remained to guard the coffins, whilst means were being brought to take them away—was Jelly. To watch Jelly's countenance when the empty shell stood revealed, was as good as a play. The jaw dropped, the eyes were strained. It was worse than even Jelly had supposed, Dr. Rane a greater villain. Not content with taking his wife's life, he had also made away with her body. Whether he had disposed of it in the manner affirmed by the mob, in that suggested by the Inspector, or in any other way, the doctor must be one of the most hardened criminals breathing—his brazen demeanour just now in the graveyard was alone sufficient evidence of that. And now the trouble was no nearer being brought to light than before, and Jelly almost wished, as she had wished many a time lately, that she might die. Hiding from the spectators stood she, her heart faint within her. When the echoes of the tramping mob had died away in the distance, Jelly turned to depart also, drawing her black shawl around her with a shudder.

"That's why she can't rest, poor lady; she's not laid in consecrated ground. At the worst, I never suspected this."

CHAPTER XXXII

A NIGHT EXPEDITION

Seven o'clock was striking out on a dark winter's night, as a hired carriage with a pair of post-horses drew up near to the gates of Dallory Hall. Apparently the special hour had been agreed upon as a rendezvous; for before the clock had well told its numbers, a small group of people might have been seen approaching the carriage from different ways.

There issued out from the Hall gates, Mr. North, leaning on the right arm of his son Richard. Richard had quitted his chamber to join in this expedition. His left arm was in a sling, and he looked pale; but he was fast progressing towards recovery; and Mr. Seeley, confidentially consulted, had given him permission to go forth. Mrs. Gass came up from the direction of Dallory; and Dr. Rane came striding from the Ham. A red-faced, portly gentleman in plain clothes, standing near the carriage, greeted them: without his official costume and in the dark night, few would have recognized him for Inspector Jekyll, who had been directing affairs in the churchyard the previous day. Mrs. Gass, Mr. North and Richard, entered the carriage. The Inspector was about to ascend the box, the postillion being on the horses, but Dr. Rane said he would himself prefer to sit outside. So Mr. Jekyll got inside, and the doctor mounted; and the carriage drove away down Dallory Ham.

Peering after it, in the dark night, behind the gates, was Mrs. North. Some one beside her—it was only a servant-boy—ran off, at a signal, towards the stables with a message, as fast as his legs would carry him. There came back in answer madam's carriage—which must have been awaiting the signal—-with a pair of fresh fleet horses.

"Catch it up, and keep it in sight at a distance," were her orders to the coachman, as she stepped in. So the post-carriage was being tracked and followed: a fact none of its inmates had the slightest notion of.

In her habit of peeping and prying, of listening at doors, of glancing surreptitiously into other people's letters, and of ferreting generally, madam had become aware during the last twenty-four hours that something unusual was troubling the equanimity of Mr. North and Richard: that some journey, to be taken in secret by Mr. North, and kept secret, was being decided upon. Conscience—when it is not an easy one—is apt to suggest all sorts of unpleasant things, and madam's whispered to her that this hidden expedition had reference to herself; and—perhaps—to a gentleman who had recently arrived in England—William Adair.

Madam's cheeks turned pale through rouge and powder, and she bit her lips in impotent rage. She could have found means, no doubt, to keep Mr. North within doors, though she had broken his leg to accomplish it; she could have found means to keep Richard also, had she known he was to be of the party: but of what avail? Never a cleverer woman lived, than madam, and she had the sense to know that a meeting with Mr. Adair (and she believed the journey had reference to nothing else) could not thus be prevented: it must take place sooner or later.

A carriage was to be in waiting near the Hall gates after dark, at seven o'clock—madam had learned so much. Where was it going to? In which direction? For what purpose? That at least madam could ascertain. She gave private orders of her own: and as night approached, retired to her room with a headache, forbidding the household to disturb her. Mr. North, as he dined quietly in his parlour, thought how well things were turning out. He had been haunted with a fear of madam's pouncing upon him, at the moment of departure, with a demand to know the why and the wherefore of his secret expedition.

Madam, likewise attired for a journey, had escaped from the Hall long before seven, and taken up her place amidst the shrubs near the entrance-gates, her position commanding both the way from the house and the road without. On the stroke of seven, steps were heard advancing; and madam strained her gaze.

Richard! Who had not yet left his sick-room! But for his voice, as he spoke to his father, madam would have thought the night was playing tricks with her eyesight.

She could not see who else got into the carriage: but she did see Dr. Rane come striding by; and she thought it was he upon the box when the carriage passed. Dr. Rane? Madam, catching her breath, wondered what private histories Mrs. Cumberland had confided to him, and how much he was now on his way to bear witness to. Madam was altogether on the wrong scent—the result of her suggestive conscience.

Almost in a twinkling, she was shut up in her own carriage, as described, her coachman alone outside it.

The man had no difficulty in obeying orders. The post-carriage was not as light as madam's. Keeping at a safe distance, he followed in its wake, unsuspected. First of all, from the Ham down the back lane, and then through all sorts of frequented, cross-country by-ways. Altogether, as both drivers thought, fifteen or sixteen miles.

The post-carriage drew up at a solitary house, on the outskirts of a small hamlet. Madam's carriage halted also, further away. Alighting, she desired her coachman to wait: and stole cautiously along under cover of the hedge, to watch proceedings. It was then about nine o'clock.

They were all going into the house: a little crowd, as it seemed to madam; and the post-carriage went slowly away, perhaps to an inn. What had they gone to that house for? Was Mr. Adair within it? Madam was determined to see. She partly lost sight of prudence in her desperation, and was at the door just as it closed after them. Half a minute and she knocked softly with her knuckles. It was opened by a young girl with a broad country face, and red elbows.

"Law!" said she. "I thought they was all in. Do you belong to 'em?"

"Yes," said Mrs. North.

So she went in also, and crept up the dark staircase, after them, directed by the girl. "Fust door you comes to at the top." Madam's face was growing ghastly: she fully expected to see William Adair.

The voices alone would have guided her. Several were heard talking within the room: her husband's she distinguished plainly: and, she thought, madam certainly thought, he was sobbing. Madam went into a heat at the sound. What revelation had Mr. Adair been already making? He had lost no time apparently.

The door was not latched. Madam cautiously pushed it an inch or two open so as to enable her to see in. She looked very ugly just now, her lips drawn back from her teeth with emotion, something like a hyena's. Madam looked in: and saw, not Mr. Adair, but—Bessy Rane.

Bessy Rane. She was standing near the table, whilst Dr. Rane was talking. Standing quite still, with her placid face, her pretty curls falling, and wearing a violet-coloured merino gown, that madam had seen her in a dozen times. In short, it was just like Bessy Rane in life. On the table, near the one solitary candle, lay some white work, as if just put out of hand.

In all madam's life she had perhaps never been so frightened as now. The truth did not occur to her. She surely thought it an apparition, as Jelly had thought before; or that—or that Bessy had in some mysterious manner been conveyed hither from that disturbed grave. In these confused moments the mind is apt to run away with itself. Madam's was not strong enough to endure the shock, and be silent.

With a piercing shriek, she turned to fly, and fell against the whitewashed chimney that the architect of the old-fashioned house had seen fit to carry up through the centre of it. The next moment she was in hysterics.

Bessy was the first to run to attend her. Bessy herself, you understand, not her ghost. In a corner of the capacious old room, built when ground was to be had for an old song, was Bessy's bed; and on this they placed Mrs. North. Madam was not long in recovering her equanimity: but she continued where she was, making believe to be exhausted, and put a corner of her shawl up to her face. For once in her life that face had a spark of shame in it.

Yes: Bessy was not dead. Humanly speaking, there had never been any more probability of Bessy's demise than there was of madam's at this moment. Dr. Rane is giving the explanation, and the others are standing to listen; excepting Mr. North, who has sat down in an old-fashioned elbow-chair, whilst Richard leans the weight of his undamaged arm behind it. Mrs. Gass has pushed back her bonnet from her beaming face; the inspector looks impassive as befits his calling, but on the whole pleased.

"I am not ashamed of what I have done," said Dr. Rane, standing by Bessy's side; "and I only regret it for the pain my wife's supposed death caused her best friends, Mr. North and Richard. I would have given much to tell the truth to Mr. North, but I knew it would not be safe to trust him, and so I wished it to wait until we should have left the country. For all that has occurred you must blame the tontine. That is, blame the Ticknells, who obstinately, wrongfully, cruelly kept the money from us. There were reasons— my want of professional success one of them—why I wished to quit Dallory, and start afresh in another place; I and my wife talked of it until it grew, with me, into a disease; and I believe Bessy grew to wish for it at last almost as I did."

"Yes, I did, Oliver," she put in.

"Look at the circumstances," resumed Dr. Rane, in his sternest tones, and not at all as though he were on his defence. "There was the sum of two thousand pounds belonging to me and my wife conjointly, and they denied our right to touch it until one of us should be dead and gone! It was monstrously unjust. You must acknowledge that much, Mr. Inspector."

"Well—it did seem hard," acknowledged that functionary.

"I know I thought it so," said Mrs. Gass.

"It was more than hard," spoke the doctor passionately. "I used to say to my wife that if I could get it out of the old trustees' hands by force, or stratagem, I should think it no shame to do it. Idle talk! never meant to be anything else. But to get on. The fever broke out in Dallory, and Bessy was taken ill. She thought it was the fever, and so did I. I had fancied her a little afraid of it, and was in my heart secretly thankful to Mr. North for inviting her to the Hall. But for putting off her visit for a day—through the absence of Molly Green—what happened later could never have taken place."

Dr. Rane paused, as if considering how he should go on with his story. After a moment he resumed it, looking straight at them, as he had been looking all along.

"I wish you to understand that every word I am telling you—and shall tell you—is the strict truth. The truth, upon my honour, and before Heaven. And yet, perhaps, even after this, you will scarcely credit me when I say—that I did believe my wife's illness was the fever. All that first day—she had been taken ill during the night with sickness and shivering—I thought it was the fever. Seeley thought it also. She was in a very high state of feverishness, and no doubt fear for her served somewhat to bias our judgment. Bessy herself said it was the fever, and would not hear a word to the contrary. But at night—the first night, remember—she had nearly an hour of sickness; and was so relieved by it, and grew so cool and collected, that I detected the nature of the case. It was nothing but a bad bilious attack, accompanied by an unusual degree of fever; but it was not the fever. 'You have cheated me, my darling,' I said jestingly, as I kissed her, 'I shall not get the tontine money.'—Here she stands by my side to confirm it," broke off Dr. Rane, but indeed they could all see he was relating the simple truth. "'Can you not pretend that I am dead?' she answered faintly, for she was still exceedingly ill; 'I will go away, and you can say I died.' Now, of course Bessy spoke jestingly, as I had done: nevertheless the words led to what afterwards took place. I proposed it—do not lay the blame on Bessy—that she really should go away, and I should give it out that she had died."

A slight groan from the region of the bed. Dr. Rane continued.

"It seemed very easy of accomplishment—very. But had I foreseen all the disagreeable proceedings, the artifice, the trouble, that must inevitably attend such an attempted deceit, I should never have entered upon it. Had I properly reflected, I might of course have foreseen it: but I did not reflect. Nearly all that night Bessy and I conversed together: chiefly planning how she should get away and where she should stay. By morning, what with the fatigue induced by this prolonged vigil, and the exhaustion left by her illness, she was thoroughly worn out. It had been agreed between us that she should simulate weariness and a desire to sleep, the better to avert a discovery of her restoration; but there was no need for simulation; she was both sleepy and exhausted."

"I never was so sleepy before in all my life," interrupted Bessy.

"The day went on. At ten o'clock, when Phillis left, I went up to my wife's room, and told her the time for acting had come," pursued Dr. Rane. "Next I crossed over to Seeley's with the news that my wife was gone: and I strove to exhibit the grief I should have felt had it been true. Crossing to my home again, I saw Frank Dallory, and told him. 'The play has begun,' I said to Bossy when I went in—and then I went forth to Mr. North's; and then on to Hepburn's. Do you remember, sir, how I tried to soothe your grief?—speaking persistently of hope—though of course you could not see that any hope remained," asked Dr. Rane, turning to Mr. North. "I dared not speak more plainly, though I longed to do so."

"Ay, I remember," answered Mr. North.

"The worst part of all the business was the next; bringing in the shell," continued the doctor. "Worse, because I had a horror of my wife seeing it. I contrived that she did not see it. Hepburn's men brought it up to the ante-room: Bessy was still in bed in the front-room, and heard them: I could not help that. When they left, I put it down by the wall with the trestles, threw some coats carelessly upon it, and so hid it out of sight. It was time then for Bessy to get up. Whilst she was dressing, I went round to the stables, where the horse and gig I use are kept, to make sure that the ostler had gone to bed—for he had a habit sometimes of sitting up late. It was during this absence of mine that Bessy went to the landing to listen whether or not I had come in. The chamber-door was open, so that light shone on to the landing. It happened to be at that moment that Jelly was at the opposite window, and—later—thought it was Mrs. Rane's ghost that she had seen."

Mrs. Gass's amused face was something good to witness. She nodded in triumph.

"I thought it might have been the effects of beer," said she. "I told Jelly what an idiot she was. I knew it was no ghost!"

"Bessy made herself ready, took some refreshment, and I brought the gig to the garden-door and drove my wife away. The only place open at that time of night—or rather morning—would be some insignificant railway-station. We fixed on Hewley. I drove her there; and there left her sitting under cover in solitary state—for I had to get back with the horse and gig before people were astir. As soon as the morning was pretty well on, Bessy walked to Churchend, about five miles' distance, and took a lodging in this very house—this very same room. Here she has been ever since—and it is a great deal longer time than we either of us ever anticipated. Poison my wife!" added Dr. Rane, with some emotion, as he involuntarily drew her towards him, with a gesture of genuine affection. "She is rather too precious to me for that. You know; don't you, my darling."

The happy tears stood in her eyes as she met his. He stooped and kissed her, very fondly.

"If my wife were taken from me, the Ticknells might keep the tontine money, and welcome; I should not care for it without Bessy. It was chiefly for her sake that my desire to possess it arose," he added emphatically. "I could not bear that she should be reduced to so poor a home after the luxury of Dallory Hall. Bessy constantly said that she did not mind it, but I did; minded it for her and for her alone."

"Couldn't you have managed all this without the funeral?" asked Richard North, speaking for the first time.

"How could I?" returned Dr. Rane. "It was not possible. When my wife was given out as dead, she had to be buried, or Mr. Inspector Jekyll, there, might have been coming in to ask the reason why. Had I properly thought of all that must be done, I should, as I say, never have attempted it. It was hateful to me; and I declare that I don't know how I could, or did, carry it through. Once or twice I thought I must give in, and confess, to my shame, that Bessy was living—but I felt that might be worse, of the two, than going on with it to the end. I hope the Ticknells will suffer for what they have cost me."

"Jelly says she saw the ghost twice," observed Mrs. Gass,

"Ah! that was Bessy's fault," said Dr. Rane, shaking his head at his wife, in mock reproval, as we do at a beloved child when it is naughty. "She was so imprudent as to come home for a few hours—walking across country by easy stages and getting in after nightfall. It was about her wardrobe. I have been over twice at night—or three times, is it not, Bessy?—and brought her things each time. But Bessy said she must have others; and at last, as I tell you, she came over herself. I think the clothes were nothing but an excuse—eh, Bessy?"

"Partly," acknowledged Bessy. "For, oh! I longed for a sight of home. Just one more sight as a farewell. I had quitted it in so bewildered a hurry. It again led to Jelly's seeing me. I was at my large chest-of-drawers, papa," she continued, addressing Mr. North. "Oliver had gone round for the gig to bring me back again; I thought I heard him come in again, and went to the landing to listen. It was not he, but Jelly; and we met face to face. I assure you she frightened me quite as much as I frightened her."

"And Bessy, my dear, what have the people here thought about it, all the time?" inquired Mrs. North. "Do they know who you are?"

"Why of course not, papa. They think I am a lady in bad health; staying here for the sake of country air—and I did feel and look very ill when I came. An old widow lady has the house, and the girl you saw is her servant. They are not at all inquisitive. They know us only as Mr. and Mrs. Oliver, and think we live at Bletchley. I want to know who pushed matters to extremities in regard to these proceedings against my husband," added Mrs. Rane, after a pause. "It was not you, papa: and Richard was doing his best to hush it all up. Richard had known the truth since an interview he held with Oliver. Who was it, papa?"

Madam tumbled off the bed, moaning a little, as if she were weak and ill. Bessy had not the slightest idea that madam had been the culprit.

"Who was it, Mr. Jekyll?" continued Bessy.

The Inspector looked up to the ceiling and down to the floor; and then thought the candle wanted snuffing. Which it certainly did. Madam cried in a shrill voice as he was putting down the snuffers, that she must depart. If the others chose to stay and countenance all this unparalleled iniquity, she could not do so.

She stood, upright as ever, tossing back her head, all her impudence returning to her. Dr. Rane quietly put himself in her path as she was gaining the door.

"Mrs. North, pardon me if I request you to give me a little information ere you depart, as it is probably the last time we shall ever meet. What has been the cause of the long-continued and persistent animosity you have borne towards me?"

"Animosity towards you!" returned madam, flippantly. "I have borne none."

The coolness of the avowal, in the very face of facts, struck them as almost ludicrous. Mr. North raised his head and gazed at her in surprise.

"You have pursued me with the most bitter animosity since the first moment that I came to Dallory, madam," said Dr. Rane, quietly and steadily. "You have kept practice from me; you have done what you can to crush me. It is you who urged on this recent charge against me—a very present proof of what I assert. But for you it might never have been made."

Madam was slightly at bay: she seemed just a little flurried. Rallying her powers, she confronted Dr. Rane and told him that she did not think him skilful and did not personally like him; if she had been biassed against him, the feeling must have taken its rise in that—there was nothing else to cause it.

Another of her shuffling untruths—and they all knew it for one. But they would get nothing better from her.

The fact was this. Madam had feared that Mrs. Cumberland could, and perhaps would, throw light on a certain episode of the past years: a contingency madam had dreaded above anything earthly: for this she had wished and hoped to drive Mrs. Cumberland from the place, and had thought that if she could drive away Oliver Rane, his mother would follow him. That was the actual truth: but no living person, excepting madam, suspected it.

She quitted the room with the last denial, conscious that she did not just now appear to advantage—for the sneaking act of tracking them this night, madam, with all her sophistry, could not plead an excuse. They let her go. Even the Inspector did not pay her the courtesy of opening the door for her, or of lighting her down the crooked old wooden stairs. It was Bessy who ran to do it.

"When you found things were going against you, sir, why did you not declare the truth?" asked the Inspector of Dr. Rane.

"I knew that the moment I declared the truth, all hope of the tontine money would be at an end; I should have done what I had done for nothing," answered Dr. Rane. "Richard North undertook to give me timely notice if things went too far; but he was disabled, you know, and could not do so. Until they were in the act of disturbing the grave, I had no warning of it whatever."

A silence followed the answer. Dr. Rane resumed.

"Ill-luck seems to have attended it from the first. Perhaps nothing else was to be expected. Jelly's having seen my wife was a great misfortune. And then look at the delay as to the tontine money! Had the trustees paid it over at once, Bessy and I should have been safe away long ago."

"Where gone?" asked Mrs. Gass.

"To America. It is where we shall go now, in any case. As I have not the money to join Dr. Jones as partner, I dare say he will take me as an assistant."

"See here," said Mrs. Gass. "I don't say that what you've done is anything but very wrong, doctor; but it might have been worse: and, compared to what a lot of fools were saying, it seems a trifle. I was once about to make you an offer of money. Finding you couldn't get the tontine paid to you and your wife; which, as I've told you, I thought was a shame, all things considered; I resolved to advance it to you myself. Mrs. Rane's death stopped me from doing it; I mean, her reported death. You won't get it now, doctor, from the Ticknells—for I suppose they'll have to be told the truth: and so you shall have it from me. Two thousand pounds is ready for you, at your command."

The red flush of emotion mounted to Dr. Rane's pale face. He gazed eagerly at Mrs. Gass, as if asking whether it could be true.

"It's all right, doctor. You are my late husband's nephew, you know, and all the money was his. You'll find yourself and your wife substantially remembered in my will; and as two thousand pounds of it may do you good now, it shall be advanced to you."

Bessy stole round to Mrs. Gass, and burst into tears on her bosom. Happy, grateful tears. The doctor, the flush deepening on his face, took Mrs. Gass's hand and clasped it.

"And I wish to my very heart I had made no delay in the offer at first," cried Mrs. Gass. "It'll always be a warning to me not to put off till tomorrow what should be done to-day. And so, doctor, there's the money ready; and Bessy, my dear, I don't see why you and he need banish yourselves to America. You might find a good practice, doctor, and not go further than London."

"I must go to America; I must," said the doctor, hastily. "Neither I nor Bessy would like now to remain in England."

"Well, perhaps you may be right," acquiesced Mrs. Gass.

"But it's a long way off," said Mr. North.

"It may not be for ever, sir," observed Dr. Rane, cheerfully. "I know I shall do well there; and when I have made a fortune perhaps we may come back and live in London. Never again in Dallory. The old and the new world are brought very near each other now, sir."

Is it of any use pursuing the interview to its close? When they went out again, after it was over, madam's carriage was only then driving off. Madam's coachman had put up his horses somewhere; and neither he nor they could readily be found. There was apparently no house open in the primitive village, and madam had the pleasure of undergoing an hour or two's soaking in a good, sound, down-pouring rain.

"I shall have to make things right with the authorities; and I suppose Hepburn may keep the coffins for his pains," quaintly remarked Mr. Inspector Jekyll.

But the carriage took back one less than it had brought. For Dr. Rane did not return again to Dallory.

PART THE THIRD

CHAPTER I

IN GROSVENOR PLACE

A well-spread dessert-table glittered under the rays of the chandelier in the dining-room of Sir Nash Bohun's town-house. Sir Nash and his nephew Arthur were seated at it, a guest between them. It was General Strachan; an old officer, Scotch by birth, who had just come home, after passing the best part of his life in India.

The winter was departing. Arthur Bohun looked better, Sir Nash pretty well. In a month or two both intended to depart for the German springs that were to renovate Sir Nash's life.

General Strachan had been intimate with Sir Nash Bohun in early life, before he went out to India. After he had gone out he had been equally intimate with Major Bohun: but he was only Captain Strachan in those days.

"And so you think Arthur like his father," observed Sir Nash, as he passed the claret.

"His very image," replied the general. "I'm sure I should have known him for Tom Bohun's son had I met him accidentally in the street. Adair saw the likeness, too."

"What Adair's that?" carelessly asked Sir Nash.

"William Adair. You saw him with me at the club-door this morning. We were going in at the moment you came up."

Perhaps Sir Nash was a little struck by the name. He called to mind a good-looking, slender, gentlemanly man, who had been arm-in-arm with the general at the time mentioned.

"But what Adair is it, Strachan?"

"What Adair? Why, the one who was in India when—when poor Tom died. He was Tom's greatest friend. Perhaps you have never heard of him?"

"Yes I have, to my sorrow," said Sir Nash. "It was he who caused poor Tom's death."

General Strachan apparently did not understand. "Who caused poor Tom's death?"

"Adair."

"Why, bless me, where could you have picked that up?" cried the general in surprise. "If Adair could have saved Tom's life by any sacrifice to himself he'd have done it. They were firm friends to the last."

Sir Nash seemed to be listening as though he heard not. "Of course we never heard the particulars of my brother's death, over here, as we should have heard them had we been on the spot," he remarked. "We were glad, rather, to hush it up for the sake of Arthur. Poor Tom fell into some trouble or disgrace, and Adair led him into it. That's what we were ever told."

"Then you were told wrong, Bohun," said the general somewhat bluntly. "Tom fell into debt, and I don't know what all, but it was not Adair who led him into it. Who could have told you so?"

"Mrs. Bohun, Tom's widow."

"Oh, she," returned the general, in accents of contempt that spoke volumes. "Why she—but never mind now," he broke off, suddenly glancing at Arthur as he remembered that she was his mother. "Let bygones be bygones," he added, sipping his claret; "no good recalling them. Only don't continue to think anything against William Adair. He is one of the best men living, and always has been."

Arthur Bohun, who had sat still as a stone, leaned his pale face a little towards the general, and spoke.

"Did not this Mr. Adair, after my father's death, get into disgrace, and—and undergo its punishment?"

"Never. Adair got into no disgrace."

"Has he not been a convict?" continued Arthur in low, clear tones.

"A WHAT?" cried the general, putting down his glass and staring at Arthur in amazement. "My good young fellow, you cannot know of whom you are speaking. William Adair has been a respected man all his life: he is just as honourable as your father was—and the world knew pretty well what poor Tom's fastidious notions of honour were. Adair is a gentleman amongst gentlemen; I can't say better of him than that, though I talked for an hour. He has come into all the family honours and fortune; which he never expected to do. A good old Scotch family it is, too; better than mine. There; we'll drop the subject now; no good reaping up things that are past and done with."

Sir Nash asked no more: neither did Arthur. Some instinct lay within both that, for their own sakes, it might be better not to do so.

But when the general left—which he did very soon, having an evening engagement—Arthur went out with him. Arthur Bohun knew, as well as though he had been told, that his wicked mother—he could only so think of her in that moment—had dealt treacherously with him; to answer some end of her own she had calumniated Mr. Adair. Cost him what pain and shame it might, he would clear it up now.

"Will you give me the particulars that you would not give to my uncle," began Arthur in agitation, the moment they were out of the house, as he placed his hand on the general's arm. "No matter what they are, I must know them."

"I would give them to your uncle, and welcome," said the plain old soldier. "It was to you I would not give them."

"But I must learn them."

"Not from me."

"If you will not give them to me, I shall apply to William Adair."

"William Adair can give them to you if he pleases. I shall not do so. Take advice, my dear young friend, and don't inquire into them."

"I will tell you what I suspect—that if any one had a hand in driving my father to—to do what he did do, it was his wife; my mother. You may tell me now."

"No. Because she is your mother."

"But I have the most urgent reason for wishing to arrive at the particulars."

"Well, Arthur Bohun, I would rather not tell you, and that's the truth. If poor Tom could hear me in his grave, I don't think he would like it, you see. No, I can't tell you. Ask Adair, first of all, whether he'd advise it, or not."

"Where is he staying?"

"In Grosvenor Place. He and his daughter are in a furnished house there. She is very delicate."

"And—you say—I beg your pardon, general," added Arthur in agitation, detaining him as he was going away—"You say that he is honoured, and a gentleman."

"Who? Adair? As much so as you or I, my young friend. You must be dreaming. Goodnight."

In his mind's tumult any delay seemed dreadful, and Arthur Bohun turned at once to the house in Grosvenor Place. He asked if he could see Mr. Adair.

The servant hesitated. "There is no Mr. Adair here, sir," he said.

Arthur looked up at the number. "Are you sure?" he asked of the man. "I was informed by General Strachan that Mr. Adair had taken this house, and was living here."

"The general must have said Sir William, sir. Sir William Adair lives here."

"Oh—Sir William," spoke Arthur, "I—I was not aware Mr. Adair had been knighted."

"Knighted, sir! My master has not been knighted," cried the man, as if indignant at the charge. "Sir William has succeeded to the baronetcy through the death of his uncle, Sir Archibald."

What with one thing and another, Arthur's senses seemed deserting him. Sir Archibald Adair had been well known to him by reputation: a proud old Scotch baronet, of a grand old lineage. And so this was Ellen's family! And he had been deeming her not fitting to mate with him, a Bohun!

"Can I see Sir William? Is he at home?"

"He is at home, sir. I think you can see him."

In his dining-room sat Sir William Adair when Arthur was shown in—some coffee on a stand by his side, a newspaper in his hand. He was a slight man of rather more than middle height, with an attractive countenance. The features were good, their expression noble and pleasing. It was impossible to associate such a face and bearing with anything like dishonour.

"I believe my name is not altogether strange to you, sir," said Arthur as the servant closed the door. "I hope you will pardon my intrusion—and especially that it should be at this late hour."

Sir William had risen to receive him. He could but mark the agitation with which the words were spoken. A moment's hesitation, and then he took Arthur's hand and clasped it within his own.

"If I wished to be distant with you I could not," he said warmly. "For, to me, you appear as your father come to life again. He and I were fast friends."

"And did you wish to be distant with me?" asked Arthur.

"I have felt cold towards you this many a year. More than that."

"But why, Sir William?"

"Ah—why. I cannot tell you. For one thing, I have pictured you as resembling another, more than my lost friend."

"You mean my mother."

Sir William looked at Arthur Bohun before replying. "Yes, I do. Will you take a seat: and some coffee?"

Arthur sat down, but it may be questioned whether he as much as heard that coffee was mentioned. Sir William rang the bell and ordered it to be brought in. Arthur leaned forward; his blue eyes solemnly earnest, his hand a little outstretched. Sir William almost started.

"How strangely like!" he exclaimed. "The look, the gesture, the voice, all are your father's over again. I could fancy that you were Thomas Bohun—as I last saw him in life."

"You knew him well—and my mother? You knew all about them?"

"Quite well. I knew you too when you were a little child."

"Then tell me one thing," said Arthur, his emotion increasing. "Was she my mother?"

The question surprised Sir William Adair. "She was certainly your mother, and your father's wife. Why do you ask it?"

"Because—she has so acted—that I—have many a time wished she was not. I have almost hoped it. I wish I could hope it now."

"Ah," cried Sir William. It was all he said.

"Did you care much, for my father, Sir William?"

"More than I ever cared for any other man. I have never cared for one since as I cared for him. We were young fellows then, he and I; not much older than you are now; but ours was a true friendship."

"Then I conjure you, by that friendship, to disclose to me the whole history of the past: the circumstances attending my father's death, and its cause. Speak of things as though my mother existed not. I wish to Heaven she never had been my mother!"

"I think you must know something of the circumstances," spoke Sir William. "Or why should you say this?"

"It is because I know part that I must know the whole. My mother has—has lied to me," he concluded, bringing out the word with a painful effort. "She has thrust a false story upon me, and—I cannot rest until I know the truth."

"Arthur Bohun, although you conjure me by your late father: and for his sake I would do a great deal: I fear that I ought not to do this."

"General Strachan bade me come to you. I begged him to tell me all, but he said no. Does he know all?" broke off Arthur.

"Every tittle. I think he and I and your mother are nearly the only three left who do know it. There were only some half-dozen of us altogether."

"And do you not think that I, Major Bohun's only son, should at least be made acquainted with as much as others know? Tell me all, Sir William: for my lost father's sake."

"The only difficulty is—that you must hear ill of your mother."

"I cannot hear worse of her than I already know," impetuously returned Arthur. "Perhaps it was less bad than I am imagining it may have been."

But Sir William held back. Arthur seemed on the brink of a fever in his impatience. And, whether it was that, or to clear the memory of Major Bohun, or that he deemed it a righteous thing to satisfy Major Bohun's son, or that he yielded to overpersuasion, Sir William Adair at last spoke out.

They sat very close together, only the small coffee-table between them. Whether the room was in light or darkness neither remembered. It was a miserable tale they were absorbed in; one that need not be elaborated here.

William Adair, when a young man, quarrelled with his family, or they with him, and an estrangement took place. His father and mother were dead, but his uncle, Sir Archibald, and other relatives, were left. He, the young man, went to the Madras Presidency, appointed to some post there in the civil service. His family made a boast of discarding him; he, in return, was so incensed against them, that had it been practicable, he would have abandoned the very name of Adair. Never a word did he breathe to any one of who or what his family was; his Scotch accent betrayed his country, but people knew no more. That he was a gentleman was apparent, and that was sufficient.

A strong friendship ensued between him and Major Bohun. During one hot season it happened that both went up in search of health to the Blue Mountains, as Indians call the beautiful region of the Neilgherry Hills. Mrs. Bohun accompanied her husband; Mr. Adair was not married. There they made the acquaintance of the Reverend George Cumberland, who was stationed at Ootacamund with his wife. Ootacamund was at that time filled, and a good deal of gaiety was going on; Mrs. Bohun was noted for it. There was some gambling nightly: and no votary joined in it more persistently than she. Major Bohun removed with her to a little place at a short distance, and a few others went also; the chaplain, George Cumberland, was one of them.

There came a frightful day for Major Bohun. Certain claims suddenly swooped down upon him; debts; promissory notes, bearing his signature in conjunction with William Adair's. Neither understood what it meant, for they had given nothing of the sort. A momentary thought arose to Major Bohun—that his wife was implicated in it; but only so far as that she might have joined in this high play; nothing worse. He had become aware that she had a passion for gambling, and the discovery had alarmed him: in fact, it was to wean her from undesirable associates and pursuits that he had come away on this holiday; health, the ostensible plea, was not the true one. But this was not known even to his best friend, William Adair. "Let me deal with this," said the major to Mr. Adair. But Mr. Adair, not choosing to allow a man to forge his name with impunity—and he had no suspicion that it was a woman—did not heed the injunction, but addressed himself to the investigation. And a nest of iniquity he found it. He traced the affair home to one Rabbetson—in all probability an assumed name—a bad man in every way; no better than a blackleg; who had wormed himself into society to prey upon it, and upon men and women's failings. This man Mr. Adair confronted with Major Bohun: and then—the fellow, brought to bay, braved it out by disclosing that his helpmate was Mrs. Bohun.

It was even so. Mr. Adair sat aghast at the revelation. Had he suspected this, he would have kept it to himself. How far she had connected herself with this man, it was best not to inquire: and they never did inquire, and never knew. One thing was certain—the man could afford to take a high ground. He went out from the interview bidding them do their worst—which with him would not be much, he affirmed; for it was not he who had issued the false bills, but the major's wife. And they saw that he spoke the truth.

Arthur Bohun listened to this now, motionless as a statue.

"I never saw any man so overcome as Bohun," continued Sir William Adair. "He took it to heart; to heart. 'And she is the mother of my child!' he said to me; and then he gave way, and held my hands in his, and sobbed aloud. 'We will hush it up; we will take up the bills and other obligations,' I said to him: though in truth I did not see how I should do my part in it, for I was a poor man. He was poor also; his expenses and his wife kept him so. 'It cannot be hushed up, Adair,' he answered; 'it has gone too far.' Those were the last words he ever said to me; it was the last time I saw him alive."

"Go on," said Arthur, without raising his head.

"Mrs. Bohun came into the room, and I quitted it. I saw by her face that she knew what had happened; it was full of evil as she turned it on me. Rabbetson had met her when he was going out, and whispered some words in her ear. What passed between her and Major Bohun I never knew. Before I had been five minutes in my rooms she stood before me; had followed me down. Of all the vituperation that a woman's tongue can utter, hers lavished about the worst on me. It was I who had brought on the crisis, she said; it was I who had taken Rabbetson to her husband. I quietly told her that when I took Rabbetson to Major Bohun, I had not the remotest idea that she was mixed up with the affair in any way; and that if I had known it, known what Rabbetson could say, I never should have taken him, but have striven to deal with it myself, and keep it dark for my friend Bohun's sake. She would hear nothing; she was as a mad woman; she swore that not a word of it was true; that Rabbetson did not say it, could not have said it, but that I and Major Bohun had concocted the tale between us. In short, I think she was really mad for the time being."

"Stay a moment, Sir William," interrupted Arthur. "Who was she? I have never known. I don't think my father's family ever did know."

"Neither did I ever know, to a certainty. A cousin, or sister, or some relative of hers, had married a doctor in practice at Madras, and she was out there on a visit to them. Captain Bohun—as he was then—caught by her face and figure, both fine in those days, fell in love with her and married her. He afterwards found that her father kept an hotel somewhere in England."

So! This was the high-born lady who had set up for being above all Dallory. But for the utmost self-control Arthur Bohun would have groaned aloud.

"Go on, please," was all he said. "Get it finished."

"There is not much more to tell," returned Sir William. "I went looking about for Bohun everywhere that afternoon; and could not find him. Just before sun-down he was found—found as—as I dare say you have heard. The spot was retired and shady, his pistol lay beside him. He had not suffered: death must have been instantaneous."

"The report here was that he died of sunstroke," said Arthur, breaking a long pause.

"No doubt. Mrs. Bohun caused it to be so reported. The real facts transpired to very few: Cumberland, Captain Strachan, myself, and two or three others."

"Did Mrs. Cumberland know them?" suddenly asked Arthur, a thought striking him.

"I dare say not. I don't suppose her husband would disclose the shameful tale to her. She was not on the spot at the time; had gone to nurse some friend who was ill. I respected both the Cumberlands highly. We made a sort of compact amongst ourselves, we men, never to speak of this story, unless it should be to defend Bohun, or for some other good purpose. We wished to give Mrs. Bohun a chance of redeeming her acts and doings in her own land, for which she at once sailed. Arthur, if I have had to say this to you, it is to vindicate your dead father. I believe that your mother has dreaded me ever since."

Dreaded him! Ay! and foully aspersed him in her insane dread. Arthur thought of the wicked invention she had raised, and passed his hands upon his face as if he could shut out its remembrance.

"What became of Rabbetson?" he asked, in low tones.

"He disappeared. Or I think I should surely have shot him in his turn, or kicked him to death. I saw him afterwards in Australia dying in the most abject misery."

"And the claims?—the bills?"

"I took them upon myself; and contrived to pay all—with time."

"You left India for Australia?" continued Arthur, after a pause.

"My health failed, and I petitioned government to remove me to a different climate. They complied, and sent me to Australia. I stayed there, trying to accumulate a competency that should enable me to live at home with Ellen as befitted my family: little supposing that I was destined to become its head. My two cousins, Sir Archibald's sons, have died one after the other."

Arthur Bohun had heard all he wished to know, perhaps all there was to tell. If—if he could make his peace with Ellen, the old relations between them might yet be renewed. But whilst his heart bounded with the hope, the red of shame crimsoned his brow as he thought of the past. Glancing at the timepiece on the mantel-shelf, he saw it was only half-past nine; not too late yet.

"May I see your daughter, sir?" he asked. "We used to be good friends."

"So I suppose," replied Sir William. "You made love to her, Arthur Bohun. You would have married her, I believe, but that I stopped it."

"You—stopped it!" exclaimed Arthur, at sea: for he had known nothing of the letter received by Ellen.

"I wrote to Ellen, telling her I must forbid her to marry you. I feared at the time of writing that the interdict might arrive too late. But it seems that it did not do so."

"Yes," abstractedly returned Arthur, letting pass what he did not understand.

"You see, I had been thinking of you always as belonging to her—your mother—more than to him. That mistake is over. I shall value you now as his son; more I dare say than I shall ever value any other young man in this world."

Arthur's breath came fast and thick. "Then—you—you would give her to me, sir!"

Sir William shook his head in sadness. Arthur misunderstood the meaning.

"The probability is, sir, that I shall succeed my uncle in the baronetcy. Would it not satisfy you?"

"You can see her if you will," was Sir William's answer, but there was the same sad sort of denial in his manner. "I would not say No now for your father's sake. She is in the drawing-room, upstairs. I will join you as soon as I have written a note."

Arthur found his way by instinct. Ellen was lying back in an easy-chair; the brilliant light of the chandelier on her face. Opening the door softly, it—that face—was the first object that met his sight. And he started back in terror.

Was it death that he saw written there? All too surely conviction came home to him.

It was a more momentous interview than the one just over. Explaining he knew not how, explaining he knew not what, excepting that his love had never left her, Arthur Bohun knelt at her feet, and they mingled their tears together. For some minutes neither could understand the other: but elucidation came at last. Arthur told her that the wicked tale, the frightful treachery which had parted them was only a concocted fable on his mother's part, and then he found that Ellen had never known, never heard anything, about it.

"What then did you think was the matter with me?" he asked.

And she told him. She told him without reserve, now that she found how untrue it was: she thought he had given her up for another. Madam had informed her he was about to marry Miss Dallory.

He took in the full sense of what the words implied: the very abject light in which his conduct must have appeared to her. A groan burst from him: he covered his face to hide its shame and trouble.

"Ellen! Ellen! You could not have thought it of me."

"It was what I did think. How was I to think anything else? Your mother had said it."

"Heaven forgive her her sins!" he wailed, in his despair. "It was enough to kill you, Ellen. No wonder you look like this."

She was panting a little. Her breathing seemed very laboured.

"Pray Heaven I may be enabled to make it up to you when you are my wife. I will try hard, my darling."

"I shall not live for it, Arthur."

His heart seemed to stand still. The words struck him as being so very real.

"Arthur, I have known it for some time now. You must not grieve for me. I even think that death is rather near."

"What has killed you? I?"

A flush passed over her wan face. Yes, he had killed her. That is, his conduct had done so: the sensitive crimson betrayed it.

"The probability is that I should not in any case have lived long," she said, aloud. "I believe they feared something of the sort for me years ago. Arthur, don't! Don't weep; I cannot bear it."

Sir William Adair had just told him how his father had wept in his misery. And before Arthur could well collect himself, Sir William entered.

"You see," he whispered aside to Arthur, "why it may not be. There will be no marriage for her in this life. I am not surprised. I seem to have always expected it: my wife, her mother, died of decline."

Arthur Bohun quitted the house, overwhelmed with shame and sorrow. What regret is there like unto that for past mistaken conduct which can never be remedied in this world?

CHAPTER II

NO HOPE

Once more the scene changes to Dallory.

Seated on a lawn-bench at Dallory Hall in the sweet spring sunshine—for the time has again gone on—was Ellen Adair. Sir William Adair and Arthur Bohun were pacing amidst the flower-beds that used to be Mr. North's. Arthur stooped and plucked a magnificent pink hyacinth.

"It is not treason, sir?" he asked, smiling.

"What is not treason?" returned the elder man.

"To pick this."

"Pick as many as you like," said Sir William.

"Mr. North never liked us to pluck his flowers. Now and then madam would make a ruthless swoop upon them for her entertainments. It grieved his heart."

"No wonder," said Sir William.

The restoration to the old happiness, the disappearance of the dreadful cloud that had told so fatally upon her, seemed to infuse new vigour into Ellen's shortening span of life. With the exception of her father, every one thought she was recovering: the doctors admitted, rather dubiously, that it "might be so." She passed wonderfully well through the winter, went out and about almost as of old; and when more genial weather set in, it was suggested by friends that she should be taken to a warmer climate. Ellen opposed it; she knew it would not avail, perhaps only hasten the end; and after a private interview Sir William had with the doctors, even he did not second it. Her great wish was to go back to Dallory: and arrangements for their removal were made.

Dallory Hall was empty, and Sir William found that he could occupy it for the present if he pleased. Mr. North had removed to the house that had been Mrs. Cumberland's, leaving his own furniture: in point of fact it was Richard's: at the Hall, hoping the next tenant, whoever that might prove to be, would take to it. Miss Dallory seemed undecided what to do with the Hall, whether to let it for a term again, or not, But she was quite willing that Sir William Adair should have it for a month or two.

And so he came down with Ellen, bringing his own servants with him. This was only the third day after their arrival, and Arthur Bohun had arrived. Sir William had told him he might come when he would.

The change seemed to have improved Ellen, and she had received a few visitors. Mrs. Gass had been there; Mr. North had come down; and Richard ran in for a few minutes every day. Sir William welcomed them all; Mrs. Gass warmly; for she was sister-in-law to Mrs. Cumberland, and Ellen had told him of Mrs. Gass's goodness of heart. She had unfastened her bonnet, and stayed luncheon with them.

Mr. North was alone in his new home, and was likely to be so; for his wife had relieved him of her society. Violently indignant at the prospect of removal from such a habitation as the Hall to that small home of the late Mrs. Cumberland's, madam went off to London with Matilda, and took Sir Nash Bohun's house by storm. Not an hour, however, had she been in it, when madam found all her golden dreams must be scattered to the winds. Never again would Sir Nash receive her as a guest or tolerate her presence. The long hidden truth, as connected with his unfortunate brother's death, had been made clear to him: first of all by General Strachan, next by Sir William Adair, with whom he became intimate.

Of what use to tell of the interview between Arthur and his mother? It was of a painful character. There was no outspoken reproach, no voice was raised. In a subdued manner, striving for calmness, Arthur told her she had wilfully destroyed both himself and Ellen Adair; her life, for she was dying; his happiness for ever. He recapitulated all that had been disclosed to him relating to his father's death; and madam, brought to bay, never attempted to deny its accuracy.

"But that I dare not fly in the face of one of Heaven's Commandments, I would now cast you off for ever," he concluded in his bitter pain. "Look upon you again as my mother, I cannot. I will help you when you need help; so far will I act the part of a son towards you; but all respect for you has been forced out of me; and I would prefer that we should not meet very often."

Madam departed the same day for Germany, Matilda and the maid Parrit in her wake. Letters came from her to say she should never return to Dallory; never; probably never set her foot again on British soil; and therefore she desired that a suitable income might be secured to her abroad.

And so Mr. North had his new residence all to himself—saving Richard. Jelly had taken up her post as his housekeeper, with a boy and a maid under her; and there was one outdoor gardener. She domineered over all to her heart's content. Jelly was regaining some of her lost flesh, and more than her lost spirits. Set at rest in a confidential interview with Mr. Richard, as to the very tangible nature of the apparition she had seen, Jelly was herself again. Mr. North thought his garden lovely, more compact than the extensive one at the Hall; he was out in it all day long, and felt at peace. Mrs. Gass came to see him often; Mary Dallory almost daily: he had his good son Richard to bear him company of an evening. Altogether Mr. North was in much comfort. Dr. Rane's house remained empty: old Phillis, to whom the truth had also been disclosed, taking care of it. The doctor's personal effects had been sent to him by Richard.

"Ellen looks much better, sir," remarked Arthur Bohun, as he twirled the pink hyacinth he had plucked.

"A little fresher, perhaps, from the country air," answered Sir William.

"I have not lost hope: she may yet be mine," he murmured.

Sir William did not answer. He would give her to Arthur now with his whole heart, had her health permitted it. Arthur himself looked ill; in the last few months he seemed to have aged years. A terrible remorse was ever upon him; his life, in its unavailing regret, seemed as one long agony.

They turned to where she was sitting. "Would you not like to walk a little, Ellen?" asked her father.

She rose at once. Arthur held out his arm, and she took it. Sir William was quite content that it should be so: Arthur, and not himself. The three paced the lawn. Ellen wore a lilac silk gown and warm white cloak. An elegant girl yet, though worn almost to a shadow, with the same sweet face as of yore.

But she was soon tired, and sat down again, Arthur by her side. One of the gardeners came up for some orders, and Sir William went away with him.

"I have not been so happy for many a day, Ellen, as I am now," began Captain Bohun. "You are looking quite yourself again. I think—in a little time—that you may be mine."

A blush, beautiful as the rose-flush of old, sat for a moment on her cheeks. She knew how fallacious was the hope.

"I am nearly sure that Sir William thinks so, and will soon give you to me," he added.

"Arthur," she said, putting her wan and wasted hand on his, "don't take the hope to heart. The—disappointment, when it came, would be all the harder to bear."

"But, my darling, you are surely better!"

"Yes, I seem so, just for a little time. But I fear that I shall never be well enough to be your wife."

"It was so very near once, you know," was all he whispered.

There was no one within view, and they sat, her hand clasped in his. The old expressive silence that used to lie between them of old, ensued now. They could not tell to each other more than they had told already. In the unexpected reconciliation that had come, in the bliss it brought, all had been disclosed. Arthur had heard all about her self-humiliation and anguish; he knew of the treasured violets, and their supposed treachery: she had listened to his recital of the weeks of despair; she had seen the letter, written to him from Eastsea, worn with his kisses, blotted with his tsars, and kept in his bosom still. No: of the past there was nothing more to tell each other; so far, they were at rest.

Arthur Bohun was still unconsciously twirling that pink hyacinth in his fingers. Becoming aware of the fact, he offered it to her. A wan smile parted her lips.

"You should not have given it, to me, Arthur."

"Why?"

Ellen took it up. The perfume was very strong.

"Why should I not have given it to you?"

"Don't you know what the hyacinth is an emblem of?"

"No."

"Death."

One quick, pained glance at her. She was smiling yet, and looking rather fondly at the flower. Captain Bohun took both flower and hand into his.

"I always thought you liked hyacinths, Ellen."

"I have always liked them very much indeed. And I like the perfume—although it is somewhat faint and sickly."

He quietly flung the flower on the grass, and put his boot on it to stamp out its beauty. A truer emblem of death, now, than it was before; but he did not think of that.

"I'll find you a sweeter flower presently, Ellen. And you know—"

A visitor was crossing the lawn to approach them. It was Miss Dallory. She had not yet been to see Ellen. Something said by Mrs. Gass had sent her now. Happening to call on Mrs. Gass that morning, Mary heard for the first time of the love that had so long existed between Captain Bohun and Miss Adair, and that the course of the love had been forcibly interrupted by madam, who had put forth the plea that her son was engaged to Miss Dallory.

Mary sat before Mrs. Gass in mute surprise, recalling facts and fancies. "I know that madam would have liked her son to marry me; the hints she gave me on the point were too broad to be mistaken," she observed to Mrs. Gass. "Neither I nor Captain Bohun had any thought or intention of the sort; we understood each other too well."

"Yet you once took me in," said Mrs. Gass.

Mary laughed. "It was only in sport: I did not think you were serious."

"They believed it at the Hall."

"Oh, did they? So much the better."

"My dear, I am afraid it was not for the better," dissented Mrs. Gass rather solemnly. "They say that it has killed Miss Ellen Adair."

"What?" exclaimed Mary.

"Ever since that time when she first went to the Hall after Mrs. Cumberland's death, she has been wasting and wasting away. Her father, Sir William, has now brought her to Dallory, not to try if the change might restore her, for nothing but a miracle would do that, but because she took a whim to come. Did you hear that she was very ill?"

"Yes, I heard so."

"Well, then, I believe it is nothing but this business that has made her ill—Captain Bohun's deserting her for you. She was led to believe it was so—and until then, they had been wrapt up in each other."

Mary Dallory felt her face grow hot and cold. She had been altogether innocent of ill intention; but the words struck a strange chill of repentance to her heart.

"I—don't understand," she said in frightened tones. "Captain Bohun knew there was nothing between us; not even a shadow of pretence of it: why did he not tell her so?"

"Because he and she had parted on another score; they had been parted through a lie of madam's, who wanted him to marry you. I don't rightly know what the lie was; something frightfully grave; something he could not repeat again to Miss Adair; and Ellen Adair never heard it, and thought it was as madam said—that his love had gone over to you."

Mary sat in silence, thinking of the past. There was a long pause.

"How did you get to know this?" she breathed.

"Ah, well—partly through Mr. Richard. And I sat an hour talking with poor Miss Ellen yesterday, and caught a hint or two then."

"I will set it straight," said Mary; feeling, though without much cause, bitterly repentant.

"My dear, it has been all set straight since the winter. Nevertheless, Miss Mary, it was too late. Madam had done her crafty work well."

"Madam deserves to be put in the stocks," was the impulsive rejoinder of Miss Dallory.

She went to the Hall there and then. And this explains her present approach. Things had cleared very much to her as she walked along. She had never been able to account for the manner in which Ellen seemed to shun her, to avoid all approach to intimacy or friendship. That Mary Dallory had favoured the impression abroad of Arthur Bohun's possible engagement to her, she was now all too conscious of; or, at any rate, had not attempted to contradict it. But it had never occurred to her that she was doing harm to any one.

Just as Arthur Bohun had started when he first saw Ellen in the winter, so did Miss Dallory start now. Wan and wasted? ay, indeed. Mary felt half faint in thinking of the share she had had in it.

She said nothing at first. Room was made for her on the bench, and they talked of indifferent matters. Sir William came up, and was introduced. Presently he and Arthur strolled to a distance.

Then Mary spoke. Just a word or two of the misapprehension that had existed; then a burst of exculpation.

"Ellen, I would have died rather than have caused you pain. Oh if I had only known! Arthur and I were familiar with each other as brother and sister: never a thought of anything else was in our minds. If I let people think there was, why—it was done in coquetry. I had some one else in my head, you see, all the time; and that's the truth. And I am afraid I enjoyed the disappointment that would ensue for madam."

Ellen smiled faintly. "It seems to have been a complication altogether. A sort of ill-fate that I suppose there was no avoiding."

"You must get well, and be his wife."

"Ay. I wish I could."

But none could be wishing that as Arthur did. Hope deceived him; he confidently thought that a month or two would see her his. Just for a few days the deceitful improvement in her continued.

One afternoon they drove to Dallory churchyard. Ellen and her father; Arthur sitting opposite them in the carriage. A fancy had taken her that she would once more look on Mrs. Cumberland's grave; and Sir William said he should himself like to see it.

The marble stone was up now, with its inscription: "Fanny, widow of the Reverend George Cumberland, Government Chaplain, and daughter of the late William Gass, Esq., of Whitborough." There was no mention of her marriage to Captain Rane. Perhaps Dr. Rane fancied the name was not in very good odour just now, and so omitted it. The place where the ground had been disturbed, to take up those other coffins, had been filled in again with earth.

Ellen drew Sir William's attention to a green spot near, overshadowed by the branches of a tree that waved in the breeze, and flickered the grass beneath with ever-changing light and shade.

"It is the prettiest spot in the churchyard," she said, touching his arm. "And yet no one has ever chosen it."

"It is very pretty, Ellen; but solitary."

"Will you let it be here, papa?"

He understood the soft whisper, and slightly nodded, compressing his lips. Sir William was not deceived. Years had elapsed, but, to him, it seemed to be his wife's case over again. There had been no hope for her; there was none for Ellen.

CHAPTER III

BROUGHT HOME TO HIM

She lay back in an easy-chair, in the little room that was once Mr. North's parlour. The window was thrown open to the sweet flowers, the balmy air; and Ellen Adair drank in their beauty and perfume.

She took to this room as her own sitting-room the day she came back to the Hall. She had always liked it. Sir William had caused the shabby old carpet and chairs and tables to be replaced by fresh bright furniture. How willingly, had it been possible, would he have kept her in life!

Just for a few days had hope lasted—no more. The change had come suddenly, and was unmistakable. She wore a white gown, tied round the waist with a pink girdle, and a little bow of pink ribbon—her favourite colour—at the neck. She wished to look well yet; her toilet was attended to, her bright hair was arranged carefully as ever. But the maid did all that. The wan face was very sweet still, the soft brown eyes had all their old lustre. Very listless was the worn white hand lying on her lap; loosely sat the plain gold ring on it—the ring that, through all the toil and trouble, had never been taken off. Ellen was alone. Sir William had gone by appointment to see over Richard North's works.

A sound as of steps on the gravel. Her father could not have come back yet! A moment's listening, and then the hectic flushed to her face; for she knew the step too well. Captain Bohun had returned!

Captain Bohun had gone to London to see Sir Nash off on his projected Continental journey to the springs that were to make him young again. Sir Nash had expected Arthur to accompany him, but he now acknowledged that Ellen's claims were paramount to his. Ellen had thought he might have been back again yesterday.

He came in at the glass-doors, knowing he should probably find her in the room. But his joyous smile died away when he saw her face. His step halted: his hand dropped at his side.

"Ellen!"

In timid, wailing tones was the word spoken. Only three days' absence, and she had faded like this! Was it a relapse?—or what had she been doing to cause the change?

For a few minutes, perhaps neither of them was sufficiently collected to know what passed. In his abandonment, he knelt by the chair, holding her hands, his eyes dropping tears. The remorse ever gnawing at his heart was very cruel just then. Ellen bent towards him, and whispered that he must be calm—must bear like a man: things were only drawing a little nearer.

"I should have been down yesterday, but I waited in town to make sundry purchases and preparations," he said. "Ellen, I thought that—perhaps—next month—your father would have given you over to me."

"Did you?" she faintly answered.

"You must be mine," he continued, in too deep emotion to weigh his words. "If you were to die first, I—I think it would kill me."

"Look at me," was all she answered. "See whether it is possible."

"There's no knowing. It might restore you. Fresh scenes, the warm pure climate that I would take you to—we would find one somewhere—might do wonders. I pointed this out to Sir William in the winter."

"But I have not been well enough for it, Arthur."

"Ellen, it must be! Why, you know that you were almost my wife. Half-an-hour later, and you would have been."

She released one of her hands, and put it up to her face.

Captain Bohun grew more earnest in his pleading; he was really thinking this thing might be.

"I shall declare the truth to Sir William—and I know that I ought to have done so before, Ellen. When he knows how very near we were to being man and wife, he will make no further objection to giving you to me now. My care and love will restore you, if anything can."

She had put down her hand again, and was looking at him, a little startled and her cheeks hectic.

"Arthur, hush. Papa must never know this while I live. Do as you will afterwards."

"I shall tell him before the day's out," persisted Captain Bohun. And she began to tremble with agitation.

"No, no. I say no. I should die with the shame."

"What shame?" he rejoined.

"The shame that—that—fell upon me. The shame of—after having consented to a secret marriage, you should have left me as you did, and not fulfilled it, and never told me why. It lies upon me still, and I cannot help it. I think it is that that has helped to kill me more than all the rest. Oh, Arthur, forgive me for saying this! But do not renew the shame now."

Never had his past conduct been brought so forcibly home to him. Never had his heart so ached with its repentance and pain.

"The fear, lest the secret should be discovered, lay upon me always," she whispered. "Whilst I was staying here that time it seemed to me one long mental torment. Had the humiliation come, I could never have borne it. Spare me still, Arthur."

Every word she spoke was like a dagger thrusting its sharp point into his heart. She was going—going rapidly—where neither pain nor humiliation could reach her. But he had, in all probability, a long life before him, and must live out his bitter repentance.

"Oh, my love, my love! I wish I could die for you!"

"Don't grieve, Arthur; I shall be better off. You and papa must comfort one another."

He was unconsciously turning round the plain gold ring on her wasted hand, a sob now and again breaking from him. How real the past was seeming to him; even the hour when he had put that ring on, and the words he spoke with it, were very present. What remained of it all? Nothing, except that she was dying.

"I should like to give you this key now, whilst I am well enough to remember," she suddenly said, detaching a small key from her watch-chain. "It belongs to my treasure-box, as I used to call it at school. They will give it you when I am dead."

"Oh, Ellen!"

"The other ring is in it, and the licence—for I did not burn it, as you bade me that day in the churchyard; and the two or three letters you ever wrote to me; and my journal, and some withered flowers, and other foolish trifles. You can do what you like with them, Arthur; they will be yours then. And oh, Arthur! if you grieve any more now, like this, you will hurt me, for I cannot bear that you should suffer pain. God bless you, my darling, my almost husband! We should have been very happy with one another."

Lower and lower bent he his aching brow, striving to suppress the anguish that well-nigh unmanned him. Her own tears were falling.

"Be comforted," she whispered; "Arthur, be comforted! It will not be for so many years, even at the most; and then we shall be together again, in heaven!"

And so she died. A week or two more of pain and suffering, and she was at rest. And that was the ending of Ellen Adair—one of the sweetest girls this world has ever known.

CHAPTER IV

CONCLUSION

The genial spring gave place to a hot summer; and summer, in its turn, was giving place to autumn. There is little to record of the interval.

Dallory, as regards North Inlet, was no longer crowded. The poor workmen, with their wives and families, had for the most part drifted away from it; some few were emigrating, some had brought themselves to accepting that last and hated refuge, the workhouse; and they seemed likely, so far as present prospects looked, to be permanent recipients of its hospitality. The greater portion, however, had wandered away to different parts of the country, seeking for that employment they could no longer find in their native place. Poole and the other conspirators had been tried at the March assizes. Richard North pleaded earnestly for a lenient sentence: and he was listened to. Poole received a term of penal servitude, shorter than it would otherwise have been, and the others hard labour. One and all, including Mr. Poole, declared that they would not willingly have injured Richard North.

So, what with one thing and another, North Inlet had too much empty space in it, and was now at peace. There was no longer any need of special policemen. As to Richard, he was going on steadily and quietly; progressing a little, though not very much. Five or six men had been added to his number, of whom Ketler was one; Ketler having, as Jelly said, come to his senses. But the works would never be what they had been. For one thing, Richard had no capital; and if he had, perhaps he might not now have cared to embark it in this manner. Provided he could gain a sufficient income for expenses, and so employ his time and energies, it was all he asked.

Madam lived permanently abroad. Mr. North—Richard in reality—allowed her two hundred a-year; her son Arthur two; Sir Nash two. Six hundred a-year; but it was pretty plainly intimated to madam that this income was only guaranteed so long as she kept herself aloof from them. Madam retorted that she liked the Continent too well to leave it for disagreeable old England.

Matilda North had married a French count, whom they had met at Baden-Baden. She, herself, made the announcement to her stepbrother Arthur in a self-possessed letter, telling him that as the count's fortune was not equal to his merits, she should depend upon Arthur to assist them yearly. Sidney North had also married. Tired, possibly, with his most uncertain existence, finding supplies from home were now the exception rather than the rule, and not daring to show his face on English soil to entreat for more, Mr. Sidney North entered into the bonds of matrimony with a wealthy American dame a few years older than himself; the widow of a great man who had made his fortune by the oil springs. It was to be hoped he would keep himself straight now.

And Mr. North, feeling that he was freed from madam, was happy as a prince, and confidentially told people that he thought he was growing young again. Bessy wrote to him weekly; pleasant, happy letters. She liked her home in the new world very much indeed; and she said Oliver seemed not to have a single care. The new firm, Jones and Rane, had more patients than they could attend to, and all things were well with them. In short, Dr. and Mrs. Rane were evidently both prosperous and happy. No one was more pleased to know this than Mrs. Gass. She flourished; and her beaming face was more beaming than ever when seen abroad, setting the wives of Richard North's workmen to rights, or looking out from behind her geraniums.

Dallory Hall was empty again. William Adair had quitted it, his mission there over. Richard North was thinking about removing the furniture; but in truth he did not know what to do with it. There was no hurry, for Miss Dallory said she did not intend to let it again at present.

Perhaps the only one not just now in a state of bliss was Jelly. Jelly had made a frightful discovery—Tim Wilks was faithless. For several months—as it came out—Mr. Wilks had transferred his allegiance from herself to Molly Green, whom he was secretly courting at Whitborough. At least, he was keeping it from Jelly. The truth was, poor Tim did not dare to tell her. Jelly heard of it in a manner that astounded her. Spending a Sunday at Whitborough with Mrs. Beverage's servants, Jelly went to morning service at one of the churches. "Pate" took her to a particular church, she said. And there she heard the banns of marriage read out, for the first time of asking, between Timothy Wilks, bachelor, and Mary Green, spinster. Jelly very nearly shrieked aloud in her indignation. Had the culprits been present, she might have felt compelled to box their ears in coming out. It proved to be true. Tim and Molly were going to be married, and Tim was furnishing a pretty cottage at Whitborough.

And that is how matters at present stood in Dallory.

One autumn day, when the woods were glowing with their many colours, and the guns might be heard making war on the partridges, Richard North overtook one of his Flemish workmen at the base of a hill about half-a-mile from his works. The man was wheeling a wheelbarrow that contained sand, but not in the handy manner that an Englishman would have done it, and Richard took it himself.

"Can't you learn, Snaude?" he said, addressing the man. "See here; you should stoop: you must not get the barrow nearly upright. See how you've spilt the sand."

Wheeling it along and paying attention to nothing else, Richard took no notice of a basket-carriage that was coming down the opposite hill. It pulled up when it reached him. Looking up, Richard saw Miss Dallory. Resigning the wheelbarrow to the man, Richard took the hand she held out.

"Yes," he said laughing, "you stop to shake hands with me now, but you won't do it soon."

"No? Why not?" she questioned.

"You saw me wheeling the barrow along?"

"Yes. It did not look very heavy."

"I have to put my hands to all sorts of things now, you perceive, Miss Dallory."

"Just so. I hope you like doing it."

"Well, I do."

"But I want to know what you mean by saying I shall soon not stop to speak to you."

"When you become a great lady. Report says you are about to marry."

"Does it? Do you still think, sir, I am going to accept a Bohun?"

"There has been some lord down at your brother's place, once or twice. The gossips in Dallory say that he comes for you."

"Then you can tell the gossips that they are a great deal wiser than I am. Stand still, Gyp"—to the shaggy pony. "I would not have him; and I'm sure he has not the remotest idea of having me. Why, he is hardly out of his teens! I dare say he thinks me old enough to be his godmother."

Miss Dallory played with the reins, and then glanced at Richard. He was looking at her earnestly, as he leaned on the low carriage.

"That young man has come down for the shooting, Mr. Richard. Frank takes him out every day. As for me, I do not intend to marry at all. Never."

"What shall you do, then?"

"Live at Dallory Hall. Frank is going to be married, to the lord's sister. Now there's some information for you, but you need not proclaim it. It is true. I shall remove myself and my chattels to the Hall, and live there till I die."

"It will be very lonely for you."

"Yes, I know that," she answered sadly. "Most old maids are lonely. There will be Frank's children, perhaps, to come and stay with me sometimes."

Their eyes met. Each understood the other as exactly as though a host of words had been spoken. She would have one man for a husband, and only one—if he would have her.

Richard went nearer. His lips were pale, his tones husky with emotion.

"Mary, it would be most unsuitable. Think of your money; your birth. I told you once before not to tempt me. Why, you know—you know that I have loved you, all along, too well for my own peace. In the old days when those works of ours"—pointing to the distant chimneys—"were of note, and we were wealthy, I allowed myself to cherish dreams that I should be ashamed to confess to now: but that's all over and done with. It would never do."

She blushed and smiled; and turned her head away from him to study the opposite hedge while she spoke.

"For my part, I think there never was anything so suitable since the world was made."

"Mary, I cannot."

"If you will please get off my basket-chaise, sir, I'll drive on."

But he did not stir. Miss Dallory played with the reins again.

"Mary, how can I? If you had nothing, it would be different. I cannot live at Dallory Hall."

"No one else ever shall." But Richard had to bend to catch the whisper.

"The community would cry shame upon me. Upon that poor working man, Richard North."

"How dare you call yourself names, Mr. Richard? You are a gentleman."

"What would John and Francis say?"

"What they pleased. Francis likes you better than any one in the world; better than—well, yes, sir—better than I do."

He had taken one of her hands now. She knew, she had known a long while, how it was with him—that he loved her passionately, but would never, under his altered circumstances, tell her so. And, moreover, she knew that he was aware she knew it.

"But Mary, since—since before you returned from Switzerland up to this hour, I have not dared to think the old hopes could be carried out, even in my own heart."

"You think it better that I should grow into an old maid, and you into an old bachelor. Very well. Thank you. Perhaps we shall both be happier for it. Let me drive on, Mr. Richard."

He drew nearer to her; made her turn to him. The great love of his heart shone in his face and eyes. A face of emotion then. She dropped the reins, regardless of what the rough pony might do, and put her other hand upon his.

"Oh, Richard, don't let us carry on the farce any longer! We have been playing it all these months and years. Let us at least be honest with each other: and then, if you decide for separation, why—it must be so."

But, as it seemed, Richard did not mean to decide for it. He glanced round to make sure that no one was in the lonely road: and, drawing her face to his, left some strangely ardent kisses on it.

"I could not give up my works, Mary."

"No one asked you to do so, sir."

"It is just as though I had left the furniture in the Hall for the purpose."

"Perhaps you did."

"Mary!"

"There's the pony going. Stand still, Gyp. I won't give up Gyp, mind, Richard. I know he is frightfully ragged and ugly, and that you despise him; but I won't give him up. He can be the set-off bargain against your works, sir."

"Agreed," answered Richard, laughing. And he sealed the bargain.

Mary said again that she must drive on; and did not. How long they would really have stayed there it was impossible to say, had not the man come back from the works with the empty wheelbarrow for more sand.

When the next spring came round, Richard North and his wife were established at Dallory Hall. Somewhere about the time of the marriage, there occurred a little warfare. Mary, who owned a great amount of accumulated money, wanted Richard to take it into his business. Richard steadily refused. A small amount would be useful to him; that he would take; but no more.

"Richard," she said to him one day, before they had been married a week, "I do think you are more obstinate upon this point than any other. You should hear what Mrs. Gass says about it."

"She says it to me," returned Richard, laughing. "There's not my equal for obstinacy in the world, she tells me."

"And you know it's true, sir."

But the next minute he grew strangely serious. "I cannot give up business, Mary; I have already said so—"

"I should despise you if you did, Richard," she interrupted. "I have money and gentility—I beg you'll not laugh, sir; you have work, and brains to work with; so we are equally matched. But I wish you would take the money."

"No," said Richard. "I will never again enter on gigantic operations, and be at the beck and call of the Trades' Unions. There's another reason against it—that it would require closer supervision on my part. And as I have now divided duties to attend to; I shall not add to them. I should not choose to neglect my works; I should not choose to neglect my wife."

"A wilful man must have his way," quoth Mary.

"And a wilful woman shall have hers in all things, excepting when I see that it would not be for her good," rejoined Richard, holding his wife before him by the waist.

"I dare say I shall!" she saucily answered. "Is that a bargain, Richard?"

"To be sure it is." And Richard sealed it as he had sealed the other some months before.

And so we leave Dallory and its people at peace. Even Jelly was in feather. Jelly, ruling Mr. North indoors, and giving her opinion, unasked, in a free-and-easy manner whenever she chose, as to the interests of the garden: an opinion poor Mr. North enjoyed instead of reproved, and grew to look for. Jelly had taken on another "young man," in the person of Mr. Francis Dallory's head-gardener. He was a staid young Scotchman; very respectful to Jelly, and quite attentive. Mr. Seeley had moved into Dr. Rane's old house, and old Phillis was his housekeeper; so that Jelly's neighbourly relations with the next door were continued as of old.

On Arthur Bohun there remained the greatest traces of the past. Sir Nash was restored to health; and Arthur, in his unceasing remorse, would sometimes hope that he would marry again: he should almost hate to succeed to the rank and wealth to which he had, in a degree, sacrificed one who had been far dearer to him than life. Arthur's ostensible home was with Sir Nash; but he was fond of coming to Dallory. He had stayed twice with Mr. North; and Richard's home, the Hall, would be always open to him. The most bitter moments of Arthur Bohun's life were those that he spent with Sir William Adair: never could he lose the consciousness of having wronged him, of having helped to make him childless. Sir William had grown to love him as a son, but it was only an additional stab to Arthur's aching heart.

And whenever Arthur Bohun came to Dallory, he would pay a visit to a certain white tomb in the churchyard. Choosing a solitary evening for it, after twilight had fallen, and remaining near it for hours, there he indulged his grief. Who can tell how he called upon her?—who can tell how he poured out all the misery of his repentant heart, praying to be forgiven? Neither she nor Heaven could answer him in this world. She was gone; gone: all his regret was unavailing to recall her: there remained nothing but the marble stone, and the simple name upon it:

"ELLEN ADAIR."

MRS HENRY WOOD (aka ELLEN WOOD) – A CONCISE BIBLIOGRAPHY

Danesbury House (1860)
East Lynne (1861)
The Elchester College Boys (1861)
A Life's Secret (1862)
Mrs. Halliburton's Troubles (1862)
The Channings (1862)
The Foggy Night at Offord: A Christmas Gift for the Lancashire Fund (1863)
The Shadow of Ashlydyat (1863)
Verner's Pride (1863)
Lord Oakburn's Daughters (1864)
Oswald Cray (1864)
Trevlyn Hold; or, Squire Trevlyn's Heir (1864)
William Allair; or, Running away to Sea (1864)
Mildred Arkell: A Novel (1865)
The Argosy (1865)
Elster's Folly: A Novel (1866)
St. Martin's Eve: A Novel (1866)
Lady Adelaide's Oath (1867)
Orville College: A Story (1867)
The Ghost of the Hollow Field (1867)
Anne Hereford: A Novel (1868)
Castle Wafer; or, The Plain Gold Ring (1868)
The Red Court Farm: A Novel (1868)
Roland Yorke: A Novel (1869)
Bessy Rane: A Novel (1870)
George Canterbury's Will (1870)
Dene Hollow (1871)
Within the Maze: A Novel (1872)
The Master of Greylands (1872)
Johnny Ludlow (1874)
Bessy Wells (1875)

Told in the Twilight: Containing 'Parkwater' and nine short stories (1875)
Adam Grainger: A Tale (1876)
Edina (1876)
Our Children (1876)
Parkwater: With four other tales (1876)
Pomeroy Abbey (1878)
Lady Adelaide (1879)
Johnny Ludlow, Second Series (1880)
A Tale of Sin and Other Tales (1881)
Court Netherleigh: A Novel (1881)
About Ourselves (1883)
Johnny Ludlow. Third Series (1885)
Lady Grace and Other Stories (1887)
The Story of Charles Strange (1888)
Featherston's Story. A Tale by Johnny Ludlow (1889)
The Unholy Wish and Other Stories (1890)
The House of Halliwell. A Novel (1890)
Ashley and Other Stories (1897)
Victor Serenus (1898)
Johnny Ludlow. Fifth series (1899)
Johnny Ludlow. Sixth series (1899)

Translations
Les Channing. Traduit de l'Anglais par Mme Abric-Encontre (1864)
Les Filles de Lord Oakburn: Roman traduit de l'anglais par L. Bochet (1876)
La Gloire des Verner: Roman traduit de l'anglais par L. de L'Estrive (1878)
Le Serment de Lady Adelaïde: Roman traduit de l'anglais par Léon Bochet (1878)